KU-009-190

Once in a Lifetime
DANIELLE STEEL

SPHERE BOOKS LIMITED

A SPHERE BOOK

First published in Great Britain by
Judy Piatkus (Publishers) Ltd of Loughton, Essex 1983
Published by Sphere Books Ltd 1983
Reprinted 1990, 1991, 1992

Printed and bound in Great Britain by
Cox & Wyman Ltd, Reading, Berks.

ISBN 0 7221 82392 91

Sphere Books
A Division of
Macdonald & Co (Publishers)
165 Great Dover Street
London SE1 4YA

To John,
Forever,
Olive.

Once in a Lifetime

It only happens once,
　　not twice,
　　　　the moments
　　　　　vanishing
　　　　　　like mice,
scurrying past,
　　　life much
　　　　too fast,
and only for
　　　the very brave,
　　　　the strong,
　　　　　the true,
and when the moment
　　comes
　　　for you,
don't let it
　　pass you by,
for in the twinkling
　　of an eye,
the love is gone,
　　the moment dead,
an empty ringing
　　in your head,
your heart will know
　　when fate
　　　has whispered
　　　　in your ear ...
oh never fear,
　　beloved friend,

for in the end
it's worth
the price,
the fee,
the cost,
when all is lost,
but love is won,
when true love
comes,
there is
but one.

d.s.

1

When it snows on Christmas Eve in New York, there is a kind of raucous silence, like bright colours mixed with snow. Looking at Central Park from a window, you can see the snow fall steadily, shrouding all in white. Everything looks so still, so quiet ... but down below, in the streets, there are the inevitable sounds of New York. Horns bleating, people shouting, the clatter of feet and traffic and excitement, only muffled, somewhat dimmed. And in the last-minute furore of Christmas Eve, there is something more, a kind of wonderful tension waiting to explode in laughter and gifts ... people hurrying home, with packages stacked high in their arms, carolers singing, the innumerable Santa Clauses, tipsy and red-faced, celebrating their last night in the deadly cold, women holding tight to children's hands, admonishing them to be careful not to fall, and then smiling, laughing. Everyone in a rush, in high spirits, in unison for this one night of the year ... Merry Christmas! ... doormen waving, happy with their Christmas tips. In a day, a week, the excitement will be forgotten, the gifts unwrapped, the liquor drunk, the money spent, but on Christmas Eve nothing is yet over, it has only just begun. For the children it is a culmination of months of waiting, for the adults the end of frenzied weeks, of parties, shopping, people, gifts ... bright hopes as fresh as falling snow, and nostalgic smiles, remembering distant childhoods and long-forgotten loves. A time of memories, and hope, and love.

As the snow fell steadily the traffic began to thin at last. It was bitter cold, and only a few hardy souls were

1

walking in the snow as it crunched beneath their feet. What had turned to slush earlier that day had now turned to ice, which slid wickedly beneath the six inches of fresh snow. It was treacherous walking, and by eleven o'clock traffic had all but ground to a halt. For New York it was unusually silent. Only an occasional horn sounded in the distance, a random voice calling out for a cab.

The sound of a dozen people leaving the party at 12 East Sixty-ninth Street rang out like bells in the night. They were laughing, singing, they had had a wonderful time. The champagne had been abundant, and there had been hot buttered rum and mulled wine, a huge Christmas tree and bowls of popcorn. Everyone had been given small gifts as they left, bottles of perfume, boxes of chocolates, a pretty scarf, a book. The host was a former book reviewer of *The New York Times*, his wife a celebrated author, their friends an interesting crew, from budding writers to concert pianists of repute, great beauties and great minds, all crushed into the huge living room in their town house, with a butler and two maids passing hors d'oeuvres and serving drinks. It had been planned as their annual Christmas cocktail party, and as always it would go on until three or four. The group that left just before midnight was small, and among them was a tiny blonde woman wearing a large mink hat and a long dark mink coat. Her whole body was enveloped in the rich chocolate fur, her face barely peeking above her collar in the wind as she waved for a last time at her friends and began to walk home. She didn't want to share a taxi with them. She had seen enough people for one evening, she wanted to be alone. For her, Christmas Eve was always a difficult evening. For years she had stayed at home. But not tonight. Not this year. This time she had wanted to see friends, at least for a while. Everyone had been surprised and pleased to see her there.

'Nice to see you, Daphne. You're back. Working on a book?'

'Just starting one.' The big blue eyes were gentle and the delicate sweetness of her face belied her age.

'What does that mean? You'll finish it next week?' She was notoriously prolific, but had been working on a movie for the past year.

She smiled again, this time with more mirth. She was used to their teasing. A touch of envy ... curiosity ... respect. She was a woman who inspired all three. Daphne Fields was intensely private, hardworking, ambitious, determined, visible in literary circles, and yet even when she was present, she wasn't always really there. She always seemed as though she was just one step back, just out of reach, and yet when she looked at you, you could feel her touch your very soul. She seemed to see everything, and yet at the same time, she didn't seem to wish to be seen. She was different than she had been ten years before. At twenty-three she had been gregarious, funny, outrageous ... protected, safe, happy. She was quieter now, the laughter of the past only showed now in glimpses in her eyes, its echo buried somewhere in her soul.

'Daphne?' She turned around quickly at the corner of Madison Avenue as she heard footsteps behind her, muffled by the snow.

'Yes, Jack?' It was Jack Hawkins, the editorial director of her current publishing house, Harbor and Jones, his face red from the cold, his eyes a brilliant blue and watering in the wind.

'Don't you want a ride?'

She shook her head and smiled, and it struck him again how tiny she was, buried in the huge mink coat, her black suede gloved hands holding the collar close. 'No, but thanks. I really want to walk. I live just down the street.'

'It's late.' As always, when he saw her, he found himself wanting to take her in his arms. Not that he ever did. But he would have liked to. So would a lot of other men. At thirty-three she still looked twenty-five, and sometimes twelve ... vulnerable, fresh, delicate ... but

3

there was something more. There was a loneliness in the woman's eyes, which tore at your very soul, no matter how spectacular her smile, how warm her eyes. She was a woman alone. And she shouldn't have been. If life were fair, she wouldn't have been. But she was. 'It's midnight, Daff...' He hesitated before rejoining the others walking slowly west.

'It's Christmas Eve, Jack. And it's cold as hell.' She grinned, her sense of humour leaping to her eyes. 'I don't think I'll get raped tonight.'

He smiled. 'No, but you could slip and fall on the ice.'

'Aha! And break my arm and not be able to write for months, is that it? Don't worry. I don't have another deadline till April.'

'For chrissake, come on. You can come home with us for a drink.'

She stood on tiptoe and kissed his cheek as she patted his shoulder with one hand. 'Go on. I'm fine. But thanks.' She waved him off then, and turned and walked quickly along the street, burying her chin in her coat, looking neither right nor left, not glancing at the shop windows, or the faces of the few people who walked past her. The wind felt wonderful on her face, and as she made her way home she felt better than she had all night. It had been an exhausting evening, it always was at parties like that, no matter how pleasant they were, how many people she knew, they were always the same. But she had wanted to be there tonight. She didn't want to be alone in her apartment, she didn't want to hold on to the memories this year ... didn't want to ... couldn't stand it anymore ... Even now, as her face tingled in the snow, the same memories came back to her, and she walked faster as though to outrun them, as though she ever could.

Almost instinctively she ran to the corner, glanced to see if there was any traffic, saw none, and assumed that the light was green ... as though if she ran fast enough, if she crossed the street, she could leave the memories behind. But she always took them everywhere with her ... especially on Christmas Eve.

Running faster across Madison Avenue, she almost lost her footing as she slipped and then regained her balance as her arms flailed wide. The corner met, she turned rapidly left, to cross the street, and this time she didn't look up in time to see the car, a long red station wagon filled with people, hurtling through the last of their green light, her red. There was a shriek from the woman sitting beside the driver, a thump, another scream from within the car, and a strange sliding noise as the car ground across the ice and stopped at last. For an interminable instant, everything was silence. And then all the car doors opened at once, and half a dozen people rushed outside. There were no voices, no words, no more screams as the driver hurried towards her and then stopped, staring down at the woman lying like a small broken rag doll, cast facedown into the snow.

'Oh, my God ... oh, my God...' He stood there helplessly for a moment, and then turned frantically towards the woman standing beside him, a look of terror mixed with fury, as though someone had to be blamed for this, anyone but him. 'For chrissake, call the cops.' He knelt beside her then, afraid to touch her, to move her, yet even more afraid that she was dead.

'Is she ... alive?' Another man knelt in the snow beside the driver, bourbon still heavy on his breath.

'I don't know.' There were no plumes of icy vapour from her breathing, no movement, no sound, no life. And then suddenly the man who touched her began to cry softly. 'I killed her, Harry ... I killed her ...' He reached out towards his friend and the two men hugged in silent agony as they knelt there, as two cabs and an empty bus stopped and the drivers ran out.

'What happened?' Suddenly all was action, talking, explanations ... she ran out in front of the car ... never looked up ... didn't see her ... icy ... couldn't stop...

'Where the hell are the police when you need them?' The driver cursed as the snow fell around him ...

5

thinking, for no reason he could understand, of the carol they had sung only an hour earlier ... 'Silent night, holy night' ... and now this woman lay in the snow in front of him, dead or dying, and there were no damn cops.

'Lady? ... Lady, can you hear me?' The bus driver was kneeling beside her, his face next to hers, trying to feel her breath on his face. 'She's alive.' He looked up at the others. 'You got a blanket?' No one moved. And then, almost angrily, 'Give me your coat.' For a moment the driver of the station wagon looked shocked. 'For chrissake, man, the woman may be dying. Take your coat off.' He hurriedly complied then, as did two others, and they buried Daphne beneath a multitude of coats. 'Don't try to move her.' The old black bus driver looked as though he knew what he was doing as he tucked the heavy coats around her and gently cradled her face, to keep it from freezing in the snow. A moment later the flashing red light appeared. It was a city ambulance and they'd had a busy night so far. They always did on Christmas Eve. A police car was just behind them, its eerie whooping siren screeching hideously as it arrived.

The ambulance attendants hurried at once to Daphne, the police moved more slowly as they took in the scene, and the driver of the station wagon hurried towards them, calmer now, but trembling horribly from the cold, as his coat lay on the street. The bus driver watched as the ambulance attendants gently rolled Daphne on to the gurney. There was no sound from her, no consciousness of pain. He saw now that her face was skinned and cut in several places, but there had been no bleeding as she lay facedown in the icy snow.

The police took a report from the driver, and explained that he would have to take a sobriety test before he could be released. All the others clamoured that he was sober, that he had drunk less than anyone that evening, and that Daphne had run out in front of the car without even looking, and against the light.

'Sorry, it's routine.' The policeman showed no

particular sympathy for the driver, nor did he show any emotion as he glanced at Daphne's face. Another woman, another victim, another case. He saw worse than that almost every evening. Muggings, beatings, murders, rapes. 'She alive?'

'Yeah.' The ambulance driver nodded tersely. 'Just.' They had just slid an oxygen mask into place, and pulled open the mink coat to check her heartbeat 'But we're going to lose her if we don't hurry.'

'Where's she going?' The policeman was scribbling on his report, 'white female of undetermined age ... probably mid-thirties.'

The ambulance driver called over his shoulder as they closed the door on Daphne. 'We're going to take her to Lenox Hill, it's the closest. I don't think she'd make it farther than that.'

'Is she a Jane Doe?' That would be another headache. They'd already sent off two unidentified murder victims to the morgue that night.

'No. She had a purse.'

'Okay, we'll follow you. I can copy it down there.'

There was a tense nod as the driver disappeared to get his charge to Lenox Hill, and the police officer turned back to the shivering driver as he struggled back into his coat. 'Are you going to arrest me?' He looked terrified now. His Christmas had turned instantly into a nightmare as he remembered the vision of Daphne lying facedown in the street.

'Not unless you're drunk. We can give you the sobriety test at the hospital. Have one of your friends drive and follow us there.' The man nodded and slipped back into his car, nodding at one of his friends, who slipped rapidly behind the wheel. There was no talking now, no gaiety: only silence as they followed the double wail of sirens towards Lenox Hill.

2

In the emergency room there was an aura of frantic activity everywhere, with armies of people dressed in white seeming to move with the precision of a fine ballet. A team of three nurses and a resident had instantly taken over as the ambulance attendants wheeled Daphne in, and another resident and an intern had been called meanwhile. The mink coat was thrown over a chair and they rapidly cut off her dress. It was a sapphire-blue velvet cocktail dress she had bought at Giorgio's in Beverly Hills earlier that winter, but it meant nothing now as it lay in pieces around her on the emergency room floor.

'Fractured pelvis ... broken arm ... lacerations on both legs...' There was a deep gash on her thigh gushing blood now. 'Just missed the femoral artery on this one...' The resident worked quickly, taking stock, checking her pulse, watching her breathing. She was in shock by now, and her face looked as pale as the ice where she had lain. There was almost a strange otherworldliness about her now, a lack of individuality, as though she no longer had a face, a name. She was just another body. Just another case. But a serious one. And if they were going to save her, they all knew they were going to have to work fast and well. One shoulder had been dislocated, and the X rays would tell them if she also had a broken leg.

'Head injury?' The other resident was quick to ask as he started an IV.

He nodded. 'A bad one.' The senior resident frowned as he flashed the beam of a narrow flashlight into her eyes. 'Christ, she looks like someone dropped her off the top of the Empire State Building.' Now that she was no longer lying on the ice, her whole face was awash with blood, and she would need stitches in at least half a dozen places on her face. 'Call Garrison. We're going to need him.' The house plastic surgeon had his work cut out for him too.

'What happened?'

'Hit by a car.'

'Hit and run?'

'No. The guy stopped. The cops said he looks like he's about to have a stroke.'

The nurses watched in silence as the residents worked over Daphne, and then wheeled her slowly into the next room for X rays. She still hadn't stirred.

The X rays showed the broken arm and pelvis, the femur had a hairline crack, and the X rays of her skull showed that there was less damage than they had feared, but there was a severe concussion, and they were watching her for convulsions. Half an hour later they had her on an operating table, to set the bones, stitch up her face, and do whatever could be done to save her life. There was evidence of some internal bleeding, but considering her size and the force with which the station wagon had hit her, she was lucky to be alive. Very lucky. And her chart showed that she wasn't out of danger yet. At four thirty in the morning she was taken from surgery to intensive care, and it was there that the night nurse in charge went over her chart in detail and then stood staring down at her quietly, with a look of amazement on her face.

'What's up, Watkins? You've seen cases like that before.' The resident on the floor looked at her cynically, and she turned and whispered with annoyance in her eyes.

'Do you know who she is?'

'Yeah. A woman who was hit by a car on Madison Avenue just before midnight ... broken pelvis, hairline crack in her femur ...'

'You know something, Doctor? You aren't going to be

9

worth a damn in this business unless you learn to see more than just that.' For seven months she had watched him exercise his craft with precision, and very little humanity. He had the techniques, but no heart.

'All right.' He looked tired as he said it. Getting along with the nurses wasn't always his strong suit, but he had come to understand that it was essential. 'So who is she?'

'Daphne Fields.' She said it almost with awe.

'Terrific. But she still has all the same problems she had before I knew her name.'

'Don't you ever read?'

'Yeah. Textbooks and medical journals.' But with the rapid-fire smart-aleck answer, suddenly a light dawned. His mother read all of her books. For a moment the brash young doctor fell silent. 'She's well known, isn't she?'

'She's probably the most famous female author in this country.'

'It didn't change her luck tonight.' He suddenly looked sorry as he glanced down at the small still form beneath white sheets and the oxygen mask. 'Hell of a way to spend Christmas.' They looked at her together for a long moment and then walked slowly back to the nurse's station, where monitors reported the vital signs of each patient in the brilliantly lit intensive care unit. There was no evidence of day or night there. Everything moved at the same steady pace twenty-four hours a day. At times there were patients who came near hysteria from the constant lights, and the hum of monitors and lifesaving equipment. It was not a peaceful place to be, but most of the patients in intensive care were too sick to notice, or care.

'Has anyone looked at her papers, to see if there's someone we should call?' The nurse liked to think that for a woman of Daphne's stature there would be a host of people anxious to be at her side, a husband, children, agent, publisher, important friends. Yet she also knew, from articles she had read in the past, how zealously

Daphne guarded her privacy. Hardly anyone knew anything about her. 'She didn't have anything on her except a driver's licence, some cash, some charge cards, and a lipstick.'

'I'll take another look.' She took out the large brown manila envelope that was going to go into their safe, and she felt both important and somewhat outrageous as she went through Daphne Fields's things. She had read all of this woman's books, she had fallen in love with the men and women born in Daphne's mind, and for years she had felt as though Daphne herself were her friend. And now she was going through her handbag as though she did so every day. People waited in bookstores on autographing lines for two and three hours just to get a smile and a signature in a book, and here she was rifling through her purse like a common thief.

'You're impressed by her, aren't you?' The young resident looked intrigued.

'She's an amazing woman with an extraordinary mind.' And then there was something more in her eyes. 'She has given a lot of people a great deal of joy. There were times...' She felt like a fool saying it, especially to him, but she had to. She owed it to this woman who was now so desperately in need of their care. 'There were times when she changed my life ... when she gave me hope ... when she made me give a damn again.'

As when Elizabeth Watkins had lost her husband in a plane crash and she had wanted to die herself. She had taken a leave from the hospital for a year, and she had sat home and mourned, drinking Bob's pension. But something in Daphne's books had turned things around for her again, as though she understood, as though Daphne herself had known that kind of pain. And she made Elizabeth want to hang in, to keep going, to fight back. She had come back to the hospital again, and in her heart she knew it was because of Daphne. But how could she explain that to him? 'She's a wise and wonderful lady. And if I can do anything for her now, I will.'

11

'She can use it.' And then he sighed and picked up another chart, but as he did so he made a mental note to himself to tell his mother the next time he saw her that he had treated Daphne Fields. He knew that, just like Elizabeth Watkins, his mother would be impressed.

'Dr Jacobson?' The nurse's voice was soft as he prepared to leave.

'Yeah?'

'Will she make it?'

He hesitated for a moment and then shrugged. 'I don't know. It's too soon to tell. The internal injuries and the concussion are still giving us a run for our money. She got quite a blow on the head.' And then he moved on. There were other patients who needed his attention. Not just Daphne Fields. He wondered, as he stood waiting for the elevator, just what made up the mystique of someone like her. Was it that she wove a good tale or was it something more? What made people like Nurse Watkins feel as though they really knew her? Was it all illusion, hype? Whatever it was, he hoped they didn't lose her. He didn't like losing any patient, but if an important, newsworthy one died, it was worse. He had enough headaches without that.

As the elevator door closed behind him Elizabeth Watkins looked down at Daphne's papers again. It was strange, there was no indication of anyone to call in case of emergency. There was nothing in her handbag of any significance at all . . . Just then, tucked into a pocket, she found a photograph of a little boy. It was dog-eared and frayed but it looked fairly recent. He was a beautiful little blond child with big blue eyes and a healthy golden tan. He was sitting under a tree, grinning broadly and making a funny sign with his hands. But that was it, other than the driver's licence and charge cards, there was nothing else except for a twenty-dollar bill. Her address was on Sixty-ninth Street, between Park and Lexington, a building that the nurse knew would be handsome and well guarded by a doorman, but who was waiting for her at home? It was strange to realise that despite her fascination with this woman's books, she knew nothing about her at all. There wasn't even a phone number for them to call. As Elizabeth mulled it over an irregularity turned up on one of the monitors, and she and one of the other nurses had to check on the man in 514. He had had cardiac arrest the previous morning, and when they reached him, they didn't like the way he looked. They ended up having to spend over an hour with him. And it wasn't until her shift ended at seven in the morning that she stopped to look in on Daphne again. The other nurses had been checking her every fifteen minutes, but there had been no change in the past two hours since she'd come up to the fifth floor.

'How is she?'

'No change.'

'Are her vitals steady?'

'No change since last night.' Nurse Watkins glanced at the chart again and then found herself staring at Daphne's face. In spite of the bandages and the pallor there was something haunting about that face. Something that made you want her to open her eyes and look at you so that you could understand more. Elizabeth Watkins stood over her quietly, barely touching her hand, and then slowly Daphne's eyelids began to flutter, and the nurse could feel her heart begin to pound.

Daphne's eyes opened slowly as in a distant haze she seemed to look around. But she still looked very sleepy and it was obvious that she didn't understand where she was.

'Jeff?' It was the merest whisper.

'Everything's all right, Mrs Fields.' Nurse Watkins assumed Daphne Fields was a Mrs. Her voice was gentle and soothing, barely audible, as she spoke near Daphne's ear. It was a practised voice of comfort. She could have said almost anything in that tone of voice, and it would have brought a sigh of relief, and the knowledge that one was safe with her.

But Daphne looked frightened and troubled as her

13

eyes struggled to focus on the nurse's face. 'My husband...' She remembered the familiar wail of the sirens from the night before.

'He's fine, Mrs Fields. Everything's fine.'

'He went to find ... the baby ... I couldn't ... I don't...' She didn't have the strength to go on then, as Elizabeth slowly stroked her hand.

'You're all right ... you're all right, Mrs Fields...' But as she said it she was thinking of Daphne's husband. He must have been frantic by then, wondering what had happened to Daphne. But why had she been alone at midnight on Madison Avenue, on Christmas Eve? She was desperately curious about this woman, about the people who populated her life. Were they like the people she wrote about in her books?

Daphne fell back into her troubled, drugged sleep then, and Nurse Watkins went to sign out. But she couldn't resist telling the nurse who took over the station. 'Do you know who's here?'

'Let me guess. Santa Claus. Merry Christmas, by the way, Liz.'

'Same to you.' Elizabeth Watkins smiled tiredly. It had been a long night. 'Daphne Fields.' She knew that the other nurse had also read several of her books.

'For real?' Her colleague looked surprised. 'How come?'

'She was hit by a car last night.'

'Oh, Christ.' The morning nurse winced. 'How bad?'

'Take a look at the chart.' There was a large red sticker on it, to indicate that she was still critical. 'She came up from surgery around four-thirty. She didn't come to until a few minutes ago. I told Jane to put it on the chart.' The other nurse nodded and then looked at Liz.

'What's she like?' And then she felt foolish as she asked it. In the condition Daphne was in, who could possibly tell? 'Never mind.' She smiled in embarrassment. 'I've just always been intrigued by her.'

14

Liz Watkins admitted her fascination openly. 'So have I.'

'Does she have a husband?'

'Apparently. She asked for him as soon as she woke up.'

'Is he here?' Margaret McGowan, the nurse who had just taken over the station, looked intrigued.

'Not yet. I don't think anyone knew who to call. There was nothing in her papers. I'll let them know downstairs. He must be worried sick.'

'That'll be a rotten shock for him on Christmas morning.' Both women nodded soberly, and Liz Watkins signed out and left. But before leaving the hospital, she stopped at central registration and told them that Daphne Fields had a husband named Jeff.

'That's not going to help us much.'

'Why not?'

'Their number's not listed. At least there's nothing under Daphne Fields. We checked last night.'

'Try Jeff Fields.' And out of simple curiosity, Liz Watkins decided to hang around for a few minutes to see what they came up with. The girl at the desk dialled information, but there was no listing for a Jeff Fields either. 'Maybe Fields is a pen name.'

'That doesn't do much for us.'

'Now what?'

'We wait. By now her family will be panicked most likely. Eventually they'll call the police and the hospitals. They'll find her. It's not as though she's just any Jane Doe. And we can call her publisher on Monday.' The girl at central registration had recognised the name too. She looked at Liz curiously then. 'What's she look like?'

'A patient who's been hit by a car.' For an instant Liz looked sad.

'Is she going to make it?'

Liz sighed. 'I hope so.'

'Me too. Christ, she's the only writer I can ever read. I'll stop reading if she doesn't make it.' The remark was

15

meant to be amusing, but Liz was annoyed as she left central registration. It was as though the woman upstairs wasn't really human, just a name on the front of a book.

As she walked out into the snow in the winter sunshine, she found herself thinking about the woman behind the name. It was rare that she took patients home with her. But this was Daphne Fields. The woman whom, for more than four years, she liked to think that she knew. And as she reached the Lexington Avenue subway at Seventy-seventh Street, she suddenly stopped and found herself looking downtown. The address on the charge cards was only eight blocks from where she stood. What was to stop her from going to Jeff Fields? He must have been half crazy by now, frantic about the where-abouts of his wife. It certainly wasn't normal procedure, but after all, they were all human. And he had a right to know. If she could tell him now, and save him some of the frantic searching, what was so wrong with that?

Almost as though her feet were moving without her telling them to, she walked along the salt spread out on the fresh snow, and turned right towards Park when she reached Sixty-ninth Street. A minute later she stood outside the building. It looked exactly as she had suspected it would. It was a large, handsome stone building, with a dark green canopy, and a uniformed doorman standing just inside the door. He opened the door for her with a look of determined inquisition and his only word was 'Yes?'

'Mrs Fields's apartment?' It was extraordinary, she said to herself as she faced him. For four years she had read her books, and now she was standing in the lobby of her house, as though she knew her.

'Miss Fields is not in.' She noticed then that he had an English accent. It was like something out of a movie, or a dream.

'I know. I'd like to speak to her husband.' The doorman knitted his brows.

'Miss Fields doesn't have a husband.' He spoke with

the voice of authority and she wanted to ask him if he was sure. Maybe he was new, maybe he didn't know Jeff. Or maybe Jeff was just her lover, but she had said 'my husband.' For an instant Liz felt confused.

'Is there someone else at home then?'

'No.' He looked at her cautiously, and she decided to explain.

'Miss Fields had an accident last night.' With a burst of inspiration she flashed open her coat then, revealing the white uniform and stockings, and she indicated the starched cap she always carried in a plastic bag. 'I'm a nurse at Lenox Hill Hospital and we couldn't find a notation of next of kin. I thought that maybe...'

'Is she all right?' The doorman looked genuinely concerned.

'We don't know. She's still on the critical list, and I thought that... Does she live with anyone at all?' But he only shook his head.

'No one. There's a maid who comes in every day, but not on weekends. And her secretary, Barbara Jarvis, but she won't be back till next week.' Barbara had told him that with a smile when she gave him Daphne's Christmas tip.

'Do you know how I might reach her?' He shook his head again with confusion, and then Liz remembered the photograph of the little boy. 'What about her son?'

The doorman looked at her strangely then, almost as though he thought she was slightly mad. 'She has no children, miss.' Something defiant and protective came into his eyes, and for a split second Liz wondered if he was lying. And then he looked into Liz's eyes with an air of dignity and distance and said, 'She's a widow, you know.' The words hit Liz Watkins almost like a physical blow, and a moment later, with nothing left to be said, she walked back out into the frigid Christmas morning and felt tears sting her eyes, not from the cold, but from her own sense of loss. It was as though she could feel her own husband's death in her bones again, as she had with such intense pain for that whole first year after he had

17

died in the crash. So she *had* known ... they weren't just stories she dreamed up in her head. She knew. She had been through it too. It made Liz Watkins feel closer to her again as she walked slowly back to the subway, at Sixty-eighth and Lexington Avenue. Daphne was a widow, and she lived alone. And she had no one, except a secretary and a maid. And Liz Watkins found herself thinking that it was a lonely existence for a woman who wrote books so filled with wisdom and compassion and love. Maybe Daphne Fields was as lonely as Liz was herself. It seemed yet another bond between them, as she walked down the stairs into the bowels of the subway beneath the streets of New York.

3

Daphne lay drifting in her own private haze as a bright light seemed to pierce through the fog from very far away. If she tried very hard to concentrate on it, it would come closer for a time, and then the fog would envelop her again, almost as though she were sailing away from shore towards a distant place, losing sight of the last, barely visible landmarks, the lighthouse blinking faintly at her in the distance. And yet there was something familiar about the light, the sounds, there was a smell she could almost remember as she lay there. She didn't know where she was, and yet she sensed that she had been there before. There was something strangely familiar about it, and even in its distant, intangible familiarity, she knew that there was something terrifying about the sounds and smells. Something terribly, terribly wrong. And once, as she lay there, dreaming, she let out a small agonised sound as, in her mind, she saw a wall of impenetrable flames. But the nurse on duty came to her side quickly, and administered another shot. A moment later there were no memories, no flames, and there was no pain. She floated out again on a blanket of soft, fluffy clouds, the kind one sees looking out of the windows of aeroplanes, unreal, immaculate, enormous ... the kind of clouds one wants to dance on and bounce on ... she could hear herself laughing in the distance, and she turned in her dream to see Jeff standing beside her, as he had been so long ago ...

'I'll race you to that dune in the distance, Daffodil.' ... Daffodil ... Daffy Duck ... Daffy Queen ... Funny Face ... he had had a thousand nicknames for her, and there was always laughter in his eyes, laughter and something gentler still. Something that was there just for her. The race was as much a lark as all their other youthful endeavours. His endless, well-muscled legs racing her thin, graceful ones, and beside him she looked like a child, dancing in the wind, a summer flower on a hillside somewhere in France ... her big blue eyes in her tanned face, and golden hair flying in the wind.

'Come on, Jeffrey ...' She was laughing at him as she raced beside him in the sand. She was quick, but she was no match for him. And at twenty-two, she looked more like twelve.

'Yes, you can ... yes, you can!' But before they reached the dune in the distance, he swept her off her feet and spun her into his arms, his mouth crushing hers with the familiar passion that left her breathless each time he touched her, just as though it were the first time, which had happened when she was nineteen. They had met at a Bar Association meeting, which she was covering for the *Daily Spectator* at Columbia. She was a journalism major, and with overwhelming seriousness and intense devotion, she was doing a series of articles on successful young attorneys. Jeff had spotted her instantly, and somehow managed to get away from his cronies and invite her out to lunch.

'I don't know ... I ought to...' Her hair had been wound into a tight figure-eight knot at the base of her neck, a pencil stuck into it, a notebook tightly clasped in her hand, and those huge blue eyes looking up into his with just a hint of laughter. She seemed to be teasing him without saying a word. 'Shouldn't you be working too?'

'We'll both work. You can interview me over lunch.' Afterwards, months later, she had accused him of being conceited, but he wasn't. He just desperately wanted to spend some time with her. And they had. They had bought a bottle of white wine and a handful of apples and oranges, a loaf of French bread and some cheese. They had gone deep into Central Park and rented a boat, and they had drifted on the lake, talking about his work and her studies, about trips to Europe, and childhood summers spent in southern California and Tennessee and Maine. Her mother had been from Tennessee, and there was something about her that suggested the delicate southern belle, until one listened to her, and realised how powerful and direct she was. It wasn't the kind of style Jeff associated with a southern belle. Her father had been from Boston and had died when she was twelve. They had moved back to the South then, and Daphne had hated it, enduring it until she left and came to college in New York. 'What does your mother think of that?' He had been interested in everything about her. Whatever she told him, he wanted to know more.

'She's given up on me, I think.' Daphne said it with a small smile of amusement, her eyes lighting up again in just the way that tore at something deep in Jeffrey's soul. There was something so damn alluring about her, at the same time so sexy and so sweet, and then at the very same time so outrageous and gutsy. 'She's decided that in spite of her best efforts, I'm a damn Yankee after all. And not only that, I've done something unforgivable, I've got a brain.'

'Your mother doesn't approve of brains?' Jeffrey was amused. He liked her. He liked her one hell of a lot in fact, he decided as he attempted not to stare at the slit in her pale blue linen skirt, and the shapely legs beneath.

'My mother doesn't approve of the overt use of brains. Southern women are very canny. Maybe wily is a better word. A lot of them are smart as hell, but they don't like to show it. "They play."' She said it with a southern drawl worthy of Scarlett O'Hara, and they both laughed in the summer sun. It had been a beautiful July morning, and the sun was hot on their bare heads at noon. 'My mother has a master's in medieval history, but she'd never admit it. "She's just a lazy southern belle, y'know..."' The drawl was back again as she smiled at him with those cornflower-blue eyes. 'I used to think I wanted to be a lawyer. What's it like?' She looked

21

suddenly very young again as she asked, and with a sigh he leaned back comfortably in the little boat.

'A lot of work. But I like it.' His speciality was publishing and that intrigued her most of all. 'You thinking about law school?'

'Maybe.' And then she shook her head. 'No, not really. I did think about it. But I think maybe writing is more for me.'

'What kind of writing?'

'I don't know. Short stories, articles.' She blushed faintly in the summer sun, and lowered her eyes. She was embarrassed to admit to him what she really wanted to do. It might never happen. It was only now and then that she thought it would. 'I'd like to write a book one day. A novel.'

'Then why don't you?'

She laughed out loud as he passed her another glass of wine. 'Simple as that, eh?'

'Why not? You can do anything you want to.'

'I wish I were that sure. And what would I live on while I wrote my book?' She had used the last of the money her father had left her to go to school, and with one more year to go, she was already worrying that the meagre funds might not hold out. Her mother couldn't help her. She was working in a dress shop in Atlanta, an elegant one, but nonetheless there was barely enough for Camilla Beaumont to feed herself.

'You could marry a rich man.' Jeffrey was smiling at her, but Daphne didn't look amused.

'You sound like my mother.'

'Is that what she'd like?'

'Of course.'

'And what do you have in mind when you finish school?'

'A decent job, on a magazine, maybe a newspaper.'

'In New York?' She nodded, and he wasn't sure why, but he felt suddenly relieved. And then he looked at her with interest, his head tilted to one side. 'Aren't you going home this summer, Daphne?'

'No, I go to school in the summer too. That way I'll finish early.' There wasn't enough money for her to take her time.

'How old are you?' It was more like he was interviewing her than she him. She hadn't asked him a single question about the Bar Association meeting or his work as an attorney, they had only talked of themselves since they had shoved off from the dock in the little rented boat.

'I'm nineteen.' She said it with a sudden spark of defiance, as though she were used to being told that she was too young. 'And in September I'll be twenty and a senior.'

'I'm impressed.' His eyes were gentle as he smiled, and she blushed. 'I mean it. Columbia's a tough school, you must have worked damn hard.' She could tell by his tone of voice that he meant it and suddenly she was pleased. She liked him. Almost too much. Or maybe it was just the sunshine and the wine, but she knew as she looked at him that it was more than that. It was the curve of his mouth, the gentleness in his eyes, the graceful strength of his hands as he pulled lazily at the oars from time to time ... and the way he watched her, with intelligence and interest ... the sensitivity of the things he said.

'Thank you ...' Her voice drifted off and sounded very soft.

'What's the rest of your life like?'

She looked confused at the question. 'What do you mean?'

'What do you do with your spare time? I mean other than pretend to interview slightly drunk attorneys in Central Park.'

She laughed at him then and the sound echoed as they passed beneath a little bridge. 'Are you drunk? It must be the sun as much as the wine.'

'No.' He shook his head slowly as they came out into the light again. 'I think it's you.' He leaned over then and kissed her, and they had both played hooky for the

23

rest of the afternoon. 'They'll never know the difference,' he assured her as they wandered south towards the zoo. They laughed at the hippopotamus, threw peanuts to the elephant, and ran all the way through the monkey house holding their noses and laughing. He wanted to put her on the pony ride as though she were a little girl, and laughing at him again, she refused. Instead they took a hansom cab ride through the park, and at last they strolled up Fifth Avenue beneath the trees, until they reached Ninety-fourth Street where she lived.

'Do you want to come up for a minute?' She smiled innocently at him, holding the red balloon he had bought her at the zoo.

'I'd love to. But would your mother approve?' He was twenty-seven years old, and in the three years since he had graduated from Harvard Law he hadn't once thought of anyone's mother or whether or not they would approve. It was a good thing too, since no one's mother would. He had been on an orgy of dating and free sex since he had left school.

Daphne laughed at him as she stood on tiptoe and put her hands on his shoulders. 'No, Mr Jeffrey Fields, my mother would not approve.'

'Why not?' He pretended to look hurt as a couple returning from work looked at them and smiled. They looked young and beautiful and perfectly matched, his hair a deeper gold than hers, his eyes a dazzling grey-green, his features as handsomely sculpted as her own, and his youthful strength in sharp contrast to her delicate size as he circled her with his arms. 'Because I'm a Yankee?'

'No . . .' She tilted her head to one side and he felt his insides melt as his hands touched the tiny waist. 'Because you're too old, and too good-looking . . .' She grinned and gently pulled free from his grasp. 'And because you've probably kissed half the girls in town' – she laughed again – 'including me.'

'You're right. My mother would be shocked too.'

'Well, then come on upstairs for a cup of tea, and I

won't tell your mother, if you don't tell mine.' Her roommate was gone for the summer, and the apartment was tiny and respectable, shabby but not ugly. She made him iced tea, which she served with mint and wonderful delicate lemon cookies. He sat beside her on the couch, and it was suddenly eight o'clock at night and he wasn't tired or bored. He couldn't take his eyes off her, and he knew that he had finally met the woman of his dreams.

'How about dinner?'

'Aren't you tired of me yet?' Her feet were curled up under her and the hours had flown like minutes. The sun had just set over Central Park, and they had been together since before noon.

'I don't think I'll ever get tired of you, Daff. Will you marry me?'

She laughed at the question, watching his face, and she noticed something strangely serious in his eyes. 'In addition to dinner or instead of?'

'I'm serious, you know.'

'You're crazy.'

'No' – he looked at her matter-of-factly – 'actually, I'm smart as hell. I graduated in the top five of my class, I have a damn good job, and one day I'm going to be a powerful and successful lawyer. You're going to write best-selling books, and' – he narrowed his eyes as though considering the matter further – 'we'll probably have three children. We should have two, but you're so damn young we'll probably sneak in a third before you're thirty. What do you say?'

She couldn't stop laughing now. 'I still say you're crazy.'

'All right, I concede. We'll make it two children. And a dog. A golden lab.' She laughed and shook her head. 'All right. A French poodle ... a Chihuahua?'

'Will you stop?'

'Why?' He looked suddenly like a little boy, and she felt the same leap in her heart she had felt all afternoon at his side. 'Don't you like me?'

'I think you're terrific. And definitely crazy. Is this the line you use on everyone, or only innocent students like me?'

He looked totally serious and perfectly calm. 'I haven't proposed to anyone before, Daphne. Ever.' He leaned back against the couch. 'When are we going to get married?'

'When I'm thirty.' She crossed her arms and looked at him with amusement as they sat looking at each other from opposite ends of the couch, but he solemnly shook his head.

'When you're thirty, I'll be thirty-eight. I'll be too old.'

'And I'm too young. Call me in ten years.' She looked suddenly womanly and sure of herself and very, very strong and he loved it, as he moved slowly towards her on the couch.

'If I walked out of here right now, I would call you in ten minutes. If I could bring myself to wait that long. Now, will you marry me?'

'No.' But her insides turned to mush as he approached.

'I love you, Daff. Even if you do think I'm crazy. But I'm not. And whether you believe me right now, or not, we're going to get married.'

'I don't have a penny to my name.' She felt a need to tell him that, almost as if what he was saying was serious, as though he really meant it. But the craziest thing of all was that she knew he did.

'I don't have a dime either, Daff. But we will one day. Both of us. And in the meantime we can live on those fabulous cookies and iced tea.'

'Are you serious, Jeff?' She suddenly looked at him with something very fragile in her eyes. Suddenly she had to know. Maybe he was only playing with her. And she hoped not.

But his voice was hoarse and powerful and kind as he touched her cheek with one hand and reached out for her hand with the other. 'Yes, I am. I know right at this moment that whatever happens between us, it'll be all right, Daff. I feel that. I could marry you tonight, and I know it would be right for us for the rest of our lives. Something like this only happens once in a lifetime. And I'm not going to let it go. If you fight me, I'll pursue you until you listen to me. Because I'm right and I know it.' And after a silent moment between them, 'And I think you know it too.'

Her gaze bored into his then, and he could see that there were tears hovering on her lashes. 'I have to think about this ... I'm not sure I understand what happened.'

'I do. We fell in love. Simple as that. We could have waited another five years to find each other, or ten, but we didn't. I found you today, at that goddamn boring meeting, and sooner or later you're going to be my wife.' He kissed her gently then, and stood up, still holding tightly to her hand. 'And now I'm going to say good night, before I do something truly crazy, like attack you.' She laughed at him then, and felt perfectly safe. There were others she would never have let into her apartment, but instinctively with Jeff she had known that she was safe. It was one of the things she instantly loved about him. She felt safe and happy and protected. She felt it just wandering at his side as they walked from the boat pond to the zoo. It was an essence of power he exuded, and quiet strength, at the same time mixed with something gentle. 'I'll call you tomorrow.'

'I'll be at school.'

'What time do you leave in the morning?'

'Eight o'clock.'

'Then I'll call you before that. Can you meet me for lunch?' She nodded, feeling suddenly awed and a little dazed.

'Is this for real?'

'Very much so.' He kissed her in the doorway and she felt stirrings she had never felt before, and that night as she lay in bed thinking of him, trying to sort out her thoughts, she felt a longing she had never known.

27

But he had meant everything he said to her on that first evening. He called her the next morning at seven o'clock, and he appeared outside the school of journalism on schedule at noon. His jacket was slung over his shoulder, his tie was in his pocket, and his golden hair shone in the sun as she came hesitantly down the steps, feeling shy for the first time. This was different from the day before. There wasn't the hubbub of the Bar Association meeting around them, there was no wine, no boat, no sunset peeking through her windows. There was only this extraordinary golden man standing in the noonday sun, smiling proudly down at her as though he owned her. And in her heart she knew he did, and always would.

They hailed a cab and went to the Metropolitan Museum for lunch, and sat by the pool as they toyed with their food, and by the time he took her back to school, she felt entirely comfortable with him again. He had a remarkable way about him, and once again she felt the same strength and safety she had felt at his side the day before.

She made dinner for him at her apartment that night, and once again he left early. And that weekend he had taken her to Connecticut to visit friends, play tennis, and sail, and they had come home golden brown from the sun, and this time he took her to his place in the East Fifties and he made dinner. It was there that he finally took her in his arms and slid his hands carefully over her silky golden flesh and made her absolutely ache for him. She spent the night wrapped in his arms, and it was only the next morning that he made love to her, with all the tenderness and caution and solemnly bridled passion of a man very much in love with a virgin. He made it beautiful for her, and that night they made love in her apartment, and this time it was she who took the lead and surprised not him, but herself, with the force of her desire and passion.

They had spent the rest of the summer in and out of bed, working their schedules around those of their

28

roommates, hers having returned in late August, until finally Jeff could stand it no longer and during the Easter vacation of her senior year, he flew to Tennessee with her, and they got married. It was a quiet ceremony attended by her mother and a dozen friends. She wore a long white organdy dress and a big hat, and carried a big bunch of wild flowers and daisies, and her mother cried, as much from relief as from the delight of seeing her daughter married.

Camilla was dying from leukaemia, but she had not told Daphne yet. Before they flew north again, she told Jeffrey. He promised her that he would take good care of Daphne forever and always. Three months later she was dead and Daphne was pregnant with their first child. Jeff flew to Atlanta with her for the funeral, and he handled everything and held her as she cried. She had no one left now except Jeffrey and the baby that was due in March.

Through the summer he watched her grieve for her mother as they furnished their new apartment with the few treasures they had shipped up from Atlanta. She had graduated from Columbia in June, and in September she got her first job, working at *Collins Magazine*, a highly respectable women's magazine. Jeffrey didn't think it made much sense to go to work since she was pregnant, but at last he agreed, and he had to admit that it did her a great deal of good. She took a leave of absence from the magazine after Christmas, and settled in for the remaining two months to wait for the baby. She was more excited every day, and finally he saw the grief of the previous summer leave her eyes. She insisted that if it was a boy she wanted to call him Jeffrey, but he wanted a little girl that looked like her. And late at night in their bed, he would touch her belly and feel the baby kick, with love and wonder in his eyes.

'Doesn't it hurt?' He worried about her a great deal, but at twenty-one she was the picture of health, and she laughed at his concern.

'No. It feels funny sometimes, but it doesn't hurt.' She

29

looked at him happily as she lay on her side, and he felt almost guilty as he reached out to touch her breasts. He always wanted her, even now, and they made love almost every night. 'Don't you mind, Jeff?'

'No. Of course not. You're beautiful, Daff. Even more beautiful than you were before.' There was something so soft and luminous about her face as her golden hair fell around her shoulders like a shaft of wheat, and her eyes lit up with a kind of inner light he'd read about and never seen. She seemed filled with promise and a kind of magical joy.

She called him at the office after the first few pains, and she sounded exuberant and almost high, and he rushed home to be with her, forgetting the client in his office, his coat behind the door, and carrying with him a law book he had had in his hand when she called, feeling more than a little frantic and more afraid than he would admit. But when he saw her waiting for him, sitting quietly in a chair, he knew that everything would be all right, as he had always known, and he caught her excitement and poured them each a glass of champagne.

'To our daughter.'

'To your son!' Her eyes teased and laughed and then became suddenly glazed with the pain. He flinched for her for a moment, reaching quickly for her hand, forgetting the champagne, and then remembering all that they'd learned in the class they'd taken for two months, helping her through each pain, timing them with the stopwatch he'd bought, until four o'clock when he sensed before she did that it was time to go. The doctor met them at the hospital, and Daphne smiled, looking almost regal, her head held high, so excited and so proud, and then just as quickly vulnerable as she leaned against him, panting softly as he coached, but her eyes still dancing at what they shared, almost impervious to the increasing pain.

'You're incredible, darling. And oh, God, how I love you.' He had helped her to the labour room, stood by and held her hand and breathed, donned a mask and gown and sped into the delivery room with her at nine o'clock that night, and at ten nineteen, with Daphne pushing with all her might, and tears streaming from Jeffrey's eyes as he looked on with astonishment and awe, their baby girl was born. Aimee Camilla Fields poked her head into the world with a giant howl as her mother gave a shout of victory and glee. The doctor held her aloft and she was quickly put into Daphne's arms as Jeffrey looked down at both of them, laughing and crying, stroking Daphne's damp hair with one hand and holding the baby's tiny fingers with another.

'Isn't she beautiful, Jeff?' Daphne was crying now, and smiling at the same time, looking up at him with all she felt as he bent to kiss her gently on the lips.

'You've never looked more beautiful to me, Daff.'

'I love you.' The nurses had stepped back, feeling, as they always did, never quite hardened to the miracles they saw each day, and the threesome stayed alone for as long as they could. And at last Daphne was brought back to her room, and when she slept, Jeffrey went home at midnight, to lie awake in their bed, thinking of their little girl, and his wife, and all that he had shared with her in two years.

The next three years had flown past. Daphne had gone back to work at *Collins* when Aimee was a year old. She had stretched her leave as long as she could, and she hated to go, but as much as she loved Aimee, she wanted to work, too. She knew that she needed that for herself, to remain who she was, and Jeff knew that it was important to her to be not only mother and wife, but someone unto herself. He always understood. They had a sitter every day, a grandmotherly woman Daphne had found after the baby was born, and Jeff helped her take care of the baby at night, and on weekends they went to the park, or drove out into the country to see friends. There was a magical quality to their life, which touched everyone they knew.

'Don't you two ever fight?' one of Jeff's friends from

work teased them when they came to Connecticut one weekend. He liked them both, and envied Jeff more than he would admit.

'Sure we fight. At least twice a week. We make appointments to fight. I kick her around a little bit, she calls me names, the neighbours call the cops, and after they leave, we watch TV.' Daphne grinned at him over Aimee's head and blew him a kiss. He was as he always had been, funny and loving and solid and everything she wanted in a man. He had remained, for her, a dream come true.

'You two make me sick.' Their friend's wife had groaned as she watched them. 'How can married people be so happy? Don't you two have any sense?'

'Not a bit,' Jeff had answered with an arm around Daphne's shoulders as Aimee leaped off her lap and ran off to chase the cat she had just seen. 'I guess we're just too dumb to know any better.' But that was the nice thing about them, they were so damn bright, so good to be with, and so much fun. 'The Perfect Couple,' their friends dubbed them, and sometimes it made Daphne nervous, for fear that it was too good to last just the way it was, but after five years things between them had only got better. They had grown into a single mould, and other than his passion for watching gory rugby matches in Central Park on Sunday afternoons, there was absolutely nothing that Daphne would have changed. It was simply a question of two people who had found precisely what suited them best, and had had the wisdom to treat it well. And the only problem that they faced was an occasional lack of funds, which never seemed to trouble either Daphne or Jeff. At thirty-two Jeffrey was making a decent salary as a lawyer. It was enough, and her money from *Collins* paid for the extras. They were thinking of a second child, and when Aimee was three and a half, they decided to try again, but so far nothing had happened.

'It's fun trying though, isn't it, kid?' He teased her on

a Sunday morning that was Christmas Day. 'Want to try again?'

'After last night? I'm not sure I've got the strength.' After getting the tree and the presents ready for Aimee, they had made love until 3 a.m. She had grinned at him and he swatted her behind. Their sex life was even better than it had been five years before. She grew prettier as she grew older, and at twenty-four she had a more womanly air as she strode across the room and stroked a single finger across his naked belly, circling slowly around the places that pleased him the most.

'If you do that, you're gonna get raped!' But Aimee had burst into the room, her arms filled with new toys, and he had quickly wrapped himself in a towel while Daphne went to help her dress the new doll Santa Claus had brought.

'Sorry, sweetheart.'

'Kids!' He rolled his eyes and went off to take a shower. It was a lazy, easy day, the three of them ate turkey and cranberry jelly and dressing till they could barely move, and when at last Aimee went to bed that night, they sat in front of the fireplace in their living room, reading the last of the *Sunday Times*, drinking mugs of hot chocolate, and looking at the tree. It had been a perfect Christmas on a relaxed Sunday afternoon and evening as Daphne stretched out on the couch and put her head in Jeffrey's lap.

'What's a mountain range in Peru?'

'I give up. What is it?' He had no knack whatsoever for the crossword puzzle she tackled every Sunday, even during the festivities of Christmas. 'How the hell do you do that damn thing, Daff? Christ, I went to Harvard Law School, did okay, and I still can't get three words right.' She finished the whole thing every week by Tuesday, and wouldn't give up until she did. He was no help at all and yet she always asked him. 'And don't ask me who Beethoven's sister was or I'll throw my hot chocolate at you.'

'That's it!' She grinned evilly and sat up. 'Violence! That's the one I couldn't get on twenty-six across.'

'You drive me nuts. Come on' – he stood up and held out a hand – 'let's go to bed.'

'Let's wait until the fire goes out.' Their bedroom and Aimee's was upstairs in the little duplex they had acquired the summer before with his last raise, and Daphne loved the fireplace but she always worried, especially now, so near to the Christmas tree.

'Turn your worry button off, it's almost out now.'

'Then let's wait.'

'Let's not.' He pinched her behind. 'I'm so horny I can hardly see straight. I think you put an aphrodisiac in my hot chocolate.'

'Bullshit.' She grinned at him and stood up. 'You've been a sex maniac ever since I met you. You don't need an aphrodisiac, Jeffrey Fields. You need saltpetre in your food just to keep you normal.' He laughed and chased her up the stairs to their bedroom, where he threw her gently into bed and began to caress her beneath her sweater and she wondered, as she had for the past two months, if she would get pregnant this time. 'Why do you think it's taking so long this time?' She looked only faintly worried. With Aimee she had got pregnant almost on the first try, but this time it hadn't taken yet. Jeffrey only shrugged and smiled.

'Maybe I'm over the hill . . . hell, maybe you ought to get a new model.'

Her eyes were serious as she looked at him across the bed as they undressed. 'I'd never find anyone like you, Jeff. I don't give a damn if we never have another baby. Do you know how much I love you?'

'How much?' His voice was deep and husky as he reached for her across their bed and pulled her slowly towards him.

'More than you'll ever know, my love.' Her words were swallowed by his lips as they kissed and held, and began to make love beneath the comforter she had bought for their big brass bed. The bed was a kind of joke

34

between them. The springs squeaked, and the bed creaked outrageously when they made love, but it was an antique they had bought at an auction and they loved it. They had bought a smaller one for Aimee, and Daphne had discovered a beautiful child's quilt her grandmother had made among her mother's things.

'Think I should check on Aimee?' She always did before they went to bed, but tonight she felt sensual and lazy as she lay sated in her husband's arms, and he felt the same, and for a prescient instant she wondered if there would be life in her womb again. Their lovemaking had had an ardour and a depth and seriousness to it that somehow seemed as though it ought to result in their longed-for second child. She was thinking of the baby they wanted, and not the one they had, as she lay sleepily in Jeffrey's arms.

'She's all right, Daph.' He always teased her because she stood so solemnly beside Aimee's bed every evening, staring down at the golden-haired little girl who looked so much like her. And if she slept too soundly, Daphne would put a finger just beneath her nose to make sure that she was breathing. 'Just stay put tonight. She's fine.' Daphne smiled drowsily then, and a moment later was sound asleep curled up within Jeffrey's comfortable clasp. She lay there like that asleep for hours, until she stirred slowly in a distant dream. They were standing beside a waterfall, all three of them, she, Jeffrey, and Aimee, and the sound of the cascading water was so loud that it disturbed her sleep, but there was something more, too, a smell in the woods that somehow she couldn't escape from, and at last she stirred beside Jeffrey, coughing, opened her eyes to flee the dream, and looked through their bedroom doorway to discover that the sound of water that had roused her was the roar of fire, and that beyond their bedroom was a wall of flame.

'Jeff! ... My God, Jeff!' She jumped from the bed feeling dazed and dizzy and he stirred slowly as she shook him and began to scream. 'Jeff! Aimee!' He was

35

awake then and saw instantly what was happening as he struggled from their bed, heading naked towards their bedroom doorway. Daphne was right behind him, her eyes wide with terror as he was forced back by the flames. 'Oh, God, Jeff, the baby!' There were tears streaming from her eyes from the pungent smoke and raw fear, but he turned to her swiftly and grabbed her shoulders tightly in his hands, shouting above the roar of the fire.

'Stop it, Daff! The fire's in the hall. We're safe, so is she. I'm going to get her now and she's going to be fine. I want you to put the blanket around you and crawl as fast as you can down the stairs to the doorway. I'm going to grab Aimee out of bed and I'll be right behind you. There's nothing to be afraid of! Do you understand me?' He was wrapping her in the blanket as he spoke, his movements quick and agile as he shoved her down towards the floor in the doorway of their bedroom and spoke clearly into her ear. 'I love you, Daff. It'll be fine.' He spoke with absolute conviction and then dashed the few feet towards Aimee's bedroom as Daphne headed down the stairs, trying not to panic, knowing that Jeff would keep Aimee safe, he always took care of them ... always ... always ... she said it over and over to herself as she crawled down the stairs, trying to glance behind her, but the smoke seemed to have grown more dense and she could barely breathe, she felt as though she were swimming in the acrid smoke, and she couldn't see, and suddenly there was the sound of an explosion behind her, but as she heard it, it seemed to come from a great distance, and she was back in the dream she had had, standing beside the waterfall with Aimee and Jeff, and suddenly she wondered if the fire had only been a dream too. She felt comforted as she realised that it was ... just a dream ... just a dream ... as she drifted off to sleep and felt Jeff at her side ... she heard voices then in the dream as she slept on and after she heard a strange and eerie wail ... that familiar sound again ... that sound ... and the lights coming at her through the fog ... Mrs

Fields, the voices said, Mrs Fields ... and then the lights had been too bright, and she was in an unfamiliar, frightening place, and she had felt terror course through her like hot blood, unable to remember how she had gotten there or why, and she had looked everywhere for Jeff ... trapped between reality and dreams ... there had been bandages on her hands and legs, and a thick coating of ointment on her face, and a doctor had looked down at her with despair as she cried ... 'no, NO! Not my baby! ... not Jeff!!! NOOO ...'

Daphne Fields called out in the night in an anguished broken voice, remembering when she had seen those bright lights before ... after the fire ... It was Christmas morning when she woke, and the day nurse in intensive care came running to see her, lying there, shaking, her eyes wild, her face frozen with remembered pain. She had waked then as she did now, feeling the same shaft of agony slice through her like a guillotine, just as it had then, nine years before, the night Jeff and Aimee died in the fire.

4

Barbara Jarvis arrived at Lenox Hill two hours after Liz Watkins had called. She had looked up Barbara's number when she got home, and Barbara came at once, shaking from head to foot at the news. It was nine o'clock in the morning, and unlike the starched nurse who led her down the hall, Barbara Jarvis looked as though she hadn't slept all night. She had been up late, and the news of Daphne's accident rocked her to the core. She had been told that her employer was in intensive care at Lenox Hill and that she could visit for fifteen minutes on the hour and should notify whatever relatives there were. Liz Watkins had wondered, after she called, if the secretary would come and what she would be like. She hadn't sounded very friendly on the phone, hadn't thanked Liz for her call, and had sounded almost suspicious in answer to the nurse's words. Liz suspected that she was a strange one, and the nurse who saw her appear at the desk would have agreed. Not strange, but far from friendly either, she had a fierce, protective way about her as she asked for Daphne's room. Her questions suggested a kind of paranoia that left the nurse feeling both angry and annoyed. She wanted to know if the press had been called, if anyone had been to see Miss Fields yet, if her name appeared on any central register, and if the general nursing staff was aware of who she was.

'Yes, some of us are.' The nurse stared down at her. 'We read her books.'

'Maybe so. But she isn't writing here. I don't want Miss Fields disturbed.' Barbara Jarvis looked ferocious as she stood to her full, rather impressive height, her dark hair pulled into a knot, her eyes deeply troubled.

'Is that clear? If any of the newspapers call, there are to be no comments, no stories, no reports. Miss Fields hates publicity, and at a time like this she is entitled to be left alone.'

The nurse on duty was quick to snap, 'We had the governor of New York here last year, Miss...' She was so damn tired she couldn't even remember the woman's name, and a sudden urge to call her Miss Bitch almost overtook her. 'And he enjoyed total privacy while he was here. Miss Fields will do the same.' But it was obvious that the dark-haired amazon standing before her didn't believe a word she said. She was in total contrast to her employer, so tiny, so frail, so delicate and blonde as she lay in her hospital bed.

'How is she?'

'There's been no change since you were called. She had a difficult night.'

Little lightning bolts of worry darted into Barbara Jarvis's eyes. 'Is she in a great deal of pain?'

'She shouldn't be. She's being well medicated, but it's hard to tell.' And then she wondered if Barbara could shed some light on the obvious terrors Daphne had suffered the night before. Her voice softened as she looked at Barbara Jarvis. 'She had a rough night.' She explained the nightmares Liz Watkins had described in the chart and something in Barbara Jarvis's eyes said that she knew, but she wasn't going to give anything up. 'She had nightmares... dreams... it could be from the concussion. I'm not really sure.' The secretary said not a single word. 'If you'd like to see her, you can see her briefly. She floats in and out of consciousness and she may not know who you are.' Barbara nodded and looked rapidly at the rooms all along the well-lit hall. There was an eerie quality to intensive care, even to a healthy person. Nowhere in the hall was there a trace of daylight, everything was brilliant and fluorescent and technical and bright. It was more than a little frightening and Barbara Jarvis had never seen an intensive care unit before. But she knew that Daphne had. She had come to her long after the tragic fire, but Daphne had told her about it one night. She knew all about it, and about Aimee and Jeffrey, and after the past three years with Daphne she knew a great deal more than that.

'May I see her now?'

The nurse nodded and led the way to Daphne's room. She walked into the room on swift, silent feet and stood looking down at Daphne, glancing at the monitors again and satisfied that all was well. She'd had another shot of Demerol an hour before and she would sleep now for several hours. The nurse glanced at Barbara and saw tears sliding slowly down her cheeks as she reached towards Daphne and took her tiny white hand in her larger one and held it as though Daphne might have been her child. Her pulse was still weak, and it was still too soon to tell if she would live. Barbara held her breath as she watched, trying not to cry but she couldn't help it. The nurse left them alone at last, and Barbara stood staring at Daphne miserably until the nurse came back and signalled to Barbara from the doorway. The tall, sturdy woman stood exactly where she had when the head nurse left her, and she gently replaced Daphne's hand on the bed, and then left the room. As she walked slowly back down the hall, she looked grief-stricken for a long unguarded moment and then put back her mask as they stood beside the desk.

'Will she be all right?' Barbara's eyes sought something they couldn't have, some encouragement, some hope, a promise. But it was difficult to believe that Daphne would make it, lying there, so still, so small, so immobile. She almost looked as though she were already gone. Liz took small comfort in knowing that Daphne inspired the same kind of passionate devotion from those who knew her as from those who read her books. But Barbara Jarvis was looking at her now, wanting an answer, an answer that no one had, save God.

'It's too soon to say. She could very well make it.' And her voice gentled with long years of practice. 'Or she might not. She has suffered a very extensive trauma.'

Barbara Jarvis nodded in silence and walked slowly away and into a phone booth. When she came out she asked when she could see Daphne again and they told her in half an hour. 'Would you like a cup of coffee? You can see her again for fifteen minutes, on the hour. Or . . .' Maybe she would leave, she was only her secretary after all.

Barbara read their minds. 'I'll stay.' She tried to smile faintly, but the effort seemed enormous. 'I'd like coffee.' And then, almost with pain, 'Thank you.' A student nurse led her to a coffee machine placed conveniently near a blue vinyl couch that had seen several lifetimes of sorrow. The couch itself seemed depressing to her as she thought of people waiting here for loved ones to live or die, more often the latter. The nurse in blue stripes poured a cup of steaming black coffee and handed it to Barbara as the taller woman stood for a moment looking into the young girl's eyes. 'Do you read her books?' Blushing, the young nurse nodded. And then she went away. And at three o'clock Liz Watkins came back, to do a double shift. Barbara was still there, looking frantic and exhausted. Liz checked the chart, and saw that there was no improvement.

Liz came to chat with Barbara after a while, and poured her a fresh cup of coffee. She wondered about Barbara then, guessed her to be about Daphne's age, and for an insane moment she wanted to ask Barbara what Daphne was really like, but she knew that to do so was to invite the secretary's hostility to rise again like an angry cloud around her.

'Is there any family who should be called?' It was all that she dared to ask.

Barbara hesitated for only a fraction of an instant and then shook her head. 'No. No one.' She wanted to say that Daphne was alone in the world, but that wasn't exactly true, and either way it was none of this woman's business.

'I understand that she's a widow.'

Barbara looked surprised that she knew, but she

41

nodded and took a sip of the hot coffee. It had come out on *The Conroy Show* once, but she had never discussed it again. She didn't want anyone to know it. Now she was known only as 'Miss' Fields, and the implication was that she never had been married. At first it had felt to Daphne like a treason to Jeff, but in the long run she knew it was better. She couldn't bear to speak of him and Aimee. She only spoke of them to ... But Barbara forced the thought from her mind, panicking at what might happen to him now.

'There've been no calls from the press?' She looked up from her coffee, suddenly worried.

'None.' Liz smiled reassuringly. 'And I'll handle those. Don't worry. We won't let them near her.'

For the first time Barbara smiled a small, genuine smile, and it was strange, for a fraction of an instant she looked almost pretty. 'She hates publicity with a passion.'

'That must be pretty rough. They must chase after her a lot.'

'They do.' Barbara smiled again. 'But she's a genius at avoiding them when she wants to. On tour it can't be helped, but even then she's very adept at dodging inappropriate questions.'

'Is she very shy?' Liz was so hungry for some piece of the real Daphne. She was the only celebrity she had actually longed to meet, and now here she was, so near, and yet Daphne was still a total enigma.

Barbara Jarvis was once again cautious, but not hostile. 'In some ways, she is. In other ways, not at all. I think "retiring" suits her better. She is very, very private. She's not afraid of people. She just keeps her distance. Except' – Barbara Jarvis looked distant and thoughtful for a moment – 'except with the people she cares about and is close to. She's like an excited happy child with them.' The image seemed to please both women, and Liz smiled as she stood up.

'I've always admired her through her books. I'm sorry to come to know her this way.' Barbara nodded, her own smile faded, her eyes sad. She couldn't believe that the woman she had worshipped might be dying. And her sorrow showed in her eyes as she looked up at Liz Watkins. 'I'll let you know as soon as you can go back in to see her.'

'I'll wait here.'

Liz nodded and hurried off. She had lost almost half an hour and she had ten thousand things to do. The day shift was the busiest of all, it was like working two shifts instead of one, and she still had to do her own shift that night. It was going to be a long, brutal day, for her, and Barbara Jarvis.

5

When the two women walked into Daphne's room again, Barbara saw her eyes open for a minute, and then flutter closed, as Barbara looked rapidly towards the head nurse who had brought her in. Barbara's face was filled with panic. But Liz was quiet and calm as she checked Daphne's pulse, and smiled as she nodded to Barbara.

'She's coming out of the sedation a little.' And almost as she said it Daphne's eyes opened again and tried to focus on Barbara.

'Daphne?' She spoke softly to her employer and friend as Liz watched, and Daphne's eyes opened again with a blank look. 'It's me ... Barbara ...' The eyes stayed opened this time and there was the faintest hint of a smile and then she seemed to drift back to sleep for a minute or two, and then she looked at Barbara again and seemed about to say something as Barbara bent near to hear her better.

'It must have ... been ... some ... party ... I have ... a hell of a headache ...' Her voice drifted off as she smiled at her own joke. Tears filled Barbara's eyes, even as she laughed. She was suddenly filled with relief that Daphne was even talking, and she turned towards Liz with a victorious look as though her firstborn had spoken her first words, and Liz's own eyes felt damp, with fatigue and emotion. She reproached herself silently for growing soft, but there was a tenderness to the scene that touched her. These two women were a strange pair, the one so small and fair and the other so tall and dark, the one so strong through her words although so tiny, the other so powerfully built, and yet so obviously in awe of Daphne. Liz watched as Daphne made the effort to speak again. 'What's new?' It was the merest whisper and Liz could barely hear her.

'Not much. Last I heard you ran over a car. They tell me it was totalled.' It was the kind of banter they exchanged every morning, but Daphne's eyes looked sad as she looked at Barbara.

'Me ... too ...'

'That's a lot of crap and you know it.'

'... tell ... me ... the truth ... how am I?'

'Tough as nails.'

Daphne's eyes looked to the nurse she could see now as well, as though she wanted reassurance. 'You're much better, Miss Fields. And you'll feel a great deal better tomorrow.' Daphne nodded, like a small, obedient child, as though she believed it, and then suddenly her eyes seemed filled with worry. She sought Barbara again with her eyes and there was something very adamant in her face as she spoke again.

'Don't ... tell ... Andrew ...' Barbara nodded. 'I mean it. Or ... Matthew ...' Barbara's heart sank at the words. She had been afraid she would say that. But what if something happened? If she didn't 'feel better tomorrow,' as the nurse promised. 'Swear ... to ... me ...!'

'I swear, I swear. But for chrissake, Daff ...'

'... no ...' She was obviously growing weaker, the eyes closed and then opened again, with curiosity this time. 'Who ... hit ... me?' As though knowing would make a difference.

'Some jackass from Long Island. The police said he wasn't drunk. The guy claimed you didn't look where you were going.'

She tried to nod but instantly winced, and it took her a moment to catch her breath as Liz watched and checked the time on her wrist. It was almost time to end the visit. But Daphne seemed determined to speak again. '... telling ... the truth ...' They waited but nothing more came, and then Barbara bent to ask, 'Who is, love?'

The voice was soft and the eyes smiled again. 'The . . . jackass . . . I . . . didn't look . . . I was thinking . . .' And then her eyes went to Barbara's. Only she knew how unbearable Christmas was for her, how painful it had been every year since Jeff and Aimee died in the fire on Christmas night. And this year she was alone, which was worse.

'I know.' And now the memory of them had almost killed her, or was it that she didn't care anymore? A horrifying thought struck Barbara. Had she stepped in front of the car on purpose? But she wouldn't. Not Daphne . . . not . . . or had she? 'It's all right, Daff.'

'. . . don't let them . . . make . . . trouble . . . for him . . . Not his fault . . . Tell . . . them . . . I said so . . .' She looked at Liz then as though to confirm it. She had been a witness. 'I . . . don't . . . remember . . . anything . . .'

'That's just as well.'

And then she looked sad and tears filled her big blue eyes. '. . . except . . . the sirens . . . it sounded like . . .' She closed her eyes and the tears slid slowly out of the corners of her eyes and on to her pillow as Barbara reached down and took her hand, tears in her own eyes.

'Don't. Daphne, don't. You have to get well now.' And then, as though to pull Daphne back, 'Think of Andrew.'

Her eyes opened then, and she looked long and hard at Barbara as Liz pointed to her watch and nodded at Daphne.

'We're going to let you rest now, Miss Fields. Your friend can come back in to see you in a little while. Would you like anything more for the pain?' But she shook her head and seemed grateful to close her eyes again. She was asleep before they left the room, and after walking halfway down the hall side by side, Liz turned and looked at Barbara. 'Is there anything we should know, Miss Jarvis?' Her eyes dug deep into Barbara's. 'Sometimes information that may seem too personal makes a big difference in helping a patient.' She wanted to add 'helping a patient choose between living or dying,' but she didn't. 'She had some awful nightmares last night.' There were a thousand questions in her voice and Barbara Jarvis nodded, but the walls went up instantly to protect Daphne.

'You already know that she's a widow.' It was all that she would say and Liz nodded.

'I see.' She left Barbara then and went back to her desk, and Barbara went back to the blue vinyl couch after pouring herself another cup of black coffee. She sat down with a sigh and she felt totally exhausted. And why the hell had she made her promise not to tell Andrew? He had a right to know that his mother was perhaps dying. And if she did,. then what? Daphne had more than amply provided for him from the books in the past years, but he needed so much more than that. He needed Daphne and no one else ... and if she died ... Barbara shuddered, and looked out at the snow beginning to fall again outside. And she felt as bleak as the winter landscape.

Daphne had told her nothing about him for the first year that she worked for her. Nothing at all. She was a successful author, apparently single, working harder than anyone Barbara had ever known, with almost no personal life, but even that hadn't seemed surprising. How could she have had time for that, putting out two major books a year? She couldn't and she didn't. But it was on Christmas Eve when Barbara had worked late that she suddenly found her in her office, sobbing. It was then that she had told her about Jeff ... and Aimee ... and Andrew ... Andrew, the child she had conceived the night of the fatal fire ... the baby who had come nine months later, when she :was so alone, with no family, no husband, no friends she would see because they all reminded her of Jeff, and his birth had been so different from Aimee's. Aimee who had been born with Jeff holding her hand, with a great gust of a cry, and her parents looking on with tears of joy intermingled with victorious laughter. Andrew had taken thirty-eight hours to come, a breech birth, with the umbilical cord threatening his every breath, until both he and his mother were finally, mercifully, released by an emergency Caesarean.

The doctor had reported that he made a strange, muted little sound when he first emerged, and he had been almost blue as they worked fiercely to save both him and Daphne. And when the anaesthetic had worn off, she had been too sick to see him, or hold him. But Barbara still remembered the look in Daphne's eyes when she spoke of the first moment she had held him. He had lain in her arms, put there by a nurse, and suddenly nothing hurt, nothing mattered in the world, except that baby, who lay staring up at her with a determined little stare, looking exactly like Jeffrey. She had named him Andrew Jeffrey Fields. She had wanted to name him after his father, but she couldn't bring herself to do it. It would have brought too many painful memories back each time she called him 'Jeff,' so instead she named him Andrew. It was a name they had chosen for a boy when she had been pregnant with Aimee. And she had told Barbara too of her shock and joy when she had discovered six weeks after the fire that she was pregnant. It was the only thing that had kept her going during those lonely nightmarish months, the only thing that had kept her from wanting to die too. And she hadn't, she had lived, as had Andrew, despite his traumatic arrival. He had been a beautiful, rosy-cheeked, happy baby. And he had Daphne's cornflower-blue eyes, but he continued to look exactly like his father.

She had rented a tiny apartment for the two of them, and she had filled the nursery with pictures of Jeffrey, so that one day he would know what his father had looked like, and in a small silver frame was a photograph of his sister. It wasn't until he was three months old that Daphne suspected that there was something different about Andrew. He was the most good-natured child she had ever seen. He was fat and healthy, but one day she dropped a whole stack of dishes as he lay peacefully in

48

a basket on the kitchen table, and he hadn't even started. She had clapped her hands at his ear after that, and he had just smiled at her. She had felt a whisper of terror run through her. She couldn't face calling the doctor, but on their next visit she had casually asked some questions, and he had instantly known what she suspected. Her worst fears had proven true. Andrew was deaf from birth. He made odd little sounds from time to time, but they couldn't know until later if he was mute as well. It was impossible to know if it had been as a result of the shocks she had sustained right after his conception, or from the medication she'd been given in the hospital for her own burns and injuries from the fire. She had been in the hospital for over a month, heavily medicated, no one had even suspected that she was pregnant. But whatever the reason for his hearing loss, it was permanent and it was total.

Daphne came to love him with a fierce, protective zeal and determination. By day she spent every waking moment with him, setting her alarm for five thirty every morning, so she could be sure to be awake before he was, ready for what the day would bring him and to assist him with each difficult moment. And they were many. At first she was obsessed with the potential hazards that constantly lay in wait for him. In time she grew accustomed to anticipating the constant dangers of warnings he couldn't hear, car horns he was never aware of, growling dogs and pans of sizzling bacon. But the stress she was under was constant. And yet there were endless precious moments, times when tears of tenderness and relief flowed down her cheeks as she shared her life with her baby. He was the happiest, sunniest child imaginable, but again and again she had to face the fact that his life would never be normal. Eventually, everything in her life stopped except her activities with Andrew. There were no friends she saw, no movies she went to. She devoted every single moment of the day to Andrew, afraid to leave him with anyone else, terrified that they wouldn't understand as well as she the dangers and frustrations that confronted him. She took every burden of his life on to her own shoulders, and each night she fell into bed exhausted, drained by what the effort had cost her. There were times too when her own frustrations in dealing with a deaf child almost overwhelmed her, when the urge to shout at him for what he could not do or hear made her clench her teeth and her fists so that she wouldn't slap him. It was not Andrew she wanted to hit, but the cruelty of fate that had deafened her beloved child. She laboured under a silent but leaden mantle of guilt, secretly feeling that it was her fault, that she should have been able to prevent it. She hadn't been able to keep Jeff and Aimee from dying in the fire, and now she couldn't keep this final brutal reality from Andrew. She was helpless to change it for him. She read every book she could find about children who were deaf from birth, and she took him to every specialist in New York, but there was nothing they could do for Andrew, or Daphne. She faced the reality of it almost with fury, like an enemy to be fought. She had lost so much, and now Andrew had too. The unfairness of it burned within her like a silent rage, and at night she would have nightmares about the fire and awake screaming.

The specialists she had seen had suggested to her that eventually she would have to put Andrew in a special school, that it would be best for him, that it would be impossible for him to deal with normal children. And they also pointed out again and again that, despite Daphne's Herculean efforts with the child, there were stumbling blocks that she was unable to get over. Although she knew him better than anyone else did, even she had difficulties communicating with him, and the specialists warned her that in time she would come to resent him for her failures. She was not a professional, after all, they insisted, and he needed more sophisticated skills than she was able to give him. In addition, his constant isolation from other children made him suspicious and hostile on the rare occasions when he did see them. Hearing children didn't want to play with him because he was different, and their cruelty caused Daphne so much pain that she hadn't taken him to a playground since he was an infant. But still she resisted the idea of his being with other children like him, so she kept him to herself, the two of them prisoners in her tiny apartment, as the specialists continued to badger her about sending him away to a special school.

'An institution?' she had screamed at the specialist she knew best. 'I won't do that to him. Ever!'

'What you're doing is a lot worse.' The doctor's voice had been gentle. 'It doesn't have to be forever, Daphne. But you have to face facts. You can't teach him at home what he needs to know. He needs totally different skills than you can give him.'

'Then I'll learn them!' She had shouted at him because she couldn't shout at Andrew's deafness, or at life, or fate, or the gods who had been so unkind to her. 'Dammit, I'll learn them and I'll stay with him night and day to help him!' But she had already done that, and it wasn't working. Andrew was living in total isolation.

'And when you die?' the pediatrician asked bluntly. 'You don't have a right to do that to him. You'll make him totally dependent on you. Give him the right to his own life, for God's sake. A school will teach him independence, it will teach him how to function in the normal world when he's ready.'

'And when will that be? When he's twenty-five? Thirty? When he's so totally used to being out of the world that he's institutionalised? I saw those people up there, I talked to them, through an interpreter. They don't even trust what they call "hearing people." They're all freaks, for chrissake. Some of them are forty years old and have never lived anywhere but an institution. I won't do that to him.' He had sat, watching them talk, fascinated by the gestures and the expressions on their faces, but Andrew had heard none of the angry words between his mother and his doctor.

For three years she had fought her private war, to the

slow but steady detriment of Andrew. It had become obvious long since that Andrew could not speak, and when he was three, her renewed efforts to introduce him to hearing children at the playground were a disaster. Everyone shunned him. It was as though they somehow knew that he was terribly, terribly different, and one day she watched him sitting in the sandbox alone, watching the other children with tears running down his face, and then looking at his mother as though to say 'What's wrong with me?' She had run to him and held him, rocking him gently as they both cried, feeling isolated and afraid. Daphne felt that she had failed him. A month later, for Daphne, the war was over. With lead in her heart she began to visit the schools she so desperately hated, feeling as though at any moment Andrew would be torn from her. She couldn't face another loss in her life, and yet she knew that not to do it would destroy him. Freeing him was the ultimate gift she had to give him. And at last she found the only school where she could bear to leave him. It was in a small, comfortable town in New Hampshire, with birch trees surrounding it, and a pretty little pond, and a small river that ran along the grounds, where she watched the children fish. And what she liked best about it was that there were no 'students' there older than twenty. They weren't called patients, or residents or inmates, as she had heard in other institutions. They were called children and students, like 'real' people. And most were sent back to their families in their late teens, to attend colleges when they could, or take jobs, and return to the families who had stood behind them for so long and waited. As Daphne walked slowly around the grounds with the director, a stately woman with white hair, she felt the weight of her loss again, knowing that Andrew might live there for as long as fifteen years, or at least eight or ten. It was a commitment that tore her heart from her. This was her last child, her last love, the only human being alive who was related to her, and she was going to leave him. Her eyes filled with tears again at the thought, and she felt

52

the same shaft of unbearable pain she had felt for months as she had come to terms with the decision, and as the tears poured down her face she felt the director's hand on her arm, and suddenly she was in the older woman's arms, being held close in a strong comforting grasp, sobbing out the pain of the past four years, since even before the birth of Andrew.

'You're doing a wonderful thing for your son, Mrs Fields, and I know how hard it is.' And then, after the sobs had finally subsided, 'Are you currently employed?' The question had come as a shock. Did they doubt her ability to pay his tuition? She had hoarded whatever money she and Jeff had had, and she had been desperately frugal. She hadn't bought so much as a new dress for herself since the few she had bought after the fire, and she was planning to use all of Jeff's insurance money for the school, for as long as it would last. But now of course, with Andrew gone, she could go back to work. She had not worked again since Jeff's death. She had had to recover herself, and then she had found out she was pregnant. She couldn't have worked anyway then, she was too distraught after their deaths. And *Collins* had given her a generous severance when they accepted her resignation.

'No, I'm not employed, Mrs Curtis, but my husband left me enough to . . .'

'That's not what I meant.' The director's smile was filled with compassion. 'I was wondering if you would be free to stay up here for a while. Some of our parents do that. For the first months, until the children adjust. And Andrew being so young . . .' There were five other children his age, which was part of what had convinced Daphne. 'There's a charming little inn in town, run by an Austrian couple, and there are always a few houses to rent. You might give it some thought.' She felt as though she'd had a reprieve. And her face lit up like a sunbeam.

'Could I see him every day?' Tears filled her eyes again.

'At first.' Mrs Curtis's voice was gentle. 'Eventually it will be better for both of you if you begin to cut the visits down. And you know' – the smile was warm – 'he's going to be awfully busy with his friends.'

Daphne's voice was forlorn. 'Do you think he'll forget me?'

They stopped where they stood and the older woman looked at her. 'You're not losing Andrew, Mrs Fields. You're giving him all that he needs for a successful life in the world again.'

A month later she and Andrew made the trip, and she drove as slowly as she could through New England. These were the last hours of their old life and she wanted to drag them out as long as she could. She knew she wasn't ready to leave him. And somehow, the beauty of the countryside made it even harder. The leaves were turning, and the hills were a riot of deep reds and bright yellows, there were cottages and barns, horses in fields, and tiny churches. And suddenly she was reminded of the big beautiful world beyond their apartment that she wanted to share with him. There were cows and lots of sights lining the road he had never seen, and he pointed and made his odd little familiar sounds to ask her questions. But how could she explain to him a world filled with people, and aeroplanes, and exotic cities like London or San Francisco or Paris? She realised suddenly how deprived he had been and how little she had actually taught him, and the familiar feeling of failure washed over her again as they drove on through the scarlet hills of New England.

All of Andrew's favourite treasures and toys were in the car, his teddy bear and a stuffed elephant he loved, and the picture books they had leafed through together, but which no one could read to him. Daphne found herself thinking of it all as they drove, and suddenly what stood out to her now was all that she hadn't accomplished rather than all that she had, and she found herself wondering what Jeff would have done in her place with his son, if he'd had the chance. Perhaps he would have had more ingenuity, or greater patience, but he could have had no greater love than she had for this child. She loved him with every ounce of her soul, and if she could have given him her own ears with which to hear, she would have.

An hour before they reached the school they stopped for a hamburger at a roadside stand, and her bleak mood brightened a little. Andrew seemed excited by the trip, and he was watching everything around him with delight. She wished, as she watched him, that she could tell him about the school, but there was no way to do that. She couldn't tell him what it was like or what she felt, or why she was leaving him there or how much she loved him. For all of his life she had only been able to meet his physical needs, or show him fire trucks racing silently by in the street. She had never been able to share her thoughts or feelings with him. She knew that he had to know that she loved him, she was with him every moment after all. But what would he think now when she left him at the school? How could she explain it to him? It only added to her private anguish to know that she couldn't. Mrs Curtis, the director at the school, had rented a little 'cottage for her in the town, and Daphne planned to stay until Christmas, so that she could visit Andrew every day. But that would be very different from what they had shared in the past, their every waking moment spent side by side. Their lives would never be the same again, and Daphne knew it. The hardest thing she had ever done in her life was letting go of this child, whom she wanted to hold on to more than life itself, but knew she couldn't.

They arrived at the school shortly after dusk, and Andrew looked around in surprise, as though he didn't understand why they were there. He looked at Daphne with confusion and she nodded and smiled as he glanced worriedly at the other children. But these children were different from the ones he had met in Central Park in New York, and it was as though he instinctively sensed that they were like him. He watched them play, and the

55

signs they made, and again and again they came over to him. It was the first warm welcome he had ever had from children his own age, and as one little girl came over and took his hand and then kissed his cheek, Daphne had to turn away so he wouldn't see the tears pouring down her face. Andrew just stared at the little girl in amazement. It was Mrs Curtis who helped him join in at last, took his hand and led him around as Daphne watched, feeling as though she had done the right thing and a new world was opening to Andrew. Something extraordinary happened as she watched, he began to reach out to these children so much like him. He smiled and he laughed and for a moment he forgot Daphne. He began to watch the signs that they made with their hands, and laughing once he imitated one of them, and then making a funny little noise, he walked over to the little girl who had approached him before and kissed her. Daphne went over to him later and waved to show that she was going away, but he didn't cry, he didn't even look frightened or unhappy. He was having too good a time with his friends, and she held him for a last moment, with a brave smile on her face, and then she ran away before the tears came again. And he never saw the ravaged look on his mother's face as she drove out of the driveway.

'Take care of my baby . . .' she whispered to a God she had long since come to fear, and this time she prayed that He would hear her.

6

Within two weeks Andrew had totally adjusted to his new life at the school, and Daphne felt as though she had lived in the cosy New England town forever. The cabin Mrs Curtis had helped her find was warm in the autumn wind, it had a perfect little country kitchen with a brick fireplace for baking bread, a tiny living room filled with a well-worn couch and deep easy chairs, there was a fireplace here too, and shining copper pots filled with plants, and in the bedroom a four-poster bed with a bright quilt. It was here that Daphne spent most of her time, reading books and writing in a journal. She had started keeping a journal when she was pregnant with Andrew, it was filled with notes about what her life was like, what she thought and felt, little essays about what life meant to her. She always thought that one day, when he was older, she would share her writings with Andrew. And in the meantime, it gave her a place to empty her soul, on long, lonely nights, like the ones in New Hampshire. The days there were bright and sunny, and she took long walks down wooded paths and beside streams, thinking of Andrew, and looking at the snowcapped mountains. This was a whole different world from New York. There were barns with horses, cows in the pastures, hills and meadows where she could walk without seeing a soul, and often did. She only wished she could share it with Andrew. For years now, he had been her only companion. And every few days she went to the school to see him. For her it was still an enormous adjustment. For four years her life had centred around him, and now suddenly he was gone, and there were times when the emptiness almost overwhelmed her. She found herself thinking more and more of Jeff, and of Aimee. She would have been eight years old by then, and at times when Daphne saw a little girl the same age, she turned away, her eyes filled with tears, her arms aching to hold her. But it wasn't as though she had lost Andrew the same way, she kept reminding herself. He was alive and happy and busy, and she was doing the right thing for him and she knew it. But time after time she would go to the school, and sit on a bench outside with Mrs Curtis, watching him play and learning to sign now. She was also learning the hand signs in order to communicate with him better.

'I know how difficult this is for you, Mrs Fields. It's easier for the children to adjust, than for their parents. For the little ones it's a kind of release. Here they are finally free of a world that didn't accept them.'

'But will it ever accept him?'

'Yes.' There was absolute certainty in the director's voice. 'It will. He'll always be different. But with the right tools there will be almost nothing he can't tackle in time.' She smiled gently at Daphne in the breeze. 'One day he'll thank you.' But what about me? she suddenly wanted to ask ... what happens to me now? What do I do without him? It was as though the older woman had read her thoughts. 'Have you thought about what you'll do when you go back to New York?' For a woman alone, like Daphne, Andrew's absence would create an enormous void, and she already knew that Daphne hadn't worked since she was pregnant almost five years before. At least most of the parents had each other, other children, jobs, activities to fill their lives in the absence of these special children. But it was obvious that Daphne didn't. 'Will you go back to work now?'

'I don't know...' Daphne's voice trailed off as she stared out at the hills. How empty it would all be without him. She almost hurt more now than she had when she first left him. The reality of it was finally sinking in. Her life would never be the same again ... never ... 'I don't know.' She pulled her eyes back from the hills and looked at Mrs Curtis. 'It's been so long. I doubt if they'd even want me.' She smiled and the passage of time showed in her eyes. The years had taught her lessons filled with pain.

'Have you thought of sharing with others what you've learned with Andrew?'

'How?' Daphne looked surprised. The thought had never occurred to her.

'There aren't enough good books on this subject. You mentioned that you were a journalism major in college, and you worked at *Collins*. Why not write a book or a series of articles? Think of how something like that would have helped you when you first found out about Andrew.' Daphne remembered the terrible feelings of being alone, of no one in the world seeming to share her problem.

'It's a thought.' She nodded slowly, and watched Andrew hug a little girl, and then chase a big red ball across the playground.

'Maybe you're just the one to do it.'

But the only thing she seemed to write now was her journal, night after night. She had nothing but time on her hands now, and she was no longer exhausted at night, as she had been for years since she had Andrew. He was just like any other small child, constantly busy, but he needed even more attention than most, to be sure that he didn't run into danger from something he couldn't hear, and there was always his frustration to deal with, at not being able to communicate with others.

When she closed her journal that night, she lay in the dark and thought again of Mrs Curtis's suggestion. It was a good idea, and yet, she didn't want to write about Andrew. Somehow it seemed a violation of him as a person, and she didn't feel ready to share her own fears and pain. It was all too fresh, just as Jeff's and Aimee's deaths had been for so long. She had never written about that either. And yet she knew that it was all bottled up inside, waiting to come out, along with feelings that she

59

hadn't faced in years. Those of being still young, and a woman. For four years now, her only close contact had been with her son. There had been no men in her life, and few friends. She didn't have time for them. She didn't want pity. And going out with another man would have seemed a betrayal of Jeffrey, and all that they had shared. Instead, she had submerged all of her feelings, locked all of those doors, and gone on year after year taking care of Andrew. And now there was no excuse left. He would live at the school, and she would be alone in their apartment. It made her never want to go back to New York. She wanted to hide in the cabin in New Hampshire forever.

In the mornings she went for long walks, and once in a while she stopped at the little Austrian Inn for breakfast. The couple who ran it were well matched – both rotund and kind, and the wife always asked about her son. She knew why Daphne was there from Mrs Curtis. As in every small country town, people knew who belonged and who did not, why they were there, when they had arrived, and when they were leaving. People like Daphne weren't so rare here, there were other parents who came to town to visit their children. Most stayed at the inn, and a few did what Daphne was doing, usually in the summer. They rented cottages and small houses, brought their other children with them, and generally made it a festive occasion. But Mrs Obermeier sensed that Daphne was different. There was something much quieter, much more withdrawn, about this tiny, delicate, almost childlike woman. It was only when you looked into her eyes that you realised she was wise well beyond her twenty-eight years, and that life had not always been kind to her.

'Why do you think she's alone like that?' Mrs Obermeier asked her husband one day as she put sweet rolls in a basket and slid a tray of cookies into the oven. The cakes and pies she prepared made everyone's mouth water.

'She's probably divorced. You know, children like

60

that can destroy a marriage. Maybe she paid too much attention to the boy and her husband couldn't take it.'

'She seems so alone.'

Her husband smiled. His wife always worried about everybody. 'She probably just misses the boy. I think Mrs Curtis said he was very young, and he's her only child. You looked like that too when Gretchen went to college.'

'That wasn't the same.' Hilda Obermeier looked at him, knowing that there was something he wasn't seeing. 'Have you looked into her eyes?'

'Yes,' he admitted with a grin and a flush of his full jowls, 'they're very pretty.' He patted his wife's behind then and went outside to bring in some more firewood. They had a house full of guests at the inn that weekend. In the dead of winter there were always those who went cross-country skiing. And in the fall, people came from Boston and New York to see the changing of the leaves. But the brilliant orange and magenta leaves were almost gone now. It was November.

On Thanksgiving Day, Daphne went to the school and shared turkey dinner with Andrew and the other children. They played games afterwards, and she was stunned when he grew angry at her and signed to her, 'You don't know anything, Mom.' The rage in his eyes cut her to the quick, and she felt a separation from him she had never felt before. She suddenly resented the school for taking him from her. He wasn't *hers* anymore, he was *theirs*, and she hated them for it. But instead she found herself taking it out on Andrew, and signing angrily at him. Mrs Curtis saw the exchange and spoke to her about it later, explaining that what they were both feeling was normal. Things were changing very quickly now for Andrew, and consequently for Daphne. She couldn't sign as quickly as he, she made mistakes and felt clumsy and stupid. But Mrs Curtis assured her that in time they would have a better relationship than the one they'd had before and it would all be worth it.

And at dinnertime she and Andrew had made friends

61

again, and they had gone to the table hand in hand, and when he signed the prayer at the start of the meal, she was so proud she thought she would burst, and afterwards he grinned at her. After dinner he played with his friends again, but as he wore down he came to sit on her lap and cuddle, as he had in years past, and she smiled happily as he fell asleep in her arms. He purred softly in his sleep, and she held him, wishing she could turn the clock back. She carried him to his room, changed his clothes, and slipped him gently into bed as one of the counsellors watched. And then, with a last look at the sleeping blond child, she walked softly out of the room and went back downstairs to the other parents. But she didn't want to be with them tonight. Once Andrew was in bed, she was anxious to get back to her cabin. She had grown used to her solitude and her own thoughts, and the comfort of spilling her soul into her journal.

She drove home by a familiar back road and gave a startled gasp as she heard something snap and the car suddenly sank forward and stopped. She had broken an axle. She was shaken but not hurt, and instantly realised how lucky she had been that it hadn't happened sometime when she was on the highway. But this was a mixed blessing too. She was alone on a deserted road and about seven miles from her cabin. The only light was that of the moon and she could see her way clearly, but it was bitter cold and it would be a long walk home in the sharp wind. She pulled her collar tightly around her, wishing that she had worn a hat and gloves and more sensible shoes, but she had worn high heels and a skirt for Thanksgiving dinner. Her eyes watered in the cold, and her cheeks tingled and her hands grew rapidly numb, even in her pockets, but she buried her chin in her coat, and with no other choice she kept walking.

It was almost an hour later when she saw headlights coming towards her on the road, and she was suddenly engulfed in panic. Even in this sleepy town something unpleasant could happen. She was a woman alone on a dark country road and if something happened to her, there would be no one to hear her screams, or come to help her. Like a frightened rabbit, she suddenly stopped in the road as she watched the headlights come towards her. And then, instinctively, she ran behind a tree, her heart pounding so loudly she could hear it as she hid there. She wondered if the driver had seen her flight. He had still been a good distance away when she ran from the road. And as the vehicle approached she saw that it was a truck. For a moment it looked as though it would drive past her, and then it ground to a sudden halt as she held her breath, terrified, waiting.

The door to the truck opened and a man stepped out. 'Hello? Anyone there?' He stood looking around for a few minutes and all she could see was that he was very tall, and she felt suddenly very foolish hiding there. As her feet and legs ached with the cold, she wanted to come out from behind the tree and ask for a ride, but how would she explain that she was hiding? It had been a stupid reaction, and now she had to stay there. He walked slowly around the truck, shrugged, hopped back into his truck, and kept going. And then he was gone, and Daphne walked slowly out from behind the tree with a foolish grin, talking to herself.

'You dummy. Now you'll freeze your ass off all the way home. Serves you right.' She began to hum then, amused by her own stupidity, and knowing that she had lived in cities for too long. There was no reason that she should have felt threatened, except that she had noticed that feeling more and more in the past few years. It was as though she had grown fearful, from her lack of contact with people. And she always felt so totally responsible for Andrew that she was suddenly desperately afraid something might happen to her.

She walked on down the road for another mile, and suddenly she was startled to hear a car behind her in the distance. Once again she thought of running off the road, and this time she shook her head, saying softly to herself, 'There's nothing to be afraid of.' She felt even more foolish for the spoken words, but she stood her ground as she moved to the side of the road and watched the same truck she had seen before come towards her. The truck stopped again and this time she could see the man as the light went on when he opened the door. He had a rugged face, grey hair, and broad shoulders and he was wearing a heavy sheepskin coat that he pulled close around him.

'Is that your car back there?'

She nodded and nervously smiled, noticing that his hands were large and rough as he took them out of his pockets. The same shiver of fear ran through her that she had felt before, but she forced herself not to run from him. If he was a decent man, he would think she was crazy. And if he wasn't, it was too late to hide from him now. She would have to deal with whatever happened in whatever way she could. She smiled, but her eyes were wary. 'Yes, it is.'

'Did I pass you awhile back?' He looked confused about it as he looked down at her. 'I thought I saw someone on the road, but when I stopped I didn't see a soul. When I saw your car back there, I figured I'd missed you.' His eyes seemed to understand something she didn't want him to know, and his voice was deep and husky and gentle. 'Broke your axle, I see. Can I give you a ride? It's an awful cold night to be walking.' They stood there like that for a long moment as she searched his eyes, and then nodded.

'I'd like that very much. Thank you.' She hoped he thought the tremor in her voice was from the cold, and by now even she wasn't sure. She was frozen to the bone, and she could barely manage the door handle with her numb fingers. He opened it for her and she slipped inside, and then a moment later he came around to his side and slipped behind the wheel, with scarcely a glance at her.

'You were lucky you weren't on the main road going fifty. Did it give you any warning at all?'

'No, it just snapped and the front end collapsed and

that was it.' She felt better now and the inside of the little truck was wonderfully warm. Her fingers ached as they thawed out and she blew on them. He handed her a pair of thick sheepskin-lined gloves without further comment and she slipped them on as they drove towards her cabin.

It was almost five minutes later when he turned to her again, with that same gentle husky voice. Everything about him suggested the rugged strength of the mountains. 'Did you get hurt?'

She shook her head. 'No. Just cold. It would have taken me a couple of hours to get home.' She remembered to tell him where she lived then.

'That's the old Lancaster cabin, isn't it?' He seemed surprised.

'I'm not sure. I think so. I rented it from a woman named Dorsey, but we never met. I did it all by mail.'

He nodded. 'That's her daughter. Old Mrs Lancaster died last year. I don't think her daughter's been back in twenty years. She lives in Boston. Married to some social lawyer.' It was all so wonderfully small-town, the details that everyone knew so well. It made Daphne smile at the memory of her terror of being attacked. All this man wanted to do was tell her the local gossip. 'You from Boston too?'

'No. New York.'

'Came up for a rest?' It was idle chitchat as they drove along, but Daphne sighed softly. She wasn't really sure she wanted to tell him, and it was as though he instantly understood. He held up a hand, smiled at her apologetically, and then turned his eyes back to the road. 'Never mind. You don't have to answer. I've been here for so long, I forget my manners. Everyone in town asks questions like that, but it's none of my business what you're doing here. I'm sorry I asked.'

He was so kind about it that she smiled in return. 'It's all right. I came up here to be near my son. I just put him in the . . . the Howarth School.' She had been about to say 'the school for the deaf' but the words stuck to her tongue and she couldn't. The man turned to her then, she might as well have said it, he knew what the Howarth School was. Everyone in town did. It was neither a disgrace, nor a secret.

'How old is your boy?' And then with a concerned glance, 'Or am I being nosy again?'

'Not at all. He's four.'

He frowned and looked at her as though he understood. 'Must be damn hard to leave him. He's awful young.'

It was strange, she wanted to ask him questions then. What was his name? Did he have children? They had suddenly become travelling companions on the dark country road. But a moment later he stopped in front of her house, and he hopped out to help her out. She almost forgot to give the gloves back, and she smiled up into his eyes. 'Thank you very much. I wouldn't have been home for hours, if it weren't for you.'

He smiled then, and she could see humour in his eyes that she hadn't guessed at before. 'Could have saved yourself at least a mile if you'd trusted me the first time.' Her face flushed in the dark and she laughed.

'I'm sorry – I almost came out – ' she stammered, feeling like a little girl beside this huge man. 'I was hiding behind a tree, and I almost did come out, but I felt like such a jerk for hiding in the first place.'

He grinned at the confession and walked her to her door. 'You were probably right. You never know who you'll meet, and there are some crazy kids in this town. There are everywhere these days, not just in New York. Anyway, I'm glad I found you and saved you the walk.'

'So am I.' She wondered for a moment if she should invite him in for coffee, but that didn't seem quite right. It was nine o'clock at night, she was alone, and she really didn't know him.

'Let me know if there's anything I can do for you while you're here.' He held out a sturdy hand and she felt its

66

strong grasp on her own as they shook hands. 'My name is John Fowler.'

'I'm Daphne Fields.'

'Nice to meet you.' She opened her door with her key and he waved as he walked back to his truck, and a moment later he was gone, and Daphne stood in the empty cabin, wishing she had invited him in. At least he would have been someone to talk to.

Even her journal held no special interest that night. She kept thinking of the rugged face, the grey hair, the powerful hands, and she found herself oddly curious about him.

7

The morning after Thanksgiving, Daphne went to the Austrian Inn and exchanged the usual pleasantries with Mrs Obermeier. She ate bacon and eggs and croissants, and after breakfast she spoke to Franz and asked him what to do about her car. He directed her to one of the local garages, where she asked them to tow the car into town, and she set off in the truck to show the man where it was. But when they got there, the car was gone, and all that was left to show that it had even been there were the tyre tracks in the dirt by the side of the road, to evidence that it had been towed.

'Someone beat you to it, ma'am.' The boy who had driven her to the spot looked bemused. 'Did you call someone else to pick it up?'

'No.' Daphne looked startled as she stared at where her car had been. This was obviously the spot but the car was gone. 'I didn't. Do you think it would have been stolen?'

'Maybe. But you ought to check the other garages first. Someone might have hauled it into town for you.'

'They couldn't have. No one knew where it was.' And she didn't know anyone in town. Unless ... but that hardly seemed likely. She didn't know him after all. 'How many other garages are there?'

'Two.'

'All right, I guess I'd better check, and then I'll talk to the police.' She remembered what John Fowler had said the night before about 'crazy kids' in town. Maybe someone had stolen it, not that it was any kind of prize, especially with a broken axle.

The boy with the tow truck dropped her off at the first

of the two garages, and before she could walk inside to inquire, she saw her car, already being worked on by two boys in parkas, blue jeans, heavy boots, and greasy hands. 'This yours?'

'Yes.' She was still a little stunned. 'It is.'

'You got plenty of trouble under here.' He looked up at her with a boyish grin. 'But we'll get it fixed for you by tomorrow. Jack Fowler said you had to have it by noon, but we can't do it if you want us to fix the rest, too.'

'He did?' Then it was he after all. 'When did he bring it in?'

'About seven o'clock this morning. Hauled it in with his truck.'

'Do you know where I might find him?' The least she could do was thank him ... and then she flushed suddenly, remembering that only the night before, she had been afraid he might rape her. And what a decent human being he had turned out to be.

Both boys shook their heads in answer to her question. 'He works out at Anderson's logging camp, but I don't know where he lives,' the freckled redhead answered, and she thanked him as she dug her hands into the pockets of her coat and began to walk back towards her end of town. She was halfway there when she heard a sudden honking and saw his blue truck pull up beside her, and she looked up at him with a wide smile.

'I owe you an enormous thank you. You were awfully nice to – '

'Never mind. Want a ride?' She hesitated for only a fraction of a second and then nodded as he swung open the door. 'Hop in.' And then as she settled herself in the wide seat she glanced at him, and his eyes were laughing. 'Sure you wouldn't rather hide behind a tree?'

'That's not fair!' She looked embarrassed and his laughter was a deep chuckle. 'I was afraid that – '

'I know what you were afraid of, and actually what you did was very smart. Still' – he smiled broadly at her – 'it's a little bit insulting. Am I that fearsome-looking?'

But as he took in her size he answered for her. 'I suppose for a little mite like you, I am, aren't I?' His voice was suddenly gentle and his eyes kind. 'I didn't mean to frighten you.'

'I didn't even see you when I hid behind the tree.' She was still blushing faintly, but there was laughter in her eyes as well. And then as they drove towards her cabin she let out a small sigh. 'I think I've gotten a little quirky since ... since I've been alone with my son. It's an enormous responsibility. If anything ever happened to me ...' Her voice trailed off and she turned her eyes back to his face, wondering why she had told him that, but there was something very comforting about him.

He was silent for a long moment and then at last he asked, 'You're divorced?'

She shook her head slowly. 'No. I'm a widow.' For five years she had hated the word. Widow. Like a spider.

'I'm sorry.'

'So am I.' She smiled so he wouldn't feel so bad, and they pulled up in front of her house. 'Would you like to come in for a cup of coffee?' She at least owed him that.

'Sure. I'd like that. I'm off till Monday, and I've got nothing on my hands but time.' He followed her inside, and they hung their coats on pegs beside the doorway, then she hurried into the kitchen to warm the coffee left over from that morning.

'The boys at the garage said that you work at the logging camp,' she said over her shoulder as she took out the cups.

'That's right, I do.' She turned to look at him and found him lounging in the doorway, watching her, and suddenly she felt very strange. He had picked her up on the road the night before, and suddenly here he was in her kitchen. A logger, a total stranger, and yet there was something about him that made her want him to stay. She was at the same time drawn to him, and yet frightened, but she realised as she turned away again that it wasn't he who frightened her, but herself. Almost as though he sensed her discomfort, he left the kitchen, and went to wait for her on the living room couch. 'Want me to start a fire?'

Her reaction was immediate and he saw something startling in her eyes. 'No!' And then as though she sensed that she had opened a part of herself to him that she hadn't intended, 'It gets too warm in here. I usually don't – '

'It's all right.' There was something extraordinary about him. It was as though he understood things before she said them, as though he saw things no one else could see. It made her faintly uncomfortable to realise that about him, and yet at the same time it was a relief. 'Are you afraid of fire?' The question was simply put and his voice was very gentle as she began to shake her head in rapid denial, and then stopping, she looked at him and nodded yes. She put the coffee cups down on the table and stood before him.

'I lost my husband and my daughter in a fire.' She had never said those words to anyone before, and he looked at her, almost as though he might reach out to her, his soft grey eyes boring into hers.

'Were you there too?' His voice was so soft and she nodded as tears filled her eyes. She looked away then, and handed him his cup of coffee. But there were still questions in his eyes. 'The little boy too?'

She sighed. 'I was pregnant then, but I didn't know it. They gave me so many drugs in the hospital during the next two months ... for the burns ... the infections ... sedation ... antibiotics ... by the time I knew I was pregnant, it was too late. That's why Andrew was born deaf.'

'You're both lucky to be alive.' He understood better now why she felt so responsible to Andrew, and how difficult it must be for her to leave him at the school. 'Life is strange sometimes.' He sat back against the couch, his coffee cup dwarfed in his hand. 'Things happen that don't make any sense at all sometimes, Daphne.' She was surprised that he remembered her name. 'I lost my wife fifteen years ago, in a car accident on an icy night. She was such a decent woman, everyone in town loved her.' His voice grew soft at the memory and his eyes looked like a morning sky. 'I never understood it. There are so many damn rotten people. Why her?'

'I felt that way about Jeff.' It was the first time she had spoken about him to anyone, but suddenly she needed to talk to this stranger about him, after five long, lonely years. 'We were so happy.' There were no tears in her eyes as she said it, only a dazed look that John watched carefully from where he sat.

'Were you married for a long time?'

'Four and a half years.'

He nodded. 'Sally and I were married for nineteen. We were both eighteen when we got married,' he smiled then, 'just kids. We worked hard together, starved for a while, did okay after that, got comfortable with each other. It was like she had become a part of me. I had a damn hard time of it when I lost her.'

This time Daphne's eyes consoled him. 'So did I, when I lost Jeff. I think I was in a stupor for about a year. Until after I had Andrew.' She smiled. 'He kept me so busy after that, I didn't think about it as much anymore ... except sometimes ... like at night.' She sighed softly. 'Did you have children, John?' There was something new and awkward about saying his name, and hearing her own on his lips.

'No. We never did. We didn't want to at first. We didn't want to be like the others, all the kids who married right out of high school and had four kids in three years, and then sat around complaining and hating each other. We made a point of not having any for the first few years, and then we decided we liked it like that. I never minded really ... until after she died. You're lucky you have Andrew.'

'I know.' Her eyes glowed as she thought of the treasured child. 'Sometimes I think he means even more to me because ... he's ... the way he is.'

'Are you afraid to say the word?' His voice was so

kind, so gentle, it almost made her want to cry, or bury her face in his chest and let him hold her in his arms.

'Sometimes. I hate what it will mean to him.'

'It'll mean he has to try a little harder, that sliding by won't be good enough for him. It may make him better and stronger, I hope it does. I think what you've gone through has done that for you. Easy roads aren't always the best ones, Daphne. We think they are, but look at the people you respect in life, they're usually the people who've made it when the going wasn't easy, people who survived and grew from all the pain. The ones who have it easy don't have a hell of a lot going for them. It's the others, the ones who climb the mountains with their heads banged up, and their faces scratched, and their shins bleeding who're worth knowing. It's not easy to watch, but it may be that way for your child.'

'I didn't want it that way for him.'

'Of course not. Who does? But he'll make it. You have. And the going can't have been easy. It must have been damn rough for you.'

She looked at him pensively, their eyes holding from across the couch. 'Sometimes it still is.'

He nodded. 'What do you do with yourself when you're not living in a log cabin?'

She hesitated for a moment, looking back over the past five years. 'Take care of Andrew.'

'And now that he'll be at the school?'

'I don't know yet. I used to work for a magazine, but that was a long time ago.'

'Did you like it?'

She thought about it for a minute and nodded. 'Yes, I did. But I was a lot younger. I'm not sure I'd like it as much now. It was a fun job when I was married to Jeffrey, but that was so long ago . . .' She smiled at him, feeling ten thousand years old. 'I was all of twenty-four.'

'And now you're what?' He grinned, amused. 'Twenty-five? Twenty-six?'

'Twenty-nine.' She said it with solemnity and he laughed.

'Of course. I had no idea you were so old. I, my friend, am all of fifty-two. Twenty-nine looks like baby years to me.' He looked it, and yet he didn't. There was something very wise and old and rare about him. Like fine cognac.

They finished the rest of their coffee and he stood up and looked around the room. 'Are you happy here, Daphne? It's a cosy little place.'

'I like it. Sometimes I think I'll stay up here forever.' She smiled and watched him. He was a beautiful male animal, even at fifty-two.

'Why would you stay here? For yourself or for Andrew?'

She wanted to say that she wasn't sure, but she was. It was for him, and he saw the answer in her eyes. 'You ought to get yourself back to New York one of these days, pretty lady. Don't waste yourself up here, in a cabin, living life for your child. You ought to be back with your own people, your own kind, busy, working, seeing friends. I get the feeling you've been in hibernation all these years, and you know what? You'd damn well better not waste it. One of these days you'll wake up and you'll be as old as I am, and you'll wonder what in hell you've done with your life. There's more to you than that, I can see it.'

Her eyes met his and all the pain of loss and time was there. 'I'm not so sure. I don't have any remarkable goals, any urge to create anything memorable, no dreams of greatness. Why couldn't I be happy here?'

'Doing what? Visiting Andrew? Hanging on to him when you ought to set him free? Walking on dark country roads when your car breaks down? Going to the Austrian Inn for Saturday-night dinner? Come on, lady, I don't know where you've been in your life, but I can tell you from looking at you, you deserve more than that.'

'Do I? Why?'

'Because you're smart as a whip and damn pretty. Whether you want to remember that fact or not.' She blushed then and he smiled at her, reaching for his jacket. 'And having talked your ear off, and made a nuisance of myself, making speeches, I will now take myself off and see what those young 'uns at the garage are doing with your axle.'

'You don't have to do that.' For a crazy moment she didn't want him to leave her. She felt comfortable with him there, and safe and happy. And now she would be alone again. For five years it hadn't really bothered her, and now suddenly it did.

But he was smiling at her from the doorway. 'I know I don't have to do it, but I want to. I like you, Daphne Fields.' And then, almost as an afterthought, 'Will you have dinner with me some night over at the inn? I promise not to lecture or make speeches, it's just that watching pretty young girls waste their lives has always bothered me.'

'I'd love to have dinner with you, John.'

'Good. Then let's do that.' He looked pensive for a moment and then smiled at her. 'Is tomorrow night too soon?' She shook her head slowly, wondering what she was doing, who this man was, and why she felt such a need to know him better, to be with him.

'That would be fine.'

'I'll pick you up at six thirty. Country hours.' He nodded to her, smiled, and then ambled out the door, closing it softly behind him as she stood and watched him from the window. He waved once as he pulled his truck out of the driveway, and then in a splash of gravel, he was gone. She stood there for a long time, watching the empty roadway, wondering where her life was going, and who John Fowler really was.

8

On Saturday evening John arrived promptly at six thirty, wearing the same sheepskin coat, but this time over a pair of grey slacks, a blazer, and a shirt and tie. The clothes were neither well cut nor expensive, and yet on him they had a certain style. His extravagantly macho build had a way of making everything about him look handsome, and Daphne was touched that he had dressed for dinner with her. There was a certain old-fashioned chivalry about the man that she couldn't help but like.

'My, don't you look pretty, Daphne.' She was wearing a white skirt and a blue turtleneck sweater that almost perfectly matched her eyes, and over it she wore a short lamb's wool coat that made her look like a tiny French poodle. Everything about her seemed soft and small, and yet there was something so intrinsically powerful about the woman, that her tiny size sometimes seemed a lie. She had worn her hair in a simple chignon, and he looked at it with interest and a shy smile. 'Do you ever wear your hair down?'

She hesitated for a moment and then shook her head. 'Not lately.' She had worn it down a lot for Jeff, cascading past her shoulders. But that was all part of another time, another life, a woman she had been for another man.

'I'd love to see it that way sometime.' He chuckled softly to himself as he watched her eyes. 'I have a great weakness for blonde beauties, I have to warn you.' But despite the teasing, and the obvious interest in his eyes, she felt safe as she left the house at his side. It was a quality she had noticed before about him. Perhaps it was because of his size, or maybe it was his almost fatherly manner, but she always felt safe beside him, as though he would take care of her, no matter what. But there was something different about her now too. She knew she could take care of herself. She hadn't known that when she married Jeff. She didn't need this man. She liked him.

He drove her to the Austrian Inn for dinner, and the Obermeiers seemed surprised to see them together, and took special care of them both. They both happened to be among their favourite people, and in the kitchen when the frantic bustle of dinner slowed, Hilda looked at her husband with intrigue in her eyes and a victorious grin. 'How do you suppose she met him?'

'I don't know, Hilda. And it's none of our business.' He chided her gently, but her curiosity and amazement could not be stopped.

'Do you realise that I haven't seen him out to dinner since his wife died?'

'Do you realise that you shouldn't be talking like that, Hilda? They're grown people, what they do is their business. And if he wants to take a pretty woman to dinner, why not?'

'Did I say it was wrong? I think it's wonderful!'

'Good. Then take them their coffee and shut up.' He patted her gently on the behind and went back to see that all his guests had what they needed, and a moment later he saw John and Daphne talking over their coffee, he was telling her something funny and she was laughing like a little girl.

'And then what did you tell them?' Her eyes still looked amused.

'That if they couldn't run a logging camp, then they should run a ballet. And you know what, damned if six months later they didn't sell the business and wind up buying some kind of dance troupe in Chicago.' He shook his head, his eyes still laughing. 'Damn fools.' He had been telling her about the pair of New York phonies who had been thinking of buying a business a few years back, and running it for a tax loss. 'Hell, I didn't get that place running like I did just for two jackasses from New York to come in and blow it. Not like that.'

'Do you like the work, John?' She was intrigued by him. He was obviously intelligent, well read, aware of what was happening in the world at large, and yet he had lived all his life in this tiny New England village, and worked with his strong back and his hands.

'Yes, I like it. It suits me. I'd never have been happy in an office. I could have. Sally's father ran a bank here and all he wanted was to get me to work with him, but it wasn't me. This suits me better, out in the air all day, dealing with the men, working with my hands.' He smiled at her. 'I'm a labourer at heart, Mrs Fields.' But it was obvious that there was a great deal more to him than that. But what the labouring had done was give him an earthiness, a strength, a sense of reality, and a chance to observe human nature. He was a wise man, and as the evening wore on she found that she liked that about him. It was over dessert that he looked at her for a long moment and then took one of her hands in his own. 'We've both lost a great deal, you and I, and yet here we are, strong and alive, we've survived it.'

'I wasn't always sure I would.' It was a relief to admit that to somebody.

'You always will. But you don't know that yet, do you?'

'Sometimes I have my doubts. Sometimes I think I won't make it another day.'

'You will.' He said it with quiet confidence. 'But maybe it's time you stopped fighting all your wars alone.' He had sensed instantly that there had been no one in her life for a very long time. She had the kind of silent sorrow of a woman who has almost forgotten the gentle touch of loving. 'Has there been anyone in your life since your husband died, Daphne, or shouldn't I ask?'

She smiled and looked shy, the huge cornflower eyes suddenly even bigger. 'You can ask. No, there hasn't. In fact' – she blushed and he felt an almost irresistible urge to kiss her – 'this is the first date I've ever had ... since...' She didn't have to say the rest. He understood.

'What a waste of a beautiful woman.' But this time his words were too much, and she turned her eyes away from his.

'It was better that way. There was more of me to give to Andrew.'

'And now?'

'I don't know...' She looked troubled as she said the words. 'I don't know what I'll do without him.'

'I think' – he narrowed his eyes as he watched her – 'I think that you're going to do something very important.'

She laughed and shook her head, amused by what he said. 'Like what? Run for Congress?'

'Maybe, if that's what you want. But it isn't. There's something deep inside you, Daphne, that's aching to come out. And maybe one of these days you'll let it.' She was stunned by his words. She had often thought the same thing, and the only release that she had for what she felt was in her journals. For a moment she wanted to tell him about them, but then suddenly she felt silly. 'Would you like to go for a walk?' They stood up after dinner, and he followed her outside the inn as Mrs Obermeier watched with obvious pleasure. 'You've made friends in this town, little one.' He smiled down at her as they walked outside. 'Mrs Obermeier likes you.'

'I like her too.' They walked side by side in silence for some time, along the deserted streets, and then he tucked her gloved hand into his arm.

'When am I going to meet Andrew?' There seemed to be no question that he would, only when it would happen. It was as though in two days this man had become a part of her life, and she wasn't sure where they were going, but she knew that she liked it. She felt released suddenly from all the bonds that had chained

79

her for years, and she felt a little bit adrift, but it was a pleasant feeling.

She turned her face up to his as they walked along and looked at the powerful profile beside her. She wasn't sure what he would be in her life, but she knew for certain that he would be her friend. 'How about tomorrow? I was going to visit him in the afternoon. Would you like to come?'

'I'd love it.'

They walked slowly back to his truck then, and he drove her home. He walked her to the door, and she didn't invite him in, and he didn't seem to expect it. She waved as she closed the door and he slipped into his truck and drove away, filled with his own thoughts of Daphne.

9

Andrew was waiting outside with two counsellors and some of the other children when Daphne and John arrived at the school, and she was quick to recognise a look of suspicion in her son's eyes. He wasn't sure who the man was, and perhaps he was threatened by John's size. But Daphne had the feeling that he wasn't sure if he liked seeing someone with his mother. He had an instinctive sense of possession about her, which she had allowed to flourish.

She folded him quickly into her arms and kissed his cheek and his neck, nestling her face beside his, feeling the familiar warmth of the child who was so much a part of her, and then she pulled away and signed to him that this was her friend, just as he had friends at the school. And his name was John. And John knelt on the ground beside him. He didn't know any of the signs Daphne had already learned, but he seemed to communicate with the little boy with his eyes and his huge, gentle hands, and in a few minutes Andrew came to him hesitantly, like a cautious puppy. Without saying a word to him, John stretched forth a hand and took Andrew's small hand in his own. He began to talk to him then, in his deep, soft voice, as Andrew watched him. The boy's eyes stayed riveted to John's and once or twice he nodded, as though he understood him. There seemed to be total acceptance between them as Daphne watched in fascination. And then, without a word to her, Andrew led John away to sit beneath a tree, and 'talk.' The child signed, and the man spoke, and they seemed to understand each other as though they had always been friends. Daphne stood in the distance, watching in total fascination as she felt a surge of emotion within her, half sorrow to have lost another little piece of Andrew, half joy to see John reach out to this child she loved with her whole soul. And somewhere deep within there was resentment, too, to see the doors to Andrew's silent world swing open so easily for John, when she had struggled for so long to unlock them. But above all there was tenderness for both John and Andrew as they returned to her at last, hand in hand, and smiling. They began to play then, and a little while later all three of them were laughing. The hours until dinnertime flew like minutes, and Daphne showed John the school, suddenly proud that she had done the right thing for Andrew. And as they walked back downstairs from the room where Andrew slept, John looked at her with warmth that washed over her like a Mediterranean summer.

'Has anyone told you how terrific you are, little one?' She blushed and he put an arm around her shoulders and held her close. It was the first time she felt him near her, and it was a powerful feeling as she closed her eyes in his embrace. 'You're brave and you're wonderful. You did a beautiful thing for Andrew, and it's going to be good for both of you,' and then in a soft voice that took her completely by surprise, 'and I love you for it.' She stood staring at him for a moment, not sure what to say, and he smiled and bent to kiss her forehead. 'It's okay, Daphne, I'm not going to hurt you.'

'Thank you.' She wasn't sure why she said it, but she suddenly slipped her arms around his waist and held him. She had so desperately needed someone to tell her what he had just told her, that she hadn't deserted Andrew, that it was all right, that she had done the right thing. 'Thank you so much.'

He gave her a quick squeeze and then walked the rest of the way downstairs, where they found Andrew and the others ready to sit down to dinner. It was time for them to go, and this time Andrew whimpered for a minute before they left, and Daphne held him close to her with tears in her eyes, breathing softly on his cheek, 'I love you.' She pulled him away from her then, so he could see her mouth the words, and he flung himself ferociously into her arms again and made a croak, which was his 'I love you.' Mrs Curtis came along then, and touched his cheek with a warm smile, signalling to him to ask if he was ready to come to dinner. He looked unsure for a minute, and then he nodded and smiled, signing yes, and then with a quick wave and a kiss, and a look of friendship towards John, he left them and joined the others.

'Ready to go, or do you want to wait awhile?' John didn't want to rush her. He could almost feel in his own gut the fresh pain she was feeling. But she nodded slowly, her eyes still riveted to her child, and then she turned and looked up at John, grateful that he was there. 'You okay?'

'Yes. Let's go.'

He followed her out, and she marvelled at how good it felt to have someone to take care of her for a change. And suddenly as the cold night air hit their faces outside, she wanted to run. The pain of leaving Andrew was already dim, and she felt more alive than she had in years. She laughed suddenly and skipped to the truck like a little girl, as John walked beside her.

'He's a terrific little kid, you know.' He looked at her almost with shared pride as he started the engine. 'You've done one hell of a fine job.'

'That's just the way he is. I'm not sure I had anything to do with it.'

'Yes, you did. And don't you forget it.' He sounded almost stern as they drove away from the school, and he saw with pleasure that she still looked happy. 'Want to go back to the inn for dinner? I feel like celebrating, and I'm not even sure what.' He glanced at her and their eyes met and held. There was a powerful bond forming between them, and she had just shared an important part of her life with him. He was touched and pleased that she had let him meet Andrew.

'How about if I make you dinner instead?'

'Can you cook?' He was teasing and they both laughed. 'I eat a lot.'

'How about spaghetti?'

'That's it?' He looked shocked and she laughed, feeling like a kid, and suddenly for no reason at all, she remembered the first time she had cooked dinner for Jeff at her apartment. That had been an eternity ago, and she was ashamed to realise that it all seemed dim now, long ago and far away and not entirely real. There were times now when she had the feeling that the memories of Jeffrey were fading. 'Just spaghetti?' John's voice brought her back to the present.

'Okay, how about a steak? And a salad.'

'I accept. With pleasure,' he added, and she laughed again.

'You must cost one hell of a lot to feed, John Fowler.'

He looked amused at the look on her face. 'Not to worry. I make a healthy wage logging.'

'Isn't it dangerous though?' Her brow creased in a small frown. And it pleased him that she was worried.

'Sometimes. Not very often. Most of us know what we're doing. It's the greenies you have to look out for. The young kids who sign on for a summer. They'll kill you, if you don't watch them.'

She nodded quietly and they pulled up in front of her house and walked inside, and for the next half hour she was busy cooking. He set the table and did the steaks. She did the spaghetti and the salad, and he looked longingly at the fireplace, and she knew instantly what he was thinking. 'It's all right, John. If you want to, go ahead. This room would be pretty with a fire.'

'We don't need that. It's pretty without it.' But suddenly she wanted him to. She wanted to leave the past behind. She was tired of the terrors and the fears and the agonies of the past.

'Go ahead. Light the fire.' There was something about him that made her feel brave.

'I don't want to upset you, Daphne.'

84

'You won't. I think it's time to leave the past.' It felt strange to say it, but at long last it did not feel like a betrayal.

He left the table to put on a log, and threw in some kindling. The fire took quickly and she sat staring at it for a long time, thinking not so much of that fateful Christmas night, but of the many times she and Jeff had sat at home on Sunday nights, reading the Sunday papers, and enjoying the fire. Without saying a word, John reached across the table and took her hand, and she found herself thinking of his arm around her shoulders at the school and how good it felt to stand beside him.

'What were you thinking just then? You looked so happy.'

Her eyes were aglow from the firelight, and he thought she had been thinking of Jeffrey.

'I was thinking about you. I'm glad you picked me up on the road the other night.'

He smiled at the memory too. 'I would have picked you up sooner if you hadn't been hiding.' They both laughed at the thought, and she brought out two cups of steaming coffee. 'You're a good cook.'

'Thank you. So are you. The steaks were just right.'

He smiled at her almost sadly. 'I've had a lot of practice. Fifteen years of doing my own cooking.'

'Why didn't you ever remarry?'

'I never wanted to. Never met anyone I cared about that much.' 'Until now,' he wanted to say, but he didn't want to scare her, and he knew it would have. 'I guess I didn't want to start over. But you're young enough to, little one. One of these days you should.'

She shook her head pensively, looking up at him. 'I don't think so. You can't do things "again" in life, you can't re-create what was. That only comes once in a lifetime.'

'That particular experience does. But other experiences come along, which matter just as much. They're just different.'

'Look who's talking. You're no different than I am.'

'Yes, I am. You're luckier.'

'Am I? Why?'

'You have Andrew.' They both smiled. 'Every once in a while I meet a kid who makes me sorry I didn't have any.'

'It's not too late.' But he laughed at that.

'I'm an old man, Daphne Fields. I'm fifty-two years old. Hell, I'm old enough to be your father.' But she only smiled at that. She didn't see him in that light, and he didn't feel that way towards her either. They were friends on a variety of levels. And she'd never had a friend like him before. Maybe because she'd never been the woman she now was. She had grown strong over the years, stronger than she had ever dreamed. She was an even match for any man. Even a man like John.

They sat on the couch looking into the fire for a while, and it was extraordinary how comfortable she felt beside him. There was something easy and unhurried about him, as though he had a lifetime ahead of him, and plenty of time to enjoy each precious moment. And the sharp sculpture of his face looked beautiful in the light of the fire.

'John . . .' She didn't quite know how to say what she felt. Maybe later she would be able to say it in her journal.

'Yes, little one?'

But she couldn't find the right words. At last, in a soft husky voice, she said what she could. 'I'm glad I met you.'

He nodded slowly, feeling all that she felt, and sensing the peace and understanding that flowed between them. He put an arm around her shoulders then, and she felt the same quiet strength that had felt so good to her earlier that evening. She liked the weight of his arm, the feel of his hand, and the scent of him beside her. It was a rich mixture of after shave and wool and fresh air and tobacco. He smelled the way he looked, like a strong, attractive man who had lived his whole life amid trees and mountains. And he looked down at her then, and saw a tear creep down her cheek. It startled him and he pulled her closer. 'Are you sad, love?' His voice was so deep and tender, but she shook her head.

'No ... I'm so happy ... just here, like this...' She looked up at him then. 'You must think I'm crazy. But I'm alive again. I feel like I've been half dead for so long. I thought...' It was hard to say the words but she had to. 'I thought I should be dead because they were. I only stayed alive for Andrew. I only lived for him.' And now she was living for herself again. At last.

He seemed to pause for an endless time, his face very close to hers, watching her. 'You have a right to your own life now, Daphne. You've paid your dues.' He kissed her gently on the lips then, and it was as though an arrow shot through her. His touch went to her very core, and she felt breathless as their lips touched and he held her. He took her face in his hands then, and sat looking quietly at her. 'Where have you been all my life, Daphne Fields?' He kissed her again, and this time she slipped her arm around his neck and held him close to her. She felt as though she wanted to cling to him for a lifetime and never let go, and he held her as though he would like her to do that.

His hands began to travel slowly over her shoulders after a little while, and then they slipped gently on to her breasts, and at last under her sweater. She uttered a soft little moan, and he held her close, sensing the rising passion within her. He stopped and pulled away after a time, and looked into her eyes. 'I don't want to do anything you don't want, little one. I'm an old man. I don't want to take advantage of you.' But she shook her head and kissed him as he pulled the pins from her hair, and loosed it from its knot to cascade down her back and over her shoulders. He let his fingers run through it, and touched her face and breasts again, and then the huge hands moved gently to her legs and she couldn't keep herself from writhing with pleasure as he touched her.

'Daphne ... Daphne...' He whispered her name as they lay on the couch beside the fire, his whole body throbbing with desire for her, and then she stood up and took his hand, and led him towards the four-poster in her bedroom. 'Are you sure?' He knew how long it had been, and she scarcely knew him. Everything had happened so quickly between them and he didn't want her to do anything she'd regret in the morning. He wanted to know her for a long time, not just for a night, or a moment.

'It's all right.' Her voice was the merest whisper as he slowly undressed her, until at last she stood before him, tiny, perfectly formed, her flesh shining in the moonlight, her blonde hair almost silver. He picked her up then and slid her into the bed, and carefully took off his own clothes, dropped them to the floor, and slid in beside her. The feel of her satin skin was almost more than he could bear, and he had a hunger for her that was impossible to control as he lay beside her. But it was she who took his face in her hands, who held him close as she arched her body towards him, as slowly, like a forgotten memory come to life with a delicious vengeance, she felt him slip inside her, and she soared to heights that, even with Jeffrey, she had never known. John was an artful and extraordinary lover, and they lay spent at last, side by side, her tiny body intertwined with his as she whispered into his neck that she loved him.

'I love you too, little one. Oh, God, how I love you ...' And as he said the words she looked up at him with a sleepy smile, pulled herself more tightly against him as her eyes closed and she drifted off to sleep in his arms, a woman again, a woman she had never been ... his woman, and her own. He was right about her. The years had made her strong, stronger than she knew.

10

'What are these?' John was holding two of Daphne's leather-bound journals in his hands as he stood naked in her kitchen at six o'clock the next morning. She had got up to make him breakfast before he left for work, but they had got delayed by another intense bout of passion.

She looked over her own naked shoulder with a smile, still amazed at how comfortable she felt with him. 'Hm? Oh, those are my journals.'

'Can I read them sometime?'

'Sure.' She looked faintly embarrassed as she put fried eggs and bacon on the table. 'They may sound a little silly though. I've poured out my soul in them.'

'There's nothing silly about that.' And then he smiled at her naked bottom. 'You've got one hell of a great ass, do you know that?'

'Shut up and eat your eggs.'

'Talk about the end of a romance.' But the romance between them had just begun. They even managed to sneak in one more 'quickie' before he left for work an hour later. 'I'm not sure I'm strong enough to work today after all that good loving.'

'Good, then stay home. I'll take care of you.'

'I'll bet you would!' He laughed out loud, zipping up the heavy parka he kept in his truck for work. 'You sure do spoil a man, Daphne Fields.'

But as she held him tight before he left, she whispered softly, 'You're the one who's spoiling me. You make me happier than I've ever been, and I want you to know that.'

'I'll remember it all day. I'll pick up some groceries

on the way home, and we'll have a quiet dinner. Sound okay to you?'

'It sounds perfect.'

'What'll you do?'

Her eyes sparkled for a moment and she smiled. 'Maybe I'll make a new entry in my journal.'

'Good. I'll check it out when I come home. See you later, little one.' And then he was off, the truck whirring on the gravel as she waved, bare-breasted, from the kitchen window.

The day seemed endless after he left, and she wondered what she had done without him. She thought about going to visit Andrew to pass the time, but it was too soon for another visit. So she stayed home, and cleaned house, and began to write in her journal, but something different rattled around in her head all morning, and after lunch she found herself writing a short story. It came out all in one piece, with a flow of its own, and when it was finished, she sat staring with amazement at the dozen pages she had written. It was the first time she had ever done anything like it.

And when he came home, she was waiting dressed in grey slacks and a bright red sweater. 'Don't you look pretty, little one. How was your day?'

'Terrific. But I missed you.' It was as though he had always been part of her life and she had waited for him every evening. They cooked dinner together again, with the groceries he had bought, and he told her the anecdotes of the day from the logging camp. It was after that that she showed him her short story, and he read it with delight as they sat by the fire.

'This is marvellous, Daff.' He looked at her with obvious pride and pleasure.

'Come on, tell the truth. Is it hokey?'

'Hell, no. It's terrific.'

'It's the first one I ever wrote. I don't even know where it came from.'

He touched the silky blonde hair on her head with a smile. 'From here, little one. And I suspect there are lots

90

more stories in there like this one.' She had tapped into a resource she didn't even know she had, and she felt an even greater release than she had ever felt when writing her journals.

They made love that night in front of the fire, and again in the four-poster bed, and once again at five thirty the next morning. And he left for work with a song on his lips, and she didn't wait until afternoon this time. She sat down as soon as he left, and wrote another story. It was different from the one she had composed the day before, but when John read it that night, he thought it was better. 'You've got a damn powerful style to your writing, Daff.' And after that he spent weeks reading all of her journals.

By Christmas they had settled into a comfortable life. He had more or less moved into the cabin with her, Andrew was growing more and more independent at the school, and she had more time on her hands than she'd had in years. It allowed her to write short stories every day. Some were better than others, but they were all interesting, and all seemed to have the same distinctive style. It was as though she had discovered a facet of herself she 'had never known before, and she had to admit that she loved it.

'It feels so damn good, John. I don't know, it's hard to explain. It's like all of this stuff has always been there, and I never knew it.'

'Maybe you should write a book.' He looked very serious as he said it.

'Don't be silly. About what?'

'I don't know. See what comes. I know you've got it in you.'

'I'm not sure I do. Writing short stories is different.'

'That doesn't mean you can't write a book. Try it. Hell, why not? You've got the time. There's nothing else to do here in winter.' And there wasn't of course, except visit Andrew. She spent two afternoons with him a week, and John went with her once every weekend. By Christmas it was easy to see that Andrew was perfectly

91

happy, and he accepted John now with ease, signing funny things to him, now that John had learned his language. And they roughhoused outside, and more often than not John ended up with Andrew on one shoulder, and one of his friends on the other. He had come to love the child, and Daphne watched them with pride, marvelling at the gifts life had brought her. It was as though all the pain of the past was swept away at last. It was easier now to live with Jeff's memory. It was only seeing little girls of Aimee's age that still hurt her so badly. But even that was better now, John had a way of soothing all hurts and making her feel peaceful and happy.

They even brought Andrew home with them for a few hours once in a while. John gave him a dozen small tasks to do around the house. They carried firewood in together, and John carved him little animals out of kindling. They baked cookies with Daphne, and once painted an old wicker rocking chair that John had found behind a deserted barn. It was obvious to all that Andrew was growing increasingly independent, and it was easier for him to communicate with them both. Daphne had grown more proficient at signing, and the tension between them had eased. Andrew was more patient with her when she made a mistake, and he giggled once or twice when she missigned a word, and then grinning, explained in sign language to John that his Mom had said she was going to cook a frog for dinner. But his silent communications with John still remained deeply touching. The two had become friends, as though they had always been part of the same life, walking side by side in silence in the fields, stopping to watch a rabbit or a deer, their eyes meeting, as though nothing needed to be said. And when it would come time to go back to the school, Andrew would sit on John's lap in the truck, and put his small hands on the steering wheel beside John's large ones, and Daphne would watch them with a smile as they drove along. He was always happy to get back to the school with the others. And leaving him was no longer as wrenching. She and John had their own little life, and she thought that she had never been as content in her entire life. And it showed in her writing.

In February she finally got up the courage to start a book, and she worked on it long and hard every day while John was at work, and at night he read the day's production, with comments and praise, and he never seemed to doubt for a moment that she could do it.

'You know, if it weren't for you, I couldn't do this.' She was lying sprawled on the couch in blue jeans and boots with a stack of work on her lap as he sliced some apples for them.

'Yes, you could. I have nothing to do with it, you know. It all comes from you. It's all there. And no one will ever be able to take that away from you.'

'I don't know ... I still don't understand where it all comes from.'

'That isn't important. Just know that it's there, within you. No one else can affect that.'

'Nope.' She took a slice of apple and leaned over to give him a kiss. She loved the feel of his face against her lips, especially at the end of a day when it felt rough from the beginnings of his beard. Everything about him was so masculine and wonderfully sexy. 'I still think it's all your fault. If it weren't for you, I'd never have written a damn thing.' They both remembered with a smile that she had written her first short story after the first time they had made love. She had sent it in to *Collins* after the first of the year, to see if they would publish it, and she was still waiting for an answer.

The answer came in March, from her old boss, Allison Baer. They wanted it for five hundred dollars. 'Do you see that? John, they bought my story! They're crazy!' She was waiting for him in the doorway that night with a bottle of champagne and the cheque, and Allison's letter.

'Congratulations!' He was as pleased as she, and they celebrated in bed until the wee hours of the morning. He teased her a lot that he never got any sleep anymore, but it was more than obvious that they both enjoyed it.

The sale of the short story to *Collins* spurred her on, and she worked harder on the book through the spring, and finished it at last in July. She sat staring at it, holding it in her hands, feeling the weight of the manuscript, and more than a little awed by what she had done, and at the same time saddened by the loss of the people who had become so real through the long months that she wrote it.

'Now what do I do?' It was a little bit like losing a job, and she was almost sorry it was over.

'That, my love, is an interesting question.' He looked at her, bursting with pride, his chest bare, his face and arms brown, drinking a beer after a long day's work. It had been a beautiful summer. 'I'm not sure, but I think you're supposed to find an agent. Why don't you ask your old boss at *Collins*? Give her a call tomorrow.' But Daphne always hated talking to her. She harped and harped on how unnatural Daphne's life was. Daphne had never told her about John, and she assumed that Daphne was staying in New Hampshire to be near to Andrew. She always insisted that Daphne should come back to New York and get a job, but Daphne always used the excuse that she had sublet her apartment until September. And after that she would find other reasons. She had no plans now to leave. She was happy with John, and she wanted to stay in New Hampshire forever. But even John occasionally argued with that, insisting that she belonged in New York, with 'her own kind' and an interesting job. He didn't think she ought to spend the rest of her life with a logger. But he didn't really want her to go, and she had no intention of leaving him, now or ever.

'How do you suppose one finds an agent?'

'Maybe you should take the book to New York and find out.'

'Only if you come with me.'

'That's silly, love. You don't need me for that.'

'Yes, I do.' She looked like a happy little girl as she sat beside him. 'I need you for everything. Haven't you figured that out by now?' He had, but they both knew how much she was capable of on her own, and she was capable of a great deal.

'What would I do in New York?' He hadn't been there in twenty years, and he had no real desire to go. He was happy in the mountains of New England. 'Anyway, why don't you call Allison tomorrow and see what she says.' But the next day Daphne didn't do it. She decided to wait until the fall. Somehow she wasn't ready to let the book go, and she claimed that she wanted to read it over a few times, to make some final changes. 'Chicken,' he teased. 'You can't hide forever, little one.'

'Why not?'

'Because I won't let you. You're better than that.' He always made her feel as though there were nothing she couldn't do. It was remarkable how much she had come into her own in the months with him.

And Andrew had changed too. He was almost five now, and no longer a baby. And in August, Daphne had plans to join him and some of the other children and parents on a camping trip, under the aegis of Mrs Curtis. It was a special event for everyone involved, and Daphne wanted John to go on the four-day trip, to share the experience with Andrew, but he couldn't get away. They had twenty college kids at the logging camp, and all of the senior men were needed to keep an eye on the 'greenies.'

'Can't you get away?' She was so disappointed.

'I really can't, love. I wish I could. You're going to have a great time.'

'Not without you.' She almost pouted and he laughed, he loved the child-woman in her.

On the third week of August they went, with sleeping bags and tents and horses. It was a new experience for the children to travel through the woods, and all around them were thrills and discoveries. Daphne had brought one of her journals along, so she could write everything down for John, all of the funny things Andrew did, and the little moments she was afraid she might not remember. But most of the time she found herself writing about John, and thinking of the night they had spent together before she left. This was the first time they had been apart in nine months, and she had ached at the prospect of being without him. Having lost someone she loved once, she had a wild fear of leaving John too. There were even nights when she had nightmares that one day she might lose him.

'You won't get rid of me that easy, little one.' He had whispered it into her neck as she shared her fears. 'I'm a tough old bird.'

'I couldn't live without you, John.'

'Yes, you could. But you won't have to try. Not for a very long time. So have a good time with the kids, and tell me all about it.'

She had lain beside him at dawn, after they made love, and had felt his smooth, cool male flesh touching her thigh. It always sent the same thrill through her.

'I may suffer withdrawal in four days.' In their lovemaking, he had spoiled her. He may have called himself an 'old man,' but there was nothing old about his passion. He had the ardour of a man half his age, blended with an experience that taught her things she had never known before. She wondered sometimes if it was so good simply because she really loved him. And it was about things like that that she wrote in her journal while she was away, whenever she wasn't playing with Andrew. She was relishing these special days with him, watching him with his friends, living together in the woods, and waking up in the morning to see that small sunny face she hadn't woken up to in so long.

They came home after four days, like any respectable bunch of campers, dirty and tired and relaxed, and pleased with what they'd done. The parents had enjoyed the trip at least as much as the children. She left Andrew at the school, and put her sleeping bag and her backpack in her car, and yawned as she slid behind the wheel. She could hardly wait to get home to John, but when she reached the cabin, she didn't find him. There were dishes in the sink, and the bed was unmade, and she smiled to herself as she stepped gratefully into the shower. She would have everything in order when he got home. But as she stood in the kitchen, washing dishes in her jeans, the knock on the door was unfamiliar. She went to open it with hands still covered with soap and she smiled when she saw one of John's friends, a man they seldom saw but whom she knew John was fond of.

'Hi, Harry, what's new?' She was tanned and relaxed and happy, but John's friend looked strained.

'When did you get back?' His face was grave and his eyes were sad, as they always were. John always teased him that he looked like his best friend had just died, but he had a fat wife and six kids, which would have been enough to depress anyone, John said. 'How's Gladys?'

'Daphne, can I talk to you for a minute?' This time he looked genuinely troubled. And suddenly somewhere behind her she heard the ticking of the kitchen clock.

'Sure.' She wiped her hands on her jeans, put down the towel, and came to where he stood. 'Is something wrong?' He nodded slowly, with no idea how to tell her. He couldn't begin to say the words, and there was an eerie silence between them.

'Let's sit down.' He moved nervously towards the couch, and she followed him as though in a dream.

'Harry? What is it? What's wrong?'

His eyes were like two sad black stones as they looked into hers. 'John's dead, Daphne. He died while you were gone.'

She felt the room spin around her as she saw Harry's face in the distance ... John's dead ... John's dead ... the words were from a bad dream, not reality, this hadn't happened, not to her ... again. And suddenly, in the stillness around them, she heard a woman laughing, hysterically, a raucous sound.

'No! No! No!' The shrill laughter turned to sobs as

Harry watched her, anxious to explain how he died, but she didn't want to hear it. It didn't matter. She'd been here before. But impervious to what she was feeling, Harry began talking. She wanted to put her fingers in her ears and scream and run. 'There was an accident at the camp the day you left. We called the school, but they said there was no way to reach you. Some of those damn college kids lost control of a winch, and a load of trees hit him...' Harry began to cry, and Daphne stared at him with wide eyes. '... broke his back and his neck. He never knew what hit him.'

Neither had Jeff. Or so they had said. What difference did it make? What did it matter now? She sat staring at Harry, and all she could think of was Andrew. What was she going to tell her son?

'We're all so damn sorry. The kids were sent home, and we had the funeral home keep the body. He has no family here, or anywhere, I think. They're all gone. And we didn't know what you'd want to do... Gladys thought – '

'It's all right.' She jumped up looking tense and white-faced. 'Never mind.' She had passed this way before. It was only when Harry left that the tears came, great rivers of silent, anguished tears. She looked around the room and sat down again. John Fowler would never be coming home again.

'You can make it on your own, little one.' She remembered his words from the past. But she didn't want to make it on her own. She wanted her life with him.

'Oh, John...' It was a soft, broken whisper in the silence of their cabin, and she remembered all that they had said before, he about losing his wife, and she about losing Jeff. This made no more sense than that had, and she understood it no better, and yet this was different, she knew the futility of hanging on. She walked out into the woods at sunset, and the tears came again as she looked into the summer sky and thought of him, the broad shoulders and big hands, the deep voice, the man who had loved her and Andrew.

'Damn you!' she shouted into the mauve and orange sky. 'Damn you! Why'd you have to do it?' She stood there for a long time, her tears flowing freely as the sky grew dark, and then wiping her cheeks on the sleeves of the logger's shirt she wore, she nodded. 'Okay, my friend. Okay. We'll make it. Just remember that I loved you.' And then, still crying, she looked at where the sun had been on the hills a little while before and whispered, 'Good-bye,' and then with her head bowed, she walked home.

11

Daphne woke before dawn the next morning, lying on the bed that suddenly seemed too large as she slept in it alone. She lay there, thinking about John and remembering their early mornings, side by side, and often their bodies joined as one before the dawn.

She lay there as the sun crept slowly through the windows, feeling leaden, wanting never to get up again. There was none of the horror and the panic she had felt when Jeff had died. There was only emptiness and loss, an abysmal kind of sorrow that weighed on her like her own tombstone as she ran the fingers of her mind over the wound again and again and again ... the words ran rhythmically through her mind ... *John is dead ... is dead ... is dead ... I'll never see him again ... never see him ...* and the worst of it was that neither would Andrew. How would she tell him?

It was almost noon when she forced herself out of bed at last, and she was dizzy for a moment when she stood up. There was a sick, empty feeling, born of not having eaten anything at all since the previous morning, and she could eat nothing now as the same words continued to echo in her head ... *John is dead ... John is dead ...*

She stood in the shower for half an hour, staring into space as the water beat down on her like angry rain, and it took her almost an hour after that to put on a pair of jeans, a shirt of John's, and a pair of shoes. She stared into their closet as though it held a lifetime of precious secrets, but she had been through this once before and could not let it demolish her again. When Jeff had died, the knowledge that she carried their unborn child had eventually pulled her through, but she wouldn't have that this time, the miracle of life to counterbalance death. What she had this time was Andrew himself. She knew she had to find her way to him now, for his sake and her own. She still had him.

She drove to the school, looking dazed and still feeling numb and strange, and it was only when she saw him happily playing with a ball that she began to cry again.

She stood watching him for a long time, trying to sift through her thoughts, and stop the tears, but they wouldn't stop now, and finally he turned and saw her, frowned, and dropped his ball, and walked slowly towards her, a worried frown in his eyes. She sat down on the grass and held out her arms towards him, smiling through her tears. He was the centre of her life now, as he had always been.

'Hi,' she signed to him, once he sat beside her.

'What's wrong?' All the love and protection they felt for each other was mirrored in his eyes.

There was an endless pause as she felt her hands shake. She couldn't bring herself to make the signs.

At last she did. 'I have something very sad to tell you.'

'What?' He looked surprised. She had sheltered him from all sorrows and disasters, and there had been none like this in his lifetime. But there was no way to keep this from him. The boy had grown very close to John. Daphne's chin trembled and her eyes filled as she put her arms around her son, and then released him to sign the words she dreaded. 'John died while we were away, sweetheart. He had an accident. I found out yesterday and we won't see him again.'

'Forever?' Andrew's eyes grew wide in disbelief.

She nodded and signed back. 'Forever. But we'll remember him forever, and love him, just like I do your Dad.'

'But I don't know my Dad.' The small hands trembled as they signed. 'And I love John.'

'So do I.' The tears rolled down Daphne's face again.

'So do I ...' And then, 'And I love you too.' They clung to each other then as the small child began to sob, great gulping broken sounds that tore at her heart as they held each other close. It seemed hours before either of them was ready to let go. They took a walk then, in silence, hand in hand, and every now and then Andrew would sign something about John, the things they had done, the way he had been. It struck Daphne again how remarkable it had been that the big woodsman had so captivated her son without a single word. He hadn't been a man who needed words. There was some rare and powerful essence within that transcended all else, even Andrew's handicap and Daphne's fears.

It surprised her when Andrew asked her later, 'Will you stay here without him, Mom?'

'Yes. I'm here for you, you know.' But they both knew that for the past six months that hadn't been entirely true. Andrew had got more and more independent and Daphne had stayed in New Hampshire because of John. But she couldn't leave now. Andrew needed her, and more than ever, she needed him.

The remaining weeks of the summer crawled by, as Daphne ached silently for John. She stopped crying after a while, and she no longer wrote in her journals. She barely touched food, and she saw no one, except Andrew. It was Mrs Obermeier who finally stopped by, and was aghast at what she saw. Daphne had lost twelve pounds from her tiny frame, her face was anguished and drawn, and the old Austrian woman took her in her arms, but even then Daphne didn't cry, she simply stood there. She was beyond pain, she was simply hanging on to survival, and she wasn't even sure why, except for Andrew. Even he didn't really need her now. He had the school, and Mrs Curtis had suggested that she cut back her visits.

'Why don't you go back to New York?' Mrs Obermeier suggested over a cup of tea Daphne barely drank. 'To your friends. It is too hard for you here. I can see that.' Daphne knew it too, but she didn't want to go back. She wanted to stay in the cabin forever, with his clothes, with his boots, with his smell, with his aura around her. He had long since given up his own apartment before he died.

'I want to be here.'

'It's not good for you here, Daphne.' The wise old woman sounded firm. 'You can't hold on to the past.' Daphne wanted to ask her why not, but she already knew all those answers. She had been through it before. But it only made it that much worse this time.

Her story came out in *Collins* in October, and Allison sent her a complimentary copy with a note. 'When the hell are you coming back? Love, Allie.' In Daphne's mind, the answer was never. But at the end of the month she got a note from her landlord in Boston. Her lease was up, and the cabin had been sold. They wanted her out by the first of November.

She no longer had the excuse that there was someone in her apartment in New York. Her tenant had moved out on the first of October. Which left her nowhere to go except to New York. She could have found another cabin or apartment where she was, but it didn't make much sense. She was only seeing Andrew once a week, and he barely paid any attention to her. He was more and more self-reliant now and Mrs Curtis had recently pointed out that it was time he turn his full attention to the school. In some ways Daphne's visits held him back, allowing him to cling to her. But in truth, it was Daphne clinging to him.

She packed all her things, as well as John's, put them on a bus to New York, and stared around the cabin for a last time, feeling a terrible catch in her throat as a terrible sound finally escaped her. The sobs racked her for an hour as she sat on the couch, crying into the silence. She was alone. John was gone. Nothing would bring him back. He was gone forever. She closed the door softly behind her, and leaned her face against it for a moment, feeling its wood on her cheek, remembering all the moments they had shared, and then she walked slowly away to her car. She had given John's truck to Harry.

At the school Andrew was busy with activities and friends. She kissed him good-bye, and promised to come back in a few weeks for Thanksgiving. She would stay at the Austrian Inn now, like the other parents. Mrs Curtis made no mention of John as Daphne left, although she had known him and was very sorry.

The drive to New York took seven hours, and there was no thrill for Daphne as she drove into town and caught the first glimpse of the Empire State Building. It was a city she didn't want to see, a place she didn't want to come home to. There was no home left. There was only an empty apartment.

The apartment was in decent shape. The tenant had left it clean, and she sighed as she tossed her suitcase on to the bed. Even here there were ghosts. There was Andrew's empty room to contend with, the games he no longer played, the books he no longer read. He had taken all the treasures he loved most to the school with him, and the rest he had outgrown.

And Daphne felt as though she had outgrown the apartment too. It had a dreary city look to it, which depressed her after months of living in the cabin, looking out over the New Hampshire hills. Here there was only a view of other buildings, a tiny kitchen totally unlike the cosy one she had grown used to, a living room with curtains that had grown dingy, an old rug too well worn by Andrew's toys, and furniture that was beginning to show signs of nicks and chips. Once, she had cared so much about it, wanting to make it a happy, cheerful home for herself and her son. Now, without him, it had no meaning. She cleaned the rug the first weekend she was home, and changed the curtains, bought some new plants, but for the rest she simply didn't care. She spent most of her time out walking, getting used to New York again, and avoiding going home to the apartment.

It was actually a beautiful time of year, the best

possible in New York, but even the cool, golden sunny weather didn't cheer her. She didn't give a damn, and there was something dead in her eyes as she got up every morning and wondered what to do with herself. She knew she should go out and look for a job, but she didn't want to. She still had enough money to live for a while without working, and she told herself that after the first of the year she would think about it. She stuck her manuscript in a desk drawer and she didn't even bother to call her old boss, Allie. But she ran into her one day in a store downtown, where she was looking for pyjamas for Andrew. He had grown two full sizes in the past year, and Mrs Curtis had sent her a list of what he needed.

'What are you doing here, Daff?'

'Shopping for Andrew.' She sounded matter-of-fact, but she looked worse than she had the year before, and Allison Baer couldn't help wondering what in hell had happened to her.

'Is he all right?' There was worry in her eyes.

'He's fine.'

'Are you?'

'Pretty much.'

'Daphne' – her old friend touched her arm, concerned by what she saw – 'you can't hold on to the child forever.' Was it possible that she was grieving to that extent, from leaving the child at the school? It just wasn't healthy.

'I know. He's fine. He really loves it.'

'And you? When did you get back?'

'A couple of weeks ago. I meant to call, but I've been busy.'

'Writing?' Allie looked hopeful.

'Not really.' She didn't even want to think about that now. That was all part of her life with John, and it was over. As far as she was concerned, so was her writing.

'What ever happened to that book you said you were

writing, and promised to send me? Did you finish it yet?'

She wanted to say no, but somehow she didn't.

'Yes. I finished it this summer. But I didn't know what to do next. I meant to call you about finding an agent.'

'Well?' Everything about Allison rang out with the staccato of New York, and Daphne just didn't feel up to it. She was already exhausted after five minutes. 'Can I see it?'

'I suppose so. I'll drop it off.'

'How about lunch tomorrow?'

'I don't think I can ... I ...' She looked away, unnerved by the crowds in the store, and the pressure of Allie.

'Look, Daff.' She gently took hold of Daphne's arm. 'Speaking bluntly, you look worse than you did when you left last year. In fact, you look like shit. You have to pull yourself together. You can't avoid people for the rest of your life. You lost Jeff and Aimee, Andrew is all squared away in that school, for chrissake, you have to do something with yourself. Let's have lunch and we'll talk about it.' The prospect was truly appalling.

'I don't want to talk about it.' But as she tried to brush Allie off, it was as though she heard John's voice somewhere in the distance. 'Come on, little one, dammit ... you can make it ... you have to ...' All that faith he had had in her, all his excitement over her book. It was like denying him some final thrill to leave the book buried in her desk. 'All right, all right. We'll have lunch. But I don't want to talk about it. You can tell me how to find an agent.'

They met the next day at the Veau d'Or, and Allie was full of helpful suggestions. She seemed to keep searching Daphne's eyes, but Daphne kept strictly to the subject. Allie gave her a list of agents to call, took the manuscript in hand, and promised to return it to her after the weekend, and when she did, she was raving. She thought it was the best thing she had read in years, and in spite of herself Daphne was pleased by her praise. She had always been damn tough with her criticism, and seldom generous with her applause. But for Daphne, she was applauding.

She told Daphne whom to call on the list, and on Monday she did, still feeling that she was doing it for John, but suddenly she was beginning to catch the fire of Allie's excitement. She dropped the manuscript off at the agent's office, expecting not to hear for several weeks, but four days later, as she was packing to go to see Andrew for Thanksgiving, the agent, Iris, called at four o'clock and asked if she could see her on Monday.

'What did you think of the book?' Suddenly she had to know. Slowly she was coming back to life, and the book was becoming important to her. It was her last link to John, and it was her only link to survival.

'What did I think? Honestly?' Daphne held her breath. 'I loved it. And Allison's right, she called me the day you dropped it off. It's the best thing I've read in years. You've got a sure winner there, Daphne.' For the first time in three months Daphne smiled a real smile and tears filled her eyes. Tears of excitement and relief, and that same old aching again, of wanting to share something with John, and realising once more that he wasn't there to share it. 'I thought maybe on Monday we could have lunch.'

'I'm going out of town...' She didn't want to have lunch, but she also knew that she would be back on Sunday. 'All right. Where?' Allison had warned Iris that Daphne wasn't easy, that she had been traumatised by her husband's and daughter's deaths years before, and she had a son who was in an 'institution' and she had never really recovered. Allison had always assumed that Andrew's being deaf meant he wasn't mentally quite 'normal.'

'Le Cygne at one o'clock?'

'I'll be there.'

'Good. And Daphne?'

'Yes?'

'Congratulations.'

She sat down on the bed after the call, her knees weak, her heart pounding. They liked her book ... the book she had written for John ... it was an amazing thought. More amazing yet if a publisher bought it.

12

Thanksgiving dinner with Andrew was its own special kind of joy, but that night, in her bed at the Austrian Inn, she lay awake and her mind roamed nervously from place to place. It was difficult to forget that a year before John had picked her up on a dark country road, and their life had begun, and now, only one year later, it was over. She had another holiday to hate now. Thanksgiving as well as Christmas. And she knew that this year Andrew had felt it too. Often she saw him looking dreamy, and once or twice with a wistful look in his eyes, he signed to her about John. They both had a lot of memories to live with. Too many, she thought to herself as she carefully avoided walking past their cabin. But she couldn't allow herself to think of John now, she had Andrew to think of, and his progress at the school.

When she left Andrew, this time it wasn't particularly traumatic. She was coming again during Christmas vacation.

She took a solitary walk in the hills where she had scattered John's ashes before she drove home. And she found herself speaking aloud to him, knowing that no one would hear her. She told him about the book and about Andrew, and then looking deep into the woods and up into the winter sky, she whispered, 'I sure miss you.' She could feel the echo of his thoughts and knew that he missed her, too. Perhaps, in a way, she was lucky to have loved him. Maybe that was all there was to know when it was over.

She got back in her car and drove to New York, and that night she fell into bed, exhausted. And the next day she got up and dressed in a white wool dress and heavy black coat and boots. It was freezing cold, and it seemed a thousand years since she had gone to one of those lunches. Now it seemed very strange to her to be meeting some woman to discuss her book. She remembered authors' lunches from *Collins*, but the funny thing now was that she was the author.

'Daphne? I'm Iris McCarthy.' The agent was red-headed and sleek, and a collection of elegant rings glittered on her well-manicured hands as they moved towards their table.

They spent the entire luncheon discussing her book, and over coffee and chocolate mousse Daphne began to talk about an idea she had for a second one. It was an idea she had discussed with John, and he had loved it. Iris did too, and Daphne smiled with pleasure. It was almost as though she could hear John whisper in her ear, 'That's it, little one ... you can do it.' By the end of lunch they had settled on titles for both books, and Daphne was delighted. The first was *Autumn Years*, the one she had written in New Hampshire, about a woman who loses her husband at forty-five, and how she survives it. It was a subject she knew well, and Iris assured her that there would be a 'tremendous market for it.' The second was to be called simply *Agatha*, a story of a young woman in Paris after the war. It was a story she had written originally as a short story, but it had wanted to grow and now she would let it. She promised to get to work on an outline right away, and then to discuss it with Iris. And by that afternoon she was sitting at her desk staring at a blank sheet of paper. And when the ideas for the book began to come, she let them. By midnight that night she had the beginnings of a very solid outline and by the time she returned from her Christmas holiday with Andrew, it was not only finished but well polished. The outline was delivered to Iris in her office, and she gave Daphne the green light. For the next three months Daphne hid out in her apartment and worked night and day. It was not an easy book to write but she loved it. She was often so engrossed that she didn't even bother to answer the phone, but when it rang one day in April, she stood up and stretched with a groan and went to the kitchen to answer it.

'Daphne?'

'Yes.' No, Dracula, she was always tempted to answer. Who else would answer the phone? The upstairs maid in a two-room apartment? It was Iris.

'I have some news for you.' But Daphne was too tired to pay much attention. She had worked on the book until 4 a.m. the night before and she was exhausted. 'We just had a call from Harbor and Jones.'

'And?' Suddenly Daphne's heart began to race. In the past four months it had all begun to matter. For her sake, for John's, for Andrew's. She wanted it to happen, and it seemed as though it was taking a very long time. But Iris assured her that four months was nothing. 'Did they like it?'

'You could say that.' At her end, Iris was smiling. 'I'd say that an offer of twenty-five thousand dollars means they like it.' Daphne stood in her kitchen with her mouth open, staring at the phone.

'Do you mean it?'

'Of course I mean it.'

'Oh, my God . . . oh, my God! Iris!' Her face broke into a grin and she stared into the spring sunshine outside her kitchen window. 'Iris! Iris! Iris!' It had happened after all, John had been right. She *could* do it! 'Now what do I do?'

'You have lunch with your editor on Tuesday. At the Four Seasons. You've moved up in the world, Mrs Fields.'

'I sure as hell have.' She was almost thirty-one years old and she was about to publish her first book, and have lunch with an editor at the Four Seasons. Now that was a lunch she wouldn't miss for the world. And she didn't. She arrived on schedule at noon on Tuesday, in a new pink Chanel suit she had bought for the occasion. The editor was a dragonlike woman with a carnivorous smile, but by the end of the lunch Daphne knew they

111

would work well together, and that she would learn a great deal from her. She began discussing her second book, as they sat at a table next to the pool in the centre of the white marble room with waiters scurrying around them. The editor from Harbor and Jones asked if she could see what Daphne had of the new book. A month later there was a second offer, and when she finished the book in late July, she went up to New Hampshire to spend a month with Andrew.

Her first book came out that Christmas, dedicated to John, and it enjoyed a modest success, but it was the second one that made her. It came out the following spring, and it hit *The New York Times* list almost at once. And the paperback rights sold for one hundred thousand dollars.

'How does it feel to be a success, Daff?' Allie took a maternal pride in her progress, and had invited her to lunch for her thirty-second birthday. 'Hell, I should make you pay for lunch.' But it was obvious that she didn't begrudge her what had happened. It had brought her back to the land of the living in a way Allison had never dreamed, and all of those who knew what she had been through in her life were thrilled for her. 'What are you working on now?' Her third book was well under way, already bought by Harbor and Jones before it was even finished, and scheduled for the following summer.

'Something called *Heartbeat*.'

'I like the title.'

'I hope you like the book.'

'I will, and so will all your readers.' Allie never doubted her for a moment.

'I'm a little nervous about this one. They're going to make me go on the road to promote it.'

'It's about time.'

'I'm glad *you* think so. What in hell do I talk about on talk shows in Cleveland?' Daphne still looked terribly young, and a little bit shy, and the prospect of television made her very nervous.

112

'Tell them about you. That's what people want to know. They always ask me.'

'And what do you say?' Allison stalled just long enough for Daphne to know the truth. 'That I've had a tragic life? That's exactly what I don't want to tell them.'

'So tell them how you write your books, all that kind of stuff.' She giggled then. 'Tell them who you're dating.' Daphne had looked so well for the past two years that she assumed there were a host of escorts. What she didn't know was that there had been no one in Daphne's life for two years, not since John died. And she was rapidly coming to the conclusion that she was going to keep it that way, for good. She couldn't have faced another loss, and she didn't plan to. 'Who is the man in your life, by the way?'

Daphne smiled. 'Andrew.'

'How is he?' But Allie was never really very interested. She liked grown-ups and careers and successful people. She had never married, and she didn't particularly like children.

'He's fine. Enormous and beautiful, and very, very busy.'

'He's still at the school?'

'He will be for a while.' Something sad came into Daphne's eyes, and Allison was sorry she had asked. 'I'm hoping that in a couple of years I can bring him home.'

'Is that a good idea?' Allison looked shocked. She still thought he was crazy. But Daphne knew that about her friend and didn't hold it against her.

'We'll see. There are conflicting theories on the subject. I'd like to put him in a regular school here at home, whenever he's ready.'

'Won't that interfere with your work?' Allison would never understand and Daphne knew it. How could a child she loved interfere with her work? Daphne knew that it could only enhance it. And it might complicate things a little, but it was a complication she longed for. 'Well, tell me about the tour. Where are you going?'

'I don't know yet. The Midwest, California, Boston, Washington, DC. The usual insanity from what everyone tells me. Twenty cities in as many days, no sleep, no meals, and the terror that you won't remember where you are when you wake up in the morning.'

'Sounds great to me.'

'It would. To me, it sounds like a nightmare.' She still longed for the life she had once had in the cabin in New Hampshire, but that was long gone now, and it would never come again. She was thinking of buying an apartment in the East Sixties.

And after lunch she went home to work on the new book, as she did every day, every night, every hour that she wasn't visiting Andrew. She had found something to fill the void. A fantasy life conducted on paper, filled with people who lived and died in her head, and delighted hundreds of thousands of readers, and millions in paperback. There was nothing in her life except her work, but it paid off. Just before her thirty-third birthday, Daphne Fields's book *Apache* made it to the number one spot on the *The New York Times* Best Seller List. She had made it.

13

'How is she?' Barbara's eyes looked wearily at the nurse as she checked all the monitors again, but it was useless asking. There was obviously no change. It was incredible to think of her lying here, so still, so lifeless, so devoid of the energy she had so richly shared with those who needed her. Barbara knew better than anyone what mountains she was capable of moving. She had moved them for Andrew, and for herself, and for Barbara, over the years.

As the nurse left the room again Barbara closed her eyes for a minute, thinking back to the beginning, and the first time she had seen her, when Barbara was still living with her mother in those long-gone nightmare days. She had gone out to buy groceries, and had returned, exhausted and breathless after the long hike up the stairs to their dismal, dingy West Side apartment where Barbara had been trapped with her invalid mother for years.

Daphne had found her through her agent, who knew that Barbara took in typing at home, to supplement her meagre secretarial income, and also secretly to give herself an escape from the life she hated so desperately and the realities she almost couldn't bear. But the manuscripts added a touch of whimsy, a glimpse into other worlds, even if they were a lot of work.

Barbara had staggered through the door with groceries in both arms, assaulted as always by the smell of cabbage and decaying flesh. And there sat Daphne, serious, quiet, nicely dressed, and something about her so fresh. Looking at her was, for Barbara, like opening a window and taking gulps of clean air. The women's eyes met almost instantly, and Barbara blushed. No one ever came here, she always went to the literary agency herself to pick up the work.

Barbara had been about to speak to Daphne as she heard the familiar plaintive wail. 'Did you buy me rice?' Barbara felt a sudden urge to scream as Daphne watched her, taking it all in. 'You always get the wrong kind.' Her mother's voice was, as usual, hideous and whiny, always angry and shrill.

'Yes, I got rice. Now, Mother, why don't you go inside and lie down while I –'

'What about coffee?'

'I got it.' The old woman began to dig through the two bags, making small clucking sounds, and Barbara's hands shook as she took off her jacket. 'Mother, please...' She looked apologetically at Daphne, who smiled, trying not to let the scene unnerve her. But there was something claustrophobic about just being there. She felt trapped just watching Barbara and her mother. Eventually the old woman had gone to a back room, and Daphne had been able to explain what she wanted. The manuscript had come back to her in two weeks, perfectly typed, without a single error. And Daphne said that she thought it remarkable that she had got it done at all with the old woman undoubtedly driving her crazy. It seemed like a ghastly life to her, and she wondered why Barbara had chosen to live with her mother.

She had brought her more work to do after that, typing rewrites and rough drafts and an occasional outline, and in time she had asked Barbara to come to her apartment and work with her there. And it was then that Barbara finally poured out her story. Her father had died when she was nine, and her mother had struggled to support her, put her through the best possible schools, and eventually helped put her through college. Barbara had gone to Smith, and had graduated with honours, but by then her mother had had a stroke and could no longer help her. Now it was Barbara's turn to struggle to support her, for two years the woman had been destitute.

116

Barbara took a job as a secretary to two attorneys, and at night she nursed her mother. There wasn't time for much else, and she told Daphne that she had been perennially exhausted. The romance that she'd had in college fell away, the young man couldn't stand the demands of her life, and when he proposed she tearfully refused to leave her mother. They couldn't afford to put her in a home, and her mother begged her not to. She just couldn't leave her, not after the years Eleanor Jarvis had spent standing on her feet night and day, working two jobs to put Barbara through school. The debt had to be repaid, and her mother constantly reminded her of it. 'After all I did, you would leave me . . .' She accused and she whined and she laid all the guilt at Barbara's feet. Barbara had no intention of leaving her. She simply couldn't. She spent two years nursing her mother back to health and working in the law firm. It was at the end of those two years that her boss left his wife and began to court Barbara. He knew about the life she led, and he felt very sorry for her. She was a bright girl with a good mind, and it irked him to see her waste her life. At twenty-five she was beginning to look and act and sound like an old woman.

It was he who urged her to get out whenever she could. He would come to pick her up, and chat with her mother. Her mother objected strenuously whenever she went out, but he was firm with Barbara about getting something out of life for herself, and she managed what time with him she could, while still trying to appease her mother. The affair lasted six months, and it was the only ray of sunshine she had, until Christmas, when he told her he was going back to his wife. She was going through change of life, and having a hard time, and the kids were giving her a lot of trouble.

'I have responsibilities, Barbara. I have to go back and give her a hand. I just can't let her go on struggling alone . . .' He was apologetic, and Barbara looked at him with a bitter little smile, tears bright in her eyes.

'What about your own life? What about the things you

said to me about getting what I need, and not just dancing to everyone else's music?'

'That's all true. I believe everything I said. But Barb, you have to understand. This is different. She's my wife. In your case, you're being strangled by an overbearing, demanding, unreasonable mother. You have a right to your own life. But my life is Georgia's too ... you just don't throw twenty-two years out the window.' And what was she supposed to do with her mother? Run out the door and never come back? He was full of shit and she knew it. He went back to his wife the next day, and the affair ended abruptly. She quit her job after the new year, and two weeks later she discovered she was pregnant. She deliberated for a week, locking herself in her room, and sobbing silently into her pillows. She had thought that she loved him, that he would be free, that he might marry her some day ... that she would be free of her mother. And what in hell was she going to do now? She couldn't take care of a child by herself, and having it aborted went against everything she believed. She didn't want to do it. In the end she decided to call him. He met her for lunch, looking very businesslike and a little distant.

'You're all right?' She nodded, looking grim and feeling desperately nauseous. 'And your mother?'

'She's all right. But the doctor is worried about her heart.' At least that was what she told Barbara, every time Barbara wanted even to go to a movie. Now she never went out. There was no point, and she didn't really feel up to it. She was constantly nauseous. 'I've got something to tell you.'

'Oh?' A wall instantly went up, as though deep in his gut he suspected. 'Didn't your last cheque arrive?' They had decided it would be better if she quit the firm and he had arranged a large severance pay for her to assuage his guilt. Yes, you son of a bitch, she thought to herself ... but this isn't about money. It's about my life. And your baby.

'I'm pregnant.' She couldn't think of a gentler way to

say it and she didn't really want to. Screw Georgia and her change of life. This was more important. At least to Barbara.

'That certainly presents a bit of a problem.' He tried to sound glib, but his eyes told her that he was nervous. 'Are you sure? Have you seen a doctor?'

'Yes.'

'Are you sure it's mine?' Even knowing her life, he didn't flinch as he said it, and her eyes filled with tears which spilled on to her cheeks.

'You know something, Stan? You're a real shit. Do you really think I was sleeping with someone else?'

'I'm sorry. I just thought – '

'No, you didn't. You just wanted to get out of it.'

For a moment he didn't answer. And then his voice was a little more gentle when he spoke again, but he didn't even reach out to touch her hand as she sat crying across the table. 'I know someone who...' She cringed at what he was about to say.

'I don't know if I can do it ... I just can't...' She began to sob and he looked nervously over his shoulder.

'Look, be realistic, Barb. You have no choice.' And without another word he scribbled a name on a piece of paper, wrote her a cheque for a thousand dollars, and handed them both to her. 'Call this number and tell him I sent you.'

'Why? Do you get a special deal?' Apparently this had happened to him before, and then with despair in her eyes she looked across at him, this wasn't the man she knew, this wasn't the man she had believed in ... the man she had thought would save her. 'Would you send Georgia to him?'

He looked stony-faced at her for a long moment. 'I sent him my daughter last year.'

She lowered her eyes and shook her head. 'I'm sorry.'

'So am I.' They were the last kind words he said as

119

he stood up and looked down at her. 'Barb, get it done fast. Get it over with. You'll feel a lot better.'

She looked up at him from where she sat. 'And if I don't?'

'What the hell do you mean?' He almost spat the words at her.

'I mean what if I decide to have the baby? I still have a choice, you know. I don't have to have an abortion.'

'If you don't, it's entirely your decision.'

'Meaning don't call you?' She hated him now.

'Meaning I don't even know if that's my child. And that thousand dollars is the last you'll see from me.'

'Is it?' She picked up the cheque, looked at it, and tore it in half before handing it back to him. 'Thank you, Stan. But I don't think I'll need it.' And with that, she stood up and walked past him out of the restaurant.

She had cried all the way home, and that night her mother had forced her way into her bedroom. 'He left you, didn't he? He went back to his wife.' She was so evil she almost gloated. 'I knew it ... I told you he was no good ... he probably never even left her in the first place.'

'Mother, leave me alone ... please...' She lay back on her bed and closed her eyes.

'What's wrong with you? Are you sick?' And then instantly she knew. 'Oh, my God ... you're pregnant... aren't you? Aren't you?' She advanced on her with a wicked look in her eye, and stood in front of Barbara.

Barbara sat up to face her mother with a look of grief in her eyes. 'Yes, I am.'

'Oh, my God ... an illegitimate baby ... do you know what people will say about you, you little whore?' Her mother reached out and slapped her and suddenly all the frustration and loneliness exploded within Barbara.

'Dammit, leave me alone. It happened to you with my father.'

'It didn't ... we were engaged ... he wasn't a married man. And he married me.'

'He married you because you were pregnant. And he

120

hated you for trapping him. I heard the things he said to you when you fought. He always hated you. He was engaged to someone else...' Her mother slapped her again, and Barbara sank back on to the bed sobbing.

For the next two weeks they barely spoke, except when her mother tormented her about the illegitimate baby. 'You'll be ruined ... disgraced ... you'll never find another job.' And the truth was that she was worried about the same thing. She hadn't been able to find a job since she left Stan's office. The unemployment rates had been soaring since the previous summer, and even with her summa cum laude degree from Smith, she couldn't find a thing. And now she was having a baby.

In the end there was nothing else she could do. Too proud to call Stan for the name of his doctor, she called a friend, got a name of a doctor, and had an illegal abortion in New Jersey. She rode all the way home on the subway in a daze, bleeding copiously on to the seat, and passed out cold on the subway platform. They called her mother from the emergency room at Roosevelt Hospital, and her mother refused to come. When she got home three days later, her mother stood in the living room and uttered two simple words. 'Baby killer.'

The hatred between them grew after that, and Barbara was going to move out. But her mother had another stroke, and she couldn't leave her. All she wanted was her own life and her own apartment. She got unemployment payments instead, since Stan allowed her to say she'd been fired, and her mother got a pension and they lived on that, but barely. She nursed her mother back to health for six months, and through it all her mother never let her forget about the abortion. She blamed the stroke on her, and her disappointment in Barbara as a human being. And without even realising that it had come, Barbara lived in a constant haze of depression. Eventually she got another job, working at another law firm. But this time there was no affair, there were no men, there was only her mother. She lost touch with all her friends from Smith, and when they called she didn't bother to return their calls. What could she tell them? They were all married or engaged or having babies. She had had an affair with a married man, had an abortion, worked as a secretary, and was a full-time nurse for her mother. And her mother was always carping at her that they needed more money. It was another secretary at the law firm where she worked who suggested that she call around to some literary agents. She could do extra typing at night, and the money was halfway decent. In fact, sometimes it was pretty good. So Barbara did, and it was thus that Daphne Fields found her, ten years after she had begun typing manuscripts at home in her spare time, a withered, lonely, nervous spinster at thirty-seven. The once handsome, well-built, athletic young girl who had been the president of the senior class at Smith and graduated summa cum laude in political science, was taking in typing in a fourth-floor walk-up on the West Side, nursing her ever more vicious mother. She hated everything Barbara was, hated her lack of spirit and fire. And yet it was she who had stamped it out. And in great part because of her, Barbara had never recovered from the tragic love affair and the abortion.

Barbara was fascinated by Daphne at first, but she didn't dare ask anything about her life. There was something very private and closed about Daphne, as though she were keeping a multitude of secrets. And it was only late one night when Barbara had delivered a manuscript to her apartment, a year after she'd begun typing for her, that the two women had begun to open up about themselves. Barbara had told her then about the abortion, and about being imprisoned by her invalid mother. Daphne had listened quietly to the long unhappy tale, and then told her about Jeff and Aimee, and Andrew. They had sat on the floor of her apartment, drinking wine and talking until the wee hours of the morning. It seemed like yesterday as Barbara watched her now, lifeless in her hospital bed, when only days before she had been so vibrant.

Daphne had been adamant, when she heard Barbara's tale, that Barbara had to leave her mother.

'Look, dammit, it's a matter of your survival.' They had both been a little drunk, and Daphne had pointed an emphatic finger at her.

'What can I do, Daff? She can hardly walk. She has a heart condition, she's had three strokes...'

'Put her in a home. Or can you afford to?'

'I could if I worked my ass off to do it, but she says she'd kill herself. And I owe her that much...' Barbara's thoughts drifted back to the past. 'She put me through school, she even put me through Smith.'

'And now she's ruining your life. You don't owe her that. What about you?'

'What about me? There's no me left.'

'Yes, there is.' Barbara had looked at her, wanting to believe her, but it had been years since she had dared to think of herself. Her mother had almost destroyed her. 'You can do anything you want to do.' It was what John had said to her in their cabin in New Hampshire. She told Barbara about him then. She was the first person she had told. There were no secrets left when the night was over. And again and again they went back to talking about Andrew. He was everything that mattered to Daphne, everything that counted, that brought life and fire to her eyes.

'You're lucky you have him.' Barbara looked at her with envy. Her own child would have been ten years old by then. And she still thought of it often.

'I know I am. But I don't "have" him in that sense.' A look of sorrow came across her face then. 'He's at the school. And I have my own life, such as it is.' Barbara suspected that in her own way Daphne was not so much better off than she was. She had her son and her work, but nothing else. There had been no man in her life since John died, and she was careful to see that there wasn't. Apparently several people had asked her out over the years, old friends of Jeff's, a writer she had met through her agent, people she met at publishing functions, but she had declined them all. In her own way she was as lonely as Barbara. And it formed a bond between the two. She confided in her more than anyone else, and after Barbara began coming to her house to work, they went to lunch now and then, or shopping on a Saturday afternoon together.

'You know something, Daphne? I think you're crazy.'

'That's not news.' She grinned up at her tall friend as they went through the racks at Saks. Barbara had actually managed to escape her mother for an entire afternoon and they had decided to spend it together.

'I mean it. You're young, you're gorgeous. You could have any man you want. What are you doing shopping with me?'

'You're my friend and I like you. And I don't want a man.'

'That's what's crazy.'

'Why? Some people never have what I've had.' She almost cringed as she said it, knowing the emptiness of Barbara's life.

'It's all right.' Barbara had looked down at her with a warm smile, looking suddenly younger. 'I know what you mean. But that's no reason to quit.'

'Yes, it is. I'll never have again what I had with Jeffrey, or John. Why settle for second best?'

'That's not a reasonable assumption.'

'In my case it is. You don't find men like that again in a lifetime.'

'Maybe not just like them. But someone else. Are you really going to give up on that for the next fifty years?' Barbara had been horrified at the thought. 'That really is goddamn crazy.' It didn't seem as crazy to her that she had given her life up to a mother she hated. But she didn't see herself in the same light. Daphne was beautiful and petite, and Barbara had sensed from the first that she was going to be very successful. Their lives were worlds apart to Barbara.

But it was Daphne who saw hope for her friend, and

she nagged her constantly to do something about it. 'Why the hell don't you move out?'

'To where? A tent in Central Park? And what do I do with my mother?'

'Put her in a home.' It became a familiar refrain between the two, but it wasn't until Daphne bought the apartment on East Sixty-ninth Street that she developed a plan, and she faced Barbara with it, her eyes filled with excitement.

'Christ, Daphne, I can't.'

'Yes, you can.' She wanted Barbara to move into her old apartment.

'I can't support us both.'

'Wait till you hear the rest of my idea.' She offered her a full-time job, at a handsome salary that she could well afford.

'Work for you? Are you serious?' Barbara's eyes had lit up like a summer sky. 'Do you mean it?'

'I do, but don't think I'm doing you a favour. I need you, dammit. You're the only thing that keeps my life running smoothly. And I'm not going to take no for an answer.' Barbara had felt her heart soar within her, but she was terrified, too. What about her mother?

'I don't know, Daff. I'll have to think it over.'

'I've already thought it out for you.' Daphne grinned at her. 'You can't have the job unless you move out from your mother. How's that for a stiff deal?' It was and they both knew it, but after a month of tormenting herself over what Daphne said, she got up the guts to do it. Daphne gave her two stiff drinks, and took her over in a cab to her apartment. She dropped her off with a hug and a kiss and told her she could do it. 'It's your life, Barbara. Don't blow it. She doesn't give a damn about you, and you've paid your debt. Don't forget that. How much more can you give? . . . How much more do you want to?' Barbara already knew the answer. For the first time in years she saw a light at the end of the tunnel, and she ran for it as hard and as fast as she could. She went upstairs and told her mother she was moving out, and she refused to accept the threats or the vengeance or the insults or the blackmail.

Her mother moved to a home the following month, and although she never admitted it to Barbara, she actually came to enjoy it. She was with people her own age, and she had a whole circle of cronies to whom she could complain about her selfish daughter. And when Daphne's new apartment was ready, Barbara took over her old place, and she felt as though she had finally been released from prison. She smiled now as she remembered the feeling. She woke up every morning with a light heart and a feeling of freedom, made coffee in the sunny little kitchen, stretched out on her bed, feeling as though she owned the world, and she used what had been Andrew's bedroom as an office whenever she brought work home, which was often. She worked for Daphne every day from ten in the morning until five o'clock, and when she went home she always took stacks of work with her.

'Don't you have anything else to do, for chrissake? Why don't you leave that here?' But as Daphne said it she was sitting at her own desk, preparing to work until the wee hours of the morning. The two were well matched, but neither of them had a normal life, and all that Barbara wanted out of life was to repay her for what she had done. She had helped her to free herself of her mother. But Daphne also realised that there was another danger, that Barbara would turn her habit for devotion and slavery towards Daphne.

'Just don't treat me like your mother!' she ranted teasingly when Barbara would appear with lunch on a tray when Daphne was working.

'Oh, shut up.'

'I mean it, Barb. You've been taking care of someone else all your life. Take care of yourself for a change. Make yourself happy.'

'I do. I enjoy my job, you know. In spite of what a pain in the ass you are to work for.' Daphne would grin at her distractedly and go back to work, working at her

126

typewriter from noon until three or four in the morning.

'How the hell can you work like that?' Barbara would
watch her in amazement. She never stopped, except
once in a great while for a cup of coffee, or to go to the
bathroom. 'You'll destroy your health working like
that.'

'No, I won't. It makes me happy.' But happy wasn't
a word Barbara would ever have used to describe her.
There was always something in Daphne's eyes that said
she hadn't been happy in years, except right after she
had seen Andrew. But the events of her life were etched
deep into her eyes, and the ache she still felt over the
people she had lost never really left her. She put the joy
and satisfaction she felt from her work between her and
the ghosts that she lived with, but they were always
there, and it showed, although she seldom spoke of it to
Barbara.

But when she was alone in her office sometimes, she
would sit and look out the window, her mind far away
. . . in New Hampshire with John, or a place she had been
to with Jeff . . . or in spite of the iron control she kept over
herself, her eyes would mist over with memories of
Aimee. It was a side of her no one saw, and she was
careful that they didn't, but she admitted her innermost
feelings to Barbara, about what her life had been like at
various times, and how much she missed it, the people
she had lost, like John and Jeff and Aimee. And always,
always, she would talk about Andrew and how much she
missed him. But, she had a different life now than she
had had when Andrew lived at home. A life filled with
work and accomplishment and success, publishers and
publicity people, and her agent. She had a good head for
business, which she hadn't realised before, and she
exercised her craft well, with a deft pen and a good sense
for what her readers wanted. The only thing she hated
about her work was the promotional appearances she
occasionally had to do, because she didn't want anyone
prying into her personal life, or asking about Andrew.

She wanted to protect him from all that. There was nothing about her personal life that Daphne wanted to share with the world, and she felt that her books spoke for themselves, but she recognised that her publishers felt the publicity was important. The issue came up again when she was asked to do *The Conroy Show* in Chicago and she hesitated, gnawing on a pencil.

'What do you want me to tell them, Daff? Do you want to go to Chicago tomorrow?' They had been bugging Barbara all morning and she had to give them an answer.

'In a word?' She grinned, rubbing her neck. She had worked late the night before on her new book and this morning she was tired. But it was a kind of tired she liked, the book was going well, and there was a sense of pleasure she always had with what she did. She didn't mind the ache in her back, or the inevitable pains in her shoulders. 'No, I don't want to go to Chicago. Call George Murdock at Harbor and ask him if he thinks it's important.' But she already knew the answer. Even though they were between books just then, publicity was always important, and the *The Conroy Show* in Chicago was a biggie.

Barbara came back five minutes later with a rueful smile. 'Do you really want to know what he said?'

'No, I don't.'

'I figured.' Barbara watched her sink into a comfortable chair with a sigh as she laid her head back against the soft white cushion. 'Why do you work so damn hard, Daff? You can't run away forever.' She still looked like a little girl as she sat there, but there was an undeniable aura of womanhood too, no matter how determined she was to deny it. She was kind to everyone who entered her life, her publishers, her agent, her secretary, her few well-chosen friends, her son, the people at the school, the other children. She was kind to everyone but herself. Of herself she demanded murderous goals, and almost unbearable standards. She worked fifteen hours a day, was always patient, interested, warm. The only warmth denied was to herself. She never really let anyone near her. There had been too much pain in her life, too much loss, and now the walls were around her forever. Barbara thought it again as she watched the still form in the hospital bed, and the echo of Daphne's words rang in her head.

'I'm not running away, Barb. I'm building a career, that's different.'

'It is? Looks the same to me.'

'Maybe so.' With Barbara she was usually honest. 'But it's for a good cause.' She was building up a fortune for Andrew. He would need it some day and she wanted his life to be easy. Everything she did seemed to centre around Andrew.

'I've heard that story before. But you've made enough for Andrew by now, Daff. Why don't you think of yourself for a change?'

'I do.'

'Oh, yeah? When?'

'For about ten seconds when I wash my face in the morning.' She smiled at her confidante and friend. There were some things Daphne didn't like to talk about. 'So they want me to go to Chicago, huh?'

'Can you get away from the book?'

'If I have to.'

'So we go?'

'I don't know.' She frowned and looked out the window before glancing back at Barbara. 'I'm worried about that show. I've never been on it, and I don't really want to.'

'Why?' But Barbara suspected the reason for her answer. Bob Conroy threw a lot of curves, and he was a prober. He had an extraordinary research team, and he had a knack for digging up bits and pieces of people's pasts, and confronting them with them on national television. She knew that Daphne was afraid that would happen. She had gone to great pains to keep her own story private. She never talked about Jeff, or Aimee, and she was violent on the subject of Andrew. She never wanted him subjected to idle curiosity or gossip. He lived a happy secluded life at the Howarth School in New Hampshire, and he had no idea that he had a famous mother. 'Are you afraid of Conroy, Daff?'

'Honestly? Yes. I don't want a lot of old stuff to come out.' Her eyes were huge and blue and sad as she looked at Barbara. 'It's nobody's business what happened in my life. You know how I feel about it.'

'Yes, but you can't keep everything a secret forever. What if it did come out, would that be so awful?'

'For me, yes. I don't want anyone's pity, and neither will Andrew. We don't need it.' She straightened her back and sat up in her chair, looking nervous and defiant.

'All it would probably do is make your readers love you more.' She knew better than anyone how much they already did. She answered all of Daphne's fan mail. Daphne had a way of pouring out her soul in her books, so that her readers felt they knew her. In fact, they knew her better than she liked to admit, the secrets of her soul were what made her books real, but she passed them off as fiction.

'I don't want them to love me more. I want them to love the books.'

'Maybe there's no difference.'

Daphne nodded silently from where she sat and then she stood up with a sigh. 'I guess I have no choice. If I don't go, I'll never hear the end of it from George Murdock. They've been trying to get me on that show for the last year.' She looked at Barbara then with a smile. 'Want to come? They have some nice shops in Chicago.'

'Do you want to spend the night?'

'Sure.' She had a favourite hotel now, as she did in almost every major city. They were always the quietest, most conservative and yet always the most elegant hotels in each city. Hotels where dowagers wore sable coats, and people spoke in hushed whispers. She ordered room service, and enjoyed the comforts of what her work

130

brought her. She had grown into it well, and she had to admit that there were aspects of her success that pleased her greatly. She no longer had to worry about money, she knew Andrew's future was secure. She had invested well, and she bought expensive clothes and antiques, and paintings she liked whenever she had the opportunity. But at the same time there was nothing showy about Daphne. She didn't use her money to flaunt her success, she didn't throw lavish parties, or try to impress her friends. It was all very quiet and simple and solid. And in a funny way, she knew that it was exactly what Jeffrey and John would have expected. She had grown up well, and knowing that pleased her.

'You're on the show at ten o'clock. Do you want to go in the morning or in the afternoon? You should rest for a while and have dinner before we go to the studio.'

'Yes, Mother.'

'Oh, shut up.' Barbara jotted some quick notes on her pad and disappeared as Daphne went back to her desk with a worried frown and stared at the keyboard. She had told Barbara that she had an odd feeling about doing the show, a strange, unhappy premonition. And Barbara had told her she was being silly. She remembered it now as she sat watching Daphne's face, so battered by the car that had hit her. It seemed a thousand years since they had been in Chicago.

14

Daphne and Barbara arrived at the studio at exactly nine thirty. Daphne was wearing a simple beige silk dress and her hair was coiffed in a quiet, elegant chignon. There were pearl earrings in her ears, and a large, handsome topaz ring she had bought earlier that year at Cartier's. She looked elegant and successful, but not opulent and showy. It was typical of Daphne. As usual, Barbara was wearing one of her navy blue suits. Daphne always teased her that she had fourteen that all looked alike, but she looked neat and trim and her straight black hair fell in a smooth, shiny sheet to her shoulders. She looked younger now that she had left her mother. And in the past year Daphne had noticed that she had become increasingly attractive. She looked more like the photographs of the girl who had been at Smith, and there was laughter in her eyes now as she looked at Daphne.

She leaned over and whispered as they were ushered into the standard waiting room, with comfortable chairs, a bar, and a maid to attend to their needs. 'Don't look so uptight. He's not going to bite you.'

'How do you know?' But she always got nervous before she went on talk shows. It was part of why she took Barbara with her. It was also nice to have a friend along, to chat with on planes, and help sort things out at hotels when things got loused up with their reservations. And Barbara had a marvellous ability for keeping everything in control. With Barbara around, the luggage never got lost, the meals arrived in Daphne's room on time, there were magazines and books and newspapers to read, the reporters were ushered to the door when she'd had enough, and her clothes were always pressed before she had an interview. She made everything seem miraculously easy.

'Do you want a drink?'

Daphne shook her head. 'That's all I need, to go on half bombed. Then I'll really tell him a thing or two.' They both grinned, and Daphne settled into a chair. Even at times like this she wasn't really a drinker.

'Miss Fields?' A production assistant stuck his head in the door. 'You're on first.'

'Oh, Christ.'

'Mr Conroy didn't want to keep you waiting.'

That was always the hardest spot, she didn't have time to relax about the show, and watch how the others handled themselves, but she also knew that tonight she had star billing. 'I wish he wouldn't do me such a big favour,' Daphne whispered to Barbara, feeling her palms begin to sweat, but Barbara whispered something reassuring.

'You'll be fine.'

'How long will I be on?' It was like setting an internal time clock for having a tooth filled at the dentist ... twenty minutes ... I can stand twenty minutes of pain ... or can I? And at least at the dentist they gave her Novocaine so she wouldn't feel the pain. This was cold turkey.

'They didn't tell me. I asked yesterday. The girl said he just wants to "let it flow." But I don't imagine it'll be more than fifteen minutes.' Daphne nodded, gearing herself up, and a moment later the production assistant reappeared and signalled for her to come with him.

'So long, kid.' She glanced over her shoulder at Barbara, thinking of the old saw 'We who are about to die salute you.'

'You'll be great.'

She rolled her eyes and disappeared and Barbara settled down with a glass of wine to watch her on the monitor.

The production assistant led Daphne to the set,

133

indicated which chair, and clipped a microphone to the neck of her dress, as a makeup artist ran up and dusted her face with powder. Her hair was perfectly in place, and the rest of her makeup was fine. The woman nodded and disappeared and the production assistant nodded and adjusted his headphones before whispering to Daphne. 'Mr Conroy is coming out now. He'll sit there.' He indicated a chair. 'He'll do the first ninety seconds alone, then he'll introduce you.' She nodded, noticing her last two books on the low table. Usually she was given some indication of what they'd talk about, but Conroy didn't work that way. It was precisely because of that that she was worried. 'Do you want a glass of water on the set?'

'Thank you.' Her eyes felt too large in her face, her mouth felt dry, and she could feel little rivers of perspiration rolling slowly down her sides as Bob Conroy appeared in a dark suit and a pale blue shirt and red tie. He was in his late forties and undeniably handsome. But there was something very cold and sharp in his eyes, something too glib and terribly plastic about him.

'Daphne?' No. Mata Hari.

'Yes.' She smiled, trying not to feel dizzy.

'Nice to have you on the show. How was the weather in New York?'

'Fine.'

He sat down and glanced out to see the angles on the camera. But before he could say anything more, the assistant producer began counting, a red light went on, and a camera moved in on Conroy's face as he smiled the sexy smile that turned American womanhood on, and told his viewers who they could expect on the show that evening. It was exactly like all of the other shows Daphne had been on. One was brought out like a dancing dog, asked to do one's act, and sent off the set with scarcely a thank you, while the host did his egocentric pirouettes to enchant his viewers.

'And our first guest this evening is a woman whose

books most of you have read, certainly you ladies' – he stopped to smile into the camera, and then picked a book up off the coffee table and then looked back into the camera – 'but I suspect that most of you have read very little about her. From all reports, Daphne Fields is a very private person.' He smiled again and turned slowly to Daphne as the camera included her and a second camera moved in slowly on casters. 'It's nice to have you here with us in Chicago.'

'It's nice to be here with you, Bob.' She smiled shyly at him, knowing the camera would cover her full front without her having to turn towards it. That was always the case except on shows in backwater towns where the only angle they ever shot was the host. She had spent an entire hour on a show in Santa Fe once, without realising that all the viewers saw was the back of her hairdo.

'You live in New York, don't you?' It was a typically innocuous question.

'I do.' She smiled.

'Are you working on a book now?'

'Yes, I am. It's called *Lovers*.'

'Now there's a title for you.' He looked deep into the eyes of his female viewers. 'Your readers will love that. How's the research going?' He gave a suggestive little laugh and Daphne blushed softly beneath her makeup.

'My work is generally fiction.' Her voice and smile were soft, and there was something wonderfully delicate about her, which made him look brash and sound harsh with his question. But he would get her for that, they always did. It was his show, and he planned to be on for a long time. Daphne was just a one-night stand. It was his ass on the line, not hers, and he never forgot it.

'Come, come, a pretty lady like you ... you must have an army of lovers.'

'Not lately.' This time there was mischief in her eyes and she didn't blush. She was beginning to think she might survive it.

But the humour faded from Conroy's voice as he turned towards her. 'I understand, Daphne, that you're

135

a widow.' It was a line she didn't expect, and for a moment she almost gasped. He had done his research well, and she nodded. 'That's a great pity. But' – his voice oozed sympathy and compassion – 'perhaps that's why you write so well. You write a great deal about surviving loss, and you certainly have. I'm told you lost a little girl, too.' Her eyes filled with tears at the shock of hearing him discuss Jeff and Aimee, and she sat there, with her guts on his cocktail table.

'I don't generally discuss my private life in association with my work, Bob.' She was struggling to regain her composure.

'Maybe you should.' The face was earnest, the voice helpful. 'It would make you more real to your readers.' Zap. He had got her.

'As long as my books are real – '

He cut her off. 'But how can they be, if they don't know who you are?' Before she could answer, he went on, 'Am I right in saying that your husband and daughter died in a fire?'

'Yes, you are.' She took a deep breath, and as Barbara watched on the monitor, tears filled her eyes. What a stinking thing to do. The son of a bitch . . . Daphne had been right to be afraid to come here.

'Was your husband the man you talked about in *Apache*?' She shook her head. It had been John. And with a sudden wave of panic she wondered if he knew about him, too, but there was no way he could have. 'What a striking character that was. I think every woman in America fell in love with him. You know, the book would make a marvellous movie.'

She began to recover then, praying for the interview to end. 'I'm awfully glad you think so.'

'Any prospects on the horizon?'

'Not yet, but my agent thinks they will come.'

'Daphne, tell us, how old are you?' Shit. There was no way around him, but she laughed softly.

'Do I have to tell the truth?' But she made no secret of her age. 'I'm working my way towards thirty-three.'

136

'Good Lord' – he looked her over appraisingly – 'you don't look it. I would easily guess you for twenty.' It was the charm that so delighted his female viewers. But as Daphne smiled he moved in on her again with that same sympathetic look she had come to distrust, and she was right again. 'And you've never remarried. How long have you been a widow?'

'Seven years.'

'It must have been a terrible blow.' With a look of innocence now, 'Is there a man currently in your life?' She wanted to scream or reach out and slap him. They never asked questions like that of male writers, but women were fair game, somehow it was assumed that a female writer's personal life was part of her work, and hence public property. A man would have told him to go to hell, but he would never have asked the question.

'Not at the moment, Bob,' with a gentle smile.

He smiled sweetly. 'I'm not sure I believe that. You're much too pretty to be alone. And then there's that book you're working on now ... what was it, *Lovers*?' She nodded. 'When will that be out? I'm sure all your readers are waiting breathlessly for it.'

'Not too breathlessly, I hope. The book won't be out until next year.'

'We'll be waiting.' They exchanged another plastic smile as Daphne waited for her reprieve, she knew it would come soon, and she could hardly wait to get off the set, and away from his questions. 'You know, there's something else I've been wanting to ask you.' She waited, almost expecting him to ask her bra size. 'Our next guest is also a writer, but not in your field. His book is nonfiction. He's written a marvellous book about autistic children.' Daphne felt herself grow pale as she saw him coming ... but surely he couldn't ... 'A good friend of mine in New York, at *Collins* where you used to work, tells me that you have an autistic child. Maybe, from a parent's point of view, you could shed some light on this subject for us.' She eyed him with open hatred, but she was thinking of Allie ... how could she have told him a thing like that? How *could* she?

'My son is not autistic, Bob.'

'I see ... perhaps I misunderstood...' She could almost envision his viewers panting. In ten short minutes they had learned that she had lost her husband and daughter in a fire, had worked at *Collins*, had no man in her life at the moment, and now they thought her only surviving child was autistic. 'Is he retarded?'

'No, he is not.' Her voice rose and her eyes blazed. Just how much did this man think he had a right to? 'My son is hard of hearing, he is in a school for the deaf, but other than his hearing impairment, he is a perfectly marvellous, normal child.'

'I'm glad for you, Daphne.' Son of a bitch. Daphne was seething inside. She felt as though she had been stripped naked. But worse than that, much worse, he had stripped Andrew. 'And I'm delighted to hear about *Lovers*, and I'm afraid that our time together is over. But we hope to see you again the next time you're in Chicago.'

'I'd like that very much.' She smiled through clenched teeth, smiled then for the benefit of the viewers, and they took a break for a collection of commercials. And with a look of barely veiled fury, she unclipped the microphone from her dress and handed it to him during the break. 'You know, I don't know how you can make excuses for yourself.'

'Why? Because I have a passion for the truth?' He wasn't smiling now. He didn't give a damn about her. He cared only about himself, his viewers, and his sponsors.

'What difference can any of that possibly make? What right do you have to ask anyone those kinds of questions?'

'Those are the things people want to know.'

'Those are the things people have no right to know. Aren't there things in your life that you don't want exposed? Is there nothing sacred to you?'

138

'I'm not at your end of the interview, Daphne.' He said it coolly as the next guest arrived to take her seat. She stood there for a moment looking down at him and she didn't extend her hand.

'Then you're very lucky.' And with that she turned on her heel and left the stage, walking quickly into the waiting room and signalling to Barbara to follow her.

They were on a plane bound for New York two hours later. It was the last flight out, and they reached La Guardia at two o'clock in the morning. At two thirty she was back in her apartment. Barbara had gone on in the cab. And on Sixty-ninth Street, Daphne closed her front door behind her, and walked straight to her bedroom without turning on the lights, threw herself on the bed, and broke into sobs as she lay there. She felt as though her whole life had been exposed that night, all her pain and her sorrow. The only thing he hadn't known about was John. It was a good thing she had never told Allie ... and tell us, Miss Fields, is it true you shacked up with a logger in New Hampshire? . . . She turned over and lay staring at the ceiling in the dark, thinking of Andrew. Maybe it was just as well he was at the school. Maybe if he were at home with her in New York, his life would turn into a sideshow. People like Allie would treat him like a freak ... autistic ... retarded ... she cringed at the words, and lay there until she fell asleep on her bed, in the beige dress she had worn, with tearstains on her face, and her heart feeling like it had been beaten with rocks. She dreamed that night of Jeffrey and John, and she awoke the next morning, at the sound of the phone, feeling a wave of terror wash over her ... terrified that something had happened to Andrew.

15

'Daphne, are you all right?' It was Iris. She had seen the show.

'I'll live. But I won't do it again. You can tell Murdock that for me, or I will. Take your choice, but that's it. My publicity life is over.'

'I don't think you should feel that way, Daff. It was just one bad show.'

'Maybe to you. But I'm not going to go through that again, and I don't have to. My books sell just fine without my prostituting myself for assholes who want to hang my underwear on their clothesline.' But most of all, what still smarted was what they had done to Andrew. She tried to keep him so protected from that world, and in one brief moment they had torn away all her protection and exposed him as 'autistic.' She still shuddered at what they had said. And every time she thought of it, she wanted to kill Allie. She had to force her mind back to what Iris was saying. She was insisting they have lunch at the Four Seasons, but Daphne really didn't want to.

'Something wrong?'

'No. A very interesting offer, but I want to talk to you about it, hash it out for a while. Do you want to come to the office?'

'Why don't you come here? I don't feel like going out.' In truth, she wanted to go into hiding. Or go back to the school, to put her arms around Andrew.

'Fine. I'll be there at noon. All right with you?'

'Perfect. And don't forget to call Murdock.' But Iris planned to wait awhile on that. Publicity on Daphne's books was just too important to take a hasty stand, and it was possible that Daphne would back down. Although knowing Daphne, it was more likely that she wouldn't. She had a stubborn streak in her a mile wide, and the one thing that mattered to her most was her privacy. Having that violated on national TV had to have been a shattering experience for her.

'I'll see you in a little while.' It was already ten o'clock, and Daphne heard Barbara's key in the door as she walked into the kitchen in her stockinged feet and the dress she had worn the night before. She looked as though she had been to a very drunken party.

'My, don't you look lovely this morning.' Barbara was wearing grey slacks and a red sweater and a bright smile, and Daphne grinned at her as she put on a pot of coffee. She wandered into the kitchen and set down her bag. It was one of the rare times when she didn't have a notebook in her hand. 'Did you get any sleep last night?' Barbara had been very worried about her, but hadn't dared to call. She was hoping that Daphne was asleep, and suspected that her friend wanted to be left alone. But this morning Daphne was fair game and Barbara pulled no punches. 'If you'll pardon my saying so, you look like shit. Did you sleep?'

'Some.'

Barbara took a sip of the steaming coffee. 'I'm sorry that happened last night, Daff.'

'So am I. But it won't happen again. I just told Iris to call Murdock.'

'She won't.' She sounded matter-of-fact and Daphne smiled.

'You have everyone figured out, don't you? You may be right. But if she doesn't, I will.'

'What are you going to do about Allison Baer?'

An ugly look came into Daphne's eyes. 'Frankly, I'd like to kill her. But I'll settle for giving her a piece of my mind and then never speaking to her again.'

'It was a shitty thing for her to do.'

'I can forgive her almost anything, but not what she said about Andrew.' They both fell silent for a moment

141

and Daphne sighed as she slid into a chair, looking exhausted and rumpled. She looked as though she needed someone to undress her, and run a hot bath, and brush her hair, and Barbara was suddenly sorry that she didn't have a husband to do it. She was the kind of woman who would have made a man a good wife, and she needed someone to take care of her. She worked too hard, worried too much, carried all of the burdens on her frail shoulders. She needed a man, as Barbara did herself, but it wasn't likely that either of them would find one. And certainly not Daphne. She didn't let anyone near enough to her to hold her coat, let alone marry her.

'What does Iris want, by the way?'

'I don't know. She said something about an interesting offer. And if it's a publicity tour' – Daphne grinned ruefully and stood up – 'I'm going to tell her to shove it.'

'That I'd like to hear. Any calls you want me to make?' Daphne handed her a list and went to take a shower. And when her agent arrived five minutes before noon, she was wearing white gabardine slacks and a white cashmere sweater.

'My, don't you look pretty.' She had a quiet elegance about her that always impressed Iris. Most authors who made it eventually got showy, but Daphne never had. She had style, and there was something very distinguished about her. It made her seem older than her years at times, but that was the way she was, and it was no surprise after all she'd been through that she seemed somehow older. Dealing with life at its most painful had given her both wisdom and poise, and a great deal of compassion.

'So, what's new?' They sat down to lunch and Daphne poured her a glass of white wine as Iris looked at her long and hard. 'Something wrong?'

'You're working too hard.' She said it like a stern mother, but she had known Daphne for long enough now to read her life through her eyes, as she did now. And she could see that Daphne was tired.

'What makes you say that?'

'You're getting too thin, and your eyes look like you're a hundred and fifty.'

'As a matter of fact, I am. A hundred and fifty-two to be exact. A hundred and fifty-three in September.'

'I'm serious, Daphne.'

'So am I.'

'All right, I'll mind my own business. How's the book coming?'

'Not bad. I should have it wrapped up in another month.'

'And then what? Any plans?'

'I thought I'd spend some time with Andrew. You know' – she looked bitterly at her agent – 'my autistic son.'

'Daphne, don't take that so hard. They say a lot of things like that on talk shows and in the papers.'

'Well, they're not going to say them about me, or my son. That's the way it is. Did you call Murdock?' Her eyes were hard as she looked at Iris.

'Not yet. But I will.' Barbara was right and she knew it. Iris was stalling.

'If you don't, I will. I meant what I said this morning.'

'All right, all right.' She held up a hand, as though begging for mercy. 'There's something else I want to discuss with you first. You've had a very interesting offer.'

'To do what?' Daphne didn't look impressed, more than anything she looked suspicious. The night before had burned her badly.

'To make a movie, on the West Coast.' Iris looked enormously pleased and Daphne watched her. 'They're interested in buying *Apache*. Comstock Studios called yesterday after you left. They want to buy the book, but they also want you to think about writing the screenplay.'

Daphne sat in silence for a long moment. 'Do you think I could? I've never done that.' Her eyes looked worried.

'There's nothing you can't do, if you want to.' It was once again an echo of John, and Daphne smiled.

'I wish I believed that.'

'Well, I do, and so do they. They offered you a very handsome fee for the package. You'd have to live out there and they'd also pay for your living expenses, within reason.'

'What does that mean?'

'A house, food, entertainment, maid, and a car and driver.'

She sat staring, looking into her plate, and then looked up at Iris. 'I can't do it.'

'Why not?' She looked shocked. 'Daphne, it's a fabulous offer.'

'I'm sure it is, and I'd like to sell them the book. But I can't write the screenplay.'

'Why not?'

'How long would I have to be out there for?'

'Probably about a year, to write it, and they want you to consult on the movie.'

'At least a year. Maybe more.' She sighed as she looked soberly at her agent. 'I can't leave Andrew for that long.'

'But he doesn't even live here.'

'Iris, I go up to see him at least once a week when I can. Sometimes I'm there for the weekend. I can't do that if I'm living in Los Angeles.'

'Then take him with you.'

'He's not ready to leave the school. I wish he were, but he's not.'

'Put him in a school there.'

'That would be too hard on him. It just wouldn't be fair.' She shook her head decisively. 'I can't. Maybe in a few years, but not now. I'm really very sorry. Maybe you can explain it to them.'

'I don't want to explain it to them, Daphne. From a

career standpoint you're dead wrong. Maybe this is a sacrifice you'll both have to make. I want you to think about it, at least until Monday.'

'I won't change my mind.' And knowing Daphne, Iris feared that she wouldn't.

'You'll be making a serious mistake if you don't do it. This really is the next important step in your career. You may always regret it if you don't take it.'

'And how do I explain that to a seven-year-old child? Tell him my work is more important to me than he is?'

'You can explain it to him, and you can fly back for a day or two whenever you have a break.'

'What if I can't get away? Then what? I can't call him on the phone and explain it.' That stopped Iris. Of course she couldn't call him. It was an aspect Iris had never thought of. 'I just can't, Iris.'

'Why don't you just wait to decide?' But Daphne knew already what her answer would have to be on Monday, and after Iris left, she discussed it with Barbara, sitting curled up in the big cosy white chair.

'Would you want to go if you could?'

'I'm not really sure, to tell you the truth. I'm not sure I could write a screenplay, and living in Hollywood for a year isn't really my style.' She looked around her pretty little apartment with a sigh and then shrugged. 'But it isn't worth thinking about anyway. I can't leave Andrew for that long, and it might not always be easy for me to get back.'

'Why not have him fly out to see you if you can't get away? I could fly back to get him if you want.' Although they had never met, she always felt as though she knew the child. And Daphne smiled at the generous offer.

'I love you for that. Thank you.'

'Why don't you talk to Mrs Curtis about it when you go up there this weekend, Daff?'

But what was there to think about? None of them understood. They just couldn't. They didn't know what it had been like to discover he was deaf when he was only a few months old, to struggle to communicate with him, to fight with every doctor she had seen about putting him in an institution. They didn't know what it had been like to pack his things and take him up to New Hampshire ... to tell him his friend John was dead. They didn't know what any of it felt like in her gut, or what it would mean to be three thousand miles away if something happened to him. They didn't know, and they never would. There was nothing for Daphne to think about, she realised again as she picked up her suitcase, put it in the car, and started the lonely trip to New Hampshire to see him.

16

Daphne made the trip in five hours, and pulled into the driveway of the Howarth School in the darkness of the winter evening. It always pulled at her heart to come back here, not only because of Andrew, but because of John. Her thoughts always drifted back to their days in the cabin. But the school was brightly lit, and she knew that in a moment she would see Andrew. She glanced at her watch and saw that she was just in time to join him for dinner.

Mrs Curtis was in the front hall when she walked in and looked instantly pleased and surprised to see her.

'I didn't know you were coming up this week, Daphne.' Over the years they had become friends, and she called Daphne by her first name, although due to her advanced years, Daphne never felt quite comfortable calling her Helen. She sent her all of her books though, and Helen Curtis admitted that she loved them.

'How's our boy?' Daphne took her coat off in the front hall and she felt as though she had come home. There was always something wonderfully warm and welcoming about Howarth. And the school was well endowed, so it was beautifully kept up. The whole place had been redone the summer before, and now there were murals in the halls that the children loved, and there were clouds painted on the ceiling.

'You won't recognise Andrew!'. Mrs Curtis was smiling at her.

'Did he cut off all his hair again?' The two women laughed, remembering how he had looked the winter before after he and two friends had had a spree with a pair of scissors. He hadn't come out of it quite as badly as the two others. The little girls with the exquisite blonde braids had been almost bald and looked like little fuzzy ducklings when they were through with them.

'No, nothing like that.' Mrs Curtis shook her head with a smile. 'But he must have grown two inches this month. Suddenly he's enormous. You'll have to do some shopping again.'

'Thank God for my royalties!' And then with a hungry look in her eyes, 'Where is he?' Mrs Curtis answered her by pointing towards the stairs. He was coming down in a pair of beige corduroy pants and a little red flannel shirt, and he was wearing the new cowboy boots she had brought him the last time. Her face exploded in a wide smile and her eyes danced and she walked slowly towards him.

'Hi, sweetheart. How are you?' She said the words now as well as signing and he read her lips with a broad grin, and then he amazed her by speaking.

'I'm fine, Mommy ... how ... are you?' The words were clumsy and he still didn't speak clearly, but anyone would have understood what he had said. 'I missed you!' And then he flung himself into her arms and she held him, fighting back the tears that came so easily when she first saw him. They were used to their life now, and the days of their shared solitude in her old apartment seemed like a distant dream. He had seen the new place too, but he had signed to her that he liked the old one better. She assured him that he'd get used to this one too, and she showed him his room and told him that one day he would live there all the time, as he had in the old one. But now all she could think of was holding his warm, cuddly little body against her own as she swung him into her arms and he clung to her.

'I missed you too.' She pulled away a little so he could see her face as she said it. 'What have you been doing?'

'I'm growing a vegetable garden!' He looked thrilled. 'And I made two tomatoes.' He was signing to her, but

148

when she spoke he read her lips, and he seemed to have no trouble doing it.

'In the middle of winter? How did you do that?'

'In a big box downstairs and it has special lights on it, and when spring comes, we're all going to plant flowers outside.'

'That sounds wonderful.'

They went into the dining room hand in hand then, and she sat with him and the other children as they ate fried chicken and corn on the cob and baked potatoes, and they laughed and told jokes, all of them signing.

She stayed until he went to bed, tucked him in, and then came downstairs to see Mrs Curtis before she left.

'Have you had a good week?' But there was something strange in her eyes as she asked the question, and Daphne instinctively knew she had seen the show. Who hadn't?

'Not really. I was in Chicago yesterday.' She hesitated to say anything more, but she didn't have to.

'I know. That was a rotten thing for him to do.'

'You saw the show?'

'I did. But I'll never watch him again. He's a bastard.' Daphne smiled at the uncharacteristic strong language.

'You're right. I told my agent I won't do any more publicity as a result. I've just had it. And what galls me is that they'd never ask a man those kinds of questions. But the worst of it of course was what he said about Andrew.'

'It doesn't really matter, you know. You and he know the truth, and the rest of the world will forget it.'

'They may' – Daphne didn't look so sure – 'and they may not. Muckrakers are amazing. Ten years from now someone will dig up a tape of that and come up with a story.'

'Yours is not an easy business, my dear. But it must be rewarding.'

'Sometimes.' She smiled but there was a troubled look in her eyes that the older woman saw.

'Is something wrong?'

'No ... not really ... but ... I need some advice. I thought maybe we'd talk later in the weekend.'

'Does it have to wait? We could talk now. Would you like to come in and sit down?' She waved towards her private quarters and Daphne nodded. It would be a relief to talk it over.

Mrs Curtis's apartment in the school was tidy and small, like the woman herself. It was filled with attractive Early American antiques she had bought herself, and there were paintings of the landscape of New Hampshire. There was a vase of fresh flowers on a low table, and a hooked rug she had bought in an antique shop in Boston. It looked like a school-teacher's house somehow, but it had an added warmth and some of her things were lovely. Most of all it was inviting. Daphne looked around, like everything else about the school, this was familiar to her. Helen Curtis looked around too this time, almost with nostalgia, but Daphne didn't notice.

She poured them each a cup of tea in her tiny separate kitchen, and she handed Daphne a delicate flowered Spode cup with a little lace napkin. 'Well, what's on your mind, my dear? Something about Andrew?'

'Yes, indirectly.' She decided to get right to the point. 'I've had an offer to do a movie. Comstock Studios want to buy *Apache*, which is very nice. It would mean my being in Los Angeles for about a year. And I just don't think I can do it.'

'Why not?' The older woman looked both pleased and surprised.

'What about Andrew?'

'What about him? Would you want to put him in a school there?' At this, Mrs Curtis looked troubled. She knew that for the moment, change would still be difficult for him. Howarth had been his home for a long time, and he would suffer.

'I think a school out there would be too much of a change for him. No, if I went, I'd leave him here. But he'd feel so deserted.'

'Not if you explained it to him properly. No more than any child his age. You could tell him that it's for your work, and that it's only for a while. He could fly out to see you, we could put him on the plane, or would you be coming back here?'

'Probably not very often. From what I understand, once a movie gets going it's almost impossible to get away. But do you really think he could come out?'

'I don't see why not.' She looked gentle and kind as she set down her cup of tea. 'He's getting older, Daphne, he's not a baby anymore, and he's acquired a great many skills that will help him. Has he ever been on a plane before?' Daphne shook her head. 'He'd probably love it.'

'You don't think the whole experience would be too hard for him? He wouldn't see me as often as he does now.'

'You know, most of the other parents don't visit as often as you do. You're fortunate that you can come up, most of the other parents can't, they have husbands and other children, jobs that tie them down ... you and Andrew are very lucky.'

'And if I go?'

'He'll adjust. He'll have to.'

It would be so damn hard leaving Andrew. She felt so terribly guilty. 'I know it won't be easy at first, but it might do you both good. It could be a marvellous experience for you. How soon would you leave?'

'Very soon. Within the month.'

'That still gives you plenty of time to prepare him.' And then she sighed and looked at her young friend. She had grown very fond of Daphne over the years, the girl had such guts and such a gentle way about her. Both of those qualities showed up in her books, it was a most appealing combination. 'I'm afraid I haven't had as much of a chance to prepare you.'

'Prepare me for what?' Daphne looked blank, her mind still full of the decision of whether or not to leave Andrew and go to Los Angeles.

'I'm leaving the school, Daphne. I'm retiring.'

'You are?' Daphne felt a rock fall through her heart. She had a hard time with change herself, and losing people she cared for. 'But why?' The silver-haired woman laughed softly.

'Thank you for asking. I would think the reason showed. I'm getting old, Daphne. It's time for me to go home, and leave Howarth to someone younger, more dynamic.'

'But how awful!'

'It won't be awful at all. It'll be better for the school. Daphne, I'm an old lady.'

'You are not!' She looked incensed.

'I am. I'm sixty-two. That's old enough. And I don't want to wait until I'm so old that you all have to shove me out of here in a wheelchair. Trust me, it's time.'

'But you haven't been sick...' Daphne looked like a child about to lose her mother...the way Andrew would feel when she told him. And how could she leave him now with Mrs Curtis leaving too? He would feel as though everyone he knew were deserting him. Daphne looked at her almost in despair. 'Who will take your place? As though anyone could.'

'Don't be so sure. The woman I succeeded thought she couldn't be replaced, and fifteen years later no one even remembers her. That's only right. The school is only as strong as the people who lead it, and you want those people to be young and strong and filled with new ideas. There's a wonderful man taking over for this year. He runs the New York School for the Deaf now, and he's taking leave for a year to see how we do things here. He's been running the New York School for eight years and feels he needs some fresh ideas so he doesn't get stale. In fact, you'll meet him. He'll be here tomorrow. He's been coming up during the week to get acquainted.'

'Won't that make too many changes for the children?' •

'I don't think so. Our board of directors was comfortable with him. His tenure is for one year.

Matthew Dane is extremely well thought of in our field. In fact, last year I gave you a book written by him. He's written three. So you'll have that in common.' Daphne remembered the book, and she had thought it made a great deal of sense. But still . . . 'I'll introduce you to him tomorrow.' And then with a gentle smile she stood up. 'And if you'll forgive me for being overly maternal, I think you need a good night's sleep. You're looking awfully tired.'

With that Daphne walked towards her and did something she had never done before, she put her arms around her and hugged her. 'We'll miss you, Mrs Curtis.'

There were tears in her eyes as she stood back from Daphne's arms. 'I'll miss you too. But I'll come to visit often.'

Daphne left her then and drove to the familiar little inn, where Mrs Obermeier showed her her room and left her with a thermos of hot chocolate and a plate of cookies. People liked Daphne in the town, she was a celebrity they knew, and a woman they respected. There were those who remembered John, and they liked seeing her strolling along with Andrew. To them, she was extremely human.

She climbed into bed with a yawn, poured herself a cup of chocolate, and finished it with a dreamy look on her face. Suddenly so much was changing. She turned off the light and put her head down on the large fluffy pillow, and five minutes later she was asleep. She didn't even move in the bed until the sun streamed in the windows in the morning.

17

On Saturday morning, after breakfast at the inn, Daphne arrived at the school in time to watch the children play tag in the garden. Andrew was laughing and playing with his friends and he hardly noticed her arrive as she watched him. There was none of the clinging and desperation she had always envisioned there would be if she left him. He understood their lives now, as well as she did, sometimes better. She almost wondered sometimes what it would be like for him when he finally left the school. He would be so lonely without the constant companionship of other children. It was something that worried her at times, when she thought of the far-off day when he would be ready to come home. But by then he would be older, and life would be different. He would have his studies and new friends, hearing children, not just children like him.

She stood looking around for a while then, unconsciously waiting for Mrs Curtis, to continue their conversation of the night before. But when she saw her again, she was deeply engrossed in a conversation with a tall, lanky, good-looking man with a boyish smile, and she found herself staring at him. He looked vaguely familiar. Mrs Curtis turned then and caught her eye and motioned her towards them.

'Daphne, I'd like you to meet our new director, Matthew Dane. Matthew, this is Andrew's mother, Miss Fields.' In the years of her success, the Mrs had somehow become Miss, even here.

Daphne held out a hand to meet him, but the look in her eyes changed slightly, from welcome to questioning

154

glance. 'It's nice to meet you. I enjoyed your last book.'

He smiled at the compliment, a broad boyish grin that made him seem younger than his forty years. 'I've enjoyed all of yours.'

'You've read them?' She looked both pleased and surprised and he was amused.

'Along with about ten million other people, I imagine.' Somehow she always wondered who read her books, she sat at her desk for hours on end, creating characters and plots and outlines and working endless hours, and yet it was always difficult to imagine that out there somewhere were real people who read them. It always surprised her when people said they read her books. And most surprising of all was to see a stranger hurrying along the street with one of her books tucked under his or her arm. 'Hey ... wait ... I wrote that ... do you like it? ... Who are you? ...' She smiled at him again, their eyes meeting, filled with questions.

'Mrs Curtis tells me that you're coming to Howarth for a year. That's going to be a big change for the children.' There was concern in her eyes as she said it.

'It will be a big change for me, too.' There was something very reassuring about the man as he stood looking down at her from his long, lanky height. There was a boyish quality about him, yet at the same time, an aura of quiet strength. 'I imagine many of the parents will be concerned that my tenure here is only temporary, but Mrs Curtis will be around to help us' – he glanced at her briefly, smiling at her and then Daphne – 'and I think we'll all benefit from this experience. We have a lot to learn from each other' – Daphne nodded – 'and there are some new programmes we want to try out, some exchanges with the New York School.' It was the first Daphne had heard of it and she was intrigued.

'An exchange programme?'

'Of sorts. As you know, most of our children are older, and there are more younger ones here. But Mrs Curtis and I have been talking, and I think it might be very useful to some of the students from the New York School to come up for a week or two, to see what it's like living in the country, maybe to establish some kind of a big brother/big sister arrangement with the children here, and then bring some of the little ones down there for a week or two. They get very isolated up here, and that might make an interesting breakthrough for them, while still in an environment that's relatively familiar. We'll have to see how the idea develops.' And then the boyish smile appeared again. 'I have a few tricks up my sleeve, Miss Fields. The main thing is to keep our eye on our goals for the children, to get them back into the hearing world again. At the New York School we put a lot of emphasis on lipreading for that reason, more so than on signing, because if they're going to get out into the hearing world eventually, they have to be able to understand what's going on around them, and despite new awareness in recent years, the fact is that very few hearing people know anything about signing. We don't want to condemn these kids to living only among themselves.' It was something Daphne had thought of often and she looked at him now almost with relief. The quicker he taught Andrew the skills he needed, the quicker he could come home to her.

'I like your thinking, Mr Dane. That's why I liked your book so much. It made sense in terms of the realities, it wasn't filled with crazy dreams.'

'Oh' – his eyes sparkled – 'I have a few crazy dreams too. Like starting a boarding school one day for the hearing and nonhearing. But that's a long way off.'

'Maybe not.' They stood looking at each other for a moment, a kind of respect dawning between them, and then something softened in his eyes as he looked at her, almost forgetting Helen Curtis standing beside them.

He had seen Daphne two days before on *The Conroy Show* in Chicago and it explained a lot of things about her that he had sensed but hadn't known. The knowledge he had gained through the show seemed somehow a violation, and he didn't want to admit to her that he had seen it. But she saw it all in his eyes as he hesitated, and her eyes were honest with him.

'Did you see me on *The Conroy Show* the other night, Mr Dane?' Her voice was soft and sad, her eyes wide open, and he nodded.

'Yes, I did. I thought you handled it very well.'

She sighed and shook her head. 'It was a nightmare?'

'They shouldn't have the right to do that.'

'But they do. That's why I won't do it again, as I told Mrs Curtis last night.'

'They're not all like that, are they?'

'Most are. They don't want to hear about your writing. They want to push themselves into something very private, your heart, your guts, your soul. And if they can get a little dirt in the bargain, they love it.'

'That wasn't dirt. That was pain, and life, and sorrow.' His voice was almost a warm embrace in the chill air. 'You know, in reading your books, one comes to know more than anything they could pull out of you, anyway. That's what I was going to tell you. I've learned something about you through your books, but more than that I've learned something about myself. I haven't had the kind of losses you have' – and he marvelled silently at how she had survived them and was still so whole – 'but we all suffer losses of our own, losses that matter to us, that seem the worst tragedies on earth to us. I read your first book when I got divorced a few years back, and it did something very special for me. It got me through it.' He looked embarrassed then. 'I read it twice and then I sent a copy to my wife.' His words touched her deeply. It was extraordinary to realise that her books mattered to anyone so much. And at that moment Andrew ran over to them, and she looked down at him happily and then at Matthew Dane, switching from spoken words to signing.

'Mr Dane, I'd like you to meet my son. Andrew, this is Mr Dane.'

But when Matthew Dane signed to him, he spoke in

157

a normal voice at the same time, moving his lips very distinctly, and making normal sounds. 'It's nice to meet you, Andrew. I like your school.'

'Are you a friend of my Mommy's?' Andrew signed to him with a look of open curiosity, and Matthew smiled, glancing quickly at her.

'I hope I will be. I came here to visit Mrs Curtis.' Again he signed and spoke at the same time. 'I'm going to be here every weekend.'

Andrew looked at him with amusement. 'You're too old to go to our school.'

'I know.'

'Are you a teacher?'

'I'm the director, just like Mrs Curtis, at a school in New York.' Andrew nodded, he had heard enough for the moment, and turned his attention to his mother, both arms around her, his blond hair blowing in the wind.

'Will you have lunch with us, Mommy?'

'I'd love that.' She said good-bye to Matthew and Mrs Curtis then and followed Andrew inside, as he leaped and skipped, waving and signing to his friends. But her thoughts were filled with the new director. He was an interesting man. She saw him again later, walking down the halls with a stack of papers in his arms. According to Mrs Curtis, he was reading everything he could lay his hands on, every letter, every file, every report and logbook, and observing the children. He was very thorough about his work.

'Did you have a nice day with Andrew?' The dark brown eyes were interested and kind.

'I did. Looks like you've got quite a load of homework.' She smiled at him and he nodded.

'I have a lot to learn about this school.'

Her voice was very gentle as they stood in the hallway. 'I think we have a lot to learn from you.' She was intrigued by his emphasis on lipreading, and noticed that he spoke to all the children as he signed, and treated

158

them as though they could hear. 'How did you ever get into this, Mr Dane?'

'My sister was born deaf. We were twins. And I've always been especially close to her. The funny thing was that we made up our own language between us. It was a kind of a crazy sign language that worked. But then my parents put her away in a school' – he looked troubled as he spoke – 'not a school like this. The kind they had thirty years ago, the kind where you stayed for the rest of your life. And she never got the skills she needed, they never taught her a damn thing that would have helped her get back into the world.' Daphne was afraid to ask him what had happened to her as he paused, but then he looked at her with that boyish grin. 'Anyway, that's how I got into this. Thanks to my sister. I talked her into running away from the school when I graduated from college, and we went to live in Mexico for a year, on the money I had saved working in the summers on construction crews. I taught her how to speak, she learned to lip-read, and we came back and told our parents. She was of age then and legally she could do what she wanted. They tried to have her declared incompetent, once they even tried to have me arrested ... it was a crazy time, but she made it.'

At last she dared to ask, 'Where is she now?'

His smile grew wide. 'She teaches at the New York School. She's going to take over for me while I'm gone this year. She's married and she has two children, both hearing, of course. Her husband is a doctor, and of course now our parents say that they always knew she'd make it. She's a terrific girl, you'd like her.'

'I'm sure I would.'

'She loves your books. Wait till I tell her I met you.'

Daphne blushed then, it seemed so silly, a woman who had conquered so much, impressed with Daphne's meagre works of fiction. It made Daphne feel very small in comparison. 'I'd like to meet her too.'

'You will. She'll be coming up here, and Mrs Curtis tells me that you come up here pretty often.'

159

Daphne looked suddenly troubled and he searched her eyes. 'I do ... I did ...' She sighed softly, and he waved towards two chairs in a corner.

'Do you want to sit down, Miss Fields?' They had been standing in the hallway for almost half an hour, and she nodded as they walked towards the chairs.

'Please call me Daphne.'

'I will, if you call me Matt.'

She smiled and they sat down.

'Something tells me that you have a problem. Is there anything I can do to help?'

'I don't know. Mrs Curtis and I talked about it last night.'

'Is it something to do with Andrew?'

She nodded. 'Yes. I've just had an offer to make a movie in Hollywood. It means moving out there for a year.'

'And you're taking him with you?' He looked suddenly disappointed but she shook her head.

'No, I really think I ought to leave him here. But that's the problem. He'll hardly ever see me ... I don't know if he could handle it, or more honestly, if I could ...' She looked up at him then, her enormous blue eyes reaching out to his brown. 'I just don't know what to do.'

'That's a tough one. For you, not so much for Andrew. He'd adjust.' And then gently, 'I'd help him. We all would. He might be angry for a little while, but he'd understand. And I'm going to keep them all pretty busy this year. I want to take a lot of field trips with them, get them back out into the world as much as possible. They're a little isolated here.' She nodded. He was right. 'What about having him fly out to see you during vacations?'

'Do you think he could do that?'

'With the right preparation. You know, eventually that's the kind of life you'd want him to lead. You want him to be able to get on planes, to go places, to be independent, to see more of the world than just this.'

She nodded slowly. 'But he's so young.'

160

'Daphne, he's seven. If he were a hearing child, you wouldn't hesitate to have him put on a plane, would you? Why treat him any differently? He's a very bright little boy.' As she listened to him she felt relief begin to flood over her, and walls she had built around Andrew in her mind slowly began to fall. 'And not only that but it's important for him that you're happy, that he see you leading a full life. You can't cling to him forever.' There was no reproach in his voice, only gentleness and understanding. 'You're no more than seven or eight hours away at any given moment. If we have a problem, we'll call you and you hop on a plane to Boston. I'll even pick you up at the airport, and in two hours you're here. It's hardly farther than New York if you look at it that way.' He had a marvellous way of solving problems, finding solutions, and making everything seem so simple. She could easily understand now how he had taken his sister out of her school and run off with her to Mexico. She smiled at the idea.

'You make it all sound so easy.'

'It can be. For you and Andrew, if you let it. What you have to base your decision on is what *you* want to *do*. One day he'll have to make decisions for himself too. Independent decisions, decisions to be free and strong and make choices for himself, not you. Teach him that early. Do *you* want to make a movie? Do *you* want to go to Hollywood for a year? Those are the issues. Not Andrew. You don't want to give up an important part of your life for him. Opportunities like that don't come along that often, or maybe they do for you. But if it's important to you, if it's what you want, then do it. Tell him, let him adjust to it. I'll help you.' And she knew he would.

'I'll have to think it over.'

'Do that, and we can talk about it again tomorrow. You'll have to brace yourself for a little anger from Andrew most likely. But you'd get that from any kid his age if you told him you were going away. Know that the anger and the reaction are normal. Being a parent isn't

161

always easy.' He smiled at her again. 'I see what my sister has been through. She had twins also. Her girls are fourteen now. And if you think a seven-year-old boy is rough, you should try doubles that age, and girls!' He rolled his eyes. 'I'd never survive it!'

'You don't have children of your own?'

'No.' He looked sorry. 'Except for the hundred and forty-six I'm leaving at the New York School with Martha, my sister. My wife never really wanted children. She was not a hearing person' – Daphne nodded, accustomed to what would have been to someone else an unfamiliar term – 'and she was very different from my sister. She was terrified her own children wouldn't hear. She had a lot of hang-ups about her deafness. In the end' – he looked regretful – 'it's what did us in. She was a model in New York, and an incredibly bright girl. I had tutored her for a while, that's how I met her. But her parents always treated her like a china doll, and she hadn't had a crazy brother like me when she was growing up. She retreated into her deafness. She's a perfect example of why you shouldn't treat Andrew any differently than any other child. Don't do that to him, Daphne. If you do, you'll rob him of everything that will ever matter to him.' They sat quietly for a moment, each with his own thoughts. He had given her a lot to think about in the last hour. He had shared an important part of his life with her, and she knew she had made a friend.

'I think you're right, Matt. But it scares the hell out of me to leave him.'

'There are lots of things in life that are scary. All the good stuff usually is. Think of all the good things you've done in your life. How much of it was easy? Probably none of it was, but it was always worth the struggle, I'll bet. And I would imagine that making a movie is an important step in your career. Which book is it, by the way?'

'*Apache.*' She smiled at him, proud of herself and suddenly not ashamed to let him see it.

162

'That's my favourite.'

'Mine too.'

And then, picking up his stack of papers, he stood up. 'Are you staying for dinner?' She nodded. 'I'll join you for coffee afterwards. I'm going to take a sandwich upstairs in the meantime, so I can do my homework.' She thought again of what he had said. The good things in life weren't easy. They hadn't been for either of them.

'I'll see you later, Matt.' They parted company at the staircase and she watched him for a moment. Sensing it, he looked down at her as she looked up. 'And thank you.'

'Any time. You'll always get the truth from me, Daphne, about what I think and what I feel. Remember that when you're in California. I'll tell you how he is, and if he needs you I'll tell you. You can fly home, or I'll put him on the next plane.' She nodded, and he waved to her and then disappeared on to the upstairs landing. It seemed strange to her that he seemed to assume she was going. Had he read her mind? How could he know her decision before she did? Or was that what she had already secretly decided, and longed for. She wasn't sure as she went into the big playroom to find Andrew. And as she saw him she felt her heart sink. How could she leave him? He was so little and so dear.

But that night as she lay in bed at the inn she thought about it all again, pulled one way and then the other, by duty, obligation, love on one side, and fascination, curiosity, ambition, career on the other. It was a tough choice, and then suddenly the phone rang and it was Matthew. She was startled to hear him and wondered instantly if something was wrong.

'Of course not. If it were something like that, Mrs Curtis would call you. I'm not official yet, you know, at least not for a few more weeks. I was just thinking about your decision, and I had a crazy thought. If you get too tied up in Los Angeles at some point and you can't have him out to visit, I could take him home to stay with my

163

sister and her kids. You'd have to give us special permission of course, but he might enjoy it. My sister is really quite something and her girls are terrific. How does that strike you?'

'I don't know what to say to you, Matthew. I'm overwhelmed.'

'Don't be. Last year I had forty-three of our students at my place for Christmas dinner. Martha cooked and her husband coached touch football in the park. It was super.' She wanted to tell him that she thought he was, but she didn't dare.

'I don't know how to thank you.'

'Don't. Just trust me with Andrew.'

She was silent for a moment, it was late, and he had been very open with her. She wanted to do the same with him. 'Matt, it's hard for me to leave him . . . he's all I've got.'

'I know that. Or at least, I suspected it.' His voice was very soft. 'He'll be all right, and so will you.' And as she listened to him she knew that, and the decision was finally made.

'I think I'm going to do it.'

'I think you should.' It made it easier for her that he said that, and it suddenly seemed amazing that she had only met him that morning and already she had come to rely on his judgement, and trust him with her son. 'When you go back to New York, I'll introduce you to my sister. Maybe you'd like to come to the school next week to meet her, if you have time.'

'I'll make time.'

'Great. I'll see you in the morning. And congratulations.'

'For what?'

'For making a tough decision. Besides, I have a selfish motive in all this. I want to see my favourite book made into a movie.' She laughed then and they hung up, and that night she slept peacefully at last.

18

'I know it seems like a long time, sweetheart, but you can come out to see me during vacations, and we can do fun things in California, and I promise I'll fly back...' She was signing desperately, but Andrew refused to watch her. His eyes were awash with tears. 'Andrew ... darling ... please...' Her eyes filled too as she sat in the garden with him, fighting to keep from clutching him to her and sobbing. He stood with his back to her, his shoulders hunched over and shaking, his head bent, and when she gently pulled him towards her, he made terrible little gurgling sounds and her heart tore in half. 'Oh, Andrew ... sweetheart ... I'm so sorry.' Oh, God, she couldn't do it. She couldn't, not to him. 'He'll adjust,' they said. Christ, it was like adjusting to double amputation, and why should he have to do that? Just because she wanted to make a film. She felt rotten and selfish as she sat beside him, hating herself for the decision she had made and what it was obviously doing to him. She couldn't do this to her child. He needed her too badly. After all ... She tried to put her arms around him and he wouldn't let her, and she stood there in despair looking at him as Matthew Dane came outside. He watched them for a moment, saying nothing, and from the look on Andrew's face he knew instantly that she had told him. He walked slowly over to them, and looked at Daphne with a gentle smile.

'He'll be all right in a little while, Daphne. Remember what I told you. You'd have had this kind of reaction from any child, even a hearing one.'

'But he isn't a hearing child.' Her eyes blazed at him and her voice was sharp. 'He's special.' She wanted to

165

add 'dammit,' but she didn't. She felt certain that he had misjudged the situation, he had given her bad advice about her son and she had let him. She was wrong to even consider going out west for a year. But Matt didn't look swayed from his earlier opinion, even now.

'Of course he's special, all children are. Special is all right, different isn't. What you're saying is that he's different. You don't have to cater to his haidicap, Daphne. That won't help him. Any seven-year-old child would be upset by his mother going away. That's normal. Other parents have situations their children have to adjust to, siblings, divorces, deaths, moves, financial problems. You can't create a perfect world for him forever. It would be impossible for you to live up to, and in the end it would hurt him. Besides, can you really live up to that? Do you want to?'

She wanted to shout at him, he didn't understand anything, least of all her responsibilities to her child. He watched her eyes and knew what she was thinking, and he smiled.

'It's all right, go ahead, hate me. But I'm right. If you stick to your guns for a little while, he'll be okay.' They both saw then that Andrew was watching them, lip-reading, and Daphne turned towards her son with sorrow in her eyes. This time she spoke to him as well as signing.

'I'm not happy about going either, sweetheart. But I think it's important for me to do this. I want to go to Hollywood to make a movie out of one of my books.'

'Why?' He signed the word.

'Because it would be exciting, and it would help my work.' How do you explain lifetime career goals to a seven-year-old child? 'I promise you could come out to see me, and I'd come back here. I wouldn't see you every week, but it won't be forever . . .' Her voice drifted off and there was a distant spark of interest in his eyes.

'Could I come on an aeroplane?'

She nodded. 'Yes. A great big one.' This seemed to spark some further interest, and then he looked down and kicked the ground. When he looked up again, Daphne wasn't sure what he was thinking, but he looked less devastated than he had earlier.

'Could we go to Disneyland?'

'Yes.' Daphne smiled. 'We could do a lot of other things too, you could watch them make the movie when you visit.' And then, suddenly, she knelt beside him and took him in her arms for a moment before moving back so he could see her lips again. 'Oh, Andrew, I will miss you so much. I love you with all my heart, and as soon as I finish my work in California, I'll come back and stay here, I promise. And Mr Dane says that he'll take you to New York to visit his sister and her children . . . maybe if we both keep as busy as we can, and learn as much as we can, the time will go very quickly . . .' She wanted it to, she wanted it to be over right now. In her heart of hearts she didn't want to leave him, but she knew she had to. For herself. It was the first time in many years that she was doing something she knew she wanted to very badly, even though it wasn't easy, and suddenly she thought of all that Matt had said the night before. The good things in life weren't easy, either for her or Andrew. Something in Andrew's face told her then that even though he didn't like her going, he'd be all right. 'Andrew . . . do you know how much I love you?' She watched him, wondering if he'd remember the game they'd played so often when he was younger.

'How much?' He signed it at her and her eyes shone with unshed tears. He did remember after all.

'As much as this.' She threw her arms wide and then threw them around him, and then whispered into his hair, 'As much as my whole life.'

Matthew left them to each other and they spent a quiet hour together, talking about things that were important to Andrew, about her trip, and how soon she would come back. She told him that she wouldn't be leaving for another month, and she'd come to visit often in the meantime, and then they talked about when he

167

would come to California, the things they'd do, and what it would be like.

'Will you write to me?' His eyes turned to hers sadly, and her heart ached again. He was still so little and California seemed as though it were on another planet.

'Yes. I promise I'll write every day. Will you write to me?'

But this time he grinned at her. 'I'll try to remember.' He was teasing and her heart felt lighter.

When she got back to New York that night, she felt as though she had climbed a mountain. She unpacked her suitcase and walked around her apartment, and at last her thoughts turned from Andrew as she looked out the window at the brilliant lights of Manhattan. She was suddenly excited about what she was doing, and for the first time in three days the reality of it came home to her. She was going to California to make a movie of *Apache*! And suddenly she stood there, smiling to herself and laughing . . . it was happening! She had really made it. 'Hallelujah!' she whispered softly, and then she walked into her bedroom, climbed into the bed, and turned off the lights.

19

'Well, kiddo,' Daphne smiled at Barbara as she came through the door the next morning. 'Hang on to your hat.'

'What's up?'

'We're going.'

Barbara looked startled. 'Where?'

'To California, dummy.'

'You're going to do it, Daff?' Barbara looked nothing less than astounded.

'I am.'

'What about Andrew?' She hated to ask, but she had to.

'I told him this weekend, and he wasn't too pleased at first, but I think we'll both survive it.' She told her then about all that Mrs Curtis had said, and about the new director at the school. 'I'm going to have Andrew fly out to see me, and I'll come back whenever I can. And Matthew says he'll bring him to New York, to visit the New York School and see his sister...' Her voice trailed off with a gust of laughter at the look of confusion on Barbara's face. 'He's the new director up at Howarth.'

'Matthew? How friendly!' Barbara's eyes were teasing. 'Do I sense the presence of an attractive man?'

'Very attractive, as a friend, Miss Jarvis, nothing more, I assure you.'

'Bullshit. You just quoted him like God, and he's bringing Andrew down to see his sister? Hell, you've never even let me meet the kid for chrissake and you're trusting him to a stranger? This guy must be pretty terrific, Daff, or you wouldn't let him do that.'

'You're right, he is terrific, and he's the smartest

human being I've ever known about the hard-of-hearing, but that doesn't mean I'm interested in him as a man for chrissake.' She was still laughing.

'Why not? Is he ugly?'

'No.' She was still chuckling. 'As a matter of fact he's very handsome. But that's not the point. Let's talk about us.'

'Us?' Barbara looked confused again. Everything was topsy-turvy this morning.

'I want you to come with me.'

'Are you kidding?' She sat down with a load of fan mail in her arms. 'What would I do there?'

'Run my life, the way you do here.' Daphne smiled.

'Is that what I do?' Barbara returned the smile. 'Run your life? I figured I had to be good for something other than answering fan mail.'

'You know damn well you are.' She knew that she was invaluable to Daphne and it meant a lot to her. And she never forgot that it was Daphne who had helped to free her from her old life. 'Now, will you come with me?'

'When do I pack? Is tomorrow soon enough?' She was beaming and Daphne laughed at her.

'I think you can wait a couple of weeks for that. First, we're going to have to get organised here, and I want you to come to Iris McCarthy's with me this afternoon, so you can hear what it's all about when I do. I think we leave next month sometime. That ought to give us plenty of time to get everything wrapped up.'

'What are you going to do with the apartment?'

'Let it sit here. I'll use it when I fly in to see Andrew, and Comstock is paying for me to rent a house out there, so I won't have double expenses. Besides, I don't want some stranger sleeping in my bed.' She made a face and Barbara laughed at her with a rueful smile.

'Listen, once in a while, I think that wouldn't be so bad . . .' The two women exchanged a smile.

They went to Daphne's agent together that afternoon, after Daphne took Barbara to the Plaza for lunch and they drank a toast to the West Coast and to Comstock.

170

It was all beginning to feel exciting, and by the time they left Iris's office at four thirty, Daphne could hardly wait to start. She turned to Barbara nervously in the cab going back to the apartment then, with a worried frown. 'Do you really think I can do it, Barb? I mean hell, I have no idea how to write a movie.'

'You'll figure it out. It can't be that much different from a book. Play it by ear, they'll tell you what they want.'

'I hope so.' There was a nervous flutter in the pit of her stomach as Barbara patted her hand.

'You can do it. It's going to be fabulous.'

'I hope so.' But whether it was or not, she knew she had to try.

She went back to see Andrew the following weekend, and he seemed by then perfectly adjusted to the idea of her going. He only complained about it once and that time only halfheartedly, the rest of the time he talked about Disneyland and her movie, and he seemed relaxed and happy and she marvelled at how quickly he had accepted it all. Children really were amazing, she decided, and she mentioned it all to Matthew when she saw him again, at dinner in the main dining room of Howarth on Saturday night.

'Will you kick me if I say I told you so, Daphne?' He smiled at her over the remains of dinner and she grinned. This week she looked relaxed and happy, and younger, with her blonde hair spilling over her shoulders, blue jeans, and a persimmon-coloured cowboy shirt.

'I may, so watch out.'

'You're scaring me to death.' But there was a pleasant banter between them. He told her about what had happened at the New York School that week, and she told him about the preliminary plans for the movie. Dinner seemed to fly as they chatted, and Helen Curtis left them alone after dinner, she said that she had work to do, and for once Matthew did not. 'I don't know how you manage to write those books the way you do, Daphne.' He stretched his long legs towards the fire after the children were in bed and they sat in the cosy living room of the school. She didn't feel like going back to the inn and it was still early. Besides, he was good company and she liked him.

He was nice to talk to, and she felt they had a lot in common. They shared Andrew, and interest in her book. 'I really don't know how you do it.' He was thinking about *Apache* and she looked at him with amusement.

'How can you say that? You've written three books yourself.'

'All of them nonfiction, about a subject I eat, sleep, and breathe. That's hardly very remarkable.' He smiled at her from where he sat.

'It's a lot harder than what I do. You have to be accurate, and you help an awful lot of people with those books, Matthew. Mine are all make-believe stories born out of nowhere, and they don't do a damn thing for anyone, except amuse them.' She was always modest about her work, and he liked that about her. One would never guess from talking to her that she was one of the nation's leading best-selling authors. She was bright and intelligent and amusing, and she did not show off.

'You're wrong about your books, Daphne, they do a lot more than just amuse. I told you, one of your books helped me a great deal, and they all taught me something' – he seemed pensive for a moment – 'about people ... relationships ... women.' He looked at her with interest. 'How do you know so much about that stuff, leading such a solitary life?'

'What makes you think I do ... lead a solitary life, I mean?' She was amused at the question.

'You told me so yourself last week.'

'Did I?' She shrugged and grinned. 'I talk too much. I suppose I don't have time for anything more than that. I work like a dog all week long, and then there's Andrew ...'

Matt looked disapproving for a moment and then his face softened in the firelight. 'Don't use him as an excuse.'

She gazed at him frankly. 'Usually, I don't.' And then she smiled, 'Only when someone puts me on the spot, like you did.'

'I'm sorry. I didn't mean to do that.'

'Yes, you did. What about you? Is your life so full?'

'Sometimes.' He was noncommittal. 'For a long time I was afraid to get involved again, after my wife.'

'And now?' It was strange questioning him this way, it was as though they were old friends, but he had that kind of quality about him, he was so warm and so open and so easy to talk to. She felt as though they had known each other for years, it was as though they were on a desert island, the rest of the world was unimportant. They just sat there by the fire, alone and comfortable with each other, and each one curious to know what made the other tick.

'I don't know ... I don't have much time for serious involvement these days. There's a lot going on in my life professionally.' And then he smiled at her again. 'And I don't suppose I'll find the woman of my life in the next year, up here.'

'You never know. Mrs Obermeier might decide to leave her husband.' They both laughed at the thought and Matthew looked at her more seriously for a moment. He had heard the story of John Fowler from Helen Curtis, but he wasn't sure if he could broach the subject with her, or if it was taboo.

'Don't you ever want to try again, Daphne?' He suspected that she was very lonely, and yet there was no sense of her reaching out towards a man, certainly not towards him. She had an easy, comfortable way about her that reminded him of his sister, and her warmth was in the same vein. But there was a sense about her that she had forgotten she was a woman, and didn't want to remember it ever again. She had obviously been very hurt.

But as she looked at him now in the glow from the embers, he saw sadness in her eyes beyond measure, and stories that he knew would never be told. 'No, I don't

173

want to try again, Matt. I've had all I ever wanted. Twice in fact.' Daphne surprised herself with how easily her secret slipped out. 'It would be wrong of me to ask for more ... and stupid ... and greedy ... and very foolish. I thought I'd never find what I had once, with my husband, and yet I did find someone else. It was very different, very special. I've had two extraordinary men in my life, Matt. I couldn't ask for anything more.'

So she was ready to talk about Fowler.

'And so you've given up? What about the next fifty or sixty years?' The prospect of her solitude depressed him. She deserved more than that ... much more ... she deserved someone wonderful who would love her. She was too good and strong and young and wise to spend the rest of her life alone. But she smiled philosophically at him.

'I don't have any trouble keeping busy. And one of these days Andrew will come home ...'

'You're using him as an excuse again.' He sounded gentler this time, less disapproving. 'He's going to be terrific and totally independent when he gets older. So don't count on basing your life on him.'

'I don't really do that, but I must admit, I think a lot about his coming home.'

Matthew smiled at her in the soft light. 'That'll be a fine day for both of you, Daphne, and it won't be too long.'

She sighed softly then. 'I wish I knew that for sure. Sometimes all of this seems like forever.'

His eyes filled with a distant memory as he thought of the years without his sister when he was young. 'I used to feel that way about Martha. She was gone for fifteen years, and not in a place like Howarth. It was awful for her. Thank God they don't have places like that anymore.' Daphne nodded silent agreement and a little while later she stood up and decided that it was time to go home. 'I enjoy talking to you, Daphne.' His eyes were gentle as he walked her to the front door, and then he said something unexpected, which startled them both.

174

He hadn't really meant to say it to her, but he couldn't help it. 'Andrew's not the only one who's going to miss you in the next year.'

Had the hall light been brighter he would have seen her blushing, but it wasn't, and she held out a small, fragile hand. He took it in his own and held it for a moment. 'Thank you, Matthew. I'm just glad to know that you'll be here with Andrew. I'm going to call you a lot to see how he's doing.'

He nodded, feeling only slightly disappointed. But he had no right to expect more. He was only the director of the school where her son lived. Nothing more. And he knew how solitary her life was, and something told him that she wasn't going to change that. She was a strong-willed woman, and she hid behind solid walls. 'You do that. Call as often as you like. I'll be here.' She smiled at him then and left with only a whispered good night.

As she drove slowly back to the inn she found herself thinking of him. He was a lovely man and they were lucky to have him at Howarth. But she had to admit, even if only to herself, that she felt something more for him. Some vague, gnawing, deeper interest, as though she wanted to know everything about him and talk to him for endless hours. She hadn't felt that way since she had met John Fowler, but she also knew that she wasn't going to let herself feel that way again. Not about any man. Two losses were enough. Matthew Dane would be an important person to her, in the life of Andrew, and for all that he could teach her in helping Andrew back into the world of the hearing. But that was his only role in her life, and she knew it, no matter how much she liked him. Those things just didn't matter anymore. She wouldn't let them. It was enough to have loved and lost, she had no desire to love that way again. Ever. And it was easy to imagine loving Matthew Dane. He was a lovable, likable, admirable man. But for that reason she'd have to keep her guard up all the higher. Just to be certain she stayed safe. It was on Andrew that she

175

showered all her love now, every feeling, every moment, every thought. She lived her life exclusively for him. And maybe a little bit for herself. The trip to California was the first sign of that.

20

Daphne all but closed the apartment on her last Friday in New York. She had done all her packing. Her suitcases for California stood waiting in the hallway, everything was ready, and all that was left was to spend one last weekend with Andrew. She would return on Sunday night, put her car in storage in the garage, and fly to Los Angeles with Barbara on Monday morning. They would stay at the Beverly Hills Hotel, in a cottage, until she found a suitable house there, and within a week of her arrival in LA, she would have to get to work on the screenplay. According to her contract she had only two months to write it, and it was beginning to give her sleepless nights.

She thought about it all the way up to New Hampshire, and made notes to herself late into the night once she got to the little inn. The next morning she spent with Andrew, and as usual joined him for lunch, and the afternoon and dinner, and it wasn't until then that she saw Matthew, and he looked almost as harassed as she felt by then.

'You look like you've had a tough week.' She smiled at him over coffee and he ran a hand through his thick brown hair and groaned.

'Oh, God, I have. Four major crises at the New York School since Monday, and this is my last weekend here as an observer. I start officially next Friday. Mrs Curtis leaves the following Monday morning for good, and if I don't have a nervous breakdown by then, I'll be doing fine.'

'Welcome to the club, I have two months to write my screenplay, and I'm beginning to panic. I have no idea what I'm doing, and every time I sit down in front of a piece of paper, my mind goes blank.' He smiled in sympathy at the image.

'That used to happen to me every time I had a deadline on a book. But eventually, out of sheer desperation, I used to force myself to tackle the problem. You will too. Probably once you get there, everything will fall into place.'

'I have to go house hunting first.'

'Where will you be in the meantime?'

'I left Mrs Curtis all my numbers. I'll be at the Beverly Hills Hotel until I find a house.'

He rolled his eyes and attempted unsuccessfully to look sympathetic. 'Tough life you lead, lady.'

'Yeah, ain't it?' She grinned.

She only chatted with him for a few moments in the hall before she went back to the inn. He had to talk to Helen Curtis on this final weekend before he moved in for good, and Daphne was exhausted from a long week's work.

The next morning, as usual, she went to church with Andrew, and came back to the school to spend the day with him. And now each moment shared with him was precious. He clung to her more than usual this weekend, but that was to be expected. And she felt a need to be as close to him as she could, to touch him, to hold him, to feel his hair slip through her fingers so that she would remember its silky touch when she was so far away, to nuzzle his neck with her lips as she kissed him, to smell the last hint of soap on his childlike flesh as they hugged. Everything about him seemed more special to her now, and somehow dearer. It was the hardest weekend of all for her, and sensing that, Matthew stayed away. It wasn't until she was ready to leave that he approached her again, watching with silent understanding as she held Andrew, wanting to reach out to them both when he saw the first tears spring to her eyes. He knew that leaving wouldn't be easy for them. But Andrew would recover more quickly. It was Daphne who would suffer, worrying about the child, keeping him in her thoughts in every spare moment, wondering how he was, and longing for him from so far away.

'How are you two doing?' He said it to her over Andrew's head, pretending not to see her tears. 'He's going to be fine, you know, Daphne, in a few hours, no matter how hard he cries when you go.'

She nodded, a sob cluttering her throat, and then finally she took a deep breath. 'I know. He'll be okay. But will I make it?'

'Yes, you will. I promise.' He touched her arm gently then. 'And you call any time you like. I'll give you all the latest information and reports.'

'Thank you.' She smiled through her tears and touched her son's head with a gentle hand, and she bent then to tell Andrew that it was time to go to bed. She sat with him for a long time that night, talking to him about California, about all the fun they'd have, and how much she would miss him. And then, sadly, with the strange little sound he had always made when he was sad, he began to cry, and he held out his arms and held her tight, signing at last.

'I'm going to miss you so much.'

'Me too.' The tears ran down her cheeks. Maybe it was just as well he saw them after all. So he would know how much she would miss him too. 'But I'll see you soon.' She smiled at him through her tears and at last he smiled too. She stayed until he fell asleep, and she walked slowly downstairs as though she had lost her best friend, and she found Matthew waiting for her in a chair at the bottom of the stairs.

'Asleep?'

'Yes.' Her eyes were huge and sad, and she didn't even attempt a smile. And he said nothing at all but followed her to the front door. She had already said good-bye to Mrs Curtis before she took Andrew up to bed, she had checked out of the inn and her suitcase was in the car, there was nothing left to do but go. As though sensing her silent mood, Matthew walked her to her car, and then watched as she unlocked the door. She turned to him then with those huge blue eyes, and he reached out and took both her shoulders in his hands.

'We love him too, and we'll take good care of him, I swear.' They always had before, but it was different now that she would be so far away. It all hurt more than it had in years and she felt ten thousand years old as she looked up into Matthew's dark brown eyes.

'I know.' She had seen so much loss in her life, so many people she had loved, and now all she had left was this one small boy. 'I'm not very good at this. I should be by now. I've had a lifetime of good-byes.' He nodded, it was all written in her eyes.

'This isn't the same, Daphne. Right now is the hardest part. And it won't be for long. A year seems like an eternity right now, but it's not.'

She smiled. Life was so strange. 'When I come back, you'll have done your year here, and you'll be ready to go.'

'And we'll all have learned so much. Think of that.'

The tears spilled over again as she shook her head. 'I can't . . . all I can think of is how he looked the first time I brought him here.'

'That was a long time ago, Daphne.' She nodded. That had been the beginning of her year with John. Why did everything always have to end in good-bye? But Matthew bent then and kissed her cheek. 'Godspeed. And call.'

'I will.' She looked up at him again and for a mad moment she wanted to fold herself into his arms, to feel the safety she had once felt, protected by a man. She longed silently for a time when she hadn't had to stand alone, when she hadn't had to be so brave all the time. 'Take care of yourself . . . and Andrew too.' And then she slid into her car, and looked up at him through the open window. 'Thanks for everything, Matt. And good luck.'

'I'll need it.' His face broke into a boyish grin. 'And

make me a great movie. I know you will.' She smiled and started the car, and as she drove away she waved and he waved back. And as she drove off into the night he stood there for a long, long time.

21

The plane touched down in Los Angeles with a small bump and seemed to soar along the runway before it stopped and taxied to the gate. Barbara was looking excitedly out the window, and Daphne smiled at her. Travelling with her had been like travelling with a little girl. Everything delighted her, and she had been excited from New York all the way to LA. Daphne had been quieter than usual and she had already written three postcards to Andrew. But now her mind was no longer on him. She was caught up in the realisation that a whole new life was about to begin.

They were met at the gate by the chauffeur Comstock had hired for her, a tall, seedy-looking man of indeterminate age in a black suit and cap, with a long, sorrowful-looking moustache. He stood holding a large card with her name written on it in red ink: 'Daphne Fields.'

'That's subtle.' She looked at Barbara with amusement, and her companion grinned.

'This is Hollywood, Daff. Nothing is subtle out here.'

It turned out to be a prophetic statement, as they discovered when they reached the Beverly Hills Hotel. It stood in pink stucco splendour surrounded by palm trees with its name splashed across the front in bright green. Inside the lobby everything was chaos, women hurried past wearing tight jeans, gold chains, silk shirts, blonde hair, and high-heeled sandals; men walked by in expensive Italian suits, or tight pants and shirts open to their waists. The aroma in the hotel was a veritable symphony of expensive perfumes, bellboys staggered under the weight of enormous arrangements of flowers, or stacks of Gucci luggage, and the hotel roster read like the Academy Awards.

'Miss Fields? Of course. We have your cottage ready.' A bellboy solemnly wheeled her cartful of luggage past the starlets and would-be producers clustered around the swimming pool, and Daphne was fascinated by the array of bodies and more gold chains, everyone drinking white wine or martinis in the middle of the day. The 'cottage' turned out to have four bedrooms, three baths, an icebox stocked with caviar and champagne, and a view of still more palm trees, and there was a huge bouquet of roses and a box of chocolates from Comstock with a note that said 'See you tomorrow.' And suddenly she turned to Barbara with a look of terror.

'I can't do it.' Her voice was tense. The bellboy had just left them, and they stood in the enormous flowery living room of their cottage. Daphne's eyes were larger than Barbara had ever seen them. 'Barb, I can't.'

'What? Eat the chocolates?' Teasing was her only hope, it was obvious that Daphne was panicked.

'No. Look at all this. It's Hollywood. What the hell am I doing here? I'm a writer. I don't know anything about all this stuff.'

'You don't have to. All you have to do is sit down at your typewriter and do the same thing you do at home. Ignore all this bullshit. It's just window dressing.'

'No, it isn't. Did you see them out there? They all think it's real.'

'This is a hotel for chrissake. They're all from St Louis. Relax.' She poured her a glass of champagne, and Daphne sat on the pink-and-green-flowered couch, looking like an orphan.

'I want to go home.'

'Well, I won't let you. So shut up and enjoy it. Hell, I haven't even seen Rodeo Drive yet.' Daphne grinned at her, remembering the life Barbara had led with her mother. It was a far cry from all this. 'Do you want something to eat?'

'I'd throw up.'

'Christ, Daff. Why don't you just relax and enjoy it?'

'Enjoy what? The fact that I've signed a contract to do something I have no idea how to do, in a place that looks like life on another planet, three thousand miles from my only child ... for God's sake, Barbara, what am I doing here?'

'Making money for your kid.' It was an answer Barbara knew would reach her if nothing else did. 'Get my point?'

'Yeah.' But it was small consolation. 'I feel like I've signed on for the foreign legion.'

'You have. And the faster you get to work, the faster we get out of here.' Not that Barbara wanted to, not by a long shot. She loved it already.

'Now there's a good idea.' She went to unpack then, and half an hour later she looked better. Barbara called Comstock and told them they had arrived safely, and after that they went out to the pool and swam. That night they shared a quiet dinner, took a look into the Polo Lounge filled with what looked like actors and models and businessmen and shady characters who might have been drug dealers, and by ten o'clock they were in bed, Barbara with a feeling of excitement and anticipation, and Daphne with a sense of awe at what lay ahead.

The next morning they went to a meeting at Comstock, and by the time they left at noon, back to the exotic splendour of the hotel, Daphne almost felt as though she might live. She had a better idea of what they wanted her to do with *Apache*, she had taken copious notes and she planned to get to work the same day. And Barbara's work was cut out too. She had the names of half a dozen real estate agents. She was going to look for a house for them to rent. She also placed a call to Daphne's agent, and got whatever messages Iris had for her. And by that afternoon things were beginning to roll smoothly. Daphne had brought her own typewriter from New

York, had shoved a table and chair into a corner, and had begun to work as Barbara went out to the pool.

When she came back an hour later, Daphne was still working, and Barbara turned the lights on for her. She was so engrossed in what she was doing that she hadn't even noticed the light grow dim.

'Mn?' She looked up with the distracted look she always wore when she was working, her hair was piled up on her head with a pen stuck through it, and she had put on a T-shirt and jeans. 'Oh, hi. Have a nice swim?'

'Very. Want something to eat?'

'Hm ... nah ... maybe later.' Barbara liked to watch her working, she got so totally involved in what she did. You could actually see the creative process at work. At eight o'clock she ordered room service for them both and when it arrived, she tapped Daphne on the shoulder. She never remembered to eat when she was working, and in New York Barbara would just set a tray on her desk and keep reminding her to eat.

'Chow time.'

'Okay. In a minute.' Which usually meant an hour, and in this case it did too.

'Come on, kiddo. You've got to eat.'

'I will.' At last she stopped pounding her typewriter and sat back with a sigh as she stretched and rubbed her shoulders. She smiled at Barbara then. 'Boy, that feels good.'

'How's it going?'

'Not bad. I feel like a virgin all over again.'

She went back to her typewriter after dinner, and stayed there until 2 a.m. And the next morning she got up at seven, and was pounding away again when Barbara got up.

'Didn't you go to bed last night?' She knew that sometimes Daphne didn't, but this time she had.

'Yeah. I think it was around two.'

'You're really smoking, huh?'

'I want to keep at it while what we talked about

yesterday is still fresh in my mind.' And she did keep at it all day. Barbara went out to see three houses, had lunch by herself, and sat at the pool. Then she came back to work in her own room answering fan mail, and they took dinner again that night on trays. In a funny way she was like a mother to Daphne, but she didn't mind it. She had had long years of training with her mother, and Daphne was a joy to work for. She was fun to be with, her work was exciting, and there was something marvellous about standing right next to that kind of genius. Daphne never saw it that way, but Barbara always did.

On the fourth day Daphne called Mrs Curtis to ask after Andrew, true to her promise she had sent him a letter every day. Mrs Curtis said he was well and happy, and had readjusted immediately after she left. She also reminded Daphne that she wouldn't be speaking to her again until Daphne returned to New Hampshire and came to visit her in her new home. The following day was her last day at Howarth. Daphne wished her luck again and hung up, thinking suddenly of Matthew, wondering how he was doing. She knew he was probably madly busy wrapping up at the New York School before he left.

'How's Andrew?' Barbara came in with a tray for Daphne, and she looked up with a smile.

'Mrs Curtis says he's fine. How are we doing on house hunting by the way?'

Barbara grinned. '"We" are doing fine. Except so far they're all lemons. Something ought to turn up soon though. Do you want a pool in the shape of a typewriter, or will one in the shape of a book do?'

'Very funny.'

'Listen, today I saw one heart shape, one oval, one in the shape of a key, and one crown.'

'Sounds very exotic.'

'It is, and it's tacky as hell, and the worst of it is that I love it. I'm discovering a whole other side to my personality.'

186

Daphne grinned at her, amused. 'Listen, if you walk in here with your shirt open to your waist, wearing gold chains, I'll know it's terminal.' And the next day, just for a laugh, she did, and Daphne roared.

'We've only been here five days and you've already been taken over.'

'I can't help it. It's in the air. It's stronger than I am.'

'Nothing is stronger than you are, Barbara Jarvis.' It was a compliment and she meant it, but Barbara shook her head.

'That's not true, Daff. You are. You're the strongest woman I know, and I mean that in a nice way.'

'Would that it were true.'

'It is.'

'You sound like Matthew Dane.'

'Him again.' Barbara watched her closely. 'I still think you missed the opportunity of a lifetime. I saw his picture on the back of his book, he's gorgeous.'

'So? What did I miss? An opportunity for a one-night stand before I left New York for a year? Come on, Barbara, what sense does that make? Besides, he didn't offer.'

'Maybe he would have if you'd given him half a chance. And you are going back after all.'

'He's the director of my son's school. That's indecent.'

'Think of him as another author.' But Daphne was trying not to think of him at all. He was a nice man and a good friend. And nothing more than that.

As usual she went back to work after dinner, and Barbara sat in her room, reading a book. It wasn't until the next day that she finally got antsy and took herself off to Rodeo Drive for a look around. She had done everything she had to do for Daphne and there were no houses that day, so she decided to play hooky.

The limousine dropped her off at the Beverly Wilshire and she stood looking around her with fascination. A long handsome street stretched ahead of her for several blocks, lined inch by inch with expensive boutiques selling clothes and jewellery and luggage and paintings for a grand total of at least several hundred million dollars. It was awesome and, she reminded herself with a feeling of amazement, a long way from the dingy West Side apartment she had shared with her mother.

Her first stop was at Giorgio's. When she wandered inside she was instantly accosted by a salesgirl wearing high-heeled lavender shoes, pearls, and a pink and mauve Norell suit that retailed for two thousand dollars. The price tags she saw on the clothes hanging on the racks were in the same league. She said she'd 'just wander around,' which she did, trying hard not to giggle. There was a men's department too in the store, offering mink trench coats and silver fox vests, beautiful suedes and leathers and silk shirts, and stacks and stacks of fabulous cashmeres. She tried on hats, looked at shoes, and at last bought herself an umbrella that said 'Giorgio's.' She knew Daphne would tease her unmercifully about it, but she hadn't brought one from New York, and she wanted to buy something. From there she wandered up the street, to Hermès and Celine and eventually to Gucci, which was an enormous store with a rich leather smell and wall after wall of the exquisite Italian leather goods in every design they made. She stood in awe in front of an entire case of handbags in black lizard. There was one particular bag that she couldn't take her eyes off. It was a large, simple, rectangular-shaped bag, with a plain gold clasp and a shoulder strap, and other than the fact that it was beautifully made in the expensive reptile, there was nothing pretentious about it. She liked it because it wasn't showy, and it was exactly the kind of bag she liked, but she didn't dare ask how much it was. She knew it had to be unbelievably expensive.

'Would you like to see the bag, madame?' A salesgirl in the simple black wool dress they all wore opened the case and handed it to Barbara. She was about to refuse, but as the bag danced beneath her eyes she couldn't resist the lure and took it from her. It had a wonderful feel to it, and glancing in the mirror, she slipped it on her shoulder. It was sheer heaven. 'For your height it has exactly the right proportions,' she lilted in her gentle Italian voice, and Barbara almost drooled, and then just for the hell of it she opened the bag and glanced at the price tag. It was seven hundred dollars.

'It's very pretty.' Regretfully she slipped it off her shoulder and handed it back. 'I'll look around some more.'

'Certainly, madame.' The pretty blonde girl smiled as Barbara began to walk away and saw that a tall, attractive man was watching her intently. She glanced at him, embarrassed that he had seen her give the bag back, and for a moment she wished that she could turn around and buy it. It was embarrassing somehow to be wandering through these gilded emporiums, totally unable to afford them. But his eyes never left her face as she walked away and looked at some scarves. She was thinking of buying one for Daphne. The woman had done so much for her, it would be fun to bring her a gift as she slaved away over her screenplay in the cottage. But as she handed a red and black scarf to one of the uniformed girls, she noticed that the man who had been watching her earlier had followed her. She turned her back and pretended not to notice, but she saw him slowly approach as she glanced in one of the long elegant mirrors. He stood behind her. He was wearing grey flannel slacks and a well-cut blue shirt, open at the neck, a dark blue cashmere sweater casually tied around his shoulders, and had she looked down she would have seen that his brown loafers were Gucci. But he didn't really have the look of LA about him, he looked more like New York, or Philadelphia, or Boston. He had sandy hair and blue eyes, she guessed he was in his late thirties or very early forties. And as Barbara glanced at his reflection again she had the feeling she had seen him somewhere before, but she didn't know who he was and she couldn't place him. He caught her eyes then in the mirror, and with an embarrassed smile he finally approached her.

'I'm awfully sorry ... I've been staring at you, but I thought...' Here it comes, she thought to herself, the old line, 'Haven't I met you somewhere before?' – a smooth line, his card pressed into her hand. Barbara's eyes were not as warm as he remembered as he walked towards her. But as he looked at her now, he was sure. She had changed a great deal, her frame was the same, but her face had a distant, almost distrustful, look. Life had apparently not been kind to Barbara Jarvis. 'Barbara?'

'Yes.' No invitation in her voice or eyes, but he smiled now, sure that it was she.

'I'm Tom Harrington. I don't think you remember me. We only met once, at my wedding... I married Sandy Mackenzie.' And then suddenly she knew, her eyes flew wide and she stared at him in amazement.

'Oh, my God ... how did you remember me? It's been...' She hated to think as she added it up. She hadn't seen him since she was twenty, almost exactly twenty years before. He had married her third-year roommate at Smith. She had dropped out because she was pregnant, and they'd gotten married in Philadelphia. Barbara had gone to the wedding and met him then. But she had never seen either of them after that. He had been a law student then, and after the baby was born they moved to California. 'How are you? How's Sandy?' They had sent Christmas cards to her for a dozen years and then finally stopped. She had always been too busy with her mother to answer, but she remembered Sandy distinctly, and Tom, too. She smiled at him warmly then. 'Is she here?' It would be fun to see her, especially now that she worked for Daphne. She hadn't wanted to write back to them then, because there was nothing she wanted to tell them. What? That she was living in a depressing little apartment with her mother, buying groceries and cooking, and working as a secretary in a law firm? What was there to be proud of then? But things were different now. 'How are the children?' She remembered that they had had another four years later.

'They're great. Robert is at UCLA, as a drama major, which doesn't have us exactly thrilled, but he's good at it, and if it's what he wants...' He sighed with a smile. 'You know how kids are. And Alex is still at home with her mother, she'll be fifteen in April.'

'Good God.' Barbara looked genuinely shocked. UCLA and fifteen years old? How did that happen? Was it that long ago? But it was. She was so stunned that she didn't even notice the way he had phrased his answer.

'What about you? Are you living out here?' She saw him glance at her left hand, but there was nothing there.

'No, I'm out here for my job. The woman I work for is writing a screenplay, and we're out here for a year.'

'Sounds like a kick. Anyone I know?'

Barbara smiled with obvious pride. 'Daphne Fields.'

'That must be an interesting job. How long have you been here?'

She grinned. 'A week. We're at the Beverly Hills Hotel, it's a tough life.' They both laughed and then a shockingly beautiful redhead in white jeans and a white silk shirt joined them. She eyed Barbara with piercing green eyes. She couldn't have been a day over twenty-five, if that. She had creamy cameo skin and the red hair fell almost to her waist. She was quite something. 'Nothing fits.' She pouted at Tom, and decided that Barbara wasn't worth worrying about. 'Everything's too big.'

Barbara smiled in frank admiration of the couple they made, wondering who she was. 'I wish I had that problem.'

But there was something kind and intelligent in Tom's eyes as he looked at Barbara. 'You look marvellous, you've hardly changed in all these years.' It was a friendly lie, but she thought that it was nice of him to say so, and he didn't look particularly bowled over by the young beauty at his side. Barbara noticed then that he

191

was already carrying a shopping bag filled with expensive goodies. She couldn't quite figure out the girl's role in his life with Sandy, but his introduction rapidly explained it. 'Eloise, I'd like you to meet Barbara.' He smiled at Barb, and then Eloise. 'Barbara is a friend of my ex-wife's.' And suddenly she understood. They were divorced. Then this was his girl friend.

'Barbara Jarvis,' she filled in for him and held out her hand, her eyes going quickly back to his, wanting to ask him more about Sandy, but this was not the time. 'It's very nice to meet you.' The young redhead didn't say much, but went off to look at a large beige lizard tote bag as Tom watched and then glanced back at Barbara with a look of amusement.

'I'll say one thing, she's got awfully good taste.' It didn't seem to bother him much, nor did he seem overly taken with her.

'I'm sorry to hear about you and Sandy.' Barbara looked genuinely sympathetic. It had been eight or nine years since the Christmas cards stopped. 'How long has it been?'

'Five years. She's remarried.' And then after a moment's hesitation, 'To Austin Weeks.' But that bit of news startled Barbara.

'The actor?' It was a stupid question, how many Austin Weekses could there be? He was a very well-known English actor, but he was at least twice her age, and had been a real Romeo in his day, but Barbara knew from his last movie that he was still breathtakingly handsome. 'How did that happen?'

'I handled a fairly large legal matter for him and we got to be friends...' He shrugged, but there was still something bitter in his eyes as he said it, and then he turned to Barbara with a forced smile. 'This is Hollywood, you know. It's all part of the game. Sandy loves it out here. It suits her to a tee.'

'And you?' Even twenty years before, Barbara had hardly known him, but she had liked him that day at the wedding. She had been the maid of honour and she had thought him intelligent and witty and decent, and she had told Sandy how lucky she was. Sandy had agreed, but there had always been something about her ... something dissatisfied, restless, greedy. She had been unhappy in college, and Barbara had always suspected that she had gotten pregnant just so she could get married. Tom had been from a Main Line family in Philadelphia, but there had been a lot more to him than just that even then. And when Barbara had driven back to school, she had thought of them both with envy.

'Do you like it out here, Tom?'

'Pretty much, but I have to admit, I've stayed out here because of the kids for the last five years. And I've been practising here for so long, it would be hard to go back.' He was in film law, Barbara remembered, and this was of course the place to be, but he didn't look as though he loved LA. 'It gets pretty plastic here after a while.' He flashed a warning smile and looked no older than he had at his wedding. 'Watch out that it doesn't get you. It's addictive.'

'I know.' Her smile answered his. 'I'm already getting to like it.'

'Oh oh, bad sign.' And with that Barbara's salesgirl returned with the gift-wrapped scarf, and Eloise returned to Tom's side; she had decided that the three thousand dollar lizard tote bag didn't suit her.

'It was nice to see you again, Tom.' Barbara held out a hand. 'And say hello to Sandy for me, if you see her.'

'I do. I see Alex a couple of times a week and I see them both then.' Again the flash of pain in his eyes. He had been betrayed by his wife and a man he had thought was his friend. It was a scar that would never leave him. 'I'll tell her you said hello. You ought to give her a call, if you have time.' But Barbara hesitated. Married to Austin Weeks, why would Sandy want to see her?

'Tell her I'm at the Beverly Hills Hotel with Daphne Fields, if she'd like, she can call me. I don't want to intrude.' He nodded, and after a moment Barbara left, thinking how interesting and strange life was.

193

'Well, did you conquer Rodeo Drive?' Daphne was sprawled out on the couch reading the day's work when Barbara wandered in, and she looked like she had put in a hard day's work. 'How was it?'

'Super.' She had lingered on for another two and a half hours, wandering in and out of Jourdan, Van Cleef & Arpels, Bijan, and a host of other shops, and at last she had stopped at a restaurant for a sandwich. That had been a whole other show to observe, and she was delighted with her afternoon. She had even bought herself a bathing suit, a hat, and two sweaters. 'I love this place, Daff.'

Daphne grinned. 'I always thought you were crazy. What did you buy?'

She showed her, and then tossed the small Gucci box on to her lap. 'And that's for you, Madam Boss. I would have bought you the white mink bathrobe I saw at Giorgio's but it wasn't your size.' She grinned happily at her.

'Oh, shit. Couldn't you order it?'

They both laughed and Daphne opened the box and was touched and pleased. Red and black were her favourite colours.

'You didn't have to do that, silly.' She looked at her friend with warmth in her eyes. 'You spoil me in so many other ways, Barb. Without you I couldn't get a damn thing done.'

'Bullshit, you'd do fine without me.'

'I'm glad I don't have to.'

'How's it coming, by the way?'

'Pretty good. But it really is a whole new skill to learn. I feel so damn clumsy most of the time.'

'You won't after a while, and I bet it reads as smoothly as your other stuff.'

'I hope they think so at Comstock.'

'They will.' They were interrupted then by the telephone, and Barbara went into her own room to answer. Daphne had the hotel switchboard answer the phone when Barbara was out, and when she was there she took the endless calls from realtors in her own room not to disturb Daphne. She picked up the phone and sat down on her bed. At least she had had one day off from looking at houses. But she wanted to find something soon. She knew it would be easier for Daphne to work in more homelike surroundings. 'Hello?'

'May I please speak to Barbara Jarvis?'

'This is she.' Out of habit she grabbed a pad and picked up a pencil.

'This is Tom Harrington.' She was surprised and her heart skipped a beat. Why would he call her? But it was silly to get excited. He was just the ex-husband of an old friend and he wanted to be friendly.

'It's nice to hear from you, Tom.' She wanted to ask him then what she could do for him. Maybe, like most other people who called, he wanted access to Daphne.

'Did you have a nice afternoon?'

'Very. I covered every inch of Rodeo Drive.'

'That's an expensive pastime.' He glanced at his chequebook lying on the bed next to him. Eloise had done a fair amount of damage, but she was no different from all the rest. There had been dozens of Eloises in his life in the past five years, and no one like Barbara, ever. 'What did you buy?'

Barbara looked embarrassed and wondered what he was leading up to. Why would he call her? 'Just some silly stuff. Nothing in your league.'

'That was a nice bag you were looking at, at Gucci.' Then he had noticed. His eyes had seemed to take everything in, and he had watched her for a long time before finally coming over to speak to her.

'I'm afraid it's not in my league. Just a little rich for my blood.' Besides what would she do with a black lizard bag like that? Carry her pencils and notepad in it?

'Tell your boss you want a raise.' She bridled silently. She didn't need to tell Daphne anything of the sort. Daphne already spoiled her rotten. 'Or find some nice man to buy it for you.'

'I'm afraid that's not my style.' She sounded suddenly cool.

'I didn't think it was.' His voice was deep and gentle. If he did, he wouldn't be calling. He had Eloise for that. But Barbara was different. 'We didn't get much of a chance to talk this afternoon. Did you ever marry?'

'No. I never did. My mother got sick when I finished Smith, and I spent a long time taking care of her.' She said it matter-of-factly, without regret. It was what had been.

'That must have been rough for you.' But there was admiration in his voice. Sandy would never have done anything like that, and he wasn't sure he would either. In fact he was sure he wouldn't. 'When did you start working for Daphne Fields?'

'About four years ago part time, and then eventually it worked into a full-time job.'

'Do you like it?'

'I love it. She's the best friend I've got and she's a dream to work for.'

'That's unusual for a successful woman.' He had seen his share and most of them weren't easy.

'Not Daphne. She's the most unassuming woman I've ever met. She just does her work, and quietly goes about her life, she's really an incredible human being.'

'That's nice for you.' He didn't sound overly interested in Daphne. 'Listen, we didn't get much of a chance to talk. How about a drink later on? I have to meet one of my partners for a quick dinner to discuss a couple of contracts. But I should be free by nine o'clock. I could meet you at the Polo Lounge if that's convenient for you . . .' His voice drifted off and he sounded somewhat nervous. He correctly sensed that Barbara was well guarded. 'How does that sound to you?'

At her end there was a long silence. She didn't really want to go out, and she suspected that his dinner date was probably the young redhead. But on the other hand, she had nothing to do, Daphne would be working and wouldn't need her, and he was a nice man. Without letting herself think about it anymore, she suddenly nodded. 'Okay. Why not?'

'I'll meet you in the Lounge at nine. If I'm going to be late, I'll call. Will you be in your room until then?' He somehow suspected she would.

'Yes, I want to order Daphne's dinner.'

'Doesn't she go out?' The image he had of writers was one of carousing and drinking and parties.

'Very seldom, and never when she's working. She's working on the screenplay now and she hasn't left the room since we got here.'

'That doesn't sound like much fun.'

'It's not. It's hard work. She really works harder than anyone I know.'

'She sounds like she's up for early sainthood.' He said it with a smile.

'In my book, yes.' It was a warning to him not to malign Daphne, at this or any later date. Barbara defended her like a priestess at the altar of her private god, whether it was reasonable or not, it was simply the way she felt about Daphne. 'I'll see you later, Tom.'

'I'm looking forward to it.' And as he showered and shaved before meeting his partner at his house in Bel-Air, he was amazed at how true that was. She was attractive, but she was not a spectacular beauty. She looked more interesting than sexy, more intelligent than pretty, and yet there was something very alluring about her, something solid, something real. She looked like the kind of woman you could talk to, and hold on to and count on and laugh with. Tom Harrington had never even known a woman like that, but they were qualities that had struck him in Barbara twenty years before, in sharp contrast to Sandy. Sandy had been a pretty little blonde debutante from New York, with dazzling blue eyes and a smile that knocked him on his ass. But she had been spoiled rotten by her parents, and later by him, and she had always let him down, especially at the last when she had run off with Austin. She had taken both kids, and called him two weeks later. He had thought of fighting her for custody for a while after they got divorced, but it would have torn the kids apart, and he didn't have the heart to. And since then there had been no one important in his life. He didn't know why, but he suddenly felt an irresistible pull towards Barbara. He had known the moment he saw her that afternoon that he wanted to see her again, even if only to talk to her.

'Daff, did you eat?' Barbara walked into her room and glanced at the tray and saw instantly that she hadn't. But Daphne was frowning at the typewriter as she clattered along, and she barely heard her. 'Daff . . . hey, kiddo, food.' Daphne looked up with a vague smile.

'Huh? Oh. Yeah, okay. Soon. I want to finish this scene.' And then, with a glance over her shoulder, 'You going out?'

'Just for a little while. Can I do anything for you before I go?'

'No, I'm fine. I'm sorry I'm not much fun.'

'I can take care of myself.' She started to tell her then about Tom, but Daphne was already typing. 'I'll see you later. And don't forget to eat.' But Daphne didn't answer. She was already miles away, working on the scene, and Barbara closed the door softly behind her.

22

Tom gave Barbara the name of his own real estate agent, and the first afternoon that she went out with him to look at houses in Bel-Air and Beverly Hills they found exactly what she needed, in Bel-Air. It was a beautiful little house on Cielo Drive, with three bedrooms that looked out on a huge well-manicured garden. The house and grounds were surrounded by a tall brick wall, overgrown by hedges and vines, so it didn't look like a prison, but it was entirely private. There was a vast expanse of lawn and a simple rectangular pool, a sauna, a hot tub, and the house itself was really lovely. The floors were a pale beige marble, there were huge white couches everywhere, a collection of very valuable modern art, and a kitchen straight out of *House & Garden*. And throughout the house was a feeling of sunshine and peace. There was a library panelled in whitewashed pine that looked out on the pool, which was a perfect place for Daphne to write. It had everything that they wanted. And although the price was high, it wasn't something that Comstock would cringe at. It belonged to a very respected actor and his wife who were in Italy on location for a movie.

Barbara stood looking around her with an ecstatic smile as the real estate agent watched. She opened every closet, every drawer, and checked out each room with great care for her employer. 'Well, what do you think, Miss Jarvis?'

'I think we'll move in tomorrow, if that's okay with you.'

They exchanged a smile. 'My clients will be pleased. They've been gone for a month.' It was a miracle that the place hadn't already been rented, but they had placed some fairly stringent restrictions on the kind of tenant they wanted. 'Do you think your employer will want to see it first?'

'I don't think so.' And as hard as Daphne was working, she would have been in such a haze that she wouldn't have noticed if Barbara had rented a grass shack. 'She's very busy.'

'Then why don't we go back to my office and sign the papers?'

Barbara signed the lease for a year an hour later, and she and Daphne moved in the next day.

That night Daphne wandered around the house, adjusting to the new surroundings. Sometimes it was difficult to work right away in a new place, and she was trying to get settled. She had unpacked all her things, and her typewriter was set up in the pretty little den. Everything was ready and waiting, but Barbara had gone out, and it suddenly occured to Daphne that she didn't know where she had gone. Lately she seemed to have gotten very independent in Los Angeles. She seemed to have blossomed since they had arrived, and Daphne was glad. Barbara's life had never been very exciting, and if she was happy here in LA, then Daphne was happy for her. But as she sat in the kitchen now, by herself, eating scrambled eggs and thinking about her screenplay, suddenly she felt lonelier than she had in a long time. All she could think of as she sat there was Andrew, the meals they had shared long ago in their apartment, the moments and the days before she had put him in the school. And then she thought of him at Howarth, and ached just to hold him, touch him, see him. As she thought of it a sob broke from her and she pushed away the plate of scrambled eggs. And feeling like a child herself, she laid her head down on the counter and cried, keening for Andrew.

She promised herself, by way of consolation, as she blew her nose at last that she would send for him at the earliest possible moment, but in the meantime she just had to tough it out. It was even worse to think about what he might be feeling, and the terror that he might be sitting alone in his room crying too reduced her to tears again. There was almost a sense of panic, of desperation, that filled her, a fear that she had failed him, that in coming to California she might have done the wrong thing. And suddenly she knew she needed reassurance, someone to tell her that her baby was all right, and there was only one person who could do that. Matthew. And without even looking at the clock to see what time it was in the East, she hurried to the telephone on the kitchen wall. With trembling fingers she dialled the familiar number, praying that he was awake. She had to talk to someone. Now.

She had dialled Mrs Curtis's old private number, and a moment later a deep, husky voice answered and just hearing him, she felt less alone.

'Matt? It's Daphne Fields.' Her throat felt tight as she heard his voice and her eyes filled with tears again as she tried to control them. 'I hope it's not too late to call.'

He laughed softly into the phone. 'Are you kidding? I'm sitting here looking at another two or three hours of work on my desk. It's nice to hear your voice. How's California?'

'I wouldn't know. I haven't seen it yet. All I've seen is my hotel room and now my house. We moved in today. I want to give you my new number.' She did and he jotted it down as she regained her composure, and she tried to sound less upset than she was as she asked him how Andrew was doing.

'He's fine. He learned to ride a bike today, a two-wheeler, Mom. He can hardly wait to tell you. He was going to write you a letter tonight.' It all sounded so healthy and so normal and suddenly the flood of guilt she had felt began to ebb. But her voice was sad as she answered. 'I wish I'd been there.'

There was a moment's silence as Matthew listened, empathising with what he suspected that she felt.

'You will.' There was a moment's comfortable silence between them. 'Are you okay, Daff?'

'I think so ... yes.' And then she sighed. 'Just lonely as hell.'

'Writing is lonely work.'

'So is leaving your only son.' She sighed deeply then, but there were no more tears. 'How are things at Howarth?'

'Hectic for me, but I'm starting to catch up. I thought I had a good grip on things before I got here, but somehow there's always another ton of files you haven't read, or a child you have to talk to. We're making some minor changes, but nothing earthshaking yet. I'll keep you informed.'

'I'd like that, Matt.' He could hear how tired she was, and she reminded him of a little girl who's been sent far from home, and is desperately homesick.

There was a moment's pause then and he tried to visualise her so far away in California. 'What's your house like?'

She told him about it and he sounded impressed, particularly when he heard who it belonged to. Their conversation was distracting her a little from her pain. He was good at that too. He was sensitive and wise and strong. But, she still felt the familiar ache for Andrew. 'I sure do miss you all.' He was touched to be included.

'We miss you too, Daphne.' His voice was warm in her ear, and she felt a stirring in her soul, and as she sat in the silent kitchen at eight o'clock at night, she reached out to this man she had known for such a brief time, yet who had become her friend before she left.

'I miss talking to you, Matt.'

'I know ... somehow I expected to see you here last weekend.'

'I wish I could have been. This seems like a million miles from home, no matter how pretty it is.'

'You'll be home soon.' But suddenly the year ahead stretched before her like a lifetime. She had to fight back her tears as he went on. 'And think of what a great opportunity this is for you. We both have a lot of important new lessons ahead of us.'

'Yes, I guess so . . . how is it for you at Howarth?' Little by little they were regaining the ease they had discovered with each other during their talks at the school, and she felt a little less lonely. 'Is it what you expected?'

'So far it is. But I have to admit . . . I feel about as far from New York as you do in California.' He smiled then and stretched back in his chair. 'New Hampshire is awfully quiet.'

She laughed softly from her seat at the counter in the kitchen. 'Don't I know that well! When I first moved up there, when I put Andrew in the school, I used to get nervous just listening to the silence.'

'What did you do to get used to it?' He was smiling, remembering the look in her eyes, and feeling the miles evaporate between them.

'I kept a journal. It became like a constant friend. I think in a funny way that that's how I started writing. The journal became essays, and then I started writing short stories, and then I wrote the first book, and now' – she looked around the streamlined white kitchen – 'and now look what's happened, I'm out on the West Coast writing a movie I have no idea how to write. On second thoughts, maybe you'd better get used to the silence and let it go at that.'

They both laughed. 'Miss Fields, are you complaining?'

'No.' She thought it over with a soft smile. 'I think I'm actually whining. I was lonely as hell tonight when I called you.'

'There's no shame in that. I called my sister the other night and I was practically in tears. I had one of my nieces relay all my complaints to her, in hope of getting a little sympathy from Martha.'

'What did she say?'

'That I was an ungrateful bastard and that I was getting paid twice what I make at the New York School and I should bloody well shut up and enjoy it.' He laughed at the memory of the words his niece had relayed over the phone. 'That's my sister. She's right, of course, but I was mad as hell anyway. I wanted sympathy and I got a kick in the ass. I guess I had it coming. That's the kind of stuff I used to say to her before we ran away to Mexico.'

'What was that like?' She didn't feel like working anymore. She just wanted to hear Matt's voice as she sat in the kitchen.

'Oh, God, Daphne, Mexico was the craziest thing I've ever done, and I loved it. We lived in Mexico City for a while. We spent three months in Puerto Vallarta, which was a sleepy little town then with cobblestone streets, where no one spoke English. Martha not only learned to lip-read, she learned to lip-read in Spanish.' His voice filled with admiration and love again at the memory.

'She must be an amazing woman.'

'Yeah' – his voice was soft – 'she is. She's a lot like you, you know. She's got guts and heart at the same time, it's a rare combination. Most people who have survived tough moments in life become tough themselves. She never did, and you didn't either.' It made her wonder again just how much he knew, how much more than she had told him. But he had already decided to confess to her. 'Mrs Obermeier told me about your friend up here. The one you referred to last time we talked.' Matt was afraid to say his name, as though he had no right to. 'He must have been a wonderful man.'

'He was,' she sighed softly and tried not to feel the pain of loss again, but it was hard not to. 'I was wondering tonight how different my life would be now if he were still alive, or if Jeff were. I suppose I wouldn't be out here, beating my brains out over my type-writer.'

'You wouldn't be half the person you are now, Daphne. That's all a part of you now. It's part of what makes you so special.' She wondered if he was right. 'I don't know if I'd say you were lucky exactly, but maybe in a funny way you are. You've had some damn tough things happen to you in your life, but you've beaten them into tools you can use, and beautiful parts of yourself. That's quite a victory.' She had never really thought of herself as victorious, just as surviving, but she also knew that in other people's eyes that was how it looked. She had won: she was successful. But there was more to life than that, as she knew only too well. Much more. Even though now she no longer had that. But whatever she did or didn't have in her life anymore, Matthew Dane made her feel better about life and herself every time she talked to him.

'You're a hell of a good friend, Matthew Dane. You make me want to run out and conquer the world again.'

'It's an awfully nice world out there to conquer.'

'Who taught Andrew to ride the bike?' But she already knew without asking.

'I did. I had some spare time this afternoon, and he had nothing much to do. I'd seen him watching some of the older kids the other day and I saw the look in his eyes, so we went out and gave it a try, and he did great.' She smiled at the vision he conjured up.

'Thank you, Matt.'

'He's my friend too, you know.'

'He's a lucky boy.'

'No, Daff.' His eyes were gentle and wise as he sat in his chair. 'He's not the lucky one, I am. Kids like Andrew make my life worth living.'

There didn't seem much else to say. 'I guess I ought to let you go. We both have work to do.' It was a comforting feeling for some reason, knowing that when she went to her desk, he would be sitting at his, both of them working into the night for the next few hours.

'Give my love to Andrew tomorrow, and a big kiss from me.'

'I will. And Daphne' – he faltered for a moment,

always unsure of just how much to say – 'I'm glad you called.'

'So am I.' He had made her feel warm and happy and as though she had a friend somewhere. 'I'll call again soon.'

They each said goodbye and afterwards she could still feel his presence beside her in the kitchen. She went to her desk, and looked down at her work, and then she walked into her bedroom, took off her clothes, slipped into a black bathing suit, and walked out to the pool. The warm water was delicious on her skin and she swam a few laps, thinking of Matthew. When she got out, she felt refreshed and went back to her desk after she changed her clothes. And half an hour later she was a thousand miles away again, lost in her screenplay. But in New Hampshire, Matthew Dane put aside his files and turned off the lights and sat staring into the fire, thinking of Daphne.

23

'What's she like, Barb?' Barbara and Tom lay stretched out beside his pool. It had been two weeks since they'd moved into the new house, and she had barely seen Daphne. She was deep in her work and hardly knew what happened around her. Barbara completed whatever tasks she had to, and every evening now she came over to see Tom. Both their lives had changed radically in two weeks, since they had become lovers. He held lightly to her hand now as they watched the sunset and lay beside his pool. He was always fascinated by stories of Daphne.

'She's hardworking, loving, compassionate, sad.'

'She must be. She's had enough rotten stuff happen to her in one lifetime to kill ten people.'

'But it hasn't killed her. That's the amazing thing about her. She's warmer and gentler and more open than anyone I know.'

'I don't believe that.' He shook his head and looked into Barbara's eyes.

'Why not? It's true.'

'Because no one is more warm or gentle than you.' As he said it she realised again how lucky she was. In truth, luckier than Daphne. She was silent for a moment as Tom watched her and then leaned over and kissed her tenderly. He had never been as happy in his life and he had watched Barbara open up before him in the past two weeks like a summer flower. She was laughing and happy and her eyes were more alive than they had been when he met her when she was in college. 'Look at you, love. You were hurting too. Nobody can be that alone and be happy. I wasn't even alone and I was miserable.'

'You didn't look all that miserable to me that day at Gucci.' She loved to tease him about that. Eloise had disappeared two weeks before, and was already reported to be living with a young actor.

But Barbara also knew now that he had been desperately lonely while he was married. It was hearing him tell her about that that had opened her heart and allowed her to trust him. He had been so badly hurt, much more so than she had been by the lawyer who'd gotten her pregnant years before. She had told him about that too, and he had held her in his arms while she cried, spilling the guilt and the sorrow she had felt for thirteen years and kept bottled up inside. And then she had admitted that what she really grieved over was that she was now too old to have children.

'Don't be ridiculous, how old are you?'

'Forty.' He was forty-two, and he looked at her with gentle determination.

'Women today are having babies at forty-five and forty-seven and fifty, for chrissake. Forty isn't even remarkable anymore. Is there any medical reason why you couldn't?'

'Not that I know of.' Except that she had always secretly wondered if the abortion had damaged her in some way and would keep her from having children. For years she had no longer wondered. It was obvious that it was irrelevant. But Tom didn't agree. 'It really is too late. It's ridiculous to have children at my age.'

'If you want them, it's ridiculous not to. My children have been the greatest joy in my life. Don't ever deprive yourself of that, Barbara.'

He had introduced her to Alexandra, and she could see why his children brought him such joy. She was a beautiful, happy, easygoing young girl, with Sandy's striking blonde looks and her father's gentle disposition. She hadn't yet met his son, Bob, but from all that she heard, he was much like his father and she was sure that she would like him too.

For six weeks Barbara kept her life secret from Daphne. Then one morning Barbara came home and found Daphne sitting in the living room with an almost drunken grin.

'What's with you?'

'I did it!'

'Did what?'

'I finished the screenplay!' She was exploding with energy and pride, her eyes alight with excitement. She had a sense of accomplishment second to none, and the secret bonus of knowing that the sooner she finished her work, the sooner she would see her son.

'Hurray!' Barbara had given her a huge hug, and had opened a bottle of champagne. It was on their third glass that Daphne looked at her with her eyes full of mischief.

'Well, aren't you ever going to tell me?'

'Tell you what?' Barbara's mind went momentarily blank.

'About where you go every night while I work my ass off.' Daphne grinned and Barbara blushed furiously. 'And don't tell me that you've been going to the movies.'

'I've been meaning to say something, but...' She looked up, with a dreamy expression in her eyes, and Daphne groaned.

'Oh, God, I knew it. You're in love.' She wagged a finger at her. 'Just don't tell me you're getting married. At least not until we finish the movie.' Barbara's heart sank, Tom had mentioned marriage for the first time that night, and her answer had been much like Daphne's admonition. He had been hurt by her loyalty to her employer, but he had agreed to wait until the propitious moment.

'I'm not getting married, Daff. But I must admit ... I'm crazy about him.' She smiled broadly and looked about fourteen years old instead of forty.

'Am I ever going to meet him? Is he respectable? Will I approve?'

'Yes, to all three questions. He's wonderful and I love him madly, and . . . he married my roommate in college, and I ran into him at Gucci, with this incredibly beautiful stupid redhead, and . . .' It all came rushing out at last and Daphne laughed at her.

'My, I've been missing a lot, haven't I? What does he do? And please don't tell me he's an actor.' She wanted the very best for Barbara, and didn't want her to get hurt again. She suddenly frowned, worried, thinking about what Barbara had said about his marrying her room-mate. 'Is he still married?'

'Of course not. He's divorced, and he's a lawyer. He's with Baxter, Shagley, Harrington, and Row.' And at that Daphne suddenly grinned.

'You know them?'

'So do you, dummy, or you should have. We haven't had to deal with them yet, but Iris said something about them before we left New York. They're Comstock's lawyers for our movie. Didn't he know?'

'He's been all wrapped up in a tax case for one of his clients.'

'What happened to his wife?'

'She ran off with Austin Weeks.'

'The actor?' Daphne looked momentarily stunned and then realised, as Barbara had two months before, that it was a foolish thing to ask. 'Never mind, that was a dumb question. Christ, that must have been a blow to your friend. Austin Weeks must be two hundred years old.'

'At least, but he's rich as the devil, and twice as good-looking.' Daphne nodded.

'What's your friend's name, by the way?'

'Tom Harrington.'

They exchanged a slow smile and Daphne looked pleased. 'I'm happy for you, Barb.' She lifted her glass of champagne to her friend and toasted her happiness with Tom. 'I hope you both live happily ever after . . .'

And then she grinned. 'But not until we finish the movie.' There was the same feverish light in her eyes Barbara had seen ever since they'd come to California. All she wanted to do was work at breakneck speed, get it over with and get home. But now that almost frightened Barbara. She was in no hurry to leave California.

She introduced Tom to Daphne the next day. They had drinks beside the pool, and Barbara could tell when they left that Daphne had liked him. The conversation had been relaxed and she kissed him on the cheek as they left and told him to take good care of Barbara. Daphne waved as they got into his car, and then walked slowly back to the pool and picked up their glasses. She was happy for Barbara. And Daphne had an odd feeling of watching precious people set sail for a long journey. She felt somehow left behind on a lonely shore.

That night as she made herself a sandwich for dinner she decided to call Matthew. As a result of her two months of nonstop work, she still didn't know a soul in LA and she called Matt from time to time. He was becoming an even dearer friend, and her only real contact with Andrew. But when she called tonight, he was out, and she wondered where he was. He had never been out before, and she suddenly wondered if he had met a woman. It felt as though everyone in the world had someone except her, and all she had was her little boy, and he was three thousand miles away in a school for the deaf. It was a desperately lonely feeling, and even the victory of having finished the screenplay did not subdue her pain as she went to bed immediately after dinner, and lay there fighting back tears, her whole soul longing for Andrew.

24

The people at Comstock Studios were overwhelmed by Daphne's screenplay. It was more powerful than the book, they told her, and everyone could hardly wait to start. The actors had long since been lined up, the sets had been built. In three weeks they were to begin, and after a round of congratulations Daphne went back to the house, feeling pleased with herself, and very excited. They had hired Justin Wakefield for the starring role, and even though she thought he might be a little too handsome, she was extremely impressed by his talent.

'Well, madam, how does it feel?' Barbara smiled at her as they got back to the house together and wandered inside.

'I don't know. I think I'm in shock. I really expected them to tell me they hated it.' She sat down on the white couch and looked around, feeling a little disoriented.

But Barbara smiled at her friend. 'You're crazy, Daff. You always think Harbor's going to hate your books too, and they always love them.'

'So I'm crazy.' She shrugged with a grin. 'Maybe I'm entitled.'

'What are you going to do with yourself for three weeks?' They wouldn't start shooting until then. Daphne was barely able to keep herself from her desk for three days, let alone three weeks, but Barbara suspected what she had in mind as Daphne smiled at her.

'Are you kidding? I'm going to call Matt tonight and have him put Andrew on a plane.'

'You don't want to fly back to New York?'

Daphne shook her head and glanced at the pool. 'I

think he'd love it here, and maybe it's time he saw a little bit more of the world than just Howarth.' Barbara nodded silent agreement, wondering what he was like, she had still never met him. And then Daphne looked up at her with a warm smile. 'Do you want to come to Disneyland with us?'

'I'd love it.' Tom had a business trip to New York coming up, and she was already lonely just thinking about it. It made her dread how she would feel when she eventually went back to New York at the end of the year. She still hadn't accepted his proposal, on the grounds that she couldn't leave Daphne. Not yet.

Half an hour later Daphne got up and went to the phone, and called Matthew Dane at Howarth.

'Hi, Matt. How are you?'

'I'm fine. How's the screenplay coming?'

'Terrific. I'm all finished, and I found out today that they loved it. We start in three weeks. They had just been waiting for me to finish.'

'You must be excited as hell.' He sounded genuinely pleased for her.

'I am. And I want to spend the next two or three weeks with Andrew. How soon do you think you can get him on a plane?'

At his end, Matt looked down at the appointment calendar on his desk with a thoughtful look. 'I can take him into Boston on Saturday if you'd like. Is that soon enough?'

She smiled at her end. 'No, but it'll do. I can hardly wait to see him.'

'I know.' He knew better than she suspected how lonely she had been. He could tell by how often she called him. And it always amazed him that a woman with her looks and her mind and her success should be alone. There should have been flocks of people at her door, especially men, but he also knew that she didn't want them. 'How's life otherwise, Daff?'

'What otherwise? All I've done is work since I got here. Now suddenly I've finished and all I do is sleep.

I went out in the world today for the first time, to go to Comstock, and it was like having been dropped on to a new planet.'

'Welcome to earth, Miss Fields. What are you and Andrew going to do while he's out there?'

'Go to Disneyland for starters.'

'Lucky kid.' Matthew smiled, knowing how Andrew would lord it over the others, but not in a nasty way, he wasn't that kind of child.

'I'll have to see after that. Maybe we'll just hang out here at the pool, although to tell you the truth, that kills me. I keep feeling I should be working every minute so I can get out of here faster.'

'Don't you ever stop and just enjoy things?'

'Not if I can help it. I'm not here to have a good time. I'm here to work.' Sometimes she sounded as though she were driven by demons, and he knew what they were. She was always pushing herself so she could see Andrew. 'Matt...' She suddenly sounded worried and pensive. 'Do you really think he'll be all right on the flight? I could fly back to get him if I had to.' But she had to admit that she was bone tired from two months of incessant work. But nonetheless she'd have done it for Andrew.

'He'll be fine. Let him be, Daff. Let him try his own wings. This is a big step for him.' But what if something happened? 'Trust him. And trust me. He'll be fine.' There was something so comforting about him that she believed him.

He called her back the next day to tell her when Andrew was arriving. He was flying nonstop from Boston to Los Angeles the next day and due to arrive at three in the afternoon. She wondered for a moment how she would get through another twenty-four hours. Suddenly she ached to put her arms around him again, every moment would be too long. Matthew smiled, 'You sound as antsy as he does.'

'I am.' And then her face grew serious again. 'Is he scared about making the trip alone?'

'Not at all. He thinks it's going to be exciting.'

Daphne sighed into the phone. 'I'm not sure I'm ready for this, even if he is.' For years he had been so protected, and now at Matthew's urging he would be trying his own wings, even for something so simple as a plane trip to California; it scared her.

'What are you afraid of, Daff? That he'll get to be independent?' His voice was gentle but it was a low blow and suddenly there was anger in the cornflower-blue eyes.

'How can you say that? You know that's what I want for him.'

'Then let him have it. Don't make him feel different all his life. He doesn't have to be, unless you make him that way.'

'Okay, okay, I've heard the speech before. I get the message.' Their long talks on the phone had brought them the kind of friendship that allowed her to get angry, and she had before, but never for long. And usually, Matthew was right.

'Daphne, he's going to feel proud of himself, and you'll feel proud too.' She knew it was true. 'But I know that doesn't make it easy at this end of the flight. Tomorrow at this time you'll both be glowing. Don't forget to call me when he arrives.' Now it was Matthew who sounded like the worried mother hen.

'I won't. We'll call you from the airport.'

'I'll do the same tomorrow from Boston.'

And the moment he did, there began a six-hour vigil for Daphne, watching the clock, sitting by the phone, terrified that something would go wrong, that something would happen to the plane, or worse, that up in the air Andrew would be unable to communicate with anyone around him, or some child on the plane would torment him as they had in the playground so long ago. It seemed terribly wrong that he should face the world again now, all alone, and yet perhaps it was fitting. Perhaps Matthew really was right and it was Andrew's battle, to win on his own, and he had a right to that victory by

215

himself, without anyone else sharing the glory or taking it from him.

'You okay?' Barbara stuck her head into Daphne's study, and saw the tension in her face. 'Any news?'

'Only that he's on the plane. Nothing since then.'

Barbara nodded. 'Want some lunch?' But Daphne shook her head. She couldn't eat, all she could think of was Andrew, winging his way towards her from Boston. She was going to the airport to meet him alone, and Barbara would meet him at the house. They had arranged a little party for him, with paper hats and a cake and balloons and a sign that said, 'We love you, Andrew. Welcome to California.'

When it was time to leave for the airport, Daphne showered and slipped into beige linen slacks and a white silk shirt, sandals, and a white silk blazer that Barbara had bought for her on Rodeo Drive. It was the perfect size and looked beautiful now as she picked up her handbag and walked out the door as Barbara watched her. She turned once in the doorway, and their eyes met and held, and then with a smile she was gone, and Barbara marvelled at what she had seen. There was a love in the woman's eyes that Barbara envied, a love for a child who was a piece of her own soul, whatever his problems, hearing or deaf he was her little boy and she loved him with all of her heart, with everything she had to give him.

At the airport Daphne looked up at the big board that listed the arrivals and heaved a sigh of relief. The plane was on time, and she hurried to the gate. She had another half hour to wait there, she had come early 'just in case,' and she stood watching at the window, watching planes land and take off, and feeling the minutes tick by like aeons. And finally, ten minutes before he was due to arrive, she walked into a phone booth and called Matthew.

'Safely arrived?' There was a smile in his voice, but Daphne still sounded tense.

216

'The plane's not due in for another ten minutes. But I can't stand it. I had to call you.'

'The last stretch, eh? He'll be fine, Daphne. I promise.'

'I know he will. But suddenly I realise that it's been two and a half months since I've seen him. What if he's different? What if he hates me because I'm out here?' She was terrified of seeing her own son, but Matthew knew it was normal.

'He doesn't hate you, Daff. He loves you. He can hardly wait to see you. That's all he's been talking about for the last two days.'

'Are you sure?' She felt like a nervous wreck.

'Positive. Come on, kid, hang in there. He's almost there.' He looked at his watch, and in the airport she saw people gathering at the gate. 'Another five minutes.'

And suddenly she grinned then, feeling silly. 'I'm sorry I called you, I just got so nervous . . .'

'Listen, I'd feel the same way. Just relax. Tell you what, don't bother to call me till you get home. If I don't hear from you, I'll assume he arrived safely. But don't louse up your first minutes with him by rushing for a phone.'

'Okay.' And then suddenly she saw the plane, taxiing slowly towards them. Tears filled her eyes and she couldn't talk anymore. 'Oh, Matt . . . I see the plane . . . he's here . . . goodbye.' She hung up and he smiled, feeling the emotions rise within him, too.

Daphne stood very still as the plane pulled up to the gate, and she clutched a railing with one hand as it stopped. And a moment later people began to pour from it, tired-looking businessmen with briefcases, grandmothers with canes, models with portfolios, and no sight of Andrew. She stood there, saying nothing, her eyes combing the crowd, and then suddenly she saw him. He was smiling and laughing, holding a stewardess's hand, and then suddenly he pointed at Daphne, and said almost clearly, 'That's my Mommy!' With tears streaming down her face Daphne ran towards him and swept him into her arms, closing her eyes tight and holding him, and then she pulled away so he could read her lips. 'I love you so much!' And he laughed with delight and hugged her again and when he pulled away he moved his lips and spoke.

'I love you too, Mom.'

He was enthralled by the limousine waiting for them at the kerb, and the sign they had made at home, and the pool and the cake. He told Barbara all about the flight, moving his lips carefully and speaking awkwardly but nonetheless so that she could understand him. After dinner they all went for a swim, and at last he went to bed, Daphne tucking him in, stroking his fair hair, and kissing him softly on the forehead as he drifted off to sleep, and tonight she watched him for a long time as he lay there near her once more. Andrew was home. It was all she could think of as she stood there, and it was a long time before she left the room, and found Barbara putting the cake away in the kitchen.

'You've got one hell of a terrific kid, Daff.'

'I know.' There was little she could say, whatever happened tonight seemed to bring tears to her eyes and they came again as she smiled at Barbara. Then she went into her office to call Matt, and when he answered, she spoke in a tremulous voice. 'He made it, Matt . . . he made it!' She tried to tell him about the trip, but halfway through she began to cry, in great gulping sobs of relief that he understood as he waited.

'It's all right, Daff . . . it's okay . . . it's okay.' His voice was gentle and soothing from three thousand miles away, and it was like being held in his arms as her sobs subsided. 'He's going to make it from now on. There will be ups and downs in his life, but he's going to be just fine. You gave him what he needed, and that's the most beautiful thing you could give him.' But she knew that Matthew and the others had given him something too, something she could never have given him. And she had only had the wisdom to let them.

218

'Thank you.' He knew what she meant, and for the first time in years he felt his own eyes fill with tears, and it was only with the greatest effort that he managed not to tell her that he loved her.

25

The trip to Disneyland was a huge success, and Barbara and Daphne enjoyed it as much as Andrew. They spent another day going to Knotts Berry Farm, went to the La Brea Tar Pits one afternoon, and Comstock Studios for a tour, and every afternoon they swam at their pool. The two weeks of his visit went all too quickly, and it seemed only moments later that their last day had come, and they sat at the pool, signing quietly. His eyes were grave as he told her all the things he had liked best, and how much he liked Barbara. Daphne smiled, told him she liked him a lot too, and then was startled at his next question.

'Are you ever going to be like her, Mom?'

'What do you mean?' She signed the answer slowly. It had never occurred to her to be 'like' Barbara.

'You know, with somebody who loves you.' He had met Tom and liked him too, 'almost as much as Matthew,' he had signed, which was the highest form of praise from Andrew. But he had just brought up a very tough question. It dawned on her too that not so long before they would never have been able to have this conversation. He was able to express himself now with extraordinary depth, by signing, and he accurately lip-read almost every conversation. There were no longer locked doors between her and her child, they had all been unlocked by the people who loved him at Howarth. But as she thought of them for a moment, Andrew repeated the question.

'I don't know, Andrew. You don't just find someone. It's a rare and special thing.'

'But it happened to you before.'

'Yes, it did.' There was a wistfulness in her eyes he had never seen as she answered. 'With your Dad.'

'And John.' He was still faithful to the memory of his friend, and she nodded.

'Yes.'

'I'd like to have a Daddy like Matthew.'

'Would you?' She smiled gently, half sad, half amused. No matter how hard she tried, there was always something she wasn't giving him, something she couldn't do. Now it was giving him a Daddy. 'Don't you think you could be happy with just me?' It was a serious question, and she watched his eyes and his hands as he signed the answer.

'Yes. But look how happy Barbara is with Tom.' She chuckled then, he was almost nagging, but he had made his point, and it was a tough one.

'What they have is very special, Andrew. You don't fall in love every day. Sometimes that happens only once in a lifetime.'

'You work too much.' He looked annoyed. 'You never go out.' How could he be so young and know so much?

'That's because I want to finish my work so I can come home to you.' He seemed appeased by that, but when they went inside for lunch, Daphne was still thinking with amazement of what he had said. He was beginning to see her as she was, with her fears and her flaws as well as her virtues. He was growing up, more than just to take an airplane alone. He was doing his own thinking. And she was even more proud of him for that.

'Maybe I don't need a man like Barbara does.' She brought the subject up again herself after lunch, as though to convince him.

'Why not?'

'I have you.' She grinned at him over dessert.

'That's silly. I'm just your little boy.' He looked at her as though she were really dumb and she laughed.

'You drive a hard bargain, don't you?'

He looked confused at the signed words, and she said, 'Never mind. We'd better get ready or we'll miss your plane.'

And this time the parting was far from easy. Neither of them knew for sure when they would see each other again, and he clung to her with tears rolling down his cheeks as Daphne fought to retain her composure.

'I promise, you'll come back soon, sweetheart. And if I can, I'll come to New York for a few days.'

'But you'll be too busy with your movie.' It was a sad little garbled wail. He had been speaking a lot since he had been there.

'I'll try though, I'll really try. And you try too ... not to be sad, and to have a good time with your friends at school. Think of all the terrific stuff you have to tell them.' But neither of them was thinking of that as the stewardess led him to the plane. He was suddenly only a seven-and-a-half-year-old boy aching for his mother, and she felt the most vital part of her being, being torn from her heart once again. How often she had known that pain, and yet each time it came again it seemed like the first time.

Barbara said nothing as Daphne cried, staring blindly at the plane, she simply put an arm around her shoulders and held her close. They waved frantically as the plane pulled away but they never knew if he saw them. And the trip back to the house was silent and sombre. Daphne went to her room when she got home and this time she didn't call Matthew, he called her. He could hear instantly from her voice how she was feeling, and he knew she would, which was why he had called her.

'I bet you feel like shit, huh, Daff?'

She smiled through her tears and nodded. 'Yeah. It was harder this time than it's ever been. It's different when I leave him at the school.'

'Look at it this way, even that isn't forever. One of these days he'll be home with you for good.'

She blew her nose and took a deep breath. 'It's hard to imagine that day will come.'

222

'It will. It won't be long. And for the next couple of months you're going to be awfully busy with your movie.'

'I wish I'd never signed the damn contract. I should be in New York, near Andrew.' But they both knew that she didn't entirely believe it. It was in part a reaction to his leaving.

'Well, then hurry up and finish the damned thing so you can come home. I wouldn't mind that either. Hell, you're the only parent I can complain to.' She laughed into the phone and lay back on her bed.

'Christ, Matt, sometimes life is so tough.'

'You've been through worse.'

'Thanks for reminding me.' But she was still smiling.

'My pleasure. Anytime.' They had a comfortable banter between them, and she seemed to tell him about all of her problems, all of which either centred around work or Andrew, there was nothing much else to tell him. 'When do you start the movie?'

'Day after tomorrow. The actors have been having fittings for costumes, "wardrobing," they call it, for the last two weeks. But they don't really start filming for another two days. I don't have to be on the set until then. I'll probably have to rewrite scenes and just watch how it's going. From here on out I'm basically just an adviser. The directors and the actors do all the work now.'

'Have you met the actors yet?'

'Yeah, all except for Justin Wakefield. He was in South America on location, and I don't think he got in until a couple of days ago.'

'You'll have to tell me what he's like.' There was something new in his voice, but she didn't recognise it.

'Probably an asshole, I suspect. Anyone that good-looking has to be spoiled rotten.'

'Maybe not. He may be a very nice man.'

'Just so he does a decent job with the movie, that's really all I care about.' It was a story about a modern-day man who was part Apache, what it meant

223

to him, and the responsibilities and problems and joys it carried through his entire lifetime, as he turned his back on what he was and then eventually embraced it. It was a story about manhood and self-acceptance, independent of racial themes. It was a powerful story, and it surprised everyone that a woman had written it. But if Justin Wakefield did it right, it could win him an Academy Award, and Daphne suspected he knew it. He was a spectacular blond hero, idolised by almost every woman in the country, and he would bring something to it that should make *Apache* a sure hit. 'At least we know he can act.'

'If you have a minute, call and tell me how it's going.'

'I will, and I want to know how Andrew is, no matter how busy I am. I should have a number at the studio where you can reach me. I'll call you as soon as I know what it is.' Eventually they would go on location in Wyoming, but that wouldn't be for several months. First they would shoot the local scenes.

'I'll call you later too, when Andrew gets in.'

'Thanks, Matt.' As usual, he had brought her comfort, and she felt less distraught at the departure of her son. 'Matt?'

'Yeah?'

'Who does this for you?'

'What?' He didn't understand.

'Comfort you. You're always there for me, it's not really fair.' He was the only person she had leaned on in years, and sometimes she felt guilty.

'You pay a price for the people you love in life, Daff. I don't need to tell you that.' She nodded silently at her end. He was right. And she had. 'I'll call you later.'

'Thanks.' They hung up then and she wondered what she had done before there had been Matthew.

26

The making of the movie *Apache* began on an indoor set on Sound Stage A of Comstock Studios at five fifteen on a Tuesday morning. It should have started on Monday but didn't because the female lead, Maureen Adams, had the flu. According to the production manager's computations, the delay cost the studio several thousand dollars, but that was calculated into the budget, and it gave Justin Wakefield an extra day he needed to study the script and confer with the director, in this case Howard Stern, an old Hollywood pro, given to cigars and cowboy boots and fits of bellowing at his actors, but also a genius recognised by his peers, and known for making brilliant films. Daphne had been immensely pleased to learn that he was the director.

Daphne got up at three thirty that morning, showered, dressed, made scrambled eggs for herself and Barbara, and was ready to leave the house at quarter to five. The limousine was waiting, and they arrived on the set at exactly the appointed hour to find most of the crew gathered there, and the director already smoking cigars and eating donuts with the cameramen. Maureen Adams was having her makeup done. Justin Wakefield was nowhere to be seen. Daphne said good morning to the studio men who had shown up just to make sure that everything was going smoothly and was introduced to the director, who stuffed his donut in his shirt pocket and looked at her piercingly for a moment before holding out his hand with a broad grin.

'Awful little, aren't you? But good-looking, damn good-looking.' And then he bent towards her, whispering to her with a smile, 'You ought to be in the movie.'

'Oh, God, no!' She held up a hand in protest, laughing. He was an amazing-looking man, well into his sixties with a face full of lines, hard won, hard earned, and somehow his face looked better for them. He wasn't a handsome man, and had been even less so in his early years, but Daphne instantly liked him. And she sensed that he liked her.

'Excited about your first film, Miss Fields?' He waved towards two chairs and they sat down together, his enormous frame filling his chair, and hers looking almost childlike as she looked at him and smiled again.

'Yes, very excited, Mr Stern.'

'So am I. I liked your book. In fact, I liked it a great deal. It's going to make one hell of a movie. And I like your script.' And then with a noncommittal look, 'Justin Wakefield does too. Have you met him before?' He eyed Daphne, thinking his own thoughts.

'No, I haven't met him yet.'

He nodded slowly. 'Interesting man. Intelligent, for an actor. But don't forget that's what he is.' He looked her over appraisingly. 'They're all the same. I know from years of working with them. There's a piece missing from them all, and something extra added, something childlike and free and wonderful. They're hard to resist. But they're selfish and spoiled and egocentric. They don't give a damn how you are, most of them, they only care how they are. It'll shock you when you first see it, but if you watch them closely, you'll see a similarity of character. After a while it's all very clear. There are exceptions of course' – he named a few, names she had heard of and seen on the screen – 'but they're rare. The rest are ...' He hesitated and smiled, as though he knew a secret she did not, but would learn soon. 'Well ... they're actors. Remember that, Miss Fields, it will help you to keep your sanity in the next months. They'll drive you crazy, and me too. But in the end we'll have a remarkable picture, and it will all be worthwhile, we'll all hold hands and cry and kiss good-bye. And the fights will be forgotten, the jealousies, the feuds. We'll

226

remember the jokes, the laughs, the extraordinary moments. There's a kind of magic to all this ... ' He waved an arm, taking in the entire stage with a majestic sweep. And then he stood up, and bowed, and his eyes laughed into hers, and off he went to confer with his cameramen again. Daphne felt more than a little in awe of him and the entire scene, and she sat watching silently as grips and extras and wardrobe people and sound men and lighting engineers came and went, performing mysterious tasks, until at last at seven thirty there was a sudden stir, a heightened sense of tension all around them, and she correctly sensed that they were about to begin.

Almost at the very moment that the flurry of activity seemed greatest, she noticed a man leave a dressing room in a T-shirt and a parka, sneakers and no socks, his thick blond hair falling across his forehead in a boyish way. He sauntered towards her looking tentative and shy, and then eventually sat down in the chair Howard Stern had sat in long before. He glanced at Daphne, at the set, and then back to her, looking taut and nervous, and she smiled at him, knowing just how he felt and wondering who he was.

'Exciting, isn't it?' It was the only thing she could think of to say and he looked amused as she gazed into deep sea-green eyes. There was something familiar about him and she wasn't sure what.

'Yeah, I guess it is. I always get sick to my stomach just before we start. Occupational hazard, I guess.' He shrugged and reached into his pocket for a piece of candy, popped it into his mouth, and then with a look of embarrassment for being rude, dug into his pocket again and held one out to her.

'Thank you.' Their eyes met again and she felt a blush creep into her cheeks at his appraising glance.

'Are you an extra in this one?'

'No.' She shook her head, not quite sure what to say. She didn't want to tell him she wrote it, it sounded so pompous, and he didn't pry. He seemed too busy

227

watching the preparations on the set, and then nervously he got up and walked away.

When he reappeared, he looked down at her with a boyish smile. 'Can I get you something to drink?' She was touched. Barbara had disappeared twenty minutes before in search of two cups of coffee. They had momentarily run out on the set, and she felt useless standing there. But now Daphne nodded.

'Sure. Thanks. I'd give my right arm for a cup of coffee.' The set was cool and draughty and she was tired.

'I'll bring you one. Cream and sugar?' She nodded and he reappeared a moment later carrying two large steaming mugs. Nothing had ever looked so good. She took hers and sipped it slowly, wondering when they would begin, and when she glanced at her benefactor he was looking at her again with those startling green eyes. 'You're beautiful, do you know that?' She blushed again and he smiled. 'And shy. I love women like that.' And then he rolled his eyes and laughed at himself. 'That's a dumb thing to say, it sounds like I audition them by the hundred every day.'

'Doesn't everyone here?' They both laughed this time and he seemed intrigued by her. He could see in her eyes that she was bright and quick, not the kind of woman you could fool, or would want to. He liked her and wondered again who she was.

'No, not everyone here does that. There are still some decent people in this town, even in this business ... maybe.' He smiled, sipped his hot coffee, and then set the mug down. 'I'm curious about you, miss. What are you doing on this set?'

It was time to tell the truth. 'I wrote the screenplay, but this is the first one I've done. So it's all new to me.'

At that he looked even more intrigued. 'Then you're Daphne Fields.' He seemed impressed. 'I've read all your books, and like this one best of all.'

'Thank you.' She looked pleased. 'And now I get to

ask the same question. What are you doing here?' But at that he threw back his head and laughed, a wondrous golden sound, and then he looked at her again, and with one hand swept the blond mane back from his face and smiled and suddenly she knew and she was stunned. He was every bit as beautiful as he had been in all his films, but he looked so different here, so out of place, so unassuming in his old parka and worn jeans. 'Oh, my God . . .'

'No, not quite.' They both laughed then. He knew she knew. He was Justin Wakefield. He held out a hand to shake hers, and as their hands met, their eyes held, there was a kind of magic to the man, a childlike glee, a magnetism in his eyes that held one spellbound for a moment before letting go. 'I am performing in your movie, madam. And I hope very much that you'll be pleased with my performance.'

'I'm sure I will.' She smiled at him now. 'I was so happy when you took the part.'

'So was I,' he admitted frankly. 'It's the best damn part I've had in years.' She beamed. 'You write like a demon.'

'You're not half bad yourself.' Her eyes said that she was teasing him, and a little voice inside her whispered that she was playing with America's favourite movie idol. It was a heady feeling sitting here beside him. And for some reason she couldn't explain, for the first time in a long time she felt like a woman, not a work horse or just a writer, or even Andrew's mother. But a woman. She had caught his attention, she sensed it in the way he talked to her. But it had been so long since she had related to a man, except to discuss Andrew with Matthew, that she wasn't sure what to say. Feeling nervous, she fell back on her work. It made her feel safe. And she didn't feel entirely safe with this man. He was watching her too closely and she was afraid she'd say too much. Maybe he would see the loneliness she always camouflaged so well, or the aching void left in her soul when John died.

'What do you think of the script?'

'I like it, very much in fact. Howard and I had a meeting about it yesterday. There's only one scene so far that doesn't work for me.'

'Which one?' She looked suddenly worried but his eyes were kind as he reached into her chair and took the copy of the script that Barbara had left there.

'Not to worry. It's a small scene.' He flipped the pages, and obviously knew the script well, and pointed to the part he hadn't liked. She glanced at it, nodded, and was frowning when she looked up at him again.

'You may be right. I wasn't sure about that myself.'

'Well, let's wait and see what Howard says. We're both going to be making a lot of changes and adjustments before we're through. Have you ever seen him work?' She shook her head and he laughed. 'You're in for a treat. And don't let the old bastard scare you. He has a heart of gold' – he smiled impishly at her – 'and a mouth full of nails. You'll get used to it after a while. We all do. And it's worth it, the man is an absolute genius. You'll learn something from him. I've worked with him twice before, and each time he gave me something different. You're lucky that he's directing *Apache*. We all are.' And then, his eyes seeming to caress her face, he whispered to her, 'But we're even luckier to have you.' And with a smile that seemed almost a kiss, he left her then, to go into his dressing room to change, and at that moment Barbara reappeared.

'I can't find any goddamn coffee.'

'Never mind. Someone else got me some.' But Daphne still looked vague. Justin Wakefield was the most extraordinary man, and she wasn't sure if she liked him or not. He was obviously bright, extremely playful, handsome as hell, amusing at times, but she found it impossible to decide if he was real. How could anyone that beautiful be real?

'You look like you've just seen a vision.'

'I think I have. I've been talking to Justin Wakefield.'

'What's he like?' Barbara sat down in the empty chair, trying not to look impressed, but she was. She had been dying to meet him and hadn't as yet noticed him on the set. 'Is he as gorgeous as he looks on the screen?'

Daphne laughed. 'I'm not sure. He's awfully handsome, but I didn't even recognise him when he sat down next to me.'

'How come?'

'He just looked like some kid. I guess I was expecting something different.' Daphne smiled at her secretary and friend.

'Are you telling me I'm going to be disappointed?' She looked crushed.

'I wouldn't say that.' Hardly, with those looks. And as she sat lost in her own thoughts about him she saw him emerge from his dressing room in the soft caramel-coloured skintight suede pants the early moments of the movie demanded, with a white turtleneck sweater, and he looked like a young, blond Marlon Brando, and Daphne heard Barbara catch her breath.

'Oh, my God, he's gorgeous!' Barbara whispered and Daphne smiled as she looked at him. He certainly was in that outfit. He was breathtaking as his muscles rippled while he walked towards them, his hair was smoothed back now as Daphne had seen it before in movies, and he looked like Justin Wakefield, the actor, not the impish boy who had offered her a mug of coffee on the set.

He walked straight towards Daphne and stopped beside her chair with a warm smile. 'Hello, Daphne.' His mouth seemed to caress her name.

'Hello.' Daphne smiled, trying to look more composed than she felt. 'I'd like you to meet my assistant, Barbara Jarvis. Barbara, this is Justin Wakefield.' He shook Barbara's hand with a warm smile, and then turned and saluted Daphne before going off to join Howard Stern and begin shooting, as Barbara sat gaping at him and Daphne leaned towards her with a grin. 'Close your mouth, Barb. You're drooling.'

'Jesus Christ. He's unbelievable looking.' She couldn't stop staring at him, and Daphne first looked at him and then at Barbara's reaction. He certainly had an effect on women. That much she was sure of, and she had to admit that she was feeling it herself. It was hard not to.

'Yes, he is. But there's more to life than being pretty.' She sounded very old and wise and Barbara laughed at her.

'Oh, yeah. Like what?'

'Like Tom Harrington, or do I need to remind you?' Barbara blushed as she grinned.

'All right, all right.'

'How's that going, by the way?'

Barbara sighed and looked dreamy for a moment. 'He's the most wonderful man, Daff. I love him, and I love his children.' But there seemed to be more she wasn't saying.

'So? What's the problem?'

'There is none.' Barbara smiled at her. 'I've never been happier in my life, except when I remind myself that one of these days we'll be going back to New York.'

'Not for a while, so enjoy it while you have it. Don't spoil your fun by worrying about six months from now, for heaven's sake. Things like this don't happen every day.' She smiled at her gently. For Barbara it had never happened before. At forty, she was deeply in love with the right man for the first time in her life.

'That's what Tom said right from the beginning. Something like this only happens once in a lifetime, so we'd better grab it while we've got it.'

Daphne looked distant and sad for a moment. 'Jeff said that to me once, right after we first met...' Her mind drifted off as she thought about her husband and then she looked back at Barbara. 'He was right. Other things come your way, and each moment, each experience, is different. Each one only happens once. And if you let the moment pass you by, it's gone forever.' She had almost let that happen with John, and had always been grateful that she hadn't. And then she forced her mind from the past back to the present. 'Even this, Barb. Even this crazy movie we're making. There will never be a first movie for me again, there will never be another first time in California for you ... we might as well enjoy it, because it's all pretty damn special. You never know what's just around the corner, or who.' And for some reason she looked at Justin Wakefield as she said it, and he turned as though he felt her eyes on him. He stopped what he was doing and looked straight at her, and she felt an almost involuntary reaction run up her spine. His gaze bored into hers and she felt herself held by his magnetic gaze.

The making of the movie began at nine fifteen, and by noon the first scene had been shot twice. Howard Stern had roared at the grips and called Justin a flaming asshole, Maureen Adams had burst into tears and insisted she was still sick, and the studio men had disappeared as Daphne and Barbara watched the whole production in fascination. The hairdresser assured them that all of this was normal, and when lunchtime was called, everyone seemed to be friends again. Howard Stern put an arm around Justin, told him he was pleased, and pinched Maureen Adams's behind as she walked past. She didn't seem to mind. She blew Howard a kiss and handed a tightly rolled joint to Justin before going to her dressing room to lie down. Daphne was standing alone by then. Barbara had gone to call Tom.

'Well, what do you think about your first morning?' Justin came directly towards her and stood in his full, extravagant beauty just before her in his tight suede pants. She tried not to let herself be overwhelmed by the attraction she felt for him.

'I am beginning to strongly suspect that you're all crazy.' She grinned at him, trying to look aloof but not succeeding. There was something so damnably beautiful about the man.

233

'I could have told you that much before. How did you like the scene?'

'It looked fine to me the first time.' She was sincere as she said it. It had looked fine to her.

'It wasn't. Howard was right. I had to get angry and I wasn't. We're going to try it again at the end of the day and we're going to start off this afternoon with the scene with Maureen in her apartment.' It was a nude scene for both of them and Daphne looked startled even though she had written it. But it came much later in the film and seemed as though it would be difficult to do right after the opening scene, totally out of context. 'Don't look so shocked, kid. You wrote it.' He seemed amused.

'I know. But how does that work out of context?'

'The whole shoot is out of context. We just do it scene by scene, according to some masterful and insane plan in Howard's head, and then later they cut it all up like spaghetti and splice it all together and somehow it works. It's a crazy business.' But it didn't seem to bother him much. And he looked as though he was more interested in Daphne than his work.

'You did a hell of a good job, you know, Daff.'

His eyes caressed her again.

'Thank you.'

'Can I interest you in some rotten commissary lunch?'

She started to tell him that she was going to have lunch with her assistant and then she realised that Barbara would probably die to sit near Justin Wakefield for an entire meal.

'Yes, if I can bring my assistant.'

'Sure. I'll go change my clothes. I'll be back in a minute.' He disappeared into his dressing room, still carrying the joint Maureen had given him and she felt herself wondering if he was going to smoke it now or later, as Barbara returned from calling Tom.

'I just made us a lunch date.' Daphne looked as though she had mischief up her sleeve.

'With whom?'

'With Justin. All right with you?'

Barbara gasped and Daphne laughed out loud. 'Are you kidding?'

'Nope.' And just as she said the word Justin strode out of his dressing room, dressed in his blue jeans and sneakers. He was still wearing makeup and had his hair combed back. This time Daphne would have recognised him, unlike their first meeting that morning, and he looked almost as handsome as he had in the white sweater and suede pants.

'Ready, ladies?' Daphne nodded and Barbara simply stared and they followed him to the enormous commissary building, where they found themselves with cowboys and Indians, two southern belles and a whole army of German soldiers, as well as two midgets and a flock of little boys.

Barbara looked around and started laughing. 'You know what? This looks like the circus!' And suddenly Justin and Daphne were laughing too. They ate hamburgers that tasted like rocks and the ketchup looked like red paint, and then Justin brought them both apple pie and coffee. And it seemed only moments later when they were back on the set, and Justin had disappeared into his dressing room.

Barbara pulled up a chair beside Daphne, and as they waited for the action to begin, Barbara found herself thinking about Justin. It was easy to discern that he was attracted to Daphne, but despite his good looks, Barbara didn't think she liked him. There was something childlike and self-centred about the man, and she had noticed that every time they passed a mirror or window in which he could see himself, he ran a hand over his hair, or looked himself in the eye. It annoyed her, but she also had the unmistakable feeling that Daphne liked him.

Before she could say anything to Daphne, Justin had emerged from his dressing room in a long white terry cloth hooded bathrobe and Swedish clogs. There was something beautiful and mysterious about him, and

235

almost monklike beneath the white terry cloth hood, which he slipped off his head with a toss of the blond mane and a smile. And then a moment later he shed the terry cloth robe entirely and strode on to the set wearing nothing but his lean, long, beautifully muscled flesh and limbs. Maureen Adams followed him on to the set a moment later, and dropped a pink satin bathrobe on the edge of the set, walking around, holding the script, and running a hand through her hair. But it wasn't Maureen who held everyone's attention. It was Justin. Aside from his obvious physical beauty there was an incredible electricity and excitement about the man. Daphne tried not to look impressed, but it was so long since she had seen a man naked that she found herself spellbound by his raw beauty and the long athletic-looking limbs. 'I hate to say it,' Barbara confessed at last, 'but he really is absolutely incredible looking.' But when she glanced at her employer, Daphne hadn't heard her. She was staring at Justin in a way that made Barbara nervous. But who could blame her? He simply was what he was. Justin Wakefield, king of the screen.

The scene as he played it was spellbinding, and after a time both Barbara and Daphne forgot that he was naked. Daphne sat riveted as she watched the scene she had written come to life. He twisted it and moved it and wove it around him like a rich brocade cloth, covering his nakedness with his genius, and several times he even brought tears to her eyes. The scene was spellbinding for everyone who watched. The man was not only beautiful, he was masterful with his craft. And then, as deftly as he had shed it, he picked up the white terry cloth robe and put it around him again, covering his head with the hood and slowly turning towards Daphne. He looked older than he had at lunch, and very tired, and very open, and his wide green eyes found her as though he had to know what she thought more than any other.

'I loved it. It was exactly what I meant when I wrote it, only more so. It was as though you took what I had in mind and you went deeper and farther.' He looked enormously pleased that she was so impressed.

'That's what I am supposed to do, Daphne.' He sounded kind and wise, and she liked what she saw in his eyes now. 'That's what acting is all about.' She nodded, still impressed with his performance. He had actually brought her book to life.

'Thank you.' It was going to be a sensational movie. And he was a sensational man. And she felt something tingle deep within her just from the thrill of having watched him.

27

For the next week Daphne watched Justin Wakefield in total fascination, spinning his web of magic around them. She and Barbara ate lunch with him every day in the commissary, and once or twice some of the others joined them, but it was rapidly becoming obvious that Justin Wakefield wanted to get close to Daphne. They talked about her books and his movies, her deeper intentions for some of the characters, her philosophies about the plot. They talked a great deal about *Apache*, and he insisted that what she told him helped him each day on the set, that it was she who made the difference, who brought something out of him that he didn't know was there before.

'It really is you, Daff.' They were sitting on the set and sharing a can of strawberry soda, a disgusting concoction they agreed, but the only thing the machine still had in it, and they were both dying of thirst. It was a hot day and they had already spent long hours on the set. 'I couldn't do this without you here. It's my best performance. Ask Howard, he'll tell you. I've never been able to dredge up this much before, not day after day like this.' He looked at her then with those intense huge green eyes of his. 'I mean it. You do something wonderful to me, Daphne.' She wasn't quite sure what to say.

'You're doing something wonderful to my book.'

'Is that all?' He looked disappointed, as though he had wanted her to say something more. But he didn't know Daphne, how cautious she was, how high the walls were built around her. And then he surprised her. 'Tell me something about your little boy.' It was as though he sensed that in talking about her son, perhaps she would let some of her guard down. And he wasn't wrong. She smiled, and thought of Andrew, so damnably far away.

'He's wonderful, and bright, and very special. He's about this tall' – she held up a hand to indicate his height and Justin smiled – 'and I took him to Disneyland a few weeks ago when he was here.'

'Where is he the rest of the time? With his dad?' He thought it unusual for a woman like Daphne to give up custody of her son, and his voice showed his surprise.

'No. His dad died before he was born.' It was easier to say that these days. 'He's in New Hampshire, in school.'

Justin nodded as though that made sense, and then he looked into Daphne's eyes again. 'You were alone when he was born?'

'Yes.' Something pulled at her gut as she said it, a lonely memory she had fled long ago.

'That must have been rough on you.'

'It was, and . . .' She didn't really want to tell him, about discovering that Andrew was deaf, and those ghastly lonely years. 'That was a pretty tough time.'

'Were you writing then?' It was the first time Justin had asked her questions about herself. They had talked about *Apache* and her other books, and his movies, all week.

'No, I didn't start writing until later. Until Andrew went away to school.'

'Yeah. I'll bet it's tough to be creative with kids around. You were smart to send him away to school.' Something pulled taut in her gut as he said that. He couldn't possibly know what she felt for the child or what it had been like to tear herself away from Andrew. And his comment reflected a selfishness that she abhorred.

'I sent him away to school because I had to.'

'Because you were alone?'

'For other reasons.' Something told her not to share the reasons with him. She still had a deep need to protect

239

Andrew. And she suddenly had the sense that Justin wouldn't understand. Maybe he wouldn't even try to, and she didn't want to find that out. 'I had no choice.' She suddenly felt very tired and old. What did this man know about that kind of heartbreak? 'You don't have children, Justin?'

'No. I never felt the need for that kind of extension of myself. I think that's an ego trip for most people.'

'Children?' She looked shocked.

'Yes, don't look so shocked. Most people want to see themselves reproduced and continued. I have my movies for that. I don't need to make kids.' It was an odd way to look at it, she thought, but maybe for him it made sense. She tried to understand his viewpoint. He wasn't an insensitive man, after all. He couldn't be, not the way he'd been living out *Apache* for the last week. And if he had different views from hers, she would listen. She at least owed him that.

'Have you ever been married?' She was curious about him now. Who was he? What made him the way he was, so able to interpret someone else's feelings, as he had hers in her book?

He shook his head. 'Not legally, at least. I've lived with two women. One for seven years, one for five. In a way, that was really no different from being married. We just didn't have the papers. It doesn't make much difference in the end. When someone wants out, they go, papers or no, and I wound up supporting them both after they left.' She nodded. After all, that was what she had had with John. But she suspected that eventually they would have got married. They might even have had children, although John had had no great need for children either. He had just wanted her. And Andrew, of course.

'Are you living with someone now?' She felt rude for probing, but they already knew so much about each other now. They had almost lived together, fifteen hours a day for the past week. It began to feel like being on a desert island or a ship, thrown together in an intimate way.

But again Justin shook his head. 'I haven't lived with anyone for a while. I've been involved with someone on and off for the past year, but it's mostly off, she doesn't understand the rigours of this business, and God knows she should. She's an actress, but she's a twenty-two-year-old kid from Ohio, and she just doesn't understand where I'm at.'

'And where's that? Or am I prying?' Daphne's voice was cautious but he smiled, he didn't mind the questions, he liked them. He liked her, and he wanted her to know what he was about.

'You're not prying, Daff. By the time we finish this movie, we'll all know each other inside out.' He hesitated for a moment, thinking of her question. 'I don't know how to explain it to you, but I just don't want to tie myself down anymore to someone who doesn't understand this business. It's exhausting having to defend yourself all the time. She's insanely jealous, and I can't answer to anyone night and day. I need space. I need time to think about what I'm doing, where I'm going, what I am and think and feel. I'm better off alone than with someone who stifles that.' It was easy to agree with what he was saying and Daphne nodded, and then he laughed and shook his head. 'Loosely translated, I think that means "she doesn't understand me." You've heard that before?'

'Yup.' She took a drag on their shared soda and laughed. 'I have. I think that may be why I stay alone too. It would be damn hard to explain to anyone why I work eighteen hours a day, then crawl into bed at six in the morning feeling like I've been beaten. It gives me sustenance, but it's not likely it would do the same for someone else. I wouldn't have it any other way. Yet no sane man would put up with that.'

'I doubt it.' He smiled, feeling a certain kinship with her. 'Except someone with the same habits. Sometimes

241

I read all night, until the sun comes up. It's a great feeling.'

'Yes, it is.' She smiled too. 'I love that. You know, maybe one gets to a point in life when it's better to be alone. I didn't used to think that, but I do now. It works for me anyway.' She handed him the soda and he finished it and set it down.

'I don't think I agree with that. I don't want to be alone forever, but I don't want to be with the wrong person. I think I've finally gotten to the point where I'd rather be alone than with the wrong woman. Yet I still believe, must believe, that there's someone out there who would meet my needs and make me happy. I just haven't found her yet.'

Daphne saluted him with the empty can. 'Good luck.'

'You think it's impossible to find?' He was surprised. Certainly her writing didn't suggest that. She seemed to believe in love and happy unions. Yet she had a clear understanding of unhappiness and loss.

'I don't think it's impossible, Justin. I found it twice.'

'And? What happened?'

'They both died.'

'That's a bitch.' He looked sympathetic.

'Yes, it is. And I don't think you get more than two chances like that.'

'So you've given up?'

They were in the mood to be honest, so she was. 'More or less. I've had everything I wanted, now I have my work and my son. That's enough.'

'Is it really?'

'It is for me. For now. It has been for a long time. And I have no desire to change it.' That was not entirely the truth. There were times when she longed for someone to hold her, but she was too desperately afraid of an eventual loss.

'I don't believe you.' He was searching her eyes but not finding the answers he wanted.

'What don't you believe?'

'That you're happy like that.'

'I am. Most of the time. No one is happy all the time, not even if you're madly in love.'

'You can't be happy alone forever, Daff. It's not healthy. You lose touch with life.'

'Have I? Is that what you read in my books?'

'I read a lot of sorrow in those books, a lot of sadness, a lot of loneliness. Some part of you is crying out.'

She laughed softly then. 'You sound just like a man, Justin, unable to believe that a woman can survive alone. You told me that you're happy by yourself, why shouldn't I be?'

'For me, it's temporary.' He was being honest.

'For me, it's not.'

'You're crazy.' The whole idea annoyed him. She was a beautiful, vibrant, intelligent woman. What the hell was she doing, determined to be alone for the rest of her life? 'The whole thing is nuts.' And it was also a challenge. He couldn't stand thinking of what she had done to her life.

'Don't let it upset you. I'm perfectly happy.'

'It just pisses me off to think of you wasting your life. You're beautiful, dammit, Daphne, and warm and loving, and you have a brilliant mind. Why have you shut yourself off?'

'I'm sorry I told you.' But she didn't look particularly upset and she wasn't. She had accepted her life. And she was relatively happy.

And with that, Howard Stern called them all back to the set for another six hours of work, and when they left the set that day, Justin had to meet a friend for a drink, and Daphne left with Barbara without seeing him again. They went back to the house, and Daphne took a shower and then went out to swim in the pool in the balmy night air, and Barbara came out to tell her that she was going to see Tom.

'And I might be home later and I might not.'

243

'Good for you.' Daphne smiled as she floated in the pool. 'Say hi to Tom for me.'

'I will. And don't forget to eat dinner, you look bushed.'

'I am. But I'll grab something to eat before I go to bed.' And she wanted to call Matthew that night before it got too late. With their strange hours on the set and the time difference between California and New Hampshire, it was getting harder and harder to call. 'Have a good time, Barb!'

'Thanks, I will!' She called it over her shoulder as she left, and Daphne floated in the pool for a while before wrapping herself in a towel, and wandering into the kitchen to take something out of the refrigerator before she made her call. She dropped the towel on the counter after a minute, and stood in a tiny red bikini, dripping water on the kitchen floor. And just as she reached for the phone to call Matthew she heard the front doorbell ring, and wondered who it was. She wondered if Barbara had come back for something and had forgotten her key.

Daphne walked out to the front hallway, and tried to glimpse through a side window to see who it was. But whoever it was had his back turned and was standing too close to the front door for her to see him. She could only see part of one shoulder, so she stood at the front door and asked who it was.

'It's me. Justin. Can I come in?'

She opened the door in surprise and stood there looking at him. He was wearing white Levi jeans and a white shirt and sandals, and his golden tan looked darker at night as he stood there looking boyish as he smiled. 'Hi. How did you find me?'

'The studio gave me your address, is that okay?'

'What's up?' She never heard from him after hours and she was more than a little surprised. She was also tired and hungry and wet, and these were her off-hours, and she felt the need to have some solitude.

'Can I come in?'

'Sure. Do you want something to drink? Wait a sec, I'll go put something on.' She was suddenly conscious of wearing only the red bikini and it made her uncomfortable in front of him.

'You don't have to, you know. You've seen me in less.' He grinned at her boyishly and she laughed.

'That was different. That was business. This isn't.'

'Some business we're in, where you take all your clothes off to go to work.'

'I can think of others like it.'

He liked her sense of humour. 'Are you suggesting that acting is like prostitution?'

'Sometimes.' She said it over her shoulder as she disappeared into her bedroom and he resisted an urge to follow her.

'You happen to be right.'

When she returned she was wearing a bright blue caftan the same colour as her eyes, and she had combed her hair and put on sandals. He looked at her approvingly and nodded.

'You look lovely, Daff.'

'Thanks. Now what can I do for you? I'm pooped. I was about to eat dinner and go to bed.'

'That's what I figured and it sounds deadly. I was on my way to a party and thought you might want to join me. At Tony Tree's. You might like it.' Tony Tree had won five Grammies in five years, and he was easily the biggest singer in the country. Any other time she might have been intrigued enough to meet him, but not tonight.

'Sounds like fun, but honest, I just can't.'

'Why not?'

'Because I'm exhausted. Christ, you worked your ass off all day today. Aren't you tired?'

'No. I love my work, so I don't get tired.'

'I love my work too but it still knocks me out.' She smiled at him then, not wanting to sound harsh. 'I'd fall asleep on my feet.'

'That's okay. They'd just think you were stoned.

245

You'd fit right in.' She laughed at his quick answer and resisted an impulse to rumple his perfectly combed blond hair.

'Don't be stubborn. I'm pooped. You want a sandwich before you go? I'm going to make one for myself. I don't have any strawberry soda, but I might be able to find you a beer.'

'That sounds good. Where's Barbara?'

'Out with friends.' She handed him a beer from the icebox, and started to make herself a sandwich. Justin hopped up on a stool in the kitchen and watched her. He could see her naked silhouette through the caftan and he liked what he saw. He had liked the bikini better, but this would have to do.

'You mean Barbara actually goes out?'

'Yes. Believe it or not, she's human too.' The two had decided several days before that they didn't like each other. Barbara thought that underneath the charm he was a heartless bastard, and Justin thought she was an aging vestal virgin. 'You're like an old schoolmarm,' he had finally told her after she'd planted herself once too often between himself and Daphne. She sensed how vulnerable Daphne was to his charm, though Daphne denied it. Barbara saw something ugly in him, which Daphne did not.

'Does Barbara have a boyfriend?' Justin pretended surprise, speaking in the same bantering tone he always used with her now.

'Yes, a very nice one in fact.' She hopped up on a stool across the counter from him. Maybe it wasn't so bad that he had dropped by after all. It was pleasant to have company while she ate her sandwich, even though it meant that by the time he left, it would be too late to give Matthew a call. 'Her friend is an attorney.'

'That figures. Probably tax law.'

'Film law, I think.'

'Oh, Jesus. He probably wears a business suit and gold chains.'

'Come on, Justin. Be nice.'

'Why? I think she's an uptight bitch. I don't like her.'

'She's a wonderful woman and you don't know her.'

'I don't want to.'

'It's entirely mutual, which is no secret. And I think you're both behaving like children.'

'She hates me.' He sounded plaintive and Daphne smiled.

'She doesn't hate you. She disapproves of you, and she doesn't really know you. She was very badly hurt a long time ago and it made her suspicious of men.'

'You can say that again.' He had sensed her distrust of him, and it annoyed him. 'I can't offer her a cup of coffee without her getting on my back.' Daphne knew all about it, and she had already told Barbara to cool it. They didn't need feuds on the set. 'Anyway, I'm glad you're alone. She protects you like the Vatican Guard whenever I'm around.'

'She's possessive, that's all. We've been through a lot together.'

'She acts like she thinks she's your mother.'

Daphne smiled. 'Sometimes I could use one.' She had had so much on her shoulders, alone, for such a long time, and Barbara was the only person in aeons that had eased at least some of the burdens.

As she spoke he slid off the stool and came around the counter. He stood in front of her and took her face in his hands. 'Daphne. You're a beautiful, desirable woman and I want you.' She felt a wave of shock run through her and at the same time a long forgotten hunger between her legs.

'Justin, don't be foolish.' Her voice was soft and scared.

'I'm not foolish.' He looked hurt. 'I've fallen for you like a ton of bricks, and you're playing this stupid game, hiding behind your walls. Why? Why won't you let me love you, Daff?' His eyes almost misted over and hers were huge in her face.

247

'Justin, please ... we have to work together ... it would be a terrible mistake to – '

'To what? To fall in love? Is that what you're afraid of? Why? We're two strong, intelligent, talented people. I can't think of a better combination. I've never met anyone like you, and you've probably never known anyone like me. Why would you pass that up? Who's keeping track of how hard you are on yourself? In the end you'll wake up one day an old woman and it'll be all over, and you can tell yourself that you've been faithful to the memory of two dead men. Why, Daphne ... why?' And then he leaned towards her and kissed her, covering her mouth with his own and forcing her lips open with his tongue until he probed inside her and she felt her breath quicken as he folded her in his arms. And then breathlessly she pulled away and stood up. She was tiny beside him, but she looked at him with imploring eyes.

'Justin, please ... don't ...'

'I want you, Daff. And I'm not going to let you run away from this. I can't believe you don't feel anything for me. We understand each other too well. I understand every word you ever wrote, and I can see from the way you watch me work that you feel my work in your gut too.'

'What difference does that make?' She was still half angry, half frightened. He had shown up on her doorstep, kissed her, and now was trying to turn her life upside down. She wouldn't let him. It was dangerous. They were making a movie together, that was all. She didn't want to let her guard down. 'What do you want out of me for chrissake? A quick lay? An affair for six months? There are ten million starlets in this town, Justin. Go fuck one.' Her eyes filled with tears and she turned away. 'And leave me the hell alone.'

'Is that what you want?'

She nodded, her back still turned.

'All right. But think over what I said. I don't just want a quick piece of ass, Daff. I can get that anytime I want, anywhere I want. But I can't have another woman like

248

you. There is no one else like you. I know. I've looked around.'

She turned to face him then. 'Then keep looking. You'll find one.'

'No, I won't.' His eyes looked sad. He had finally found what he wanted, but she didn't want him. It wasn't fair, and he wanted her right there in her kitchen, but he wouldn't push her. He knew that that way he'd lose her forever. Maybe if he waited, there was a chance. 'I want you to think over what I've said to you tonight, Daphne. We'll talk about it again.'

'No, we won't.' She walked towards the front door with long strides and pulled it open for him. 'Good night, Justin. I'll see you tomorrow on the set and I don't want to discuss this. Ever. Is that clear?''

'You don't make all the rules, Daphne. Not for me.' His eyes blazed at her for an instant and then the boyish twinkle shone through the anger.

Daphne was not going to be swayed. 'I make my own rules. And you can either respect them or stay away from me. Because I won't deal with you at all if you won't respect how I feel.'

'What you feel is all wrong.'

'You can't tell me that. I've made my own choices in life, and I live by them. I made up my mind a long time ago.'

'And you were wrong.' He brushed her lips again with his then and he left, and as she shut the door behind him she leaned against it, her whole body trembling. And the most terrifying thing of all was that she believed in what she had told him, had for years, and yet her body had cried out for him each time he kissed her. But she didn't want to hurt again and love again and lose again. She wouldn't do it, no matter what he told her. But as she walked back into the kitchen she looked at where they had been sitting, and she felt her whole body begin to tremble again at the memory of his kiss, and with a moan of anguish she took his empty beer bottle and threw it against the wall.

28

'How was the party last night?' Daphne tried to look casual as they sat at the empty table at the commissary. Everyone else had finished early and gone back to the set and they were suddenly left alone. But Justin's eyes looked haunted as they met hers.

'I didn't go.'

'Oh. That's too bad.' She tried to change the subject. 'I thought the scene went pretty well today.'

'I didn't.' He pushed away his plate and looked at her. 'I couldn't think straight. You drove me nuts last night.' She didn't tell him that she had also lain awake half the night, fighting what she was feeling, and wondering if he would call. She had insanely mixed emotions about him, and it was the vehemence of them that upset her most. She didn't want to feel any of what she was feeling. She had never wanted to feel any of it ever again. 'How can you do this to us?' He looked like a small boy robbed of Christmas, but she put down her sandwich and glared at him.

'I'm not doing anything to "us," Justin. There is no "us," for chrissake. Don't create something that will only make life more complicated for both of us in the end.'

'What the hell are you talking about? What's so complicated? You're available, I'm searching. So what's your problem, lady? I'll tell you what it is.' He was speaking to her in a hoarse whisper and she hoped that no one overheard, but there was plenty of activity around them, and no one seemed to be watching, much to her relief. 'Your problem is that you're too fucking scared to let yourself feel again. You've got no balls left. You must have had them once, because I can see it in your books. But now suddenly you don't have the courage to come out from behind your walls and be a woman. And you know what? It's going to show up in your writing sooner or later if you don't watch out. You can't lead the life you do and expect to remain human. You won't. Maybe you already aren't. Maybe I'm just in love with an illusion ... a fiction ... a dream ...'

'You don't even know me. How can you be in love with me?'

'You think I don't see you? You think I don't hear you in your books? You think I don't understand *Apache*? What do you think I'm doing up there every day? I'm living out the whispers of your soul. Baby, I know you. Oh, yes, I know you. It's you who don't know yourself. You don't want to. You don't want to remember who you are, or what you are, that you're a woman, and a damn fine one, with real needs, and a heart and a soul, and even a body, that's just as hungry for mine as mine is for yours. But at least I'm honest. I know what I want and who I am, and I'm not afraid to go after it. Thank God for that.' And with that he stood up and walked away from the table, slammed the door to the commissary, and stalked back to the set. And as Daphne followed him a few minutes later she had to smile to herself. Not many women in the country had the guts to turn down Justin Wakefield. It was funny and sad all at the same time.

She watched him work on the same scene over and over and over again that afternoon and evening and well into that night. Howard Stern was shouting at everyone; he even had her make several changes in the scene to see if it would work. But the problem was not with her writing, it was with Justin's mood. She could tell that he was desperately unhappy, and it was as though he wanted the whole world to know it.

And at last, at ten o'clock that night, seventeen hours after they'd all shown up for work that morning, Howard Stern threw down his hat with disgust. 'I don't know what's wrong with you bastards today, but this whole

251

day has been shot. Wakefield, get over your snivelling moods and long face. I want everyone back here at five o'clock tomorrow morning, and whatever the problem is, you'd better fucking work it out.' It was the last they heard from him before he left, and Justin slammed into his dressing room without giving Daphne a second glance. But he made sure to walk directly past her, so that she could see how rotten he felt.

She walked silently back to the limo with Barbara and lay back against the seat with an exhausted sigh.

'Nice day, huh?' Barbara smiled as they wended their way home, but Daphne wasn't in the mood to talk. She was thinking about Justin, and wondering if she was wrong.

The next day was scarcely better, only this time she and Justin didn't speak at all. Howard let them off the set that night at seven thirty. He said he'd had enough of all of them to last him for a year.

But the next day it was as though there was magic in the air. When Justin arrived on the set, there was something hungry and angry and soulful burning in his eyes, and he tore everyone's guts out with his performance. At the end of a four-hour stretch with scarcely any retakes, Howard rushed over and kissed him on both cheeks, and the whole crew gave a cheer. For whatever reason, Justin had revived, and Daphne felt less guilty as she strolled over to the commissary for lunch. She was surprised when he sat down at her table, and she looked at him with a shy smile.

'You did a beautiful job today, Justin.' She didn't ask what had changed his mood, but whatever it was, she was glad it had happened.

'I had to. I felt I owed it to Howard. I was making everyone pay for what I felt.'

She nodded, looking first at her plate and then at him. 'I'm sorry I upset you.'

'So am I. But I happen to think you're worth it.' She wanted to cry as he said it. She had been hoping that he'd given up. 'But if this is the way you want it, Daff,

I guess I'll have just to accept it. May I be your friend?' He said it with such humility and tenderness that tears filled her eyes and she reached for his hand and held it in one of her own.

'You already are my friend, Justin. And I know I'm not easy to understand, but a lot of very painful things have happened in my life. I can't help that. Just accept me as I am. It will be easier for both of us.'

'That's hard for me to do, but I'll try.'

'Thank you.'

'I can't stop what I feel, though.' She still felt that he didn't know her, and it made her unhappy that he was being so tenacious, but maybe that was just the way he was, and if they were truly going to be friends, then she had to accept him, too.

'I'll try to respect that.'

'And I'll respect you.' And then he chuckled and whispered, 'But I still think you're crazy.' She laughed at the look on his face then and she couldn't help telling him of what she had thought the other day.

'Do you realise that I'm probably the only woman in America who would keep you out of her bed?'

'You want a presidential award for it?' He looked amused and she laughed.

'Are you giving one out?'

'Hell, why not, if it'll make you happy.' And then they went back to talking about the making of the movie, but that night he showed up on her doorstep with a plaque he'd had made by the guys in the prop room. It was a bronze plaque, carefully mounted, and exquisitely engraved. It was a presidential award to Miss Daphne Fields, for bravery above and beyond the call of duty, in keeping Justin Wakefield out of her bed. She roared with laughter when she saw it, kissed him on the cheek, and invited him in for a beer.

'You wanted a plaque, so I took you at your word.'

She propped it up on the kitchen counter and handed him a glass and a beer. 'Have you eaten?'

'I had a hamburger after work. How about a swim in

your pool?' It was already eight o'clock, but it was a beautiful night and Daphne was tempted.

'Can I trust you?'

'What? Not to pee in your pool?' For a man of his age he was more like a boy than an adult, but she liked that about him. It was refreshing at times, and sometimes it drove her crazy.

'You know what I mean, Wakefield.' She looked at him sternly.

'Yes, I do, Fields.' He returned the look with mock grimness. And then he laughed. 'Yes, you can trust me. Christ, you're a twit, Daff. You put a hell of a lot of effort into stifling your feelings. Is anything worth that much trouble?'

'Yes.' She smiled at him. 'I think so.'

'Well, no one can say you're easy. At least I can't.' And then with a sad, lonely look on his face, 'Or is it just me?'

'Oh, Justin' – she didn't want him to believe that – 'of course not, you dummy. I've just lived this way for a long time, and I'm happy like this. I don't want to change that.'

'I got the message.'

'I got the plaque.' She smiled at him gently, and then waved towards her bedroom. 'I'll go put my bathing suit on.' She put on a modest navy blue bikini, and when she came out, he was already in the pool.

'The water is fabulous.' He dove deeper into the pool and she could vaguely glimpse that he had a white suit on, and she dove in neatly, and met him at the bottom of the pool. It was then that she realised that the white suit was only the small strip of flesh on his buttocks devoid of suntan, and when they came to the surface she looked at him in disapproval.

'Justin, it's about your suit...'

'I don't like to wear one. Do you mind?'

'Do I have a choice?'

'No.' He grinned happily and dove again, tickling her feet as he went, and then he came up like a dolphin and he grabbed her and pulled her down with him. She resisted, pulling against him. He playfully pulled back. For ten minutes they played the game until finally Justin slowed down.

'Do you always have this much energy after work?'

'Only when I'm happy.'

'You know, for a grown man you act like a little kid.'

'Thank you.' No one would have guessed that he was over forty, but Daphne had to admit that in his company she felt younger too. 'You know, you look great in a bikini, Daff. But you'd look better without one.'

'Don't be a pest.' She swam a few laps then and slowly climbed the ladder and got out of the pool. And as she wrapped herself in a towel she turned her back, having noticed that he was getting out of the pool too. 'There's a towel on the chair.'

'Thanks.' But when she turned around, he hadn't used it. Instead, he stood before her in all his dripping naked beauty with the moonlight above them and a sky filled with stars. They said not a word for an endless moment, and he took one step forward and took her in his arms. He kissed her with all the gentleness of his childlike soul, and he held her, and she felt him tremble as she did, not sure if it was from desire or the cold. And for reasons she couldn't explain to herself as she stood there, she let him hold her, and felt her mouth respond to his as they kissed. It seemed hours before he turned away from her, and wrapped himself tightly in the towel she had provided, hoping to quell the ardour that had sprung to him. 'I'm sorry, Daff.' It was the voice of a small boy as he stood with his back turned to her, and she wasn't quite sure what to say. She had wanted him very badly for a moment, and she touched his back gently with her hand.

'Justin ... it's all right ... I ...' He turned to face her then and their eyes met.

'I want you, Daphne. I know you don't want to hear it. But I love you.'

255

'You're crazy. You're a wild, crazy boy in the body of a man.' And once again she remembered Howard's warning ... remember that actors are children. And Justin was. Or was he? He didn't look like one now as he took a step towards her and held her face in his hands.

'I love you. Can you really not believe that?'

'I don't want to believe it.'

'Why not?'

'Because if I do believe it' – she hesitated, her whole body trembling in the warm air – 'and I let myself love you too ... one day we'll get hurt and I don't want that.'

'I won't hurt you. Ever. I swear that.'

She sighed and leaned her head against his naked chest as he folded her into his arms. 'That's something no one can promise.'

'I'm not going to die like the others, Daff. You can't be afraid of that forever.'

'I'm not. I'm just afraid of losing what I love ... of hurting and getting hurt...'

He pulled her away from him then and looked into her eyes so she could see his, just as she did with Andrew when she wanted him to read her lips.

'You won't get hurt, Daff. Trust me.' She wanted to ask him why but she could no longer fight it, the words didn't sound right anymore. Not even to her. She let him kiss her and hold her, and a little while later he carried her into her bedroom, and they lay on her bed and made love until dawn. They got up together the next morning, and he made her coffee and toast and they stood in the shower, kissing and laughing, and Daphne could no longer remember why she had fought so hard and so long to stay alone.

And when Barbara came home from Tom's at five o'clock to go to the studio with Daphne, there was shock in her eyes when she found Justin in the kitchen in his white jeans and bare feet.

'Have a good night, Barb?' His eyes locked into hers

as they stood there. She had a wild instinct to protect Daphne from him, but she knew it was too late for that now.

'Yes, very, thanks.' But her eyes said all that she thought and he understood her.

And at five fifteen they all got into Daphne's limo and rode to the studio. Justin put in a brilliant performance, and when everyone went to lunch, they snuck into his dressing room and made love until two o'clock in the afternoon, when everyone came back to the set to work on the movie.

29

Working on a movie set is like being trapped in an elevator for an entire summer, and there can be no secrets from the others. Within a week everyone on the set knew that Daphne and Justin were lovers, and only Howard dared to make comment, one morning over coffee and donuts.

'Don't say I didn't warn you. They're all children. Spoiled children.' But Daphne was already under Justin's spell.

He sent her flowers on the set, baked her cookies at midnight in her kitchen, bought her countless small, thoughtful gifts, and made love to her whenever and wherever they could. At night they lay beside her pool, and he recited love poems to her that he had learned as a child, and told her funny stories about the making of other movies that made her laugh until she cried.

The movie itself was going beautifully, well ahead of schedule, much to Howard's delight, and there were few problems on the set. Daphne had learned more about making a film in the last three weeks than she had hoped to in the entire year.

'And when we finish this one, my love, we'll make another, and another ... and another... We're an unbeatable team, kid.' And she was inclined to agree. The only trouble with their affair was that she knew that Barbara didn't like him and it was causing tension between them that was a constant strain. Barbara tried not to say anything about it, but it was obvious in all that she didn't say. At night, at Tom's place, she would talk to him about it and he would try to calm her, but it was useless.

'She's a grown woman, Barb. And she has decent judgement. You've said so yourself. Why not just stay out of it? We have our life, let her have hers.'

'Her judgement happens to stink in this instance. The guy is out to use her, Tom, I know it.'

'No, you don't, you suspect it. You have no evidence of that.'

'Stop sounding like a lawyer.'

'Then stop sounding like her mother.' He tried to kiss her into silence, but he couldn't quell her fears. She was terrified that Justin was using Daphne. There was something that made her not trust him and she was never quite sure what it was. He had all but moved in with Daphne, and he was constantly with her, at the set, in the house, out to dinner, at parties. It was a new life for Daphne and she seemed to enjoy it, but there still wasn't total bliss in her eyes. The years before had left their mark. And she was unhappy that she didn't have enough contact with Andrew. She still wrote to him every day, but there seemed to be no break scheduled in the shooting, when she could go back to see him, or have him come out to her. And there were long gaps between her phone calls to Matthew at the school. She never seemed to have enough time to call now. It seemed as though every time she told Justin she was going to call, he would distract her with a kiss, or a caress or a problem.

Finally one night Matthew caught her at home. 'Has Hollywood won your heart, Miss Fields, or are you just too busy to call?' She had felt guilty when he had called her, and for a moment she feared that something had happened to her son.

'Is Andrew all right?' Her heart was pounding but he put her mind quickly to rest.

'He's fine. But I have to admit that I was getting lonely. How's the movie coming?'

'Fine. Terrific, in fact.' But he also heard something else in her voice and he wasn't sure what it was. There was a distance between them that hadn't been there

259

before, and he found himself anxious about what it was. Maybe it was just the movie, but he didn't really think so. And then the second time he had called her, Justin had answered the phone.

'What school?' Justin sounded vague. He was reading the next day's lines, and Daphne was in the tub. 'Ho – what?'

'Howarth. She'll know.' He was desperately sorry he had called her.

'Oh.' Justin suddenly remembered. 'Her kid. Well, she can't come to the phone. She's in the bathtub.' Matthew inwardly cringed. So that was the reason for her distance and her silence. There was a man in her life. It grieved him, but he hoped that at least he was a nice man. She deserved someone wonderful because she was wonderful. 'Should I give her a message?'

'Please tell her that her son is fine.'

'I will.' He hung up and looked at his watch then. It was eleven thirty in New Hampshire. It was a hell of a strange time for them to call. He wandered into the bathroom and told Daphne that someone had called her from her kid's school. 'He said to tell you that your son is fine.' And then he looked at her strangely. 'It's awfully late for him to call. Who is that?'

'Matthew Dane. The director.' But there was a look of regret in her eyes, as though she were sorry Justin had answered the phone. And suddenly he laughed at her and sat on the edge of the tub.

'Don't tell me that my little vestal virgin had an affair with the headmaster at her kid's school.' The idea seemed to amuse him and she looked annoyed.

'No, I won't tell you that, Justin, because it's not true. We happen to be friends.'

'What kind of friends?'

'Talking friends. Like you and I would have been if you had had any sense.' Her voice softened. 'He's a nice man and he's been a big help to Andrew.'

'Oh, Christ, all those guys in boarding school are

260

fruits, Daff. Don't you know that? He's probably in love with your kid's ass.'

There was suddenly fury in her eyes as she looked at him. 'That's a disgusting thing to say, and you don't know anything about this. This is a special school, and the people there are absolutely wonderful to those children.'

'I'll bet they are.' He did not look convinced, and then he glanced at her with an unspoken question. 'What do you mean it's a "special" school? Does he have some kind of a problem?' He remembered suddenly her saying that she had had to leave Andrew there, that she had no choice. A feeling of horror swept over him as he wondered if her son was retarded and she was watching his eyes, as though measuring how much she could trust him. There was a long pause and she nodded.

'Yes, he does. Andrew was born deaf. He's in a school for the deaf in New Hampshire.'

'Jesus Christ. You never told me that.'

'I don't usually talk about it.' She looked sad as she sat in the tub.

'Why not, Daff?'

'Because it's my business and no one else's.' She looked almost defiant as she sat there.

'That must be a bitch having a deaf kid.'

'It isn't,' and as she watched his eyes she knew that he didn't understand, but if he cared about her, he would learn to. 'He's a wonderful child, and he's learning all the things he needs to know to function in a normal world.'

'That's nice.' But he didn't seem to want to know more about it. He bent to kiss her, and then walked back into their bedroom to continue reading his lines.

Daphne got out of the tub, dried herself off, and went to call Matthew from the den. When he answered, he apologised profusely for having called.

'Don't be silly, Matt. I would have called myself, but I've been so damn busy.' She didn't explain Justin and she wasn't sure how to, but it was embarrassing to have

261

him find out that he had been there. And Justin had told her that he had said she was in the tub, which she didn't consider an appropriate way of handling her phone calls. What if the press called? But Justin didn't seem to worry particularly about that. He was a lot more accustomed to their harassment than she was, and a lot less worried about his reputation. He already had tarnished that years before. 'How's Andrew?'

'He's fine.' Matthew gave her all the latest news, but there was a strange awkwardness between them, and the conversation gave neither of them what they had shared before. She wondered if she had talked to him so much because she was lonely, and she felt suddenly guilty for using him to fill her empty nights on the West Coast. And now there was Justin and things were different, but she felt a sense of loss when she hung up.

'Did you call your friend?' Justin teased her when she came back to the bedroom.

'Yes. Andrew's fine.' And her eyes told him not to pursue the subject further, and he very wisely did not. Instead he gently unravelled the towel she held around her, and ran a hand slowly up her leg and drifted it to her inner thigh. He pulled her gently towards him then, and they both forgot about her phone call as he pulled her slowly on top of his hungry body and they became one. But after they had made love, and he had gone to sleep, snoring softly beside her, she lay there and thought of Matthew.

30

The making of *Apache* moved relentlessly on for the next two months, with no break in sight, and at last Howard gave them all four days off to rest.

'Hallelujah, baby!' Justin was thrilled. 'Let's go to Mexico for a few days.' But Daphne had other plans.

'I can't. I have to see Andrew. I haven't seen him in almost three months.'

'Andrew? Oh, for chrissake. The kid can wait. Can't he?' Daphne looked shocked.

'No, he can't. I wanted him to come out here.' Her voice was both hurt and hard. Nothing was going to come between her and Andrew. Not even Justin. And by now she expected him to take an interest in her son, but he didn't. There were some things that mattered to him not at all, and children were one of them. He had no interest in anyone's kids, not even hers. And yet their loving was lavish and there were times when they would talk into the wee hours and she felt certain that she was in love. But she had the feeling sometimes that he was only in love with part of her, and there were other parts that he didn't know at all. Most especially Andrew, who was the major part of her life. 'Justin, what do you think? Would you like to meet him?' Maybe if she made him part of her plans he would begin to respond.

'Maybe. But to tell you the truth, babe, I need the rest and in my experience, kids aren't very restful.' He sounded neither apologetic or enthused. And she herself wasn't sure if it was wise to fly Andrew out. It was a big trip for four days. In the end she called Matt and asked him what he thought.

'Honestly, Daff. I think that's a long way for him to

come just for four days. For any kid his age.' Daphne had thought the same thing. She had just wanted him to meet Justin, but maybe it was too soon. Maybe neither he nor Justin was ready. Maybe it would be best to let Justin go his own way for the four days. They could live without each other for four days, and she could have Andrew to herself. The prospect of that didn't displease her, but she was still disappointed in Justin.

'I think you're right, Matt. I'll fly to New York and drive up.'

'That's dumb.' She was stunned. She hadn't seen him in almost three months. But he instantly understood her silence and laughed. 'I don't mean flying East. I mean flying to New York and driving up. Fly to Boston, and I'll pick you up.'

'I can't do that to you. You've got enough to do up there without chauffeuring me around.'

'And you've been working almost nonstop for the last five months. Can't I do a favour for a friend?' She had to admit that it would make life easier for her, but it didn't seem fair. Matthew was always thinking about her. 'I'm serious. It's no trouble at all.' She knew it was, but the offer touched her.

'Then I accept.' She checked the schedule she had got from the airline in advance, told him what flight she'd be on the next day, and went into the bedroom to pack. She was suddenly excited to see them both, and she could hardly wait to get her hands on Andrew again. She was smiling from ear to ear when she went into the bedroom, and Justin looked at her with his sexy boyish grin.

'You're really crazy about that kid, aren't you, Daff?'

'Yes, I am.' She sat down on the bed next to him and planted a soft kiss in the palm of his hand before looking up. 'I'd like you to meet him too.'

'One of these days,' and then after a pause, 'Can he talk?'

She nodded. 'Yes. Not always clearly, but most of the

264

time.' There was an expression in Justin's eyes that troubled her, but somehow she had to ask. 'Are you afraid of that? Of dealing with a deaf child, I mean?'

'Not afraid. I'm just not much into kids, normal or abnormal, I guess.'

'He's not abnormal. He's deaf.'

'Same thing.' She wanted to lash out at him then, but she restrained herself.

'I'm going to have him come out in the fall, when we finish the film. You'll meet him then.'

'That sounds fine.' Because it was three months off? She didn't like his reactions about her child, but there were so many other things about him she did like. And once she knew Andrew, she suspected that his reluctance would be overcome. Andrew was hard to resist, deaf or not.

'What are you going to do while I'm gone?' They all needed the rest, he most of all, and she looked at him with a warm smile.

'I don't know. I wanted to go to Mexico with you.' He touched the inside of her thigh. 'Sure I can't change your mind?' She smiled. He really didn't understand, and she shook her head.

'Nope, not a chance. Not even like that.'

'He must be some kid.'

'He is.'

'Well, tell him I'm crazy about his mom.'

'I will.' But she knew she wouldn't tell him about Justin yet. He wouldn't understand that. And in Andrew's eyes she belonged to him, always had and always would. 'Are you going to stay here, love?'

'I don't know. Maybe I'll go to San Francisco for a few days to stay with friends.'

'Well, let me know where you are, so I can call.' They hadn't been apart for a day or an hour in almost three months, and suddenly the thought of being so far away from him made her feel sad. 'I'm going to miss you, sir.'

'I'll miss you too, Daff.' He took her in his arms then

and they made love until almost dawn, and then she got a few hours' sleep before she had to get up and catch her plane.

Daphne went to the airport alone in the limousine, Barbara was with Tom and there was no reason for her to go, and Justin said he had things to do. Everyone in the cast and crew was using each precious hour of the four days. She boarded the plane at ten o'clock, and expected to arrive in Boston at seven o'clock in the evening, East Coast time.

The plane came in on schedule, and Daphne was among the first off, looking around for Matthew. She didn't see him at first, but then she spotted him standing twenty feet away, his dark eyes combing the crowd. Suddenly their eyes met and held, and she felt a strange little tug at her heart, which she didn't understand. In six short months he had become her friend, mostly over the phone, but she suddenly realised how happy she was to see him. A warm smile lit his eyes, and he walked slowly towards her.

'Hello, Daff. How was the flight?'

'Too long.' And then, without knowing why, she reached up and hugged him. 'Thanks for coming, Matt.' There was a moment of awkwardness between them.

'You look great.' He also noticed that she looked very thin. She'd been working too hard and it showed, but she also looked very happy. There was a smile in her eyes, and something more. Something that troubled him now. There was something different about her than there had been, more womanly perhaps, more overtly sexy. And his thoughts went at once to the male voice that had answered the phone. He tried to force it from his mind, but he couldn't as they went to pick up her luggage. 'What have you been doing out there, other than work?' She looked prettier than ever, and something inside him wanted to know why, even though he knew he had no right to. And as she looked at him she smiled, realising how isolated he was in New Hampshire, and how totally wrapped up in his work. There had been a number of

266

items about her and Justin in the paper, but he had apparently seen not a one. Knowing Matthew as well as she did, she knew he wasn't being facetious.

She smiled again as he picked up her bag. Her eyes teased him gently and he stopped and looked down into her face. 'You're looking awfully serious, Matt.' She didn't want to explain to him about Justin.

'I'm just happy to see you, Daff . . . I'm not quite sure what to say . . .' Her eyes gently touched his face and she nodded.

'Tell me about Andrew.' She felt the questions in his eyes, and she didn't want to answer them. Her life in California was totally separate from this. This was a different life for her. A life she shared with her son. The world of Justin Wakefield seemed ten thousand miles away, and in a way this felt like coming home. She had come home alone, and she wanted to enjoy it.

As they left the airport and made their way north, Matthew told her about the changes at the school, the two new people they had hired, the field trips they'd made, and the camping trip they were all going on in July. She desperately wished that she could be there.

She sighed as she sat beside him in the car. 'I feel like I've been there forever, Matt.' He wanted to tell her that he felt that way too, but it didn't seem right.

'How much longer do you think it will be?'

'I wish I knew. Three more months, maybe six. It's been going pretty smoothly till now. But everyone tells me that you have to expect it to stretch out. Howard doesn't like that to happen, no one does, but it can't be helped, and I guess that sooner or later there will be some kind of problem. I'll be home by Christmas for sure.'

He nodded, disappointment in his eyes. 'I'll be ready to leave by then. The new director from London is scheduled to take over on January first.'

'You don't think you'll stay, Matt?' She looked sad as she asked.

'No. Howarth is a wonderful place, but I want to get

267

back to the New York School' – he grinned at her then
– 'I'm not sure I'm cut out for country life. Sometimes
I think I'll go nuts up there.'

She laughed and watched his face. It was such a
strong, handsome face, so different from Justin's golden
beauty, but Matt had a beauty of his own, a kind of
rugged, solid quality about him that made him more
man than idol. 'I know what you mean. When I stayed
up there for a year, there were times when I even missed
the dirt and the noise of New York...' She thought of
John then and her eyes grew vague.

'Well, I'll tell you.' He flashed his smile at her. 'I miss
the resources we have for the kids in New York. The
museums, the ballet...' His voice drifted off. 'My crazy
sister.'

'How is she?'

'Martha? She's fine. The twins turned fifteen last week
and they both got stereos for their birthdays. She says
she's finally truly grateful that she's deaf. She can feel
the furniture tremble when they play them and Jack says
he's going nuts.' Daphne smiled, wishing it was a
problem she would one day have with Andrew. 'I still
want you to meet her when you have time.' They both
silently wondered when that would be. For the moment
it seemed like never.

He told her then that Mrs Curtis sometimes visited
the school, she was well and always asked to be
remembered to Daphne.

'I wish I had time to see her this time, but all I have
is four days.' He felt his heart sink again.

The drive seemed to speed by as they talked and
shortly after nine o'clock they reached the school. She
knew that Andrew would be in bed, but she wanted to
see him, just to cast her eyes on his face, kiss his cheek,
touch his hair. She hurried inside, and ran upstairs. He
was sound asleep in his bed, and she stood for a long time
in his room, looking over him in his bed. It was a long
time before she noticed Matt standing in the doorway.
She smiled and bent to kiss Andrew's cheek. He stirred

268

but didn't wake, and she went downstairs, with Matthew behind her.

'He looks so good. I think he's grown.'

'He has. And you should see him ride the bike you sent him.' She smiled and looked up at Matt.

'I feel like I'm missing so much.'

'It won't be long, Daff...' Their eyes met and held, and suddenly Justin Wakefield no longer seemed real. He seemed part of a distant dream. It was Matthew who seemed real now as he stood before her.

And suddenly in spite of all the promises he'd made himself, Matthew looked at her with searching eyes, and had to ask. 'There's someone important in your life out there, Daphne, isn't there?' She hesitated as he felt his heart pound and then, slowly she nodded.

'Yes. There is.'

A little child in him wanted to cry, but nothing showed in his eyes except concern for her. 'I'm glad for you. You needed that.'

'I guess I did.' But she wanted to tell him then about her concerns about Justin and Andrew. What if Justin couldn't accept a nonhearing child? But she was afraid to ask. Somehow it seemed out of place to ask him. And then she looked into Matthew's eyes again. 'It doesn't change anything here, Matt.' He wondered what that meant, but only nodded and opened the door to the little sitting room he had inherited from Mrs Curtis.

'Do you have time for a cup of coffee, or do you want me to drive you to the inn now?'

'No. I'm wide awake.' She glanced at her watch with a smile. 'It's only seven o'clock for me.' It was ten o'clock at night in New Hampshire though, and the school was very quiet, everyone had gone to bed. 'I'd love a cup of coffee with you. It's nice not to be just talking to you on the phone.' He smiled at her as he poured her a cup from his constantly brewing pot, and he wondered how serious the affair in California was, and if he was a good man. He hoped so, he hoped that very much, more than she would ever know. He handed her the cup of coffee

269

and they sat down. He kept searching her face for unspoken answers.

She told him then about the making of the movie, the scenes they had already shot, the parts that remained to be made when they went back. 'I think next month we'll be going up to Wyoming.' The location they had chosen was Jackson Hole, a place Matthew had always longed to see.

'I envy you that.' He spoke with a slow, easy smile, his long legs stretched towards the fire. 'I hear it's a beautiful place.'

'So they tell me.' But she wasn't thinking of the movie as they talked, or even of Justin. She wondered if perhaps it was because now she was so close to Andrew. It was a relief not to be three thousand miles away, but right there, just beneath his bedroom. But maybe it wasn't Andrew at all. It was odd how Matthew pushed him from her head, she didn't really understand it, but there was a quality about this man that enveloped her with a sense of safety and well-being and comfort, and a kind of warmth that lulled her. She didn't feel tense or tired or overworked, she just felt peaceful and happy as they sat by the fire. Maybe that was why now she felt so content, and so happy. 'What about you, Matt? Will you get away this summer at all?'

'I doubt it. I may join Martha and Jack and the girls for a few days at Lake George. But I'm not sure I can get away from here.' He smiled ruefully at her, brushing back a lock of dark hair. 'I'm not even sure I want to. I always worry when I leave the kids. Mrs Curtis said she'd cover for me for a few days if I want to get away, but I don't want to impose on her.'

'You should. You need the rest too.' She noticed then that his eyes were more tired than when she'd left, and there were fresh lines that hadn't been there before. He looked young, but responsible and mature. It was something she liked about him. He didn't have the smooth, perfect beauty of Justin, but sometimes, constantly staring into that exquisite face grew tiresome. It was staggering how gorgeous the man could look day after day. His physical appearance was like a country without rain or snow, only brilliant sunshine all the time. 'It's hard to believe that you've already been here for six months, Matt.' Harder still to believe all the things that had happened in her life since then.

But Matthew was laughing softly. 'Sometimes it feels more like six years.'

She laughed too. 'That's how I feel after fourteen hours on the set.'

'How's Barbara holding up?' They hadn't met, but he felt he knew her from all that Daphne said. She told him then about her romance with Tom. 'Is she liable to get married and stay out there? That would be rough on you.' He knew how much Daphne depended on her and had for years.

'I don't know if it's that serious yet.' But it was a possibility she had considered too.

And then suddenly he asked her, 'What about you?'

Daphne looked puzzled at the question, and then she understood, and she wasn't sure what to answer. She looked at Matthew thoughtfully. 'I don't know, Matt.' His heart trembled at her words. 'I ... it's difficult to explain.' She wasn't always sure what she felt for Justin. She loved him, to a certain point, but there was still a great deal she didn't know about him. Even though they were together every hour of every day, she sensed that there were unopened doors that she had yet to discover, and there was still the question of his lack of interest in Andrew. She decided to tell Matt, maybe he could help her handle it better. 'I'm not sure about him, Matt. He isn't very interested in getting to know Andrew.'

'Give him time. Does he know he's deaf?' She nodded, still looking pensive. 'How does he feel about that?'

'He won't admit it, but I think it scares him, and as a result he just pretends that Andrew doesn't exist, forgets his name, makes believe he isn't there...' Her voice drifted off and Matthew shook his head.

'That won't work, Daff. Andrew is too important to

you for the man in your life not to share him.' He wanted to be fair to her, to give her the best advice he could. 'Is that why you didn't bring him out this time and flew back here yourself instead?'

'Partly, and also I think it would have been too much of a trip for Andrew in only three or four days.' Matt had said that much himself on the phone. 'But it was because of Justin too.' Matthew looked suddenly shocked then. It couldn't be. But of course that made sense. He felt his heart sink as he asked her.

'Justin?'

She blushed, it was embarrassing to admit that she was having an affair with the actor starring in her movie. It sounded so Hollywood, so typical, so unreal, but it was more than that, she knew it. It just so happened that they had met there, and had had a chance to get to know each other because of the film, and the romance had grown as a result ... 'Justin Wakefield.' Her voice was soft, her eyes bright in the firelight.

'I see. That's quite a catch, Daff.' He took a long, slow, deep breath. He hadn't even thought of that. He had assumed it was some ordinary mortal, not the golden god of every woman's dreams. 'What's he like?'

She sat and stared into the fire, seeing Justin's face as though he were with them in the room. 'Beautiful, of course. Very beautiful, and bright, and funny, and sometimes very kind.' And then she looked back at Matthew again, she had to tell him the truth. 'And totally self-involved, and often very selfish and unaware of those around him. He's forty-two years old and sometimes he acts more like fifteen. I don't know, Matt, he's a lovely man and at times he makes me very happy ... and at other times it's like talking to someone who doesn't hear you. Like when I talk to him about Andrew, he's just not there.' It was why she still called from time to time for comfort, to talk about her son, or other things. It was something she had wondered about often, there were parts of her life that Justin simply didn't relate to. 'He's very understanding about my work, which is

272

important to me, he cares about that, but in other ways' – she shook her head – 'he just isn't there. I sometimes wonder if it would work.' She sighed softly. 'And I have to admit that there are times when I'm not sure. It's interesting, he and Barbara absolutely hate each other. She sees a side of him I just don't see, a cold, empty, calculating side she insists is there, but I think she's misreading him. She doesn't know him as well as I do. He isn't calculating, it's just that at times he's unthinking. You can't hate a man for that.'

'No, but it could be mighty hard to live with.'

'Yes, it could.' She had to agree and then she smiled dreamily into the fire. 'But sometimes he makes me so happy. He takes away all those awful memories, all that hurt and loneliness I lived with for so long.'

'Then maybe it's all worth it.'

'Right now I think it is.'

He nodded and sighed again. 'I figured that there was someone when he answered the phone that time I called.' It had only happened once, but he had had a premonition, and she wasn't the kind of woman to indulge in one-night stands. If he answered the phone it was because he lived there and she wasn't afraid to let the world know. 'I just didn't imagine that it was him.'

'Justin?' He nodded, and she smiled. 'Fortunately, the press hasn't devoted too much time to us, an item here and there but not much. But we haven't been anywhere because we've all been working so hard, but one of these days they'll figure out that we're living together and it'll be all over the papers.' She didn't look pleased.

'How do you feel about that?'

'Not very happy, and my readers will be shocked, but I guess I'll have to face it sooner or later.' They both thought of *The Conroy Show* she had done months before, and their eyes met. 'I really don't want to have to explain it, not until I'm sure.' Sure of what? He was terrified of the answer to that one. Maybe she would marry Justin and decide to stay in California. But he had to tell her

273

what he knew, for Andrew's sake, that was his role in her life after all, in spite of the friendship that had grown between them in the past six months.

'If you decide to stay out there, there's a terrific school for Andrew in LA.' He told her about it and she listened, but after a while she began to feel sleepy. She stood up.

'I'm not to that point yet, but if I get there, I'll talk to you about the school.' Somehow the thought depressed her. She wasn't ready to think about marrying Justin, and he hadn't mentioned it either, but sooner or later the subject would come up. Eventually she would have to decide if she was going back to New York, or staying in LA. 'Right now, all I have to do is finish the movie. Then I'll think about my own life.'

'Do what's best for you, Daff. And for Andrew.' His voice was so sad, so gentle, and she suddenly wondered about him. Once or twice she had called and he was out and she had wondered if he had met a woman that he liked, but this didn't seem the time to ask. He walked her to the car and drove her to the inn. They had left her key out on the desk with a note of welcome, and he left her there with a thoughtful smile in his eyes. 'I'm glad you flew back to see Andrew.'

'So am I, Matt.' They said good night and he left, and as she walked upstairs to her room she thought about their conversation and wondered why she felt suddenly so unhappy about Justin. Why couldn't he be more like Matt? Why couldn't he listen to her about Andrew? But maybe in time he would. It was Matt's business, after all, to care about children like Andrew. But there was more to him than that and she knew it. Much, much more.

31

The visit with Andrew passed all too quickly, he was ecstatic to have her near him, and he rode his bike for her, and showed her his garden, introduced her to his new friends, and bragged about her movie. They took long walks in the sunshine and went back outside after dinner. They were glorious June days, and she felt revived just being near him. It was as though the spirits of her soul had leaked out slowly in the past three months and she hadn't noticed. She had been so busy in California with Justin and the film. But now, once again, she knew how desperately she needed her son, and how important she was to him. He asked her again and again now when he would come back to California, when she was coming home, when they could be together.

He had just gone inside to take his bath after dinner, when Matthew found her, watching the sunset from the comfortable old-fashioned swing.

'May I join you, Daff?' She looked so peaceful and pensive, he hated to break into her thoughts. But he had seen her there and had been irresistibly pulled towards her.

'Sure, Matt.' She patted the seat beside her with a smile. 'Andrew just went in for his bath.'

'I know. I met him on the stairs and he told me you were out here.' They exchanged a long, slow smile and the sun disappeared behind a hill in a burst of flame. 'It's done him a lot of good to see you. He needs you more again these days. He's turning his attention to the world outside now, and you're a big part of it for him.'

'It's done me good too.' He could see that now. The worry was gone from her eyes, and her face was relaxed and happy. She looked like a little girl sitting in the swing, in blue jeans and an old sweat shirt, her long blonde hair fanned out down her back, and a pale blue ribbon the colour of her eyes keeping it off her face. And yet he saw concern in her eyes too, concern for Andrew. 'I feel as though I should be here with him, Matt.'

'You can't right now. He understands that.'

'Does he? I'm not sure I always do.' She fell silent and he watched her.

'You look like a little kid today.' His eyes were gentle. 'No one would suspect you of being a bestselling author.' Or the mistress of the movie star who lived in every woman's dreams.

She looked at Matthew happily. 'Up here I'm not anyone but me. And Andrew's Mommy.' It was an important facet of her life and they both knew it. 'I'm going to try and come back soon.'

'How soon is that?'

'Either right before or right after Wyoming, depending on what Howard says.'

'I hope it's before.' And then he had to be honest with her, he almost always was. 'Not so much for Andrew's sake, but for me.' She looked into his eyes then, and she felt something stir deep inside her. She was never quite sure what she felt for Matt, or if she should even let herself think it over. It was so comfortable the way things were. But it was strange how important he had become to her, how much she needed to know that he was there somewhere, that she could talk to him if she had to. She couldn't imagine life without him now, especially for Andrew's sake, but for her own, too. 'You mean a lot to me, Daphne.' His voice was husky in the twilight and she nodded, looking into his soft brown eyes.

'You mean a lot to me too.'

'It doesn't make much sense, does it? We've really never spent much time together. A bunch of talks at night in front of the fire, here at the school, and a lot of hours on the phone...' His voice drifted off.

'Maybe that's enough. I feel as though I know you

better than anyone else.' It was that that was so amazing about him. She did know him. And she knew that he also knew her, as she really was, with her scars and fears and private terrors, and all her victories and strengths as well. She had let him see more of her than anyone else she'd ever known, even Justin. Justin saw the funny side, the bright side, the solid, strong part of her being, but he didn't know what Matthew knew, and she wasn't sure she'd trust him to yet. But she knew that she trusted Matthew with all her secrets and her entire soul. And yet it was Justin she lived with, Justin who slept on the other side of the gigantic bed in Bel-Air.

'Maybe one day, Daff...' Matthew started to say something, and Daphne looked at him, startled, almost frightened. He changed his mind then. It wasn't time. 'We'll have more time to spend together.' It was a safe thing to say, yet nothing felt safe now. They were both treading on fresh ground and she sensed it. She watched him, and he leaned over and kissed her cheek. 'Be good to yourself in California, Daphne. Be happy. I hope things work out with your friend. And if you need me, I'm always here.'

'You don't know how comforting that is, Matt.' And she meant it. 'I always know that if I need you, I can call.' And then she smiled. 'And if you need me, you call too.'

'What does your friend think of that?' His eyes were only slightly worried.

'He teased me about it once.' She laughed, it seemed foolish now. 'He accused us of being lovers, but he didn't seem too upset by it. He's led kind of a...' She searched for the right words, she didn't want to be unkind to Justin. '... a liberated life, shall we say, until he met me. I don't think he's too concerned about the past.' Matthew felt a pang of something close to disappointment. 'Don't ever be afraid to call me, Matt.'

'I won't.' He smiled, feeling as though his heart had been torn out. They walked inside then and she went upstairs to Andrew, and when she came downstairs again an hour later, Matthew could see the tears in her eyes.

'Boy, it's tough to leave again.' She smiled at him bravely and he put an arm around her shoulders. 'I'll be back soon.'

'We're counting on it. And you know Andrew will be fine.' She nodded, and he drove her to the inn a few minutes later to change and pick up her bags to go back to the airport. She had insisted that she could take a taxi to Boston, but Matthew wouldn't hear of it. He drove her back, just as he had driven her to New Hampshire a few days before, and they stood at the gate for a long moment, her eyes holding him tight and his searching hers.

'Take care of my baby for me, Matt.' It was a lonely whisper as she tried not to cry, and then he threw caution to the winds and pulled her towards him, holding her for a long time like that as she drew on his strength and his friendship. She said nothing to him as she left, except as she stood in the doorway of the plane she signed to him, 'I love you.' He smiled broadly and signed back, and then she disappeared, back to LA and to Justin. And as Matthew walked back to his car he told himself he was crazy. Her life was too different from his, and always would be. He was nothing more than a teacher of deaf children, and she was Daphne Fields. For a moment he hated Justin Wakefield for everything he was, and everything Matt knew he wasn't, and then with a sigh he slipped into his car and went home, thinking every mile of the way of Daphne.

32

The plane touched down in LA at 1.30 in the morning LA time, and Daphne awoke with a start as they landed. For her it was 4.30 a.m. And she awoke with a heavy, lonely feeling, she had been dreaming of Matt and Andrew, playing in the garden with them at Howarth, and now she realised how far away she was again. For an instant she felt the same unbearable pain she had felt when she first left Andrew at Howarth. But as they landed she forced her mind back to Justin. She had to force her mind back to the present and what lay ahead, or she couldn't go on. But the memories of Andrew and Matthew seemed to stay with her. They were still too fresh in her head and she wasn't ready to let go. She didn't really want to be back yet. And yet, she reminded herself, she was coming home to Justin and all the thrills she felt in his arms. It was strange though, she felt as if she had been away not for three days, but for three months. Her two lives were so entirely separate that it was difficult to imagine leading both lives within the same week. And suddenly the thought of Justin was like thinking about a stranger.

She hadn't told the limousine to meet her at the airport, and she had told Barbara not to worry, that she would get home herself. She hadn't been able to reach Justin in three days because she didn't know the people he was staying with in San Francisco. But as she rode home in a cab she knew that in a few hours they'd all be back together. It was 2.00 a.m. by then, and they all had to be at the studio by 5.30. She realised as she walked in the front door that it wasn't even worth trying

279

to go to sleep for two hours. She'd have to make do with the nap she'd taken on the plane.

The house was dark save for the lights that went on automatically each night to make the house look lived in even when it was deserted, and she walked inside thinking how strange it all looked. It seemed like someone else's house, not her own, and she realised again how far she'd flung herself. She walked into the living room and sat down, staring at the pool all lit up in the dark, and wondered how soon Justin would come home. And then she wandered slowly outside and thought of taking a swim. She looked down and saw a well-sculpted blue and white bikini top, two empty glasses, and a bottle of champagne. She wondered who might have left them there, and wondered if Barbara and Tom had used the pool while she was gone, but he had his own, and as she picked it up she saw that the brassiere was far too large for Barbara. She held it for a moment as her heart began to pound, and then she shook her head. It couldn't be. He wouldn't do a thing like that right here. She left it on a chair, trying not to think, and took the glasses and the champagne bottle into the kitchen and there she found a white lace blouse draped over one of the kitchen chairs. She smiled an ironic smile to herself, feeling like the Three Bears. 'Who's been using my pool? ... Who's been sleeping in my bed? ...' She wandered into her bedroom with the thought, and found him there, the golden god, sprawled out naked and beautiful in their bed. He looked less than half his age, and she marvelled at his looks again as she stood watching him and he didn't stir. Maybe he'd had a party before she came back and he'd been too tired to clean up the last of the debris. She felt suddenly guilty for what she'd thought, wondering if her confused feelings about Matthew made her want to think the worst of Justin. But that was wrong. She was in love with Justin, the golden god. As she took off her travelling clothes with a sigh, she felt an overwhelming longing for him. She lay down on the bed beside him for a time, but

280

she couldn't sleep, and she didn't want to wake him by tossing around. At last she got up, and put on coffee at four o'clock, and half an hour later Barbara came in.

'Welcome home.' She gave Daphne a hug with an enormous smile. 'How's our boy?'

'Absolutely wonderful. You should see him ride his bike, and he's grown again, and he sent you his love.' She looked sad for a moment as she sat down on the chair still draped with the lace blouse. 'It was so hard to leave, Barb. I wish we weren't working so damn hard so he could come out for a visit. And yet, I know that if I work my ass off, I can move back to New York sooner. It's a kind of Catch-22, isn't it?'

Barbara nodded, she felt what Daphne was going through. 'Maybe before or after Wyoming, Daff.'

'That's what I told Matt.'

'How was he?' Barbara searched her eyes, but there was nothing there she hadn't seen before, warmth, affection, interest, but nothing more. She was still in love with her Greek god, much to Barbara's chagrin.

'He's fine. As nice as ever.' She said nothing more, and Barbara poured them both coffee and when Daphne got up she glanced at the chair.

'Is that yours?' Her eyes were suddenly grim.

'No. Justin must have had friends in to swim.' The silence between them seemed to fill the room. 'Have you and Tom been around?'

Barbara shook her head. 'I came in every day to pick up the mail. You got two cheques from Iris yesterday, but other than that it was all junk and bills.'

'The new contract didn't come in yet?' She was signing with Harbor to do another book.

'No. They said not to expect it till next week.'

'No rush, I can't touch it till we finish the movie anyway.' Barbara nodded again and fought with herself for the hundredth time. Tom had told her to keep her mouth shut when Daphne got back, but every time she thought of Justin her stomach turned, and she had told Tom that she didn't owe the son of a bitch a thing.

'What made you ask if we'd been here?' Barbara averted her eyes and filled Daphne's cup again.

'Just curious. Someone used the pool. I found some wineglasses and an empty bottle of champagne.' She didn't mention the bra.

'Maybe you ought to ask Justin about that.' Her voice was unusually smooth and Daphne looked up at her. She was too tired to play games.

'Is there something I ought to know?' Her heart began to pound again. It wasn't a matter of Goldilocks this time. But Barbara said nothing at all, never taking her eyes from her friend's.

'I don't know.'

'Was he here? I thought he went away.'

'I think he stayed.' But she was too vague. Barbara would have known if he had stayed in LA, especially if she picked up the mail every day.

'Barb . . .'

She held up a hand, fighting back a rush of pent-up fury once again. 'Don't ask me, Daff.' And then through clenched teeth, 'Ask him.'

'What exactly should I ask?'

Barbara couldn't take it anymore. She held up the blouse. 'About this . . . and the bra at the pool' – then Barbara had seen it too – 'and the underpants in the front hall . . .' She was prepared to go on but Daphne stood up, feeling her knees go weak.

'That's enough!'

'Is it? Just how much shit are you going to take from him, Daff? I wasn't going to say anything when you got back, Tom told me it was none of my business but it is' – her eyes filled with tears – 'because I love you, dammit. You're the best friend I've ever had.' She turned her back on Daphne for a moment and when she turned to face her again her eyes were bleak. 'Daphne, he had a woman staying here.' There was an interminable silence in the room as Daphne listened to her heart pound and the clock tick and then her eyes met Barbara's with an expression Barbara had never seen.

'I'll take care of this, but I want to make one thing clear. You were right to tell me, Barb. And I appreciate what you feel. But this is between Justin and me. I'll handle it myself. And whatever happens, I don't want to discuss this with you again. Do you understand?'

'Yes. I'm sorry, Daff...' Her tears spilled on to her cheeks, and Daphne went to her and hugged her for a moment.

'It's okay, Barb. Why don't you go on to the studio in your car.' It was almost five o'clock and Tom had been letting her use one of his cars. 'I'll meet you there in a while. And if I'm late, tell them that I just flew in from the East Coast.'

'Will you be all right?' She dried her eyes, frightened by Daphne's sudden calm.

'I'm fine.' Her eyes held Barbara's meaningfully, and then she walked out of the kitchen and closed the bedroom door. She walked over to where Justin lay and she touched him on the shoulder with a trembling hand. He stirred sleepily then, squinted his eyes, looked at the clock, and then realised she was in the room.

'Hi, babe. You're back.'

'I am.' She looked down at him and there was nothing friendly in her voice or face. She sat down in a chair across from the bed because she could no longer stand up and she stared at him. 'What exactly went on around here while I was gone?' She got right to the point and he sat up, barely rumpled by a night's sleep, with a look of innocence and curiosity in his eyes.

'What do you mean? How was your kid, by the way?'

'He was fine. But right now I'm more interested in you. What have you been up to around here?'

'Nothing. Why?' He stretched and yawned, and smiled invitingly as he reached out and touched her naked leg. 'I missed you, babe.'

'Did you? What about the woman who stayed here while I was gone? I'll say one thing, she's got big tits. Her bra would fit over my head.' But funny as she may

283

have sounded, she was not amused, her eyes were hard as rocks and she pushed his hand away from her leg.

'I had some friends in, that's all. What's the big deal?' Suddenly she wondered if Barbara had been wrong. She would feel like a total jerk if he was telling the truth and had been falsely accused. Her eyes faltered for a moment and then she saw one of his discarded rubbers under the bed. She reached over, picked it up, and held it aloft like a trophy of sorts.

'What's this?'

'Beats me. Maybe someone slept here.'

'Are you telling me it's not yours?' Her eyes never left his.

'Oh, for chrissake.' He stood up in all his splendour and ran a hand through his golden hair. 'What's with you? I was here alone for four days and I had some friends in. What's the matter, Daff' – his eyes glittered nastily – 'don't I get pool privileges unless you're here?'

There was no other way to find out. 'Barbara tells me there was someone staying here.' But at her words he started, he hadn't known she was around.

'That bitch! How the fuck does she know anything? She wasn't here.'

'She picked up my mail every day.'

'She did?' His face grew pale. 'Oh, Christ.' He sat back down on the bed and dropped his face into his hands. He said nothing for a while and then he looked into Daphne's eyes. 'All right, all right. I got a little crazy. That happens to me sometimes after I work that hard. It doesn't mean anything to me, Daff ... for chrissake ... you have a lot to learn about this business ... it drives you nuts after a while.' But they were lame words and he knew it. There wasn't much he could say to her.

'Apparently it does. Nuts enough to sleep with someone else in my house, in my bed.' Tears filled her eyes. 'Does that seem right to you?' She felt betrayed and hurt. She had suffered loss before, but she had never

284

suffered this ... brassieres left by the pool ... spots on the couch ... condoms under the bed ... and all in three lousy days. 'What the hell's the matter with you, dammit?' She got to her feet and paced the room. 'Can't you keep it in your pants for three days? Is that all I mean to you? A convenient piece of ass and when I'm not around you sleep with someone else?' She stood before him, her eyes blazing, and he looked sad.

'I'm so sorry, Daff ... I didn't mean – '

'How could you?' She began to sob. 'How *could* you? ...' She was beyond words and she lay facedown on the bed as she sobbed, and gently he stroked her back and hair. She wanted to tell him to go to hell, but she didn't have the strength. She couldn't believe what he had done, and the callousness of doing it in her own house and letting her find out made it even worse. This wasn't a quick screw he'd picked up at some bar, this was a girl he'd moved right into her house, her bed. The humiliation of it was almost more than she could bear. And what it told her about him was very painful.

'Oh, Daphne, baby ... please ... I got drunk, I snorted some coke. I just flipped out. I told you I didn't want you to go. I wanted to go to Mexico with you, but you insisted on flying East to see your kid. I just couldn't take it, I ...' He began to cry too, and turned her over gently to face him. She felt as though all her bones had melted into the bed. She didn't have the strength to fight. She almost wished that she were dead. 'I love you so damn much. This doesn't mean anything.' He wiped the tears from his eyes. 'I was crazy. It'll never happen again. I swear.' But her eyes said that she didn't believe a word as tears streamed down her face and she said not a single word to him. 'Daphne ...' He lay his head down on her slender thighs. 'Oh, God, baby ... please ... I don't want to lose you ...'

'You should have thought of that before your friend left her bra at my pool.' Her voice sounded defeated and she sat up slowly in the bed, feeling ten thousand years old, but not yet hating him. She was too hurt even to feel

285

anger yet. All she felt was pain. 'Is this how you always behave during a shoot?' Or was this how he behaved in real life? She was beginning to wonder. And it made her feel like hell.

'This has been a rough shoot. You don't know how much of myself I've been pouring into this, Daff... how desperately I've wanted to please you ... to make this movie of yours a major hit ... Oh, Daff...' His eyes looked so childlike and so sad, he looked as though his best friend had died. The fact that he had killed her himself didn't seem to enter his mind as he grieved. 'Baby, can't we start fresh?'

'I don't know.' Her eyes went to the rubber she had tossed on to the bed and he picked it up and threw it in the john. When he came back, he looked at her.

'Maybe you'll never forgive me. But I swear I'll never do it again.'

'How do I know that? I can't sit on you for the rest of your life.' She sounded so tired and so sad and he smiled for the first time since he had seen her in the room.

'I wish you would.'

'I want to go back and see my son again. What happens then? I worry myself sick for three days while I'm gone that you're out screwing around again?' She was suddenly overwhelmed by a mindless, wordless, bottomless lonely feeling. Who in hell was he? And what did she mean to him? Did he care about her at all? It was hard to believe he did now.

'If you want, I'll come with you.' But suddenly she wasn't sure if that was what she wanted. She wanted him to meet Andrew, but there was more in New Hampshire than that. There was Matt. And suddenly she didn't want Justin to be part of that life, especially now. Suddenly, she didn't trust him. Not enough to expose Andrew to him.

'I don't know. I don't know what I want right now. I think I might want you to move out.' But she knew that

286

if he did, they would never work it out. He shook his head slowly and reached for her hands.

'Let's not do that yet. Please, Daff. Give me a chance.' It was like watching a little boy beg to get his privileges back, but this was a lot more important than that. 'I need you.'

'Why?' It seemed strange to hear him say that, she had thought that it was she who needed him. 'Why me and not someone else, like your friend with the big tits?'

'You know who she is? A twenty-two-year-old cocktail waitress from Ohio, Daff. That's all she is. She isn't you. No one is.' But Daphne narrowed her eyes. Something rang a bell.

'Isn't that the girl you were going out with before?' He hesitated at length and then nodded, dropping his head into his hands again.

'Yes. She heard through the grapevine that we were taking a break and she called.'

'Here? How did she know where you were?' The question struck fear in his heart, he was caught. Either he had let her know where he was before, or he had called her.

'All right, dammit, if you're so fucking smart, so I called her.'

'When? After I left or before?' She got out of bed and stood facing him. 'Just exactly what has been going on with you?'

'Nothing, dammit! I've been with you night and day for the last three months. You know I haven't seen anyone else. How could I? When?' It was true.

'You told me she was an actress.' It was a minor point, but everything mattered now.

'She is. She's out of work, so she's waiting on tables. Daphne, dammit, she's a nothing, a child. You're worth fifty thousand of her or any other woman in this town. I know that. But I'm human. I do crazy things sometimes. I did it, I confess, I am desperately sorry, it won't happen again. What more can I tell you? What do you want me to do to atone for my sins? Cut off my balls?'

'It's a thought.' She sat down in the chair again and looked around. Suddenly she hated this room, the whole house. He had poisoned it while she was gone. She looked up at him then, 'I don't know if I could ever trust you again.'

He sat down from her across the bed, trying to keep his voice calm. 'Daphne, every couple goes through these things. At some point or other, everyone screws up. Maybe one day you will too. We're all human, and at some moment in time, we all get weak. Maybe it's better to have it out now, to have some giant tear in hearts that we can sew up and make them stronger. We'll be better for all this if we make it through and we can, if you let us. Give me a chance. I'm telling you, it won't happen again.'

'How do I know?'

'Because I'll show you. And in time you'll come to trust me again. I know what you feel. But it doesn't have to mean the end. He reached out gently and touched her cheek with his fingers. She faltered for only a fraction of a second and he sensed it and moved in quick, reaching out and pulling her into his arms. 'I love you, Daff, more than you'll ever know. I want to marry you someday.' To him that was the ultimate statement – the beginning and the end – but Daphne still looked sad.

'This is a hell of a way to start out.' It had never happened to her with Jeff, or John. Maybe she had been right to hide behind her walls. Justin sensed her thoughts.

'You can't be half alive all your life, Daff. You have to be out here with the rest of us, get hurt, make mistakes, pick yourself up, and make it again. Otherwise you're only half a human being, and that's not you. You're a lot more than that. I'm sorry. I'm sorrier than you'll ever know.'

'So am I.' But she didn't look as vehement as before.

'Will you let it ride for a while? I swear to you, you won't be sorry.' She didn't answer. 'I love you. What more can I say?' There wasn't much. In the last hour and a half he had said it all, that he loved her, that he had been a fool, that he wanted to marry her someday. It was the first she'd heard of that, and she looked at him now, with a thousand questions still in her eyes.

'Were you serious about wanting to get married?'

'Yes. I've never said that to anyone before. But I've never met anyone like you.' His eyes were so gentle and her heart still felt as though it had been torn in half.

'You've never met my son.' It was out of context, but not really.

'I will. Maybe next time I'll fly East with you.' She didn't answer and he watched her. He didn't want to remind her that they were over an hour late for work. He knew what a crazy bastard he had been, and he knew also that he had to make it right with her before anything. He didn't want to give her more time to think. 'We have a lifetime ahead of us, my love.' It was an awesome thought. 'Will you give me another chance?'

Her eyes searched his but she didn't speak, and he leaned down and kissed her gently on the mouth, as he had so long ago when they came together in love. 'I love you, Daff. With all my heart.' And then the tears began to flow again and she held him tight, aching over what he had done while she was gone. Justin held her as she sobbed, cooing and soothing and comforting and stroking her hair. He knew he had won her back when she stopped crying at last. She was unable to say what she felt, but he knew that in time she would forgive him for what he had done, and he sighed softly to himself as he stood up and gently led her from their bed. 'I hate to say it, babe, but we have to get to work.' She groaned at the thought, it was the last thing on her mind. But she knew that he was right.

'What time is it?'

'Six fifteen.'

She winced. 'Howard's going to have a fit.'

'Yeah.' Justin smiled at last. 'But as long as he is anyway, let's make it worthwhile.' And then without another word he laid her on the bed again and began to make love to her.

She wanted to object, it wasn't what she had in mind, not after what he had done . . . not so soon . . . not yet . . . but his skill was greater than her resolve and a moment later he plunged inside her and she gave a moan of sorrow and joy and knew herself to be his once again. And perhaps he was right, she told herself afterwards, maybe everyone suffers something like that. Maybe they'd be stronger for the pain.

33

When Justin and Daphne appeared on the set at eight fifteen, Howard was nearing an apoplectic fit. He turned to stare at them in disbelief as they walked in.

'I don't believe it . . . I don't believe it!' His voice rose to a crescendo and Daphne cringed. Justin looked unimpressed. 'What is it with you two? You can't get your goddamn asses out of bed to come to work? Doesn't anyone give a shit around here? *Three hours* late on the set and you walk in like you're coming to a tea party? The hell with you!' He grabbed a copy of the script and threw it as Justin went off to put his costume on and Daphne searched frantically for Barbara.

'You okay?' Barbara sat down next to her, looking at the tired little face, the ravaged eyes, but Daphne averted her gaze and nodded. Even now she had to fight back tears. Between the emotions and the lack of sleep, she was exhausted and overwrought.

'I'm fine.' She looked up at her friend with a tired smile. 'Everything's all right.' Or at least it was going to be. Barbara realised that Justin must have sold her a bill of goods.

'Do you want a cup of coffee?'

'Yes, if you're sure Howard didn't put arsenic in my cup.'

Barbara smiled, still watching her. She hated the sorrow she saw on her face, and hated Justin for putting it there. 'Don't feel so bad, Daff. Half of the crew came in late, that's why he's so pissed off. Apparently it always takes a couple of days to settle down after a break.'

'That's the understatement of the year.' For the first time since she had come home, Daphne grinned. And it

291

was the only mention she made of the havoc she had found in her own house. Barbara brought her the coffee and slowly she began to revive, but between the long flight the night before, the lack of sleep, and the trauma she had had with Justin before work, she felt like a zombie all day long. They knocked off at six o'clock that day and Justin took her home and put her to bed. He brought her a cup of tea right away and dinner on a tray. It was like being an invalid, and she knew why he was doing it, but she had to admit she didn't mind. He was in the kitchen afterwards, putting things away, when Matthew called, and Daphne sank into the pillows with a sigh. It was a relief to hear his voice.

'Hi, Matt.' Her voice was small and she was glad that the bedroom door was closed.

'It must have been some day. You sound beat.'

'I am.' But he sensed instantly that there was more. 'Are you okay?'

'More or less.' She fought with herself not to tell him what had happened. She didn't want to. It had nothing to do with him. And yet she needed to reach out to him, she needed to know that there was still something solid left, somewhere, even if it was three thousand miles away. She didn't trust Justin yet, no matter how contrite he was. But she knew for certain that Matthew was her friend. 'How was Andrew today?'

'Not bad, considering that you only left yesterday How was the flight?'

'Okay. I slept.' For an instant she was reminded of her calls from Jeff when he went on business trips. There was comfort in the trivia of everyday life. It was all on a much smaller scale than what was happening to her, and that was a relief. What was happening in California was just too much. She fell silent then, and at his end Matthew frowned, he had known instantly when he heard her voice that something was wrong.

'Daff? What's the matter, little one?' No one had called her that since John and she felt her eyes fill with tears as she struggled with the emotions of the past eighteen hours. 'Can't I help?'

'I wish you could.' He could hear her crying now. 'It's just something that happened out here ... while I was gone ...'

'Your friend?'

She nodded and choked on her tears. It was stupid to cry now, she told herself. They had made up. But it still hurt. It all hurt so damn much. And she wanted to tell it all to Matt, as though his comforting arms around her could change anything now. 'I found kind of a mess when I got back.' He waited and she went on. 'He had a woman staying here while I was gone.' It was shocking to be telling him about that, and yet she didn't feel shocked. She just felt sad. 'It's a long story, and he feels like hell about it now. But it was kind of a lousy homecoming.' She blew her nose and something within him began to burn.

'Did you throw the bastard out?'

'No. I was going to, but ... I don't know, Matt. I think he's sorry. I think he was just a little out of his head from the pressure of so much work for the past three months.'

'What about you? You've been working harder than he has, you wrote the screenplay first. Does that sound like a reasonable excuse to you?' He was mad as hell. And madder still that she wasn't, that she was willing to give the guy another chance.

'No. Nothing sounds like a reasonable excuse, but it happened. I'm just going to wait and see what happens now.' He wanted to shake her right out of her bed, but he knew he didn't have the right. He didn't want her to get hurt. But he was helpless. She was in love with someone else, and he was only her friend.

'Do you think he's worth it, Daff?'

'I do now. This morning I wasn't sure.' Matthew was sorry he hadn't called earlier then, but he knew it wouldn't have made any difference. She wasn't ready to give Justin Wakefield up, but Wakefield was a formidable opponent. Anyone in his right mind would have told him he was nuts even to hope that she'd give him up. 'I just don't know...' She sounded so fragile and so sad, it tore at his heart. '... I ... I've lost so much in the past, Matt...' He could hear her crying.

'Then don't cheapen what you had by accepting this.'

His reaction shocked her. 'You don't understand. Maybe he's right, maybe people do make mistakes. Maybe actors are different.' She was crying harder now. 'Dammit, how many times do you think I can start over?'

'As many times as you have to, you've got the guts, lady. Don't forget that.'

'Maybe I'm getting tired of having guts. Maybe they're all used up.'

'I don't believe that.'

'And besides, we have a commitment to each other. He said so.'

'Commitment? Was he thinking of that commitment while you were here?'

'I know, Matt, I know. I can't make excuses for him.' She was suddenly sorry she had told him at all. She didn't want to defend Justin to anyone, and yet she felt she should. 'I know it doesn't make sense, but I'm going to stick it out for a while.' She sighed and dried her eyes.

'It's all right, Daff, I understand. You have to do what's right for you. Just please, don't get hurt.' But she already was, and after she hung up, she began to cry again. Justin found her lying in bed, sobbing into her pillows, and not even sure why. She was still upset over the other girl, but there was something more. She was suddenly desperately lonely for Andrew and Matt and she wanted to go home.

'Oh, babe, don't ... everything's all right...' But it wasn't and she wasn't fooled. She lay in his arms and sobbed and at last fell asleep on his chest and he turned off the light. He lay looking at her as she slept, wondering if he had done the right thing. He cared about this woman more than he had cared about anyone else before, but he wasn't sure if he could live up to what she expected of him. He wanted to, he really did, but he felt a ripple of fear run through him as he looked down the years. She was so serious and so straight and she had been through so much. And his life was built on other things, excitement, and new people, and acting and having fun. He also knew he didn't have her knack for commitment.

And in New Hampshire, Matthew sat in the dark, staring at the fire, thinking himself a fool, and hating Justin Wakefield's guts, wondering if there was any hope at all as he ached for Daphne.

34

For the next month the making of *Apache* went smoothly and they were all scheduled to leave for Wyoming on the fourteenth of July. Howard had decided that they didn't have time off until they got back to LA before doing the final scenes on the Hollywood set. For Daphne, it meant that she wouldn't have time to fly back and see Andrew but Matt assured her that he was all right, he had his pack trip to look forward to, and as soon as she got back from Jackson Hole, she would fly back to see him. She was almost too busy to dwell on feeling guilty about it. There was a lot of material to rewrite for the scenes in Jackson Hole and she seemed to spend every waking hour on the set and all the rest of her time typing late into the night. And Justin had been marvellously supportive, he read over everything she wrote, told her when it was good and what didn't work and why. He was teaching more than she had ever hoped to learn about writing a screenplay and making it hold up for the characters involved. He sat up every night with her, bringing her sandwiches and coffee, rubbing her neck, and then they would fall into bed and make love. They were existing on almost no sleep, but she had never been happier in her life. She had a working relationship with him that she had never dreamed could happen, and she knew now that she had been right to stick it out with him after the fiasco in June. Even Barbara had to admit that he was behaving like an angel, but she still didn't trust him, as she told Tom often when they were alone.

'You never liked him from the first, Barb. But if he's good to her, what's wrong with that?'

'If he pulled a stunt like that on her once, then he'll do it again.'

'Maybe not. Maybe it was just a hangover from his old life, before he met her. He may have learned a lesson.' Tom didn't see anything wrong with him when he met him, and Barbara was so rabidly anti-Justin that he often suspected she was just jealous of someone else having that much influence over Daphne. The two women had been so close during their solitary lives at one time that maybe it was just hard for Barbara to let go, even though now she had Tom. He didn't really understand it, but he always urged her to keep her mouth shut if she valued her job. 'If she's serious about him, Barb, you'd better lay off.' He suspected, as the Hollywood press had finally come to do, that Justin and Daphne would get married.

'If she does, I'll throw rocks instead of rice,' Barbara snarled. 'That man is going to hurt her. I know it.'

'All right, Grandma, just relax. Hell, I hope he does marry her, then she'll have to stay out here.' It was now a frequent subject between them. He wanted Barbara to stay in LA and marry him, but she refused to decide until the making of *Apache* was over. 'But after that, my love, there are no more excuses. I'm not getting any younger and neither are you, and if you think I'm going to wait another twenty years to see you again, you're crazy. I want to marry you and get you pregnant, and watch you sit on your ass by the pool and spend my money for the next fifty years. How does that sound, Miss Jarvis?'

'Too good to be true.' But everything about him had been since the day she had met him at Gucci. It had been a storybook romance from the first. And he had long since surprised her with the handsome black lizard bag he had watched her covet that first day. And there had been other gifts too, a gold Piaget watch, a beautiful beige suede blazer, two jade bracelets, and countless other trinkets that amazed her. She still couldn't believe her good luck in having found Tom, and was constantly amazed to realise how much he loved her. And she loved

297

him just as much. As the two parted, there were tears in her eyes when she left for Jackson Hole, but he was going to fly up every weekend while she was on location.

Daphne and Justin flew up in a chartered plane, the rest of the crew went in buses hired by the studio, and the shoot took on an aura of summer romance once they were up there. Couples formed in the romantic setting, people sat outside at night, looking at the mountains and singing songs they remembered from their childhoods from camp. Even Howard mellowed. Justin and Daphne's love flourished. On breaks from the set they went on long walks, picked wild flowers, and made love in the tall grass. It was all like a beautiful dream, and everyone was sad when it was over and they had to go back to LA. Only Daphne felt less regret than the others, because she knew she would see Andrew, she was flying to Boston again in a few days. Justin hadn't decided whether to come with her or not. It was the day before she was due to leave that he finally appeared in their bedroom doorway, a nervous look on his face as he sat down on the edge of the bed.

'I can't do it, Daff.'

'Can't do what?'

'I can't go to Boston with you.' He looked miserable and she was instantly suspicious.

'Why not? Did Miss Ohio call?' It was the first time she had made mention of it all summer and he looked crushed.

'Don't be like that. I told you. That will never happen again.'

'Then why won't you come?'

He sighed and looked desperately unhappy. 'I don' know how to explain it to you without sounding like a total asshole. Or maybe I should just accept the fact tha I am, but ... Daff ... a whole school of deaf kids ... ... I ... have this thing about handicaps, blindness deafness, cripples ... I just can't handle it. It makes m physically sick.' She felt her heart sink as he said it. I

298

it was true, they had a serious problem on their hands. Andrew was deaf. It had to be faced.

'Justin, Andrew isn't a cripple.'

'I know that. And I'd probably be fine with just him ... but all of them...' He actually looked pale and Daphne saw that he was trembling. 'I know that it's nuts for a grown man to feel like this, but I always have. Daphne, I'm sorry.' Tears filled his eyes and he hung his head. Now what in hell was she going to do, but then she had an idea. They had to meet each other. It was important. The affair with Justin looked as though it were going to last and he had to meet Andrew.

'All right, darling, look ... we'll fly him out here.'

'Do you think you could?' The colour began to come back to his cheeks and relief flooded his face. He had dreaded telling her for days, but he just knew he couldn't do it.

'Sure. I'll call Matthew and have him put on the plane. He did it last spring and Andrew loved it.'

'Great.'

But when Daphne called Matt, he told her that Andrew had had a slight ear infection the week before and he couldn't fly out to see her. She had no choice then. She had to fly East by herself, and leave Justin alone in California. When she told him, she looked unhappy and there was a vague look of suspicion in her eyes. She suddenly wondered if he had cooked up the story about his fear just so he could stay in LA and raise hell, as he had the last time, and just thinking about it made her angry.

'Daff, don't look like that. Nothing's going to happen this time.' But she didn't answer. 'I swear it. I'll call you five times a day.'

'What does that prove? Will Miss Ohio dial for you?' She sounded bitter and he looked genuinely hurt.

'That's not fair.'

'Neither was making love to her in my bedroom.'

'Look, dammit, can't we forget that?'

'I don't know, Justin. Have you?'

299

'Yes, as a matter of fact, I have. We've had three beautiful months since then. And I don't know about you, lady, but I've never been happier. Why do you have to keep throwing that shit in my face?' But they both knew the answer. She still didn't trust him, and going East was a painful reminder of what had happened when she was away in June.

She sighed then and sank into a chair as she looked at him bleakly. 'I'm sorry, Justin. I really wish you'd come with me.' That would solve the problem. But would it? All it would mean was that she could keep tabs on him, it didn't mean that she could trust him.

'I can't come with you, Daff. I just can't do it.'

'Then I guess I have no choice but to trust you, do I?' But now all the happiness of the past three months seemed suddenly dim.

'You won't be sorry, Daff. You'll see.' But she wondered as she packed her bags and they drove to the airport.

In New Hampshire the leaves were turning early, there had been a cold spell, and she had never seen the countryside more beautiful than this year. She and Matthew drove in silence for a time, and her thoughts drifted back to Justin, wondering what he was doing, and if he would be true to his word. Matt noticed that she was quieter than usual, and he glanced at her once or twice before she turned to him and smiled. She looked more peaceful than she had before, but she still looked tired. Even in Wyoming the shoot had been gruelling. Howard Stern worked harder than any other director in town.

'How's my favourite movie?' He was afraid to ask her about Justin. She seldom spoke of him lately and he wasn't quite sure what it meant. He knew that when she wanted to she would tell him. And he waited. But he also had other things on his mind.

'The movie's going fine. We're almost finished. Howard thinks it'll take another six or eight weeks of studio work on the set and then that'll be it, we'll wrap it.' She had learned all the jargon in the last nine months, and he tried to tell himself that she wasn't different than she had been when they'd met. But in some subtle way, he knew that she had changed. There was a nervousness about her, a tension, that hadn't been there before, as though she was always watching, waiting, he wasn't sure for what. He wondered if living with Justin had done that to her, or just working on the film, or perhaps being away from Andrew. But she was different than she had been when her solitary life revolved around her books. Even here she seemed to have a hard time letting go of the frenzy, but he reminded himself that she had just got off the plane. 'I'm going to have Andrew come out for Thanksgiving.' She had already planned it. She would do an old-fashioned Thanksgiving dinner at the house in Bel-Air, and she wanted Barbara to bring Tom and his children. It was something she hadn't done in ten years, not since she was married to Jeffrey. But somehow, now she knew it was time to start again. Her years of solitude were over, for better or worse, and she wanted to make a real life with Justin. And it was definitely time he met Andrew. She was sorry he hadn't made it this time. But as she glanced over at Matthew she felt a small shaft of regret slice through her. She sensed now that things were different with him.

'What happens after Thanksgiving, Daff?' He looked at her as they drove through New England, and Daphne grew pensive.

'I'm not sure.' She wasn't yet, but she suspected that she and Justin would get married, if nothing ghastly happened in the meantime. In some ways, this trip was the test.

'Will you stay out there?' His eyes searched her face. He needed an answer. It was time for him, too.

'Maybe. I'll know more in the next couple of months.' And then she looked at him gently, she owed him some kind of explanation. She had told him the worst of it three months before, now she owed him the rest. It was

301

strange this friendship they had, it was platonic, and yet there was always just the faintest hint of something more. 'Things settled down a lot with Justin this summer. I think maybe I was wrong to tell you what happened while I was away last time.' Somehow, it didn't seem quite fair. Justin had never done it again and it coloured what Matthew thought of him, Daphne knew. Even now.

'There's no harm done.' He smiled as he drove. 'I won't tell the papers.'

She smiled in answer. 'I guess it was just an aberration.' She closed her eyes and sighed. 'But God, it was so awful. When I talked to you that time, I thought I would die.' He remembered and said nothing.

'Yeah ... I know. Have you looked at the school for Andrew?'

'Not yet. I suppose I should as soon as we finish the movie. I really haven't had time to do anything. I feel like I've been living in suspended animation for months.'

'Yeah.' He smiled again. 'I know the feeling. Me too.' It was strange to realise that in three months he would leave Howarth and go back to the New York School. It was difficult to remember a time when he hadn't been at Howarth, a time when she hadn't called him, when he hadn't been her friend.

There was something sad between them this time that Daphne couldn't quite put her finger on while she visited Andrew. She saw Matthew watching her from the window of his office, and then he would quickly turn away. It wasn't until he drove her back to the airport that she finally asked him.

'Matthew, is something wrong?'

'No, little one, nothing. I just had a birthday. I think maybe I'm just feeling old.'

'You need to get back to New York.'

His sister had said the same thing, but she knew more than Daphne, because she knew her brother was in love.

'Maybe.' He was strangely noncommittal.

'It's too lonely for you at Howarth. It was different for Helen Curtis. She's an old woman, she doesn't mind being locked up all alone.'

'You didn't mind it either when you did it, and you were half her age.'

'I wasn't alone the whole time I lived there.' As always, her voice was tinged with gentle memories of John.

'Neither am I, all the time.' It was the first time he had said anything like that. Daphne looked at him in surprise. He knew so much about her life that she had no hesitation about asking.

'Are you seeing someone up there, Matt?' Somehow she had always assumed that he was alone. And she was suddenly shocked to realise that she hadn't known more. Why hadn't he told her?

'Not really. From time to time.'

'Nothing serious?' She wasn't sure why, but it bothered her, which was ridiculous, she told herself. She was thinking of marrying Justin. Why shouldn't Matt have a woman in his life? He was just her friend after all.

He looked pensive. 'It could be serious if I wanted it to be. But I haven't wanted that.'

'Why not?' Her blue eyes were all innocence, and he turned towards her, marvelling at how blind she was.

'For a lot of foolish reasons, Daphne. Very foolish.'

'Don't be afraid, Matt. I was. And I was wrong.'

'Were you? Are you that happy now?' He sounded so sad.

'Not always, but some of the time. Maybe that's enough. At least I'm alive.'

'How do you know that's better? Is it good enough just to be alive?'

'You can't have perfection, Matt. I gave up after John died, because I knew I'd never find that again, but who's to say that we'd always have been that happy. Maybe even Jeffrey and I would have had our problems after a while. My career would be hard for any man to swallow. Look at this year, for instance. How would I have managed that if I were married, in a conventional marriage?' It was a question she had thought of often.

'You could swing it if that was what you wanted and your husband was understanding. You also didn't have to write the screenplay.' There was no reproach in his voice, he was just thinking aloud.

'I'm glad I did though.'

'Why? Because of Justin?'

'Partly. But mainly because I've learned a lot doing it. I don't think I'd do it again. It takes too much time away from my books, but it's been a marvellous experience. You were right to encourage me to go.'

'Did I do that?' He looked startled.

'You did.' She smiled. 'The first night I met you, and so did Mrs Curtis.'

Matt looked at her strangely. 'Maybe we were both fools.'

'What makes you say that?' She didn't understand what he was saying. Maybe because she didn't want to.

'Nothing. Martha tells me I'm getting soft in the head. She's probably right.' They exchanged a smile then as they drove on.

'So tell me about your new friend. Who is she?'

He might as well tell her. There was no harm now. 'A schoolteacher in town. She's from Texas, and she's very pretty and very young.' He smiled sheepishly at Daphne, this was a strange friendship that they shared. 'She's twenty-five years old, and frankly, I feel like a dirty old man.'

'Bullshit. It's good for you. Christ, there's nothing else to do up here except read. No wonder everyone here loves my books.'

'So does she. She's read them all.'

Daphne looked amused. 'What's her name?'

'Harriet. Harriet Bateau.'

'That sounds exotic.'

'I wouldn't call her that, but she's a nice girl, with a good mind, good values.'

Daphne looked at him then with a curious expression. 'Do you think you'll get married, Matt?' It was hard to think of him no longer there to take her phone calls, but he couldn't be forever. What they had had been a phenomenon of two lonely lives and kindred souls. The latter would always be the same, but her life had already changed and his was changing. The calls wouldn't go on forever. They both knew it. And they were facing it now.

But he shook his head. He wasn't ready to think of marriage. 'I haven't even thought of that yet. We've just been out a few times.' It was more than that, but in his mind it wasn't, though he knew how in love with him Harriet was. He didn't want to play with her heart, and he suspected that she knew what kept him distant from her. Sometimes he wondered if everyone did except Daphne.

She smiled at him now. 'Well, let me know.'

'I will. And you do the same.'

'About Justin?'

He nodded.

'I will.'

He stood looking down at her just before she got on the plane. 'Take care of yourself, little one.' More than ever before, this time his words had the ring of goodbye. She reached up and hugged him and he hugged her back, trying not to cling to her, and silently wishing her luck.

'I'll send Andrew out to you at Thanksgiving.'

'I'll be talking to you long before that.' But he wasn't so sure, and when he waved for the last time he had to turn away so she wouldn't see his eyes fill with tears at her going.

35

When Daphne stepped off the plane in Los Angeles, she found Justin waiting at the gate, and he swept her into his arms with a hungry look of glee. Four people recognised him before they reached the limousine, but as usual he denied who he was, and Daphne sat laughing with him in the backseat. He seemed ecstatic to see her, and when they got home, she found everything spotless and in order, and Justin looked very proud of himself.

'See! I told you I had reformed.'

'I apologise for all my evil thoughts.' She was beaming. Maybe he was for real after all. She felt relief sweep over her like a flood of cool, fresh water. Now she could let go again and trust him. She adored him, and everything was all right, but he looked down at her with serious eyes.

'No, Daphne. I apologise for my evil past.'

'Don't say that, darling ... it's all right.' She kissed him tenderly on the mouth and he picked her up in his arms and deposited her on the bed and they made love until morning without even going back to the car to get her luggage or turn off the living room lights, which, like their ardour, burned brightly until morning.

The movie got back to the usual grind the next morning and the next nine weeks flew by like magic. Daphne barely had time to call Matthew, and lately she felt reluctant to call him. It was beginning to feel like a betrayal of Justin to be pouring out her soul to Matt. He didn't seem to mind it, and he never seemed to notice when she called, but still it didn't feel right now, and several times when she did call, Matt was out. She assumed, correctly, with Harriet Bateau.

They wrapped up the last scene of *Apache* in the first week of November, and as Justin walked off the set for the last time there were tears in everyone's eyes. There were kisses and hugs, and Howard grabbed her and hugged her. Champagne flowed and they all left each other with regret, feeling like lost souls. It was impossible to imagine what they would all do without the filming of *Apache*. It had taken seven months, during which time they had become brothers and sisters and lovers. And now it was over, and the sense of loss was overwhelming. There was still plenty of work for Howard and the technical people. They would spend months on editing and cutting and splicing, the music and the sound would be worked on for a long time. But for Daphne and the actors it was all over, a dream come to an end, which had at times seemed like a nightmare, but now all the pains were forgotten. Like childbirth, it all seemed very dim, except the final burst of exhilaration at the end, and at the wrap party the next day everyone got roaring drunk and generally unruly. They didn't have to worry about being at work on time at five o'clock the next morning, or Howard screaming at them. It was over. *Finito*. Finished. Daphne stood, holding a glass of champagne and beaming at Justin, as Howard made a farewell speech and she felt tears fill her eyes.

'It's a beautiful movie, Daff. You're going to love it.' She had already seen rushes on a regular basis, but she had to admit that it would be the thrill of her life when she saw the finished film, and now she looked happily up at Justin.

'You did a great job.'

Everywhere, in every corner, were people congratulating each other and kissing. It was three in the morning before they went home.

And the next morning Daphne sat in her office with Barbara feeling lost and a little sad as she grinned. 'Christ, you know, I'm as bad as Justin. I don't know what to do now.'

'You'll figure out something.' Barbara smiled. 'Not to

mention the new book.' She had three months left to write it, and after Thanksgiving she had to get down to work. 'When's Andrew coming out?'

'The night before Thanksgiving. And that reminds me' – she handed Barbara a list – 'you and Tom and the kids are still coming, aren't you?' She looked suddenly worried. She knew that Barbara had never really made peace with Justin, and she was afraid that at the last minute they'd back out.

'We wouldn't miss it.'

'Good.'

She and Justin spent the next week doing the kinds of things film people do when they aren't working. They played tennis once or twice, went to a couple of parties, had dinner at Ma Maison and The Bistro and Morton's. The papers mentioned them several times, their romance was no longer a secret, and Daphne was feeling happy and relaxed. Justin seemed to look younger by the hour, and four days before Andrew was due to arrive he read the morning paper and smiled at Daphne.

'Guess what? There's snow in the Sierras.'

'Am I supposed to get excited about that?' She looked amused. Sometimes he still reminded her of a little boy.

'Hell, yes, kiddo. It's the first snow of the year. How about going skiing this week?'

'Justin' – at moments like this she spoke as though she were his extremely patient mother – 'I hate to remind you, my love, but Thanksgiving is next Thursday and we're having Barbara and Tom and his kids, and Andrew here for Thanksgiving dinner.'

'Tell them we can't make it.'

'I can't do that.'

'Why not?'

'Because for one thing Andrew is arriving on Wednesday, and this will be special for him. Come on, sweetheart, this is important to me. I haven't had a real at-home Thanksgiving in ten years.'

'We'll do it next year.' He looked petulant as he said it.

'Justin, please...' Her eyes pleaded with him and he threw down the paper and got up.

'Oh, shit. Who the hell cares about Thanksgiving dinner for chrissake? That's for preachers and their wives. It's the best snow they've had at Tahoe in thirty years and you want to sit here with a bunch of kids eating turkey. Christ.'

'Is that really so awful?' She was hurt by his words.

He looked down at her from his great height. 'It's extremely bourgeois.'

She laughed at the expression he had used, and took his hand in hers. 'I apologise for being so boring. But this is really important to all of us. Especially Andrew and me.'

'All right, all right. I give up. I'm obviously outnumbered by all you straight folks.' He kissed her then and didn't mention it again. She had promised him that as soon as Andrew went back to school, they would go skiing, even if it meant postponing her book. Justin wasn't starting a movie for several months, so they had plenty of time to go skiing. And Andrew was only staying for a week.

But on Tuesday night, as they lay in bed, Justin rolled over and kissed her and she saw that he was hemming and hawing about something. It was obvious that he had something to say.

'What's up, love?' She suspected that he wanted to ask her about Andrew. She knew that he was still nervous about his deafness. And she had tried to reassure him that Andrew was easy to talk to now, and she would be there to help. 'What's on your mind?'

He sat up in bed and looked down at her with a sheepish smile. 'You know me too well, Daff.'

'I try to.' But she didn't. She was in for a big surprise. 'So?'

'I'm leaving for Tahoe in the morning. I couldn't

resist, Daff. And to tell you the truth, I really need to get away.'

'Now?' She lay there and stared at him and then she sat up. He wasn't kidding. She couldn't believe it. 'Do you mean it?'

'Yes. I figured you'd understand.'

'What made you think that?'

'Well ... look ... I have to be honest. Family turkey dinners just aren't my style. I haven't done that kind of shit since I was in high school, and it's too late to start again now.'

'What about Andrew? I just can't believe you'd do this.' She got out of bed and walked around the room, torn between disbelief and fury.

'What's the big deal? I'll meet him at Christmas.'

'Will you? Or will you go skiing then, too?'

'Depends on how the snow is.' She stared at him then in total disbelief. The man who had pretended he loved her for the past eight months, and had finally convinced her, despite one aberration, was actually going skiing instead of staying home for Thanksgiving to meet her son. What in hell was in his head, or his heart? Again she found herself wondering 'Who is he?'

'Do you know how important this is to me?'

'I think it's stupid.' He didn't even look apologetic. He was totally comfortable about what he was about to do, and again Howard's warning that actors were all selfish children came to her mind. He had been right about everything, even the tears at the end of the movie. Maybe he was right about that, too.

'It's not stupid, dammit. And you want to get married one of these days and you haven't even taken the trouble to meet my only child. You didn't bother to come East with me in September and now this.' She stared at him in furious stupefaction, but beneath the fury was hurt beyond measure. He didn't want what she wanted in life, but more important than that, he didn't want Andrew. She was sure of that now, and that changed everything between them.

310

'I need time to think, Daff.' He looked suddenly very quiet.

'About what?' She was startled. It was the first time she'd heard that.

'About us.'

'Is something wrong?'

'No. But this is an enormous commitment. I've never gotten married, and before I tie myself down for good, I want some time alone.' It almost sounded right, but not quite, and she didn't really buy it.

'Well, your timing stinks. Couldn't you wait until next week?'

'I don't think so.'

'Why not?'

'Because I'm not sure I'm ready to meet your son.' It was painful, but honest. 'I don't know what to say to a deaf kid.'

'You start with hello.' Her eyes were cold and hurt and empty. She was sick and tired of his neurotic games about Andrew. And maybe Andrew was only the excuse. Maybe he didn't really want her. Maybe he didn't want anyone in his life except cocktail waitresses and starlets. Maybe that was all he was up to. He was suddenly diminishing in her eyes at a frightening rate, like a balloon with a hole the size of a fist in it.

'I just don't know how to talk to your kid. I've seen people like that, they make me nervous.'

'He lip-reads and he talks.'

'But not like a normal human being.' She suddenly hated him for what he was saying, and she turned her back on him and looked out the window. All she could think of now was Andrew. She didn't need this man. She needed her son, and no one else. She turned to him.

'All right, never mind, dammit, go.'

'I knew you'd understand.' He sounded perfectly happy and she shook her head in amazement. He understood nothing of what she felt. None of the disappointment or the hatred or the hurt he had just inflicted on her.

And then, suddenly, she wondered about something. 'Just when did you make these plans?'

At last he looked somewhat embarrassed, but not very. 'A couple of days ago.'

She stared at him for a long moment. 'And you didn't tell me?' He shook his head. 'You stink.' She slammed the bedroom door and slept that night in Barbara's bedroom, which she no longer used. She had moved in with Tom, and she came in every day, as she had in New York.

The next morning Daphne got up when she heard Justin making breakfast, and she walked into the kitchen to find him already dressed. She sat staring at him as he poured them each a cup of coffee. He looked relaxed and happy and she looked at him in open disbelief.

'You know, I just can't believe you'd do this.'

'Don't turn it into a major crisis, Daff. It's not such a big deal.'

'To me it is.' And she knew that to the others it would seem like one too. How was she going to explain his disappearance? Thanksgiving bored him so he'd gone skiing instead? She was suddenly grateful that she had said nothing at all to Andrew. She had been planning to have a talk with him on the way in from the airport. But now she wouldn't have to. Their meeting was going to have to wait until Christmas, if Justin didn't pull another disappearing act then. She was beginning to wonder about him, and as she watched him eat eggs and toast, she had an unpleasant thought.

'Are you going alone?'

'That's a strange question.' He kept his eyes on his eggs.

'Then it's appropriate, Justin. You're a strange man.' He looked up at her then and saw something unpleasant in her eyes. She was not only angry at him, she was livid. And she was looking for points against him. It startled him to realise that about her. But he didn't realise how deeply he had hurt her. In rejecting Andrew, he had

312

rejected her. In fact it was worse, but he didn't understand that.

'Yes, I'm going alone. I told you, I need some time to think up in the mountains.'

'I need some time to think too.'

'What about?' He actually looked surprised.

'You.' She sighed then. 'If you aren't going to make the effort to get to know Andrew, this isn't going to work out.' Not to mention the fact that if he ran off and did exactly what he pleased whenever he felt like it, it wouldn't suit her either. She hadn't a chance to see that side of him yet. They had been too busy working on the movie but now new sides of him were coming out. Sides that she suspected she couldn't live with. He disappeared for endless hours at times, never showed up when he said he was going to, and had a slapdash, easygoing way about him that he insisted was the only way he could balance the discipline and tension he felt when he was working. She had made excuses to herself, but suddenly she was no longer inclined to.

He tried to kiss her when he left, but she turned away and walked back into the house. And when Barbara arrived, she found Daphne in her study, lost in thought. Daphne looked a million miles away and Barbara had to speak to her twice before she heard her.

'I just picked up the turkey. Biggest mother you've ever seen.' She grinned. But there was no response at first and then Daphne seemed to force herself back to the present.

'Hi, Barb.'

'You seem far away. Already thinking about the new book?'

'Sort of.' But Barbara hadn't seen that vague, trancelike state in a long time.

'Where's Justin?'

'Out.' She didn't have the heart to tell her yet, but before she left for the airport to pick up Andrew, she decided she had to. She couldn't keep up the game forever, and why should she? She didn't owe it to him

313

to make him look good. 'Barb, Justin's not coming to Thanksgiving dinner.' Daphne looked grim.

'He's not?' She looked as though she hadn't understood. 'Did you two have a fight?'

'Sort of. But not until after he told me he was going skiing for the next week instead of staying for Thanksgiving.'

'Are you kidding?'

'No. And I don't want to discuss it.' And the look on her face told Barbara that she meant it. She locked herself in her study then until it was time to go to the airport.

Daphne drove to the airport alone, her face set in a grim expression. She parked her car in the garage, and walked to the gate, her mind still reeling about Justin's behaviour. He had simply, flatly, walked out to do his own thing, as he pleased, without giving a damn about what mattered to her. And she was still running the exchange over again and again in her head as they announced Andrew's flight and she waited for the plane to pull into the gate. But when it did, suddenly all thoughts of Justin vanished. It was as though suddenly he no longer mattered, and everything came back into perspective. All that mattered was Andrew.

She felt her heart begin to beat faster as people came off the plane, and then in the midst of the crowd she saw him, holding a stewardess's hand, his eyes busily searching for her, and for an instant she was too stricken to move. This was the child Justin had rejected. This was the child she had built her whole life on. She began to move towards him then, no obstacle could stop her.

He saw her as she approached, and wrenched himself free from the flight attendant, running into her arms with the little sound he made when he was most pleased, and her whole life seemed to well up and spill from her eyes. He was all she had left from a lifetime of loss, and in truth he was the only human being who truly loved her. She clung to him like a life raft in the milling crowd,

314

and when he looked up at her face it was drenched with tears as she smiled at him.

'It's so good to have you back.' She mouthed carefully at him and he smiled in answer.

'It'll be gooder when you come home.'

'Much,' she agreed. And she suspected that that might come sooner than she had planned. They went to pick up his bags hand in hand and she seemed reluctant to let go of him even for a moment.

He had lots to tell her on the drive to her house, even a casual mention of Matthew's new girl friend, which, for some reason, cut her to the quick. She didn't want to hear about that now.

'She comes to see him at the school every Sunday. She's pretty and she laughs a lot. She has red hair and she brings us all candy.'

Daphne wanted to be pleased for Matthew, but somehow she wasn't. And she made no answer as they drove home, and the conversation moved on to other subjects. They had lots to do when they got to the house, they swam and talked and played cards, and Daphne began to feel herself return to the land of the living. They barbecued chicken in the backyard, and at last she put him to bed. He was yawning and could hardly stay awake, but he looked at her questioningly before she turned out the light.

'Mom, does someone else live here?'

'No. Why? Aunt Barbara used to.'

'I mean a man.'

'What makes you ask that?' She felt her heart skip a beat.

'I found some man's clothes in your closet.'

'They belong to the people who own the house.'

He nodded, seemingly satisfied, and then, 'Are you mad at Matt?'

'Of course not.' She looked surprised. 'Why would you ever think that?'

His eyes searched her face. Andrew was a very perceptive child. He was eight years old now, no longer a baby. 'I thought you got mad when I talked about his girl friend.'

'Don't be silly. He's a nice man, he should have a nice lady.'

'I think he likes you.'

'We're good friends.' But she was suddenly dying to ask him what made him think so.

As though he read her mind, he answered with sleepy signs. 'He talks about you a lot, and he always looks happy when you call. Happier than when Harriet comes to visit on Sundays.'

'That's silly.' She smiled, brushing it off, but in some secret place in her heart she was pleased. 'Go to sleep now, sweetheart. We have a big day ahead tomorrow.' He nodded and his eyes were closed before she turned off the light, and went into her room, thinking of Matthew. She realised then that she still had to call him to tell him Andrew was all right. As usual, he answered his private line on the second ring.

'How's our friend? Safely arrived?'

'Very much so. And full of mischief.'

'That's nothing new.' Matthew smiled. 'He's just like his mother. And how are you?'

'Okay. Getting ready for Thanksgiving.' The conversations were always more impersonal now. Things were different since the advent of Justin and Harriet Bateau, particularly lately.

'Are you having a big turkey dinner at home?'

'I am.' There was a moment's hesitation in her voice, but she decided not to tell him. It wasn't his problem that Justin had skipped out, and maybe it didn't matter anymore that Justin refused to relate to Andrew. But she didn't want to drag Matthew into her decision, and she was beginning to think about going home. 'What about you, Matt?'

'I'll be here.'

'You won't be with your sister?'

'I didn't want to leave the kids.' And Harriet? But she didn't dare ask him that. If he wanted her to know more,

316

he'd tell her. And he didn't. 'Are you coming to New York one of these days, Daff?' He sounded like the old Matt as he said it, and there was something lonely and gentle in his voice, but Daphne only sighed.

'I don't know. I've been thinking a lot about that.' It was time to make some decisions, and she knew it. 'I'm taking Andrew to visit the LA school next week.' At least that was what she'd been planning. But that was before Justin had shown his colours and gone to Tahoe.

'You'll love it. It's a great place.' But he sounded sad nonetheless. 'Everyone sure would miss him here.'

'You'll be gone anyway, won't you, Matt?'

But suddenly he sounded vague. 'I'm not sure.' Was he staying in New Hampshire then? Was it serious with Harriet Bateau after all? She felt a sinking sensation as she realised that was probably the case. What did Andrew know? He was only eight years old. Maybe Matthew was thinking of getting married.

'Let me know what you're going to do.'

'You too.'

She wished him a happy Thanksgiving then, and forcing herself not to think of Justin, she went to bed. The phone rang at midnight and woke her. It was Justin, happily ensconced in Squaw Valley, he told her, but the place where he was staying didn't have a phone. He started to tell her about the snow and how much he missed her, and then suddenly, in the middle of the conversation, he told her that he was freezing in an open phone booth, and had to hang up. And Daphne sat up in bed, staring at the phone, confused by the phone call. Why had he called her like that? And if he'd been freezing, why had he been so chatty before? She decided that she didn't understand anything about him, and forcing him from her mind once again, she went back to sleep, and oddly enough that night she dreamed of Matthew.

36

Thanks to Barbara and Tom's daughter, Alex, the Thanksgiving dinner turned out better than Daphne had dreamed. The three women worked together in the kitchen talking and laughing, and Tom and both boys putted golf balls around the lawn. He was amazed at how bright Andrew was and how funny he could be, even with his stilted speech. He discovered that he had a wonderful sense of humour, and when Daphne said grace before they began dinner, she felt more grateful than she had in years. Everyone ate tons of food, and sat by the fire after they were finished, and the Harrington troupe was sorry to leave when the time came. Both the teenagers kissed Daphne and hugged Andrew, and he promised to come visit them at their pool the next day, which they did. It was a comfortable, relaxed weekend, and other than missing Justin, Daphne was perfectly happy. The night before Andrew was to leave, Justin called her to check in, but hung up abruptly again, which annoyed Daphne. She didn't understand why he'd call, only to hang up a few minutes later. It didn't make any sense, at least not to her, but she thought about it at night after Andrew went to bed, and then suddenly it dawned on her. It was as though someone had approached him, and he'd hung up before he was found out. Suddenly she knew, and she sat up in bed livid. It was hours before she fell asleep. In the morning she was busy with Andrew. She put him on the plane and called Matt, and then went back to the house. For the next three days she tried to work on her new book, but nothing would come. All she could think about was Justin.

He drove in about two in the morning. He opened the front door with his key, propped his skis up in the hall, and then walked into the bedroom. He expected Daphne to be asleep, and was surprised when he saw her sitting up in bed with a book. She lifted her eyes to his without a word and looked at him.

'Hi, babe, what are you doing up?'

'I was waiting for you.' But there was no warmth in her voice.

'That's nice. Your kid get off okay?'

'Fine, thanks. And his name's Andrew.'

'Oh, Christ.' He knew then what he had in store. Another speech about Thanksgiving, but he was wrong. She had other things on her mind.

'Who were you with in Squaw Valley?'

'A mountain full of people I didn't know.' He sat down and pulled off his boots. After a twelve-hour drive he was in no mood for her interrogation. 'Could we just let it go until tomorrow?'

'No. I don't think we can.'

'Well, I'm going to bed.'

'Are you? Where?'

'Here. Last I heard I lived here.' He stared at her from across the room. 'Or has my address changed?'

'Not yet, but I think it might if you don't answer some questions. Honestly, for a change.'

'Look, Daff, I told you ... I needed to think...' But as he spoke the phone rang, and Daphne picked it up. She was instantly afraid that something was wrong with Andrew. Why else would anyone call at two thirty in the morning? But it wasn't Matt at the other end, it was a woman's voice, and she asked to speak to Justin. Without another word Daphne handed it to Justin.

'It's for you.'

Slamming the door, she left the room, and he found her in her study a few minutes later. 'Look, Daphne, please, I know how this looks but ...'

And then, suddenly, as he stood there, tired from the trip, he realised that the pretence was too much trouble.

He was too tired for more lies. His voice was quiet as he sat down. 'All right, Daphne. You're right. I went skiing with Alice.'

'Who the hell is that?'

'The girl from Ohio.' He sounded desperately tired. 'It doesn't mean a hell of a lot, she likes to ski, so do I, I didn't want to stay here for your little family event, so I took her up there for a week. That's all there was to it.' To him it was normal.

There was no point fighting it anymore. It wasn't going to work. It was all over. She looked at him with tears in her eyes, and she felt so disillusioned that it was like a piece of her had been removed – the piece that loved him. 'Justin, I can't do this anymore.'

'I know. And I can't do it to you. I'm not made for this kind of thing, Daff.'

'I know.' She began to cry and he came to her.

'It's not that I don't love you. I do, but in my way, and my way is different from yours. Too different. I don't think I could ever be what you want. You want an honest-to-God regular husband. That's not me.' She nodded and turned her face away.

'It's all right. I understand. You don't have to explain.'

'Will you be okay?'

She nodded as the tears flowed, looking up at him, he was even more beautiful with his mountain tan, but that's all he was, all he had ever been, pretty to look at. Howard Stern had been right, he was a beautiful, spoiled child, who did exactly what he wanted in life, no matter who it hurt, or what it cost.

When she saw that he was going, for a mad instant she wanted to beg him not to go, to stay, that they could work it out, but she knew that they wouldn't. 'Justin?' The whole question was in the single word.

He nodded. 'Yes. I think I'll go.'

'Now?' Her voice trembled. She felt lonely and frightened. She had brought it to this, but there was no other way and she knew it.

320

'It's better like this. I'll pick up my stuff tomorrow.'

It had to end sometime and the time was now. He looked down at her with a sad smile. 'I love you, Daff.'

'Thanks.'

They were empty words coming from him, he was an empty man. And then the door closed and he was gone, and she sat alone in her study, crying. For the third time in her life she had lost, but this time for very different reasons. And she had lost someone who didn't really love her. He was capable of loving no one but himself. He had never loved Daphne. And as she grieved through the night she wondered if that was worse or better.

The next day she looked subdued when Barbara arrived and there were dark circles under her eyes as she sat in her study, working. 'You feeling okay?'

'More or less.' There was a long pause as Barbara searched her eyes. 'Justin moved out last night.'

She wasn't sure what to say in answer. 'Should I ask why, or should I mind my own business?'

Daphne smiled a tired smile. 'It doesn't matter. It had to be like this.' But she didn't sound convinced. She knew she would miss him. He had meant something to her for nine months and now it was over. It was bound to hurt for a while. Daphne knew that. She had lived with pain before. She'd live through it again.

Barbara nodded and sat down. 'I feel bad for you, Daff. But I can't say that I'm sorry. He would have screwed you over for the next hundred years. He's just like that.'

Daphne nodded. She couldn't disagree now. 'I don't think he even knows he's doing it.'

'I'm not sure if that's better or worse.' It was a hell of a statement about the man.

'Either way, it hurts.'

'I know.' Barbara walked towards her and patted her shoulder. 'What are you going to do now?'

'Go home. Andrew didn't like the school here anyway, and I don't belong here. I belong in New York, in my own place, writing my books, and being near Andrew.'

321

But it would all be different now. She had opened new doors since she'd left. Doors that would be hard to close, and she wasn't quite sure she remembered how to do it. It had been a lonely life for her in New York, and there had been a lot of joy at times with Justin.

'How soon do you want to leave?'

'It'll take me a couple of weeks to wrap up. I have some meetings at Comstock.' She smiled ruefully then. 'They want to talk to me about buying another book for a movie.'

Barbara held her breath. 'Will you write the screenplay?'

'Never again, my friend. Once is enough. I learned what I wanted to learn. But from now on, I write the books, they write the movies.' Barbara looked depressed. She had figured that. Even if Daphne had stayed with Justin on the West Coast, it was unlikely she would have done it again. She hadn't written a book in a year, and Daphne had complained about it often. 'So, we go home.' It was an assumption that Barbara didn't dare counter, and that night she told Tom as she fell apart in his arms, sobbing.

'For God's sake, Barb. You don't have to go with her.' He looked like he was going to cry too.

But she shook her head. 'Yes, I do. I can't leave her now. She's all broken up over Justin.'

'She'll survive. I need you more.'

'She has no one but me and Andrew.'

'And whose fault is that? Her own. Are you going to sacrifice our life for hers?'

'No.' She only cried harder as he held her, and then at last she quieted down. 'It's just that I can't leave her now.' It was in a way what she had gone through years before with her mother, and now Daphne wasn't there to help her gain her freedom. Her mother had died the year before in the home and now Barbara was tied to Daphne.

Tom looked unhappily at the woman he loved. 'Then how soon can you leave her?'

'I don't know.'

'That's not good enough, Barb. I can't live with that.' And then with a look of total despair he poured himself a stiff drink. 'I just don't believe you'd do this. After what we've had for the last year, you're going back to New York with her. For chrissake, dammit, that's crazy!' He was shouting at her and she started to cry again.

'I know it is. But she's done so much for me, and Christmas is coming and...' She knew how hard Christmas was every year for Daphne. And she also knew that Tom didn't understand. There was no reason why he should, but she didn't want to lose him. That was too high a price to pay, even for Daphne. 'Look, I promise, I'll come back. Just give me some time to get her settled in New York again and then I'll tell her.'

'When?' The word came at her like a shot. 'Tell me a day, and I'll hold you to it.'

'I'll tell her the week after Christmas. I promise.'

'How much notice will you give her?' He wasn't giving an inch.

She wanted to say a month, but she quailed at what she saw in his eyes. He looked like a wounded beast, and she hated to leave him more than she hated leaving Daphne. 'Two weeks.'

'All right. So you'll be back here six weeks after you leave?'

'Yes.'

'Will you marry me then?' His ferocious expression never changed.

'Yes.'

He smiled slowly then. 'All right, dammit. I'll let you go back to New York with her then, but don't ever do anything like this to me again. I can't take it.'

'Neither can I.' She folded herself into his arms.

'I'll come to New York on the weekends.'

'You will?' She looked up at him with wide happy eyes, and she looked half of forty.

'I will. And with any luck at all, I'll get you pregnant

before you even come back, and then I know you'll have to keep your word.' She laughed at the radical suggestion, but the idea didn't displease her. He had long since convinced her that she wasn't too old to have at least one or two babies.

'You don't have to do that, Tom.'

'Why not? I'd enjoy it.'

They spent every minute together that they could, and Tom came to the airport when they left. Daphne looked very New York in a black suit and a mink coat and hat, and Barbara was wearing the new mink jacket he had bought her. 'You two certainly look chic.' There was no trace of Los Angeles about them. And when he kissed Barbara, he whispered, 'See you on Friday.' She smiled and held him close and then they boarded the plane and took their seats and Daphne glanced at Barbara.

'You don't look too upset. Do I sense a plot afoot?' Barbara blushed and Daphne laughed at the truth. 'How soon is he coming to New York? On the next flight?'

'Friday.'

'Good for you. If I were halfway decent I'd can you right here and now and throw you off the plane.' Barbara watched her face but it was obvious that she didn't mean it. Daphne was looking very pale beneath her dark fur hat, and Barbara knew that she had seen Justin the night before. She suspected that it wasn't an easy meeting. Eventually, after lunch, Daphne told her about it.

'He's already living with that girl.'

'The one from Ohio?' Daphne nodded. 'Maybe he'll marry her.' And then she was instantly sorry she had said it. 'I'm sorry, Daff.'

'Don't be. You may be right, but I doubt it. I don't think men like Justin marry anyone at all. I just wasn't smart enough to know that.' They talked about Andrew then, and Daphne said she was going up to see him that weekend. 'I was going to ask you to come, but now that I know you've got better plans...' They exchanged a smile, and then Barbara decided to tackle something she had thought of for a long time.

'What about Matthew?'

'What about him?' Daphne's eyes were instantly guarded.

'You know what I mean.' They had been together for too long to play games.

'Yes, I do. But he's just a friend, Barb. It's better that way.' And then she smiled. 'Besides, Andrew says he has a girl friend. And I happen to know he's right. Matt told me about her in September.'

'I have the feeling that if he knew you were free, he would dump her in about ten minutes.'

'I doubt that, and it's not important. Andrew and I have a lot of catching up to do when I get back, and I want to start the new book before Christmas.' Barbara wanted to tell her that that wasn't good enough, but she knew Daphne didn't want to discuss it. They each sat lost in her own thoughts. Barbara was relieved about the silence. She felt uncomfortable lying to Daphne about Tom and she wasn't ready to tell her they were getting married.

They arrived in New York, and Daphne grinned broadly as they drove into town. 'Welcome home.' But it no longer felt like that to Barbara. She already missed Tom. All Daphne could think of was Andrew. She talked about him nonstop for the next few days, and at the end of the week she took her car out of storage and drove up to see him. She could hardly wait as she drove along, singing and smiling. There was snow on the ground almost all the way up and it was a long tedious drive, but she didn't mind it. She had to stop and have chains put on her tyres, but never for a moment did she long for the balmy sunshine of California. All she wanted was to be near Andrew. She arrived in town well after nine, and she drove straight to the inn and called Matt to tell him that she had arrived and would be over in the morning. But one of the teachers answered his phone and told her he was out. So be it, she whispered to herself as she looked out the window. It was no longer time to think of him, he had his own life now, and she had Andrew. And the next morning when she got to the school, they had a grand reunion.

'And now we'll never be apart anymore.' It was amazing to think that the year was over. 'I'm going to come and get you in two weeks and we'll spend the whole Christmas vacation together at my apartment.' The visits to California had proven beyond any doubt that he was ready to leave the school for long periods of time, but he looked at her and shook his head.

'I can't, Mom.'

'You can't?' She looked shocked. 'Why not?'

'I'm going on a field trip.' Barbara was right. He had his own life, even now.

'Where?' Daphne felt her heart sink. She was going to spend Christmas alone.

'I'm going skiing.' And then he grinned. 'But I'm coming back before New Year's. Could I come then?'

'Sure you can.' She laughed softly. How life had changed in a year.

'Can we blow horns on New Year's Eve?'

'Yes.' But it struck her as a funny request, he wouldn't be able to hear them.

'I love the way they feel, they tickle my mouth, and everyone else will hear the noise.' There was definitely the eight-year-old inside him, despite his new independence.

And then Matthew joined them and Daphne smiled. 'Hi, Matt. I hear you're taking Andrew skiing.'

'I'm not. I'm staying here to finish up. But there's a whole bunch of them going to Vermont with some of the teachers.'

'That ought to be fun.' But he was watching the sadness he saw in her eyes.

'You wanted him in California for Christmas?' She hadn't yet told him that she'd moved back. She had just had Barbara call and tell them at the school that Daphne was in New York for the moment.

326

'No. I thought I'd stay in New York.' She searched his eyes but she saw nothing there. 'Andrew says he'll come down for New Year's.'

'That sounds great.' Their eyes met and held over the boy's head and a thousand thoughts went unspoken.

'When are you leaving, Matt?'

'On the twenty-ninth. For a while I thought I'd stay here, but they need me too much at the New York School.' He smiled. 'That doesn't sound very humble, but Martha says she'll quit if I don't come back, and they can't afford to lose us both. She's the one who's really valuable to them.'

'Don't be so modest. They're going to miss you like crazy up here.'

'No, they won't. The new director is arriving from London next week, and judging from her correspondence, she's terrific. And I'll be coming up pretty often, to visit the troops on weekends.' With that, Daphne understood that Harriet Bateau was still in the picture. It gave her her cue for the next moves, and she was careful with them. For a mad moment she had wondered if Barbara was right, that she should let him know she was free, but she had no right to do that to him now, and the fact was that there was no reason to think it would make any difference to him.

'Why aren't you going skiing with the kids?' But she assumed that she already knew.

'I want to stay here with the kids who can't go.' She nodded, but she understood the real reason. He went back to his work then and she only saw him in brief moments during her visit. He was desperately busy, getting things ready for the new director. And as had often happened before, it wasn't until her last night that they had time to sit down and talk after Andrew went to bed. She had decided to tackle the roads and drive home on Sunday night. For the first time in a long time, being in New Hampshire depressed her.

'So how's California these days, Daff?' He handed her a cup of coffee and sat down in his familiar chair.

327

'It was all right the last I saw of it. I've been in New York since Monday.'

'That's nice for Andrew that you're staying through Christmas. I gather your friend still isn't anxious to meet him. Or is he here with you?' It was the perfect opportunity to tell him, but she didn't.

'No, he's not. I have to get started on my next book.'

'Don't you ever relax?' His smile was gentle, but he was vaguely distant.

'No more than you do. From what I've seen in the last two days, you're entitled to a nervous breakdown.'

'I am. But I don't have time to collect it.'

'I know the feeling. The last few weeks of making *Apache* were absolutely nuts, but the wrap was great.' She told him about the last day and the wrap party, and he smiled as he listened. She had a nice way of weaving a tale and she was keeping the conversation from coming too close. She was still hurting too much to open up very much, even to him. It wasn't so much that she missed Justin. But she felt defeated. By Justin and the twenty-two-year-old girl from Ohio. Nothing like that had ever happened to her before. Or would again, she promised herself daily.

'What'll you do for Christmas with Andrew gone?' There was concern in his eyes, but maybe Justin would come in to be with her. The last time he had talked to her about him, she had said that they would probably get married.

'I'll have plenty to do.' It seemed an adequate answer and he nodded. There was a long pause then as they both sat lost in their own thoughts, and he found himself thinking of Harriet. She was a nice girl, but she wasn't for him, and they both knew it. She had started seeing someone else a few weeks before, and he suspected that any day he would hear of her engagement. She was ripe to get married, and there were plenty of people who would jump at the chance, but he wasn't one of them. He didn't love her. And she deserved better than that, he had told her that the last time he saw her. Daphne was watching him as he sat lost in thought. 'You look awfully serious, Matt.'

He glanced at the fire and then at her. 'I was thinking how times change.' Daphne wondered how deeply involved he was with that girl. Maybe he was getting married. But she didn't want to ask him now. She had enough with what she was going through, and when he wanted to, he would tell her.

'Yes, they do. I can't believe this year is over.'

'I told you it wouldn't be forever.' He looked quiet and wise, and she noticed that there was more grey in his hair now than there had been a year before. 'And Andrew did just fine.' He smiled at her then. 'You didn't do too badly either.'

'Andrew did well, thanks to you, Matt.'

'That's not true. Andrew did well because of Andrew.' She nodded then, and after a little while she stood up.

'I'd better go if I'm going to tackle those roads tonight.'

'Are you sure you should?' He worried and she smiled. He had given her so much comfort in the past year, it was difficult not to reach out to him now, but she knew it wouldn't be right for him. He seemed content, and he had said himself that times had changed. It was better left at that.

'I'll be fine. I'm indestructible, you know.'

'Possibly, but there's a hell of a lot of snow on those roads, Daff.' And then as he walked her to the door, 'Why don't you call me when you get home?'

'Don't be silly, Matt. It'll be three or four in the morning. That's my time of day, not any other normal human being's.'

'Never mind that, just call. I'll go right back to sleep. I want to know you're okay. If you don't call me, I'll stay up and keep calling you.' It was an offer above and beyond the call of duty, and reminiscent of their old friendship.

'All right, I'll call. But I hate to wake you.' She

thought about it again as she drove slowly south on the icy roads. It took her even longer than she thought and she didn't get home until five in the morning. It seemed a crime to call, and yet she had to admit that she wanted to. She dialled his number from her desk, and a moment later he picked up the phone, sounding sleepy.

'Matt? I'm home.' She spoke in a whisper.

'Are you okay?' He glanced at the clock as he asked. It was five fifteen in the morning.

'I'm fine. Now go back to sleep.'

'That's all right.' He rolled over in bed with a sleepy smile. 'This reminds me of when you used to call from California.' She smiled too, it was an odd sort of hour and it was easier to let one's guard down. 'I've missed you, you know. Sometimes it's strange when you pop in here. I'm busy and there are ten thousand people around.'

'I know. I feel awkward too.' They sat in silence for a moment and she thought she ought to let him go back to sleep. 'Are you happy these days, Matt?' She wanted to ask him about Harriet but she still didn't dare.

'Pretty much. I'm too busy to ask myself that most of the time. What about you?'

For a moment she faltered, then her guard went up again. 'I'm all right.'

'Getting married?' He had to ask.

'No.' But she didn't offer any further information. 'I think Barbara is, though.'

'The guy in LA?'

'Yes. He's just super. She deserves someone like that.'

'So do you...' The words had sneaked out and he instantly regretted them. 'I'm sorry, Daff. That's none of my business.' Why not?

'It's okay. I've cried on your shoulder a lot in the last year.'

'You're not crying anymore, are you, Daff?' He sounded sad and Daphne knew he was asking about Justin.

330

'Not lately.'

'I'm glad. You deserve good things in your life.'

'So do you.' Her eyes filled with tears then and she felt stupid. He had a right to be happy with that girl, but she knew she was going to miss him. Once he left Howarth she would have no excuse to call him. They might have lunch once in a while, but that would be all, and maybe not even that if he was married. 'Go back to bed now, Matt. It's so late.'

He yawned and glanced back at the clock. It was almost six o'clock, and he had to get up. 'You get some sleep too. You must be bushed after that drive.'

'A little.'

'Good night, Daff. I'll talk to you soon.'

She had called to leave a message for Andrew when he left to ski, but Matt was out, and she was planning to call him on Christmas Day, but she never got to. The car hit her on Madison Avenue on Christmas Eve, and instead of calling Matt she was lying in Lenox Hill as Barbara watched her, with tears coursing silently down her face. She couldn't believe this had happened to Daphne. And what was she going to tell Andrew? Daphne had made her promise not to call, but sooner or later she knew she'd have to. And especially if ... she couldn't bear the thought as Liz Watkins signalled to her that it was time for her to go back out in the hall, and when she checked her pulse, she noticed that Daphne was running a fever.

'How is she now?'

Liz Watkins watched Barbara's eyes, wondering if she could take the truth, then they went out into the hallway. 'Not good, to be honest with you. The fever could mean a lot of things.' Barbara nodded, her eyes filling with tears again. She went to call Tom, he had waited all day in her apartment. It was a rotten way to spend Christmas, but she had to be here with Daphne.

'Oh, babe ...' He thought that the worst had come, but Barbara was quick to reassure him. It was the tenth

331

time she had called, and he worried when he heard her crying.

'She has a fever, and the nurse looks worried.'

He sat silently as his end for a long time. 'Is there anyone you should call, Barb?' It was an enormous responsibility for her to take on her own shoulders.

'The only family she has is Andrew.' She began crying softly then, thinking of him, it would kill him if he lost his mother. She knew that she would take him back to California with her to live with Tom, but that wouldn't be the same. He needed Daphne. They all did. 'And I can't call him. He's skiing. Besides, he's only eight years old. He shouldn't see this.'

'Does she look that bad?'

'No, but . . .' Barbara choked on the words. 'She may not make it.'

And then he had a thought. 'What about the guy at the school, that director who's her friend at Andrew's school?'

'What about him?'

'I don't know, Barb, but it may mean something to him. I've always had the feeling from what you've said that there was more going on than she admitted.' One thing was for sure, she wouldn't bother to call Justin.

'I don't think there was.' She thought about it for a while. 'But maybe I should call him.' Even Barbara didn't realise how close they had become, and maybe he would have some thoughts about whether or not they should contact Andrew on his ski trip. 'I'll call you back.'

'Do you want me to come over?' She was about to say no, and then suddenly she broke down again. She couldn't take it anymore. She needed him there. 'Never mind. I'll be there in ten minutes.' She told him what floor and he told her he'd bring something for her to eat. She wasn't hungry, but he knew that she needed some food to get her through the night, food and a lot of black coffee. He had a feeling that things weren't going to end well for Daphne and Barbara was going to take it very hard if she died.

Barbara sat in the phone booth for a long time, trying to decide if it was right to call. In one of her few lucid moments Daphne had told her not to. But something even stronger told her to now. She had Daphne's handbag and she looked in the little address book she carried. The private number was there next to the name Matthew Dane.

He sounded distracted, as though he had been working.

'Mr Dane, this is Barbara Jarvis in New York.' She could feel her heart pound and her palms sweat. This wasn't going to be easy.

'Yes?' He sounded surprised. Daphne's official calls didn't usually come in at night, let alone on Christmas. He recognised the secretary's name at once. Maybe she was just calling to leave a message for Andrew.

'I ... Mr Dane, this is a difficult call. Miss Fields has had an accident. I'm at the hospital with her now...'

'Did she ask you to call?' He sounded shocked and Barbara fought back tears as she shook her head.

'No, she didn't.' He could hear that she was crying. 'She was hit by a car last night, and ... Mr Dane, she's in intensive care and...' The sobs broke from her then.

'Oh, my God. How bad is it?' She told him all she knew and she could hear that his voice was shaking when he answered.

'She didn't want me to tell you or Andrew, but I thought...'

'Is she conscious?' He sounded relieved.

'She was for a little while, but she isn't now.' Barbara sighed deeply and told him what she had told Tom. 'She just started running a fever.' She also told him what it could mean, and he had to control his voice when he asked the next question. Suddenly he understood as he never had before, what it had been like when she had lost

333

Jeffrey and then John. And he didn't want to know more than he did now. He couldn't bear it.

'Is there anyone with her, Barbara, other than you?' He wasn't sure how else to ask her.

'No, but my ... my fiancé will be here any minute. He's here from LA...' And then she realised that she wasn't telling him what he wanted to know. She decided to take the bull by the horns. 'Mr Dane, she ended it with Justin a month ago.'

'Why didn't she tell me?' He sounded even more shocked than he had before.

'She thought you were in love with some girl up there, and she didn't think it would be fair to tell you about Justin.'

'Oh, my God.' And he had sat by the fire telling her how times had changed. He almost groaned as he remembered the conversation verbatim. He had been assuming that she and Justin were almost married.

'Do you think we should tell Andrew?'

'No, I don't. There's nothing he can do. And he's too young to deal with this, if he doesn't have to.' He looked at his watch then and stood up, beginning to pace the room with his phone in his hand. 'I'll be down in six hours.'

'You're coming?' She sounded stunned. She wasn't sure what she had expected.

'You didn't think I would?' He sounded hurt.

'I don't know. I don't know what I thought. I just knew I had to call you.'

'You were right. And I don't know if it matters now, but just for the record, I've been in love with her ever since I met her. And I was too stupid to get up the guts to say it.' He felt a lump rise in his throat and he could hear Barbara cry softly into the phone. 'I'm not going to lose her now, Barb.'

She nodded. 'I hope you never will.'

37

Matthew drove to New York as fast as he could, thinking every moment of Daphne. Every phone call, every meeting, seemed indelibly etched in his mind, and now it all ran through his head like a movie. Once in a while he smiled at remembered words, but most of the time his face was grim. He couldn't believe this had happened. Not to her. Not to Daphne. So much had already happened in her life, so much sorrow and pain, so many events that required unlimited courage. This couldn't happen to her now. It couldn't end like this, but he knew that it might, and the thought that she might die before he arrived made him drive even faster.

After driving to New York as fast as he could in the snow, Matthew arrived at Lenox Hill at two thirty in the morning. Most of the lights were out in the lobby and there was no one in the halls as he went upstairs. He went straight to the desk at intensive care, and then Barbara saw him. She had sent Tom home long before and insisted that she wanted to stay. The nurse had told them a little while before that the night would be decisive. Daphne couldn't hover much longer where she was, either she would start to improve, or she wouldn't make it.

'Matt?' He turned at the sound of Barbara's voice, wishing it were Daphne. She couldn't believe how quickly he had come. He must have flown over the icy roads. He was lucky he hadn't wound up in the same state as Daphne.

'How is she?'

'The same. She's putting up one hell of a fight.'

He nodded grimly, and there were deep grooves under

his eyes. He had been working like a demon, and now this. He was still wearing the old cords and heavy sweater he had been wearing when Barbara called him. He had left a hasty note for the night staff and run out the door, grabbing his coat and his keys and his wallet.

'Can I see her?' Barbara's eyes searched those of the familiar nurse and she looked at her watch.

'Why don't we wait a few minutes?'

'Nurse' – he turned to her and gripped the desk with powerful hands – 'I've just driven seven hours from New Hampshire to see her.'

'All right.' It didn't matter now. And maybe an hour later it would be too late. Liz Watkins led the way down the hallway to the open door, and there she lay, immobile, swathed in plaster and gauze, hooked up to all her machines in the bright light. Matthew felt an almost physical shock when he saw her. It had been only two weeks since her last visit to Howarth, and suddenly she looked so different. He walked slowly into the room and sat down in the empty chair at her side and gently stroked the pale hair as Barbara watched. She turned and left the room behind Liz. She didn't want to intrude, and the nurse searched her eyes. But she felt better now that she knew there was a man. It wasn't right for a woman like Daphne to be alone. And the man with the soft brown eyes looked perfect for her.

'Hello, little one.' He touched the delicate cheek with one hand, and then sat and looked at her for a long time, wondering again why she hadn't told him about Justin. Maybe he was even foolish to hope now, maybe she had never cared about him, and never could. But if she ever woke up again, he was going to tell her that he loved her. He sat there looking at her face for close to an hour and at last Liz returned to the room to check her. 'Any change?' She shook her head. The fever had gone up slightly. But he never left the room, and she didn't ask him to. He sat there until the shift changed at seven, and Liz told the morning nurse what was going on.

'Why don't you leave him in there, Anne? He's not doing any harm, and how do we know? Maybe it makes a difference. She's fighting for her life.'

The other nurse nodded. They both knew that at times people survived who originally seemed like they would never make it, and if having someone she knew in the room would help, they wouldn't stop it. Liz stopped in to say good-bye, and took a last look at Daphne. She thought she looked a trifle less pale, but it was hard to say. He certainly looked like hell, a shadow of beard had appeared on his face and the circles under his eyes were even darker than they had been.

'Can I get you anything?' she whispered to him. It was against the rules, but she could bring him a cup of coffee. But he only shook his head. And when she left, she saw Barbara asleep on the couch. She went home, wondering if Daphne would still be there when she got back. She hoped so. She thought about her all day, and found herself rereading parts of *Apache*, which was her favourite. And when she came back on at eleven o'clock that night, she was afraid to ask. But the nurse told her that he was still there, and so was Daphne. Barbara had finally gone home that afternoon to get some rest. And Daphne was still holding her own, but barely.

Liz walked silently down the hall until she reached her door and looked in, and she saw him standing over Daphne, looking into her face, almost begging her with his eyes not to let go.

'Would you like a cup of coffee, Mr Dane?' She whispered the name they had told her. Apparently he hadn't eaten all day, he had just drunk a steady stream of coffee.

'No, thanks.' He smiled at the door, the beard was thicker now, but his eyes were strong and alive and his smile was gentle. 'She's doing better, I think.' The fever was gone, but she hadn't stirred all day. He had watched them change her assorted tubes and he hadn't flinched. He had stood there and stroked her hair as he did now while Liz watched him.

She walked slowly to the bed. 'It's amazing, you know. Sometimes I think people like you make the difference.'

'I hope so.' They exchanged a smile and she left and after a while he sat down again, watching Daphne's face, and the sun was coming up over New York when she finally moved. He sat very tense in his chair and watched. He wasn't sure what kind of sign it was, but then she opened her eyes and looked around the room. She seemed puzzled when she saw him and then she drifted off again, but only for a few minutes. He wanted to ring for the nurse, but he was afraid to move, and for a moment he was afraid that he might have drifted off himself, and possibly dreamed it. But she opened her eyes again, and looked long and hard.

'Matt?' Her voice was barely more than a whisper.

'Good morning.'

'You're here?' Her voice was thin and thready and she didn't seem to understand, but she smiled and he took her hand.

'Yes, I am. You've been asleep for a long time.'

'How's Andrew?'

'He's fine.' He was speaking to her in a whisper. 'And you're going to be fine too. Do you know that?'

She smiled faintly at him. 'I don't feel so hot.' He chuckled at the understatement. He had kept his vigil for twenty-eight hours, fearing for her life. 'Not feeling so hot' was certainly one way to say it.

'Daphne . . .' He waited for her to open her eyes again. 'There's something I have to tell you.' He felt a lump in his throat and he stroked her free arm as she looked at him and nodded slightly.

'I already know.'

'Do you?' He seemed disappointed. Had she known all along and didn't want to hear?

'You're . . . getting . . . married . . .' Her eyes were big and blue and sad as she looked at him and he stared at her in amazement.

'Do you actually think I've been sitting here, waiting

338

for you to wake up, to tell you that I'm getting married?'

A small smile dawned on her face. 'You've always been very polite.'

'Not that polite, you dummy.' The small smile grew and she closed her eyes and rested for a minute. When she opened them again, he was watching intently. 'I love you, Daff. I always have and I always will. That's what I wanted to tell you.'

'No, you don't.' She tried to shake her head but winced instead. 'You love Harriet ... Boat ... or whatever her name is...'

'Harriet Boat, as you call her, doesn't mean shit to me. I stopped seeing her after I told her I didn't love her. She knew the truth. The only one who's never known it is you.'

She looked at him for a long time, taking it all in. 'I used to feel guilty for what I felt for you, Matt.'

'Why?'

'I don't know ... I thought it wasn't fair to ... to you ... or to Justin.' She looked at him again for a long time. 'I left him.'

'Why didn't you tell me?'

'I thought you were in love with someone else.' They were both still speaking in whispers. 'And you said...'

'I know what I said. I thought you and that Greek god of yours were getting married.'

She smiled at him then, a lifetime showing in her eyes. 'He's a jerk.'

'So were we. I'm in love with you, Daff. Will you marry me?'

Two huge tears crept from her eyes, and she coughed as she began to cry. He kissed her eyes then, and put his face next to hers. 'Don't cry, Daff ... please ... it's all right ... I didn't want to upset you ...' Then she didn't love him at all. He felt like crying too, but he only stroked her hair as she tried to regain her composure. 'I'm sorry ...' But then he heard her voice again and he froze where he stood.

'I love you too ... I think I fell in love with you the first day I met you ...' Her eyes looked into his, and the tears ran slowly down his cheeks.

'I love you more than I can tell you.'

Liz Watkins came in then, to say good-bye to him before she left, and she stopped as she stood in the doorway. She had heard Daphne's voice and she saw their heads close together. She knocked softly then and came into the room. She was going to ask how Daphne was, but she could see as she approached the bed. They were both crying, and Daphne was smiling.

'This looks like a happy group.'

'It is.' He answered for his future wife. 'We just got engaged.'

'Can I see the ring?' Her eyes glowed. She could tell instantly from looking at Daphne that she would make it. The crisis was past and the worst was over. 'Where's the ring?' she teased in her soft voice.

'She ate it. That's why she's here.' Liz laughed and left them alone again and Matthew looked down at Daphne with a smile. 'Is next week too soon?'

'Will I still have this headache by then?' She looked very tired but incredibly happy.

'I hope not.'

'Then next week is fine. Will Andrew be home?'

'Yes, and that's another thing I want to talk to you about. How about putting him in the New York School?'

'And have him live at home?'

'I think he's ready.'

She was still smiling as the morning nurse rolled in a cot, and opened it next to her bed with a determined smile. 'Doctor's orders. He said that if you don't get some sleep, Mr Dane, he's going to give you a general anaesthetic.'

When the nurse left the room, he stretched out on the cot, and reached up to hold Daphne's hand. She had gone back to sleep, but it was no longer an ominous sign. He knew she would be all right, and as he drifted off to

340

sleep he smiled to himself. What fools they had been. He should have told her a year before, but it didn't matter now ... nothing did ... except Daphne.

ZOYA

DANIELLE STEEL

One woman's odyssey through a century of turmoil
. . .

St Petersburg: one famous night of violence in the
October Revolution ends the lavish life of the
Romanov court forever – shattering the dreams of
young Countess Zoya Ossupov.

Paris: under the shadow of the Great War, émigrés
struggle for survival as taxi drivers, seamstresses
and ballet dancers. Zoya flees there in poverty . . .
and leaves in glory.

America: a glittering world of flappers, fast cars
and furs in the Roaring Twenties; a world of
comfort and café society that would come crashing
down without warning.

Zoya – a true heroine of our time – emerges
triumphant from this panoramic web of history
into the 80s to face challenges and triumphs.

0 7221 8315 1   GENERAL FICTION

FINE THINGS

DANIELLE STEEL

Bestselling author of WANDERLUST

Living on the crest of a highly successful career, he was moving too fast to realise that he had everything – except what he wanted most . . .

Sent to San Francisco to open the smartest department store in California, Bernie Fine becomes aware of the hollowness of his personal life. Despite his success he grows increasingly disenchanted with his existence – until five-year-old Jane O'Reilly gets lost in the store.

Through Jane, Bernie meets her mother Liz, who finally offers him the possibility of love. But the rare happiness they find together is disrupted by tragedy and Bernie must face the terrible price we sometimes have to pay for loving . . .

0 7221 8308 9   GENERAL FICTION

Sphere Books now offers an exciting range of quality titles by both established and new authors which can be ordered from the following address:
Little, Brown and Company (UK) Limited,
P.O. Box 11,
Falmouth,
Cornwall TR10 9EN.

Alternatively you may fax your order to the above address. Fax No. 0326 376423.

Payments can be made as follows: cheque, postal order (payable to Little, Brown and Company) or by credit cards, Visa/Access. Do not send cash or currency. UK customers and B.F.P.O. please allow £1.00 for postage and packing for the first book, plus 50p for the second book, plus 30p for each additional book up to a maximum charge of £3.00 (7 books plus).

Overseas customers including Ireland, please allow £2.00 for the first book plus £1.00 for the second book, plus 50p for each additional book.

NAME (Block Letters) ....

....

ADDRESS ....

....

....

☐ I enclose my remittance for _____

☐ I wish to pay by Access/Visa Card

Number ☐☐☐☐☐☐☐☐☐☐☐☐☐☐☐☐☐

Card Expiry Date ☐☐☐☐